Fire

Fire

Deborah Challinor

HarperCollins*Publishers*

National Library of New Zealand Cataloguing-in-Publication Data

Challinor, Deborah.
Fire / Deborah Challinor.
ISBN 978-1-86950-703-9
I. Title.
NZ823.3—dc 22

First published 2007
First published in this format 2008
HarperCollins*Publishers (New Zealand) Limited*
P.O. Box 1, Auckland

ISBN (10-digit): 1 86950 703 7
ISBN (13-digit): 978 1 86950 703 9

Cover design by Natalie Winter, HarperCollins Design Studio
Internal text design and typesetting by Vincent Reynolds
Printed by Griffin Press, Australia
50gsm Bulky News used by HarperCollins*Publishers* is a natural,
recyclable product made from wood grown in sustainable plantation
forests. The manufacturing processes conform to the environmental
regulations in the country of origin, New Zealand.

Dedication

This one is for Kim Reilly,
August 1961–December 2005,
a talented artist and a true friend.

Acknowledgements

This story was inspired by the fire at Ballantynes department store in Christchurch, which occurred in 1947 and resulted in the loss of forty-one lives. The events in this novel are not intended to reflect or relate what actually happened at Ballantynes, and neither are any of the characters in this novel based on real people, except for those who already appear in the history books. To add another dimension to my story, I have taken a little bit of licence by moving the advent of the 'milkbar cowboys' and 'teddy boys' forward to the end of 1953, when actually their rise in Auckland didn't really begin until the year after that.

I would like to thank Kevin Broadfoot, Special Projects Manager at Smith & Caughey's department store in Auckland, for very kindly allowing me to go through the store's archives, and Cecilie Geary, who wrote *Celebrating 125 Years, 1880–2005: Smith & Caughey's* (Auckland: Smith & Caughey's, 2005). Cecilie also provided me with information based on her experiences as a fashion copywriter in department stores in New Zealand and overseas.

Thanks also to my mother, Pat Challinor, and my aunt, Elaine Stuart, who shared memories of Orakei, of Milne & Choyce, George Court's, John Court's, Smith & Caughey's and Farmers department stores in the 1950s, and of the trams, and of Auckland in general.

I'd also like to thank Lorain Day and the team at HarperCollins who, as always, have been helpful, supportive and enthusiastic, and Anna Rogers who, without fail, always manages to make my books just that little bit better.

Prologue

When Isobel and Edward Dunbar emigrated to New Zealand in 1874 to escape what Isobel considered to be a grimy and depressing life in Manchester, Edward was unwittingly carrying the seeds of a malady that would eventually ruin him. Isobel was twenty and Edward was twenty-four.

They settled in Wellington, where Edward did various jobs and spent increasing amounts of time in drinking establishments, while Isobel made hats for a well-known milliner. One day in 1878, Edward overheard a group of men talking about the gold strike at Waihi. Seduced by the lure of untold riches, he informed Isobel that the Coromandel was where their fortunes lay.

Edward didn't strike it rich, however, and before long he was working at the Martha Mine, spending most of his pay and all of his spare time in one or other of the town's numerous hotels. Isobel, who found Waihi even less appealing than Manchester, concentrated on making hats, which she sold to flush miners' wives, and a handful of local whores with an eye for fashion. It wasn't long before Edward was fired for being drunk on the job, and the couple packed up their meagre belongings and moved to Hamilton.

Naturally, Edward's problems went with them, and by the following year Isobel was wishing that he would either quietly disappear or die. Edward obliged her one night in 1881 by staggering home from the Hamilton Hotel, falling off the Union Bridge and drowning in the Waikato River.

Isobel moved to Auckland in 1882 and set up as a

milliner in Victoria Street, where she caught the eye of draper Horace Jones, a widower with three young children. He wanted a wife and she wanted a business partner, so they married in 1883, although Isobel refused to take his name. Their first real argument occurred over the title of their new, bigger and better, store in Queen Street: in the end, Isobel was forced to tell Horace that if he declined to call the store Dunbar & Jones she would not consent to sexual relations with him again. He capitulated and Dunbar & Jones it was.

They diversified quickly. To their stock of basic fabrics and Isobel's very popular hats, they added a range of mercery and fine laces, hosiery, mantles and shawls, footwear for men and ladies, haberdashery, umbrellas, manchester and soft furnishings. All imported, of course: Isobel had determined very early on that her store would stock nothing but the finest of products.

By the turn of the century, Dunbar & Jones was one of Auckland's most exclusive stores. Ten years later, in a new building towards the lower end of Queen Street, its only North Island rivals were Smith & Caughey's, unfortunately also located in Queen Street, and possibly Kirkcaldie & Stains in Wellington.

After Horace died in 1922, Isobel was free to run Dunbar & Jones completely unfettered. She began to import a selection of very fine furniture, china, silver and crystal from England and Europe, linens and tweeds from Ireland, Belgian lace, Oriental silks, cosmetics from America, men's and women's clothing from Paris and London, and a line of luxury continental chocolates and condiments. She also purchased the buildings on either side of Dunbar & Jones, and added another two floors to the lot. This gave her two cavernous basements for storage, three floors of retail space across three buildings, and a large uppermost floor to accommodate administrative offices as well as dressmaking, tailoring, millinery and soft furnishings workrooms, and a staff cafeteria. Beneath the gleaming panelling and new paint, however, many of the interior walls were little more than flimsy matchlining, and the various stairwells and narrow, behind-the-scenes passageways created a rabbit warren in which even longtime staff could become disoriented. But the buildings were essentially sound, and Dunbar & Jones continued to present the elegant, sometimes almost magical, environment to which its customers had become accustomed.

When Isobel died in 1928, the business went to her eldest stepson Charles and his younger brother James. To celebrate, Charles went out and purchased a brand-new Stutz Vertical 8 motor car, which mildly annoyed James and turned Charles's friends green with envy. Two weeks later, however, Charles killed himself in the car on the way to the Ellerslie races, leaving James the sole owner of Dunbar & Jones.

Under James's management the store continued to prosper. He enlarged the first-floor tearoom, redecorated it in white with gold accents and rechristened it the White Room. The dinner menu was extensive, and the morning and afternoon tea selections were said to be the finest in the city. A tiny salmon sandwich, a miniature brandy snap filled with chantilly cream, and a steaming cup of fragrant imported tea were just the thing to round out a day's shopping.

When James died in 1950, the business passed to his eldest son, Maxwell, who soon decided that Dunbar &

Jones was becoming a tad old-fashioned, and set about modernizing the interior. He replaced the rather antiquated Lamson wire cash-delivery system with a pneumatic one that made satisfying whooshing sounds as the capsules whizzed through a maze of shiny brass tubes around the store, and a year later he installed Auckland's first escalator, a novel device that would be sure to attract even more customers. He left the stately, brass-caged lifts at the rear of the store, however, aware that his more staid customers might be uncomfortable with the moderate level of agility needed to ride an escalator. He also altered the layout of the store, allocating to the ground floor departments for tableware, china, glass and silver, linens and manchester, gifts, menswear, boyswear and school uniforms, men's shoes and hats, and women's accessories, cosmetics and jewellery. The first floor housed, as well as the White Room, ladies' fashions, shoes, hats and lingerie, dress fabrics and patterns, Mother-to-be and Young Miss, and children's and infantswear, while the second floor was dedicated wholly to furniture, flooring and soft furnishings. The third floor's administrative offices, staff cafeteria and workrooms remained unchanged.

And, because customer service was still of paramount importance at Dunbar & Jones, the personnel department took on more staff, including four girls — Allie Roberts, Louise Taylor, Daisy Farr and Irene Baxter.

This story is about them.

12

Part One

Seven Days

Chapter One

The staff cafeteria was particularly noisy — people chattering and laughing, cutlery clattering against plates, chairs scraping across the linoleum floor. The girls at the table behind Allie burst into raucous laughter at a shared joke, and she had to lean forward to hear better.

'Sorry, Daisy, what was that?' As if she couldn't guess, because Daisy's wide grey eyes had gone all dreamy again.

Her friend sighed and said for the umpteenth time, 'Do you think she'll be wearing her crown when she gets off the ship?'

Allie smiled, because Daisy was doing what she did best — being sweet and unsophisticated.

Unlike Irene, who snorted.

'Well, she might,' Daisy countered, not at all offended. 'She is the new queen, after all, and queens always wear their finery in public.'

'Only in *The Big Book of Children's Fairy Stories*,' Irene said.

'What's that about a fairy story?' Louise asked as she slid her lunch tray on to the table and sat down.

15

Like Allie, and because she worked in the lingerie department, she wore the uniform of a Dunbar & Jones sales assistant: a plain, fitted black dress that zipped up the side with three-quarter-length sleeves and a small white collar, nude stockings and low-heeled black court shoes. Irene wore street clothes because she was a typist in accounts, and so did Daisy because she worked behind the scenes in the millinery workroom. There was a small, green feather clinging to her sleeve, which indicated she must be doing 'embellishments' that day.

'Daisy's telling us one,' Irene said, reaching for the salt. But she smiled to show she wasn't being deliberately mean.

Daisy shrugged. 'I was only saying, I wonder if the queen'll have her crown on when she arrives.'

Louise thought for a moment. 'I wouldn't think so. They're priceless, those royal crowns. Imagine if it fell off halfway down the gangplank and ended up in the harbour!'

Daisy shook her head, loosening the hair clip that was holding her white-blonde curls off her face. 'She won't come down a gangplank,' she said, sliding the clip back in. 'She'll come down a . . . well, something much more grand than a gangplank, anyway. And she'll be wearing all her jewels and a purple velvet cloak trimmed with ermine and a gown encrusted with precious stones and she'll be carrying that ball thing with the cross on it.'

Allie swallowed a mouthful of fly-cemetery biscuit. 'It's an orb.'

Daisy frowned. 'Pardon?'

'It's called the sovereign's orb,' Allie elaborated, 'and it's part of the Crown Jewels.'

Daisy extended her left hand and appraised her engagement ring, a tiny diamond set in a narrow platinum band. 'Well, it's not as nice as my jewels,' she said as her other hand crept down over her belly, over the secret she had so far shared only with Allie. And her fiancé Terry, of course. Oh God, and sort of with her parents.

The wedding was set for the end of January. Daisy's mother had given her a shocked and very suspicious look when she'd told her about the engagement and the early wedding date, but Daisy had been too scared to tell her the truth outright. Agnes Farr was a proper sort of woman but not at all stupid, and there was now an unspoken agreement between them — if Daisy wasn't going to mention the reason for the hasty wedding out loud then her mother certainly wasn't, and that way Agnes could pretend to herself and everyone else that her daughter was legitimately entitled to walk down the aisle wearing white.

Daisy tried not to think about her mother's silent recrimination, preferring to daydream about her new life with Terry. He worked in the Dunbar & Jones despatch office, and because it was only down the corridor from the millinery workroom they saw each other frequently. So far they hadn't had a single argument and they'd been going out now for a year. And if their first baby was arriving a little earlier than planned, it didn't really matter because they would have got married anyway. Daisy was sure of that and knew without a doubt that Terry was too.

'I still think eighteen's too young to be getting married,' Louise said, frowning at the tissue-thin slice of ham in her sandwich.

But Daisy only smiled.

Irene nudged Allie's arm. 'There he is, staring at you again.'

Allie, who was surreptitiously eyeing Daisy's rounded stomach and wondering how long it would be before people started noticing, glanced up. 'Who is?'

'That boy from stores, the smooth one,' Irene said, nodding towards a group of young men at a table on the other side of the crowded cafeteria. Above them on the wall hung a huge tinsel star with two of its points missing, clearly deemed too tatty to make an appearance this Christmas on the shop floor. 'Don't look, he'll see!'

But it was too late — Allie *had* looked and he was now waving cheerily back.

He was handsome, dark-skinned and had the sort of hair that behaved at the roots but obviously got out of hand towards the ends, because he'd wrestled it into submission with a generous application of Brylcreem. The resulting quiff sat softly gleaming above his forehead, over laughing brown eyes and a very wide smile. He reminded Allie of Montgomery Clift. No, his cheekbones were broader than that — Frank Sinatra perhaps, but with a browner face. But not as shifty-looking. It was a bit long really, his hair. No doubt Keith Beaumont, Dunbar & Jones's not particularly popular manager, would be having a word to him about it soon.

'What's his name, do you know?' Allie asked, while affecting to look completely uninterested.

Irene shrugged, but Daisy said, 'Sonny someone. He only started a few months ago. Terry knows him; he's in the basement.'

Which, Allie knew, meant that he worked in the storage areas in the very bowels of the store.

On Sonny Someone's plate sat two pies, a scotch egg and a sausage roll, all liberally covered with tomato sauce. He cut enthusiastically into a pie, speared a lump of pale pastry with his fork and shovelled it into his mouth. After at least ten seconds of purposeful chewing he swallowed, then waved at Allie again. Suddenly aware she'd been staring, she whipped her gaze away.

'I think he fancies you,' Irene said, and smirked.

Allie went pink. 'Oh, don't be silly!'

'What? You could do worse,' Irene said. 'Or would it not be the thing to take a Maori boy home?'

Mostly because she wasn't sure of the answer to that question herself, Allie replied sharply, 'I don't know, I've never asked.'

Sometimes Irene got on her nerves with her worldly-wise attitude and the things she came out with, things most other people would only ever think. Usually, though, she was good fun, big-hearted and generous. Too generous at times: Allie wondered how many people knew that Irene was having a 'flirtation' with Vincent Reynolds, floorwalker and head of furnishings. If it was any of her business, Allie thought, she'd be telling Irene she'd soon come a cropper, and probably lose her job — and possibly her husband as well. She couldn't understand what Irene saw in Vincent Reynolds: he was oily and had a nasty little moustache that he clearly thought made him look like Errol Flynn. And he was old, at least forty. And married.

In retaliation she said to Irene, 'Did you and Martin have a nice weekend?'

Irene faked a yawn, raising a manicured hand to her mouth. 'Same as usual. Martin read the *Herald* all Saturday morning, then spent the afternoon in the garden. Yesterday

19

we went to his mother's house for afternoon tea and that bloody little dog of hers shed hairs all over my new black wool skirt.'

'You didn't go out?' Louise asked.

Irene rolled her eyes. 'I wanted to. I wanted to go dancing, but Martin was too tired so we stayed in and listened to the radio. How being an accountant can make you so exhausted I don't know. Why, did you?'

Louise nodded. 'On Saturday. Mum said she'd take Susan for the whole night, so we made the most of it and went to the Peter Pan.'

'Good band?' Allie asked.

'Very. We danced until they kicked us out. God, my feet were sore. I wore my new platforms and they gave me blisters and poor old Rob just about had to carry me home.'

Daisy turned her teacup around in its saucer. 'Your mum babysits for you a lot, doesn't she? That must be a big help.'

'Oh, it is. Well, I couldn't work if she didn't, could I?'

Allie said, 'How are the savings going? Have you got your deposit yet?'

Louise was married to Rob, a motor mechanic, and they had one child, Susan, who was three years old and the cutest little thing Allie had ever seen. With her shiny chestnut hair and brown button eyes, Susan looked just like a miniature version of Louise. Rob and Louise were saving hard to buy their own home, which was why Louise had returned to work after her mother had offered to mind Susan during the week.

'Nearly,' Louise said. 'Another six months and I think we might actually have enough.'

Irene drummed her red fingernails on the table, as if to imply that saving for a house was one of the most boring things a person could possibly do. 'Has your mother-in-law stopped giving you a hard time yet?'

'What, the Wicked Witch of the West?' Louise muttered.

They all laughed. Rob's mother was on at Louise constantly about how a woman's place was in the home — especially a woman with a child — and think how confusing it must be for poor little Susan and how did Rob's work shirts get ironed if no one was at home to do them? Louise insisted that she'd pointed out dozens of times that Rob wore overalls to work, and that poor little Susan was as happy as a sandboy with her other grandmother, and if anyone was suffering it was her, Louise, because she missed her daughter.

Louise added, 'Nothing's changed. I don't think it ever will. Mind you, Rob's mum thinks it's common to eat shop-bought cakes. She's just that sort of person.'

For a moment the four of them silently pondered the awful notion of not eating shop-bought cakes.

'Well, they say you can't choose your relatives,' Allie said eventually.

'No, unfortunately, you can't,' Louise agreed. She looked at her watch. 'Oh God, only five minutes left. Is everyone else really busy today?'

'We're rushed off our feet,' Daisy said. 'We're mostly doing hats for the queen.'

They nodded. Daisy and the other milliners were flat out making hats for wealthy women to wear to receptions when the queen finally arrived in Auckland in just over a week's time. Between Christmas shopping and the royal visit, everyone at Dunbar & Jones was busy, from the office staff on the top floor down to the storemen in the basement.

Allie dug in her handbag for her cigarettes. Irene and Louise did the same: only Daisy didn't smoke. After they'd lit up, inhaled deeply and relaxed back into their chairs to enjoy a last, peaceful few minutes before returning to work, Allie asked, 'Is everyone going to the staff picnic?'

'We are,' Daisy said. 'I've made a new sundress specially.'

Louise said, 'So are we. Susan can't wait. Rob told her Santa Claus will be there. I hope to God he is this year.'

Allie frowned. 'Is she old enough to know who Santa is?'

'Crikey, yes,' Louise replied. 'She knows *exactly* where presents come from at Christmas time. Santa's house at the Norf Po, apparently.'

'And I suppose Mr Max will be Santa again this year,' Irene said. 'He needn't think I'm sitting on his knee.'

I bet you would if you could, Allie thought, still smarting slightly.

Irene read her mind and laughed. 'Look at him, though, he's fifty if he's a day! His heart would give out!'

Louise, who believed very strongly in the sanctity of marriage and knew about Irene and Vincent Reynolds, looked disapproving.

'He's forty-eight, actually,' Daisy said. 'Terry told me.'

'And how would Terry know?' Irene asked.

Daisy just smiled, comfortable in her conviction that her beloved fiancé, who was only a year older than her, knew everything.

'Apparently he really enjoys it, Mr Max,' Louise said,

'handing out presents to all the kids. It's very generous of Dunbar & Jones, isn't it?'

Irene slid the ashtray closer and stubbed out her cigarette. 'I'm off to the loo, then it's back to the salt mines.'

On their way out they met Vincent Reynolds coming in. His hair was immaculately pomaded and as black as nugget, and his moustache bracketed his top lip like a set of spare eyebrows. He slowed as he passed Irene and gave her a long, greasy wink. She simpered and Allie looked away, annoyed at the stab of envy in her stomach. But Vince Reynolds was repulsive and Allie wouldn't touch him with a ten-foot barge pole. It was more that Irene, of whom she was genuinely fond, already had a perfectly nice husband, and it wasn't right that she was, well, dallying.

Allie hurried down the two flights of stairs to the first floor where she worked. Before nine in the morning and after five at night, when the store was empty, she rode on the escalator because it was such fun, but during opening hours staff were supposed to use the stairway behind the scenes at the rear of the store that zigzagged from the third floor all the way down to the basement. Mr Beaumont believed that, ideally, sales assistants should only be seen standing at their counters, ready and politely waiting to be of help, not tripping about as if they owned the place. But unlike the grand marble public stairs that ran from the ground floor to the second floor on the south-western side of the building, and had views of Wyndham Street below, the staff stairs were narrow, wooden and somewhat rickety. And as customers never went up to the third floor anyway, and Mr Max and Mr Beaumont had their offices on the first floor just off the foyer outside the White Room, the staff stairs had never been refurbished. They did make a very satisfying, echoey racket, however, if you ran down them fast enough.

Allie loved the store at Christmas. Last year, her first Christmas at Dunbar & Jones, had been an exciting and magical time, not least because of the magnificent decorations that went up halfway through December. She adored their glittering promise of everything to come. At home they always had a real tree with a handful of shiny shop-bought balls, stars and tinsel, plus the decorations she and her sisters had made when they were little. The latter were getting very tatty now — Allie's cotton-wool Santa had lost one of his eyes and the paint was flaking off his red hat — but they were the most cherished of the lot, unpacked every year with squeals of delight and cries of 'Oh, look, remember this one?', and put carefully away again when the tree came down. Allie always felt sorry for the tree, lying outside on the back lawn, unloved and unwanted, going brown with its needles falling off until her father got around to disposing of it.

But Dunbar & Jones's Christmas decorations, many imported from overseas, were in a class of their own. There were the miles of red, green and gold swags of organza intertwined with Christmas lights, caught up every twelve feet with red velvet bows and suspended from the ceilings of all three shopping floors. Then around the walls were dozens of enormous wreaths, their glossy green-painted leaves, gold bows and red holly berries reflected in the hanging mirrored balls.

On the ground floor, just inside the main front door, was a huge artificial tree that twinkled and gleamed with glass and tinsel and coloured electric lights, though these wouldn't be turned on until the weekend before Christmas. Surrounding the tree's base were piles of beautifully wrapped parcels, which almost every child who entered the store picked up and shook, then dropped disappointedly because the boxes were empty. In the end, Mr Beaumont had a velvet rope erected around the display. The children weren't completely discouraged, however, as in the furniture department on the second floor the bedroom suites had been moved over to make room for Santa's Magic Grotto, a cave made of papier mâché over chicken-wire, decorated with artificial ferns and rows of tiny electric 'glow-worms'. Santa Claus (not Mr Max, but a bloke hired especially) sat in the cave from nine until five each day, with morning and afternoon tea breaks and forty minutes off for lunch so he could go for a smoke, dispensing yuletide cheer and the exhortation that, if children were good, Santa might bring them something from the wonderful selection of toys Dunbar & Jones had stocked especially for Christmas.

But most impressive of all, as far as Allie was concerned, was the massive model of Santa, his sleigh and his four reindeer, which usually sat above the verandah extending over the footpaths on both the Queen Street and Wyndham Street frontages. This year, however, because of the royal tour, Santa had been relegated to the Wyndham Street side, and an equally enormous crown flanked by a huge kiwi holding the New Zealand flag and a giant lion waving the Union Jack had pride of place above the front door on Queen Street.

Coming a close second were the Christmas window displays, an annual spectacular showcasing the skills and imaginations of Dunbar & Jones's windowdressers. This year the windows contained frothy, glittering tableaux depicting 'The Sleeping Beauty', 'The Snow Queen', 'The Twelve Dancing Princesses' and 'The Princess and the Pea', all lit with thousands of tiny lights that stayed on all night, providing a dose of after-dark Christmas magic. Dunbar & Jones didn't, however, put on a Christmas parade: Farmers had cornered the market on that one.

On the first floor, Allie slid her handbag into the cupboard under the main counter of the ladies' dress department. When she straightened up, Sonny Someone was leaning on the other side of it. In his blue work shirt and no tie he looked very out of place, slouched in the middle of the pale pink and cream dress salon.

He smiled at her, his brown eyes twinkling in a way that made Allie take a short, involuntary breath.

Flustered, she said, 'You'll get into trouble if Miss Willow sees you. You're not supposed to be on the shop floor.' And then she felt silly for sounding so insipid.

'Who's Miss Willow?' he asked. He had a nice voice, soft and rich, and he held her eye a moment longer than was necessary.

'Head of the dress department. My supervisor.'

'The old biddy with her hair in a bun?'

'Well, I don't think she's that old,' Allie said, praying that Miss Willow wasn't within earshot.

He shrugged, and nodded at a box on the floor. 'It's all right, I brought a parcel up for her.'

'Oh. Did you?'

'I did. Arrived just before lunch. Had "Urgent" on it so I thought I'd better deliver it pronto.' He was still leaning on the counter, his shirtsleeves rolled to his elbows revealing muscled forearms, and he didn't appear to be in a hurry to leave.

'Oh,' Allie said again. 'Right then.'

Feeling self-conscious and rather unnerved by his steady gaze, she smoothed her shoulder-length golden-blonde hair, wishing she'd taken the time after lunch to brush it. She felt short of breath.

He looked at her thoughtfully. 'You look worried,' he said finally.

'No, I'm not,' Allie replied too quickly, her face heating up. 'Look, I'm sorry, but did you want something else?'

'Yep.'

She waited, trying to avoid his amused look, but finding, to her annoyance, that her gaze kept creeping back to his. 'Well, what is it?' she said, more tersely than she meant to.

'Do you want to come to the flicks with me on Wednesday night? *High Noon*, at the Civic?'

Allie stared at him. 'But I don't even know your name!'

'It's Sonny Manaia: so now you do. Will you?'

She opened her mouth to say she didn't really think so, and was startled to hear herself say yes, thank you, that would be nice, and she would meet him outside the picture theatre just before eight o'clock.

He grinned even more widely, nodded at her and sauntered over to the escalator. The last she saw of him was a waving brown hand as he descended to the floor below.

'Cheeky monkey,' Miss Willow said, coming to stand beside Allie. 'I heard all that. And Mr Beaumont won't be very happy if he sees him joy-riding on the escalator.'

Allie eyed Miss Willow, not sure how to respond. She wasn't a bad old stick, but she'd worked for Dunbar & Jones for ever and had an abiding respect for Max Jones, as she had had for his father James and grandmother Isobel Dunbar before him. And she believed in the rules imposed by the store's management to which, these days, she belonged.

According to staff who had been with Dunbar & Jones for some time, Ruby Willow never changed. A child of the new century, the same age as the year, she had surprisingly smooth skin — which she attributed to a daily application of Elizabeth Arden face cream — and unfailingly wore her long hair pulled back in a severe bun at the nape of her neck. Her lips were painted with the same coral shade of lipstick every day of the year, and she wore no jewellery except for discreet clip-on pearls at her ears. Her only other accessory was a pair of reading spectacles which, when not in use, hung against her modest bosom on a long, gold-plated chain. Unmarried, she had for years shared a small house with Beatrice Button, another Dunbar & Jones spinster who was head milliner.

Allie finally mumbled, 'Yes, he was a bit cheeky.'

'But not a bad sort, by all accounts,' Miss Willow said. 'A hard worker, I hear, and honest. But I'd watch myself, if I were you,' she cautioned. 'And you know of course that liaisons between staff are not allowed.'

Allie nodded. But that hadn't stopped Daisy and Terry getting together, and several other members of staff, not to mention Irene and the oily Vince Reynolds.

The lift doors rattled open: Miss Willow glanced up and gave a barely audible sigh. 'Allie, go and serve Mrs Goodman, please.'

Allie stepped out from behind the counter to greet Mrs Goodman, a wealthy Dunbar & Jones customer who was well known for dithering for ages over a purchase, then choosing the exact item of clothing that suited her least. Allie and the other girls had entertained each other at the lunch table for hours inventing the most hideous outfits for Mrs Goodman to wear during the royal visit. Her shopping expedition was not unexpected, and Allie had been dreading it.

'Good afternoon, Mrs Goodman,' she said. 'May I help you with something today?'

Too vain to wear spectacles, Mrs Goodman regarded Allie through small, short-sighted eyes. 'Hello, dear. Yes, actually, I'm looking for something to wear to the civic reception at the town hall on the twenty-third. It's for the queen, you know.'

Allie did know — at least a battalion of well-heeled women had been in over the past few weeks looking for outfits for that particular social engagement.

Cautiously, she asked, 'Did you have anything specific in mind, Mrs Goodman?'

'Well, obviously something very elegant, don't you think? But still discreet, of course. I don't want to outshine Her Majesty!'

As if, Allie thought.

'Perhaps something from Christian Dior?' Mrs Goodman suggested hopefully.

Allie thought of the tiny waists, tight bodices and very full skirts on the Dior gowns currently in stock, and her heart sank; Mrs Goodman didn't have a hope in hell of shoe-horning herself into anything remotely approaching a Dior.

At Allie's hesitation, Mrs Goodman made a *moue* of indecision. 'What have other people been buying?'

Allie seized the opportunity. 'Well, for the civic reception, we've been selling a lot of very smart formal dress-and-coat ensembles.'

'Long or short?'

'Short, mostly, because it's a daytime event.'

'Mmm.' Mrs Goodman thought for a moment. 'Well, perhaps Dior would be more suited to evening. What else can you show me?'

'What about something in a nice delustred satin? That's been very popular. We have some lovely lines off the peg.'

'Well, I don't know. I really should have had something made.'

As there obviously wasn't time left for that, Allie pressed on. She took a coffee-hued dress off a rack and draped it over a nearby chair. 'This would look wonderful on you, Mrs Goodman. And we have a coat in a very pretty brocade that would go beautifully over it. What do you think?'

'What size is it?'

This was the difficult part. Allie pretended to look at the label inside the dress. 'Actually, I think this one would be just about right for you.'

Mrs Goodman looked doubtful. 'It seems rather large. I have quite a neat waist, you know.'

'Yes, you do,' Allie lied. 'But this particular style is designed to just skim the waist and hips, rather than deliberately emphasize the figure. I think you'll find it's very complimentary on. And extremely elegant.'

'Mmm, well, perhaps. Hold onto that one, dear. What else can you show me?'

After a further gruelling half-hour of Allie selecting options and having most of them dismissed out of hand, Mrs Goodman was finally ready to enter the dressing rooms and try something on. Eventually, and despite

Allie doing her tactful best to dissuade her, she chose a shantung silk in a vibrant jade that did nothing for her complexion, and which was too tight around the waist (although the princess-line skirt did help to disguise the size of her bottom), and featured a self-fabric stole that fastened across the front with a bow that made her bust look monolithic.

'Charge that to my account, please,' Mrs Goodman said.

Allie laid the dress across the counter for packing and delivery, wrote out the credit docket and put the bottom copy with the dress. The top copy she tucked into a brass capsule and placed it into the Lamson tube, to be whizzed off to the credit office on the first floor.

Mrs Goodman looked thoughtful. 'I'll need a hat, of course, and gloves. And shoes, too, I think. I have nothing to wear with that shade of green. And probably a handbag as well. What can you show me in hats?'

'I'm very sorry, Mrs Goodman, but I don't have any expertise in the millinery department,' Allie said, extremely grateful that this was the truth.

Mrs Goodman's face fell. 'But you have such an eye for putting things together. Surely you could take a minute to help me pick something out?'

Allie glanced helplessly at Miss Willow, who said helpfully, 'I'm sure we can manage without you for fifteen minutes, Miss Roberts.'

Stifling a sigh, Allie followed Mrs Goodman over to millinery, where she eventually chose a net half-hat covered in navy-blue feathers that made her head look like a hard-boiled egg. 'Just something small so I don't block other people's view of Her Majesty. We're seated very near the front, you know,' Mrs Goodman said for the third time as she signed another credit docket.

Then it was on to shoes. Mrs Goodman jammed her feet into at least a dozen pair before finally settling on navy suede pumps. Fortunately, the shoes came with a matching handbag, so Allie was spared the agony of watching Mrs Goodman dither for another hour.

Finally, it was time to select gloves. As the glove counter was on the ground floor, Allie escorted Mrs Goodman, who did not 'trust' the escalator, down in the lift. She had to look away when Walter, one of the store's two lift boys, resplendent in his black and charcoal uniform with gold buttons, winked at her behind Mrs Goodman's back.

At the glove counter, Allie pulled out one of the high wooden chairs for Mrs Goodman and waved at the sales assistant, a girl with the rather exotic name of Simone.

'Good afternoon, Mrs Goodman,' Simone said a little too brightly. 'How may I help you?'

'I want some gloves, to go with my new outfit,' Mrs Goodman said, awkwardly hoisting her bulk up onto the chair and settling her elbows on the glass counter top. Beneath was a display of white lace and crocheted gloves, elegantly arranged on disembodied hands. 'It's green.'

'Jade green,' Allie added.

'Day or evening, Mrs Goodman?' Simone asked.

'Oh, day, but formal.'

'French?'

'Preferably.'

'Leather, cotton or fancy?'

'Fancy. Or maybe leather. I don't know. What do you think?' Mrs Goodman asked Allie.

'I think fine leather would be more sophisticated.'

Lace or crocheted gloves might be a tad frivolous for the occasion.

'Show me some leather ones then, dear,' Mrs Goodman said to Simone.

'Would you prefer kid, suede, doeskin or nappa?'

'Probably suede. My new shoes and bag are suede.'

Simone turned to the shelves behind her. 'In the French suede we have yellow, grey, white, beige, black and navy.'

'Beige,' Mrs Goodman said.

Oh no, Allie thought, not with jade green. Simone selected a stack of small, flat boxes from the shelves and began to open them. 'What size glove do you normally take?'

Mrs Goodman told her and Simone stretched each glove in turn, dusted them inside with talcum powder, then slid a pair of velvet cushions under Mrs Goodman's elbows before beginning to ease a glove onto her hand.

'Are you sure this is your size?' Simone said after several minutes.

Before Mrs Goodman could reply, Allie said, 'I think beige can make a lady's hands look bigger than they really are, as white sometimes does. What about trying navy, Mrs Goodman? Then your shoes, bag and gloves will all match.'

Mrs Goodman brightened. 'Oh, that's a good idea, isn't it? Yes, I'll try the navy.'

It took longer to wrestle the beige glove off than it had to get it on, and while Mrs Goodman was struggling, Simone readied a pair of navy suedes — in a bigger size. They went on no more snugly than they should have, and Mrs Goodman was pleased with the effect.

'Very smart,' she said, admiring her hands. 'I'll take

these.' Then, glancing at Allie's trim waist, flat stomach and pert bosom, she added, 'And I might just treat myself to some new lingerie as well.'

Allie almost groaned. 'Well, in that case,' she said, 'I really do recommend that you have one of our trained corsetières help you. I'll take you up to lingerie, shall I?'

So up they went again in the lift to the first floor, where Allie was profoundly relieved to hand Mrs Goodman over to Louise. Back in her own territory, Allie resisted the urge to collapse dramatically across the counter.

Miss Willow looked amused.

'Whew,' Allie said, 'I think I've really earned my pay this afternoon.'

'You always earn your pay, Allie,' Miss Willow replied. 'And it *is* what we're here for, after all, to give our customers the best shopping experience possible. I know that Mrs Goodman can be a . . . challenge, but she's a very good customer. We can't afford to have her disappointed.'

'She wanted beige gloves, to go with jade and navy!' Allie said in a horrified whisper.

Miss Willow pursed her lips. 'That's as may be, but we're not here to cast judgement upon other people's taste.' She paused. 'I hope you persuaded her to go with navy.'

Allie nodded.

'Good girl. And at least she won't glow like a beacon,' Miss Willow said, recalling a startling cadmium-yellow coat Mrs Goodman had once purchased.

34

Chapter Two

The rest of the afternoon passed in a busy blur, and by the time Allie caught the bus home to Coates Avenue in Orakei she was almost asleep on her feet: the last two-hundred-yard trudge to her front gate felt like miles. She followed the steep concrete path down past the hydrangeas around to the back of the house, felt the washing on the line to see if it was dry — not quite — then climbed the steps and subsided onto the nearest kitchen chair.

Her father, reading the paper at the table in his singlet and braces, barely looked up. 'Rough day, love?'

'Very,' Allie agreed, easing her shoes off and wriggling her aching toes. 'I've been rushed off my feet all day.'

'Be thankful you've got a job to go to,' her father responded in a flat tone that suggested he'd said the same thing a hundred times before, which indeed he had.

Allie glanced at her mother standing at the kitchen sink, and rolled her eyes. Sid Roberts had lost his job on the waterfront during the 1951 lockout, and never missed a chance to let anyone forget it. But these days, between the TAB, his bad leg, the pub and a bit of casual work, he didn't really have the time to do a forty-hour week, although he insisted that he most certainly would if something suitable came up.

Wordlessly, Colleen Roberts set a cup of tea in front of her husband.

He glanced at the dark brew. 'Christ, Col, you could trot a mouse across that.'

Colleen ignored him: the tea was exactly the way Sid liked it, and he made the mouse comment at least once a day.

'What about you, Dad?' Allie asked. 'What did you get up to today?'

Sid shook his paper. 'Bit of this and a bit of that. Put in a new row of lettuces, went out with Bill and did a bit of painting on some old biddy's house, had a few beers in the pub after lunch.'

Allie nodded. Bill was a mate of her father's, also an ex-watersider, but unlike Sid, Bill had done something about his unemployed status and set himself up in the house-painting business. He gave Sid as much work as he could, which amounted to about four half-days a week, but it wasn't quite enough to pay the bills. Which was why Allie's mother also went out to work from nine until two, four days a week, behind the counter at a tearoom near the beach at Mission Bay. Allie's board helped, and she gave her mother extra money whenever she could, but they sometimes only just managed to pay the rent, her father's battered Morris 8 had been parked outside the house for the past six months because there was no money to fix it, Allie's younger sisters were continually demanding new clothes, and Colleen would kill for one of the new electric washing machines she'd seen at Farmers, instead of the copper she laboured over twice a week.

They'd moved into the state house in Coates Avenue three years ago, and it was much more comfortable than the old place but they didn't own it, which quietly irked Colleen. Her dream was that she and Sid would have their own home before they retired — though it seemed that Sid had almost reached that point. Colleen hadn't wanted to move into a state house at first, believing it would be nothing more than a glorified railwayman's cottage — poky, in a row that were all the same — but she'd changed her mind after she'd been to see one. They'd put their names down straight away but had had to wait for over a year. Theirs was red brick with three bedrooms with built-in wardrobes, a separate lounge, a proper bathroom, a washhouse and a toilet off the back porch, and its own semi-underground bomb shelter that a previous tenant had built on the long back lawn.

And then the lockout had happened, and for five very unpleasant months there had been no money at all and they'd had to live on handouts. When it finally ended, Sid, as a militant and now deregistered watersider, found himself unofficially barred from the waterfront, and any other industry run by 'those fascist bastards', the National Government. Then one afternoon, coming home from the pub, he'd been hit by a car and badly hurt, and couldn't even walk for six months, never mind work, so when Allie got a job after she left school and then Colleen had found work as well everyone had been very pleased. Colleen had high hopes for her daughters, and Allie being taken on at Dunbar & Jones was a very good start because everyone knew that their salesgirls were a cut above the rest.

Allie sipped her own tea, noticing how quiet the house was. 'Where're Pauline and Donna?'

'In the bomb shelter, I think,' Colleen replied, reaching into one of the kitchen cupboards and sorting through a bag of potatoes for some that hadn't sprouted. 'Your nan's coming for tea tonight.'

'Is she?' Allie was pleased; she was very fond of her grandmother — unlike her father. 'That'll be nice, won't it, Dad?'

Sid grunted behind his paper and muttered, 'Bloody harridan.'

Allie laughed. 'What'll it be tonight, do you think? No job, no money or no car?'

Her father turned a page and pretended he'd gone deaf.

'No job, probably,' Colleen said. 'It was no money last week.'

It was no secret that Rose Murphy had never been keen on her son-in-law, and when he'd lost his job it had only proved what she'd been saying for years — even before he'd had his accident and regardless of his impressive war service — that he was good for nothing and certainly not equipped to take care of either her daughter or her granddaughters. When Colleen had come home twenty years ago at the age of nineteen and told her mother she was in trouble, Rose had hit the roof. But there was nothing that could be done about it; as Rose said to her husband Patrick, Colleen would have to marry Sidney Roberts or live the rest of her life with the stigma of being an unmarried mother. So they had galloped down the aisle and Allie had been born a scant six months later, surprisingly big and healthy for such a premature baby. Rose had never really forgiven Sid for making her daughter pregnant, but she'd long ago forgiven Colleen, whom she preferred to think had been bedazzled by Sid's undeniable good looks and charm. Not that there was much of either left now, in Rose's opinion, though Colleen was always very loyal to Sid, and quick to defend him whenever things weren't going well, which, as far as Rose could see, was nearly all of the time.

'Take it with a grain of salt, Dad,' Allie suggested. 'She's only trying to look out for us.'

'She doesn't need to,' Sid said, looking up at Colleen. 'We're not doing too badly, are we, love?'

Colleen smiled at him with real affection. 'No, love, we're not.'

Allie felt a nice, round, warm feeling spread through her chest: she loved it when her parents were like this. Sometimes there were yelling matches and occasionally her mother threw the odd thing, and she knew she was the reason her parents had had to get married, because she'd sat down one day and worked out the dates, but she also knew that, no matter what went wrong, they really did love each other.

Loud bickering from the back porch announced the arrival of Allie's younger sisters Donna and Pauline — fifteen and fourteen, respectively, and both going on twenty-five.

Donna came in first. Like her sisters, she had her mother's pretty face and fair hair, matched by a set of brows that were currently almost touching in the middle, so deeply was she frowning.

'Mum!' she said as she threw her cardigan at a kitchen chair, taking no notice when it missed and landed on the floor, 'Pauline says that sweater you're knitting is for her!'

'That's right,' Colleen said, rinsing a peeled potato

under the tap and dropping it into a pot on the stove. 'It is. And it's a jumper, not a sweater. Only Americans wear sweaters.'

'Ha ha!' Pauline taunted as she followed Donna inside. 'I told you!'

'But purple's *my* favourite — it's my signature colour!' Donna complained.

Colleen stared out of the kitchen window at the lemon tree on the back lawn. She really must get out there with some copper one of these days and spray it — there were rust spots all over the leaves. She sighed. Donna and Pauline had been fair little madams since Allie had been bringing home stories about the models at Dunbar & Jones's fashion shows. If they didn't give it a rest soon she'd give them signature colours, all right.

'Mum? It's *my* favourite colour,' Donna whined again.

'I heard you the first time, love. But you got the last thing I knitted.' Colleen turned away from the window. 'And where is it, that jumper? I haven't seen it for months.'

Donna went very quiet.

'You've lost it, haven't you?' Colleen said. At the look on her daughter's face, she exclaimed, 'Oh, for God's sake, Donna, do we look like we're made of money? That was expensive wool!'

Looking sheepish now, Donna muttered 'Sorry, Mum' and disappeared into the hall.

Allie stood up. 'Is there anything I can help with?'

'Yes,' Colleen said, 'you can shake some sense into that girl's head. Pauline, bring the washing in, please. And then take your sister and go and wait at the bus-stop for your nan.'

'I'll do that if you like,' Allie offered, looking in her

handbag for her cigarettes — she'd have one while she was waiting. There was something she wanted to ask Nan before they got back to the house.

At the bus-stop Allie sat down on a low wall and lit up. It wasn't very ladylike, she knew, smoking on the street, but too bad. She shifted slightly, trying to find a more comfortable spot on the sharp scoria and settled down to wait, inhaling the smoke deeply and blowing it languorously out through her nose in the manner of the movie stars she'd seen at the pictures. She liked it here: she could smell the saltiness of the sea and knew that if she stood on the wall she'd be able to glimpse the sparkling blue Waitemata Harbour itself.

By the time the bus was approaching she'd finished the cigarette and flicked the butt into the garden behind her. She could see Nan standing just inside the door, swaying gently as the bus rattled to a halt. Then the door flapped open and out she stepped, looking as regal as ever despite her height, which was only five foot two. She always said she didn't know how Colleen had managed to grow to be five foot six, because neither she nor Patrick had come from tall stock.

As she almost always did, Rose Murphy was wearing a dark dress belted at the waist, a black cloth coat despite the warm weather, sturdy lace-up shoes and a dusty black cloche hat from the 1930s, which her granddaughters always referred to as 'Nan's po'. An umbrella poked out of her large crocodile carry-all, alongside a bunch of something green and leafy.

Allie gave Rose a kiss on the cheek, loving the smell of the lily-of-the-valley talcum powder that seemed always to surround her.

'Hello, Nan, you look nice today.'

'Thank you, Allison dear,' Rose said. 'And so do you. Are they treating you well?'

Allie knew she meant at Dunbar & Jones, for whom her grandmother had always had a great respect, even if she did do a fair bit of her shopping at Farmers now because she was only on a pension.

'Yes, they are. Very busy, though.'

'Christmas shopping or the royal tour?'

'Both.' Allie took Rose's bag. 'Is this spinach?"

'Fresh from my garden.'

'Yum,' Allie said, even though she hated the way spinach always seemed to get stuck in your teeth.

They walked in silence for a moment, then Rose asked in a confidential tone, 'How's your mother?'

'She's good. Busy, too, at the tearooms.'

Rose hmmphed. 'And your father?'

'He's been out painting nearly every day.'

Rose made a face that suggested she found that hard to believe. 'And Pauline and Donna?'

'Same as always.'

'Oh, well,' Rose said.

They walked on, dawdling as they passed a garden vibrant with summer flowers.

Rose closed her eyes and breathed in though her nose. 'Stock always reminds me of your grandfather. He used to give me lovely great bunches of it.'

'It's pretty, isn't it?' Allie said. She waited a second, then asked, 'Nan?'

'Mmm?'

'I've got a bit of a problem. Well, it's not a problem really. But it might be.'

42

Rose kept walking, but inclined her head to show she was listening.

'There's a boy at work and he's asked me out, to the pictures on Wednesday night.'

'Well, that sounds nice, dear.'

'Yes. But he's . . .' Allie struggled to find the right words. 'Well, his name's Sonny, Sonny Manaia.'

'Ah. A Maori boy?'

Allie nodded. 'And I was wondering, what do you think Mum and Dad would say? If I went out with him.'

Rose stopped, withdrew a spotlessly clean handkerchief from her sleeve, removed her glasses and started polishing them. 'Are you keen on him?'

'Yes,' Allie said, startling herself by how emphatic she sounded.

'Well, you know how narrow-minded your father is.'

'But not always, Nan. And he used to work with plenty of Maoris on the wharves and he often said what good blokes they were.'

'That's not the same as letting your daughter go out with one, though, is it?'

'I suppose.' Allie felt herself growing more and more uncomfortable, talking about Maori people as though they were . . . well, not like everyone else.

Rose put her glasses back on. 'Does he come from around here?'

'I don't know, I haven't asked.'

'Because they've had a lot of trouble lately, you know, those people from the pa, and they're not at all happy about it.'

Allie did know — vaguely — but Sonny hadn't seemed . . . like that.

'If he is local,' Rose went on, 'I'm surprised he would want to step out with a European girl, given everything that's gone on.' She blew her nose daintily and tucked her handkerchief back into her sleeve. 'Still, if he asked you to go out with him, I suppose that means he does.'

Allie nodded, though she still hadn't had her question answered. 'But what do you think Mum and Dad will say?'

Rose started walking again. 'The only way you'll find that out is by telling them, isn't it?'

Allie stifled a sigh of both frustration and resignation, because she'd suspected Nan was going to say that. 'Well, what do *you* think? Should I go?'

'I'm probably not the best person to ask, dear. I married an Irishman.'

'I'm not sure what you mean, Nan.'

Rose gave a sad little smile. 'Of all the people in this world, the Irish are probably regarded as being closest to the bottom of the heap. Or they used to be, back when I was a girl. My mother nearly had a fit when I took Patrick home. And these days the Maoris seem to be in the same boat. But I married my Irishman, and I'm very glad I did. I spent the best part of my life with your grandfather and I don't regret a second of it. So, though I should be telling you to go to bed early on Wednesday night with a cup of tea and a good book, I won't. Allie, if you like this boy, go out with him. You only have one life to live, and you never know when they're going to drop an H-bomb on us.' She looked up at the clear sky as if one might be hurtling down right now. 'But don't tell your mother and father I said that, all right?'

And then they were at the gate and the subject seemed to be closed.

Irene leaned back in her seat, looking out the window and listening absent-mindedly to the soothing *snick* of the overhead wires as the tram swayed down Parnell Road. As usual Martin had gone to work ridiculously early and she'd missed catching a lift with him. She had an enormous pile of typing to do at work today and really couldn't be bothered with it. In fact, she couldn't be bothered with anything. She felt . . . flat.

She'd had another argument with him last night, about money, as usual. She'd told him about the gorgeous mink-dyed marmot coat she'd seen at work and he'd said she couldn't have it. So she'd asked why not and he'd said because they couldn't afford it. Then she had said why didn't he ask his boss for more money, and he'd said they wouldn't need it if she didn't keep spending it like water. And it had gone on from there, escalating as it always did into something quite unpleasant and then, ultimately, pointless.

It drove her to distraction sometimes, the way they argued. Not so much the quarrel itself, because she quite enjoyed a good barney, but it was the way Martin invariably conducted his side of it. Whereas she always got worked up and angry, he never seemed to lose his temper and he never, ever raised his voice. He simply sat there, in his comfortable chair by the fireplace, reading his paper and smoking his pipe in his woollen vest and grey flannel work trousers and his slippers, and reasoned it calmly out with her, pointing out that he would buy her all the fine things she wanted when they had the money but not before.

It wasn't as if they didn't have any. But Martin had earmarked the money in the bank for the house he insisted they should buy as soon as they'd finished paying off their flat. His flat, actually. He'd already bought it well before Irene met him, when he was only twenty-two and hadn't long been working for Hart, Bullock & Associates. That had been ten years ago and, Martin being Martin, he'd already paid most of it off. But until it was freehold, he said, and he'd secured a partnership in the firm so that there was enough money for a hefty deposit on something bigger that would suit them better when children came along, there was little money for anything but essentials.

Irene didn't agree with this. For a start, so far as she was concerned there weren't going to be any children. She genuinely liked them, and adored cuddling little babies, but she didn't like what giving birth seemed to do to many women's bodies. One minute they were trim and shapely, then they were pregnant, and nine and a bit months later they had flabby stomachs, pendulous breasts and enormous backsides. Her figure was spectacular and she knew it, and had no intention of spoiling it by producing offspring. And she was sure there would be plenty of nieces and nephews around for her to enjoy and spoil: she had four younger brothers and sisters who would probably breed like rabbits, and Martin had a sister who had recently married and talked about nothing but having babies. No, she wouldn't need any of her own.

She actually could see the point of buying a better house, and knew that what Martin had in mind wasn't too far from her own vision of something at least modestly affluent — it was just that it was all taking so frustratingly long! He had promised her all sorts of things when they'd been courting, and it was true he'd spent quite a lot of money buying her pretty gifts and taking her out to dinner, and her engagement ring had cost rather a lot. He'd paid for most of the wedding, too, because her family didn't have two bob to rub together, and he'd let her have everything she'd wanted for her big day. If she were honest, she did vaguely recall him saying things like 'a penny saved is a penny earned' and 'good things come to those who wait', but she'd dismissed all that as just part of his staid and careful character, which, back then anyway, she'd thought she could live with.

The tram stopped: several people got off and some more got on. A girl inched her way past the men strap-hanging in the aisle and Irene put up her hand to indicate that there was a spare seat.

The girl sat down beside her. 'Thanks. Whew, crowded today, isn't it?'

'I'll say,' Irene replied, shifting over to give her more room.

'Must be everyone coming into town to do their Christmas shopping.'

'Probably. Though I'm off to work.'

'So am I,' the girl said glumly.

'Where do you work?' Irene asked, though she knew, from the girl's uniform.

'Smith & Caughey's. What about you?'

'Dunbar & Jones.'

'Busy?'

'Flat out,' Irene said.

'Us too,' the girl said. 'My feet are still aching from yesterday.'

Irene smiled, then turned back to the window and her thoughts.

She'd discovered quite quickly, actually, that she couldn't live with Martin's cautious and measured attitude towards life, and it was driving her around the bend. And it wasn't just the money, it was everything. They hardly ever went out, and when they did it was usually only to family gatherings or dinners with Martin's work colleagues, all of whom Irene found deeply uninteresting, particularly the wives, who all seemed to look down their noses at her. And they never went dancing, which Irene loved, so lately she'd started going out to the Peter Pan with some of the girls from work, which often ended up irking her, because she had to go without Martin. He could be quite a lot of fun on the rare occasions he let his hair down — witty, affectionate and very entertaining — and she loved being with him when he was like that. And it was embarrassing, having to tell people that your husband didn't want to take you out. It made her feel as though he didn't care enough about her. But when she told him she was going out with the girls, in the hope that he'd feel jealous enough to accompany her, all he'd ever say was have a lovely time!

And the most annoying thing of all was that most of Martin's flaws were products of his good intentions. He wouldn't spend money because he wanted them to have a nicer house, he worked very hard to earn what was actually a good salary, and because he worked so hard he was always tired. She was a night owl, but he went to bed at nine o'clock most nights to read. If she wanted to have sex, she would have to go to bed at the same time, or she'd miss her chance. If she left it much later than that she would invariably find him asleep with his book on his face. And she did quite often feel like having sex, partly because that was just the way she was, and partly because, in spite of all the frustrations, she loved him. He wasn't unattractive, he was kind and clever, he was good to her — even if his budget decreed that he could only occasionally buy her flowers or the odd box of Queen Anne chocolates — and she was in no doubt that he loved her. He said so often enough, and he frequently told her how beautiful she was and how lucky he was to have such a lovely wife, and on the rare nights that he did manage to stay awake their lovemaking was quite passionate and fulfilling. It's just that he was so . . . boring. It was all boring.

And the one thing she couldn't stand was being bored. It ate away at her, nibbling at the edges of her consciousness until finally there was a yawning great hole, which she would feel compelled to rush off and fill with anything that might blot out the vast, fierce emptiness. It made her lose her patience, it made her say quite inappropriate things at times, it made her spend money she didn't have on things she didn't need, and it led her into 'intrigues' with people — men, to be specific — that she knew were wrong. But, God, they made her feel alive! So far she hadn't had an actual affair with anyone, but she knew it was very likely to happen. She certainly hadn't been a virgin when she'd married Martin, though poor old Martin hadn't known that, and probably still didn't.

The tram turned off Customs Street and into Queen Street, stopping and starting to let people off until it drew level with Dunbar & Jones. The wide front doors of the store were closed but not locked. Irene pushed on one of the heavy brass handles and went inside.

'Morning, Ted,' she said to the little man standing just inside.

Ted Horrocks had been Dunbar & Jones's commissionaire

since 1927. He was short, straight-backed and red-faced, and had a handle-bar moustache admired by many. He was also sixty-four, but Mr Max hadn't the heart to tell him he was too old for the job. And he wasn't; every morning he arrived at exactly eight o'clock, dressed in his beautifully pressed charcoal grey uniform, complete with braided cap, gold buttons and the various medals he'd been awarded during the Great War. He would stand at the door and greet each staff member as they arrived for work, give the brass handles a quick polish, then open them to the public at nine o'clock on the dot. He knew every regular customer's name, could be relied upon to carry even heavy parcels to vehicles outside when required, and could also manage boisterous children as the need arose, though he was sometimes a bit beleaguered regarding this last duty during the school holidays.

'Good morning, Miss Lamarr,' Ted replied, tipping his cap and winking.

Irene laughed: he reckoned she looked just like the film star Hedy Lamarr and had been calling her that ever since she'd started work at Dunbar & Jones.

The store was waking up, getting ready for another hectic day. Irene waved as she passed the girls at the cosmetics counter, busy setting up their displays and dusting yesterday's powder off the glass surfaces, and headed toward the escalator in the centre of the shop floor. Keeping the heels of her suede shoes well clear of the gap between the steps, she stepped on and gripped the handrail, watching as the ground floor receded beneath her.

On the first floor she saw that Allie was already there, and made a quick detour across the ladies' dress department.

'Hi, Allie.'

'Hi, Irene. Busy day ahead?'

Irene nodded. 'Huge pile of typing waiting for me, as usual.'

'At least you can sit down all day.'

'Yes, but in ten years' time my backside will be twice the size of yours,' Irene said, sounding as though she really didn't find the notion amusing at all. 'See you at morning tea, then, eh?'

She was walking away when Allie blurted, 'I'm going out with someone tomorrow night. What do you think I should I wear?'

Irene stopped in her tracks and turned back, her eyebrows raised in delight. 'Well, that's interesting news, isn't it?' she said, knowing that Allie hadn't been out on a date for ages. 'Who's the lucky bloke?'

'It's that Sonny Manaia. You know, the one—'

'—who's been ogling you for the past fortnight in the caf? Really? When did he ask?'

'Yesterday afternoon. In front of Miss Willow and everything. I nearly died.'

'I *told* you he was a smooth one!' Irene said gleefully, pleased that her assessment of Sonny Manaia had been accurate. 'Where's he taking you?'

'To the pictures.'

Irene crossed her arms and frowned in mock concentration. 'Well, let's see. How far are you planning to let him go?'

Embarrassed, Allie exclaimed, 'I'm not planning to let him go anywhere! It's only the flicks, *and* it's a cowboy film. *High Noon*, apparently.'

'Gary Cooper, though,' Irene said appreciatively. 'That'll get you hot under the collar.'

Allie laughed. 'I doubt it. Gary Cooper's not my type.'

'Ah, but Sonny Manaia is?'

'Actually, yes,' Allie admitted, feeling herself reddening.

'In that case, wear something a bit special. What have you got?'

'Well,' Allie said, 'there's my good dress, the claret nylon, and a satin skirt, but they'd be too flash just for the pictures. I've got a few other skirts, though, and I've just finished paying off my new pale pink crêpe de chine blouse. I could wear it with my cream skirt. What about that?'

'Pencil or full?'

'The skirt? Full.'

'No, you'll look like Doris Day.'

Allie frowned. 'My navy cotton shirtwaister?'

Irene looked as though Allie had just suggested wearing her father's winter pyjamas. 'You've got a pencil skirt, haven't you, a dark one?'

'A grey one. It's a bit tight, though.'

'Sounds just the thing. You can borrow my kingfisher blue sweater to go with it, if you like. It's snug on me so it should fit you perfectly.'

Allie glanced at Irene's generous breasts, then down at her own rather more modest ones, and they both laughed.

'And my black heels?' Allie added.

Irene nodded enthusiastically. 'To put just enough wiggle in your walk. I'll bring the sweater in tomorrow.' Then, sounding thoughtful, she asked, 'Are you going out at lunchtime today? No? Good, we'll grab something to eat, then have a bit of a practice with your make-up. How does that sound?'

It sounded like an excellent idea to Allie, who seldom

wore much more than lipstick and a quick dusting of face powder.

Irene felt very pleased with herself. If *she* couldn't get dressed up and go out with someone exciting, then at least she could help Allie do it. And Allie really was rather pretty, with her gold-blonde hair, big cornflower eyes and turned-up nose, though in Irene's opinion she never did much to enhance her looks. Not that she could at work, because Dunbar & Jones salesgirls weren't allowed to wear much make-up, not even on the cosmetics counter. Still, Allie could at least get rid of that awful tangerine lipstick that made her skin look so sallow and try something a little more . . . sophisticated.

Irene waved out to Louise as she dashed past lingerie then skipped onto the escalator, resisting the temptation to take the moving stairs two at a time in case she scuffed her shoes. She stepped off at the second floor, which was as far up as the escalator went, and headed for the rugs and rolls of carpet and linoleum in the floorings department, behind which was the staff door to the stairs leading to the top-floor administration offices and workrooms. Unfortunately, halfway there, she spotted the most divine little Indian rug — just the thing for a wedding present for Daisy and Terry. She bent down and turned the ticket over. Christ, seven pounds and thirteen shillings, just for the smallest size! Oh, well, Martin wouldn't find out if she put it on her staff credit account, and what he didn't know wouldn't hurt him.

'Can I help you, madam?' a voice asked, except that 'madam' was pronounced 'mo*dom*'.

'Vince! You gave me a fright!' Irene exclaimed, straightening up.

'Sorry,' Vincent Reynolds said insincerely. He lowered his voice. 'My God, Irene, you're looking *ravishing*.'

Irene felt a surge of the brittle excitement she craved and her heart soared with elation. Her Spanish red skirt was tight enough to mould her full buttocks, but not so tight that the typing pool supervisor would give her dirty looks all day, and the matching jacket sat nicely over her bust and hugged her small waist, giving her the sort of hourglass figure most women would die for. She also knew that the colour contrasted fabulously with her shining black hair, and she'd worn the suit deliberately today with the specific aim of tantalizing Vince. Obviously she was succeeding.

He reached out to touch her, but stopped himself just in time and stuffed his hands in his trouser pockets. He glanced quickly around then whispered hoarsely, 'Meet me in the basement at lunchtime.'

Irene didn't think so. She'd made other plans, but she wouldn't have gone down to one of the warren-like basement storerooms with him today anyway because the longer she made him wait, the better it would be. So far they had only kissed — a snatched but rather exciting clinch in one of the small rooms to the rear of the second-floor lifts — but she was prepared to be as patient as necessary to get him exactly where she wanted him.

'Oh, Vince, I'm sorry, I can't. I've arranged something with the girls today.'

'Tomorrow, then?' he suggested, aiming for a nonchalant tone but not quite achieving it. His eyes kept darting down to the twin cones of her bosom and a thin sheen of sweat had appeared on his forehead.

Irene pretended to think, though she knew she had

nothing planned. 'Tomorrow? I'm not sure. Shall we see at morning tea?' She didn't need to tell him what time that would be: he seemed to know exactly when she took her breaks.

Vince nodded.

She felt his eyes on her as she walked away and, letting her hips sway just a little more than usual, she couldn't help smiling.

Chapter Three

Do you think I'll find it in a pattern book? Or something like it?'

Daisy had a picture of a wedding dress she had cut out of a magazine and was studying it intently as she picked at her sandwich.

Louise looked at the illustration. 'I expect so. It's quite classic, isn't it, but still modern with the rolled neckline and the cap sleeves.'

'I was going to have long sleeves, but Mum said not to because they'd be too hot for January,' Daisy said, a hint of disappointment in her voice.

'Then get married in the winter, if you want long sleeves,' Irene suggested. She eyed Daisy speculatively for a moment. 'Or can't you wait that long?'

Daisy looked down at the table top. 'No, I can't,' she replied, her face flaming.

There was a long silence.

Then Louise said, 'Oh, Daisy. Why didn't you tell us?'

But Daisy didn't say anything. Irene reached across the table and patted her hand, then surprised everyone by offering some very sensible advice.

'Look, it happens to the best of people, and we all know you think the sun shines out of Terry's backside and the pair of you would have got married anyway. So make yourself the wedding dress *you* want to wear, hold your head up when you walk down the aisle, and to hell with everyone else. What difference does it make, really, eh?'

'You should tell that to my mother,' Daisy said. She was smiling again, but her eyes glistened with unshed tears. 'She won't come out and say it, but she thinks I'm a trollop. And an idiot.'

Louise ferreted in her handbag for a handkerchief and passed it to Daisy. 'I'm sure she doesn't. I expect she's just disappointed. Most mothers would rather everything happened in the right order, but like Irene said, it doesn't always work out like that, does it?'

Daisy shook her head and honked into the handkerchief.

Louise put on her talking-to-a-three-year-old voice. 'So come on then, finish your sandwich and cup of tea and we'll go and look at patterns with long sleeves, shall we? It's your day and you should wear what you like.' She turned to Irene and gave her a small, grateful smile. 'Do you want to come?'

Irene shook her head. 'I would, but Allie's got a date tomorrow night and we're going to work on her make-up.'

'Have you?' Louise said to Allie excitedly. 'Who's the lucky man?'

'Everyone's asked that!' Allie tried to sound annoyed but failed.

Just then Sonny sauntered past their table, a food-laden tray casually balanced on one hand. He inclined his head and winked at her.

57

Why was it, Allie thought, that when Sonny Manaia winked it was clean and fun and like a breath of fresh air, but when Vince Reynolds did it, it was like yesterday's chip fat? She wanted to wink back but knew she wasn't very good at it and would only end up pulling an ugly face, so she smiled instead, and then he was gone.

Grinning, she confessed, 'It's him. Sonny Manaia.'

'Why am I not surprised?' Louise said.

'I don't know, why *are* you not surprised?' Allie was laughing.

Louise nodded. 'Well, good for you. It's about time you went out with someone nice. In fact, it's time you went out, full stop. It's not good for a girl to sit at home night after night.'

'I don't!'

'Oh, stop being everyone's mother, Lou,' Irene admonished. 'Come on, Allie, let's go and get stuck into this war paint.'

The light was quite good in the staff restrooms, because the row of handbasins and mirrors against one wall reflected the light from the high windows opposite.

'It's important, you know,' Irene said, 'to have the right light. You need to see every tiny imperfection.'

'I'd rather not,' Allie replied, scrutinizing her face in one of the mirrors. 'I'm covered in freckles. Oh God, is that a pimple starting? There, on my chin?'

Irene looked. 'A little one, maybe. And you're not covered in freckles, there's only a few across your nose. They make you look . . .' she struggled for an appropriate description, 'sun-kissed!'

'Sun-kissed, my bum. It's not fair, I'm twenty years old and still getting pimples.'

'Are your monthlies due?' Irene asked.

Allie had to think for a second, then nodded. 'In a couple of days.'

Irene waved her hand dismissively. 'You'll be all right for tomorrow night, then. Safe as houses.'

Allie opened her mouth to ask Irene what she meant, then caught on. 'There won't be anything like that! It's only the pictures and I hardly know him.'

'But you'd like to, though, wouldn't you?'

'I'd like to what?'

Irene laughed at the look on Allie's face. 'Know him. Isn't that why you're going out with him?'

'I suppose so.'

'There you are, then.'

Irene used one of the toilets, then came out and washed her hands. She reapplied her lipstick then eased her skirt up around her hips, hitched up her stockings and reattached them to the clasps on her suspender belt. 'Bloody things,' she said. 'They've just about had it. Right, are we ready?'

Allie nodded and Irene took her make-up kit out of her handbag and spread the contents across the bench.

'All right, first we'll start with foundation, then a bit of rouge and some powder, some eyeshadow, and just a touch of mascara, I think.'

Alarmed, Allie said, 'I don't wear eyeshadow.'

'You don't wear anything,' Irene replied. 'Don't worry, I won't make you look like a tart.'

And Allie didn't think she would, either. Though Irene did habitually wear quite a lot of make-up, she always looked beautifully groomed and never overdid anything.

Well, hardly ever. She never needed to — she already had lovely looks, even with no make-up on at all.

Allie closed her eyes and let Irene do whatever she wanted.

When she opened them again and studied her reflection in the mirror, she looked a different person. Well, no, not a *different* person, but certainly a noticeably more glamorous version of herself. Her freckles had disappeared and her complexion was the same colour all over, even her nose, which was often a bit pink from the sun. And her eyes looked bigger and darker, and her mouth was a pretty shade of rose.

Irene stood back and appraised her work. 'Not bad, but you really should do something with your eyebrows,' she said eventually.

'Such as?'

'Pluck them.'

'I wouldn't know where to start,' Allie admitted.

'Well, I would.' Irene rummaged in her bag. 'Here we are,' she said, producing a pair of tweezers. 'I'll just tidy them a bit for you.'

Allie eyed the tweezers nervously. 'Don't make me look like Greta Garbo, though, will you? Mum will kill me.'

'Well, hardly. Greta Garbo's look is very dated. It's all a lot more natural now. Well, a lot fuller, at any rate.'

She leaned in close, pressed a thumb against Allie's temple so the skin there was pulled taut, clamped an errant hair with the tweezers and pulled.

'Ow!'

'Keep still, will you?'

'That really hurt,' Allie complained, rubbing her eyebrow and blinking back tears.

'Do you want me to do this or not?'

'Not really.'

Irene sighed in exasperation. 'Don't be such a baby, Allie. It only stings for a second.'

'For God's sake, Irene, it's only—'

'—the pictures, I know. But you want to make a good first impression, don't you?'

'He's already seen me with untidy eyebrows, you know. Every day at work, remember?'

'Yes, but not up close.'

Allie rolled her eyes.

'Trust me,' Irene insisted. 'This will really make a difference.'

So Allie suffered for another ten minutes, and when Irene had finished she had to admit that the result was quite pleasing, apart from the angry red blotches that Irene guaranteed would be gone before she knew it.

Allie had to wash everything off again because of Dunbar & Jones's no make-up rule, but the marks beneath her eyebrows stayed until afternoon tea.

Fortunately, Sonny wasn't in the cafeteria.

Daisy felt sick again. She knew about morning sickness — from her older married sister Iris who'd had it with both her babies — and she'd certainly been getting that. But it wasn't morning now, it was almost three o'clock. She wondered if feeling sick all day was God's way of punishing her for falling pregnant before she was married, but decided this was stupid. God wouldn't be that mean, surely — or that interested in Daisy Farr.

But then she often had stupid thoughts, or so everyone

in her family continually told her. Terry never did, though. Terry only laughed, but in a nice way, when she came out with one of her questions or observations. And her boss, Miss Button, definitely thought she was stupid. When Daisy had started off stitching orange and red feathers onto one side of a hat and had somehow ended up with bright blue ones on the other side, Miss Button had said, 'No, *no*, Daisy! That hat is supposed to be a symphony of sunset hues, not something you might mistake for a parakeet! Get those blue feathers off as quick as you can. We're behind already and we can't be doing with silly mistakes like that!'

Daisy suspected that Miss Button probably thought she was too busy dreaming about her wedding dress to pay attention to her work, but that wasn't it at all. She was focusing all her will on not being sick, and at least she'd only sewn the wrong coloured feathers on the hat, not thrown up on it. It was a dreadful hat anyway; whoever had ordered it obviously couldn't care less that they were going to look like their head was on fire.

Daisy burped quietly, pressed her fingers to her mouth and swallowed bile. God, she wished this would go away. All of it, not just the morning sickness. She wished she and Terry were already married and living in their own little house somewhere all comfortable and happy. He would mow the lawns in the weekends and she'd cook delicious roasts for Sunday lunch and in the evenings they'd think up names for their baby, which would be arriving at the very earliest nine months after their wedding day, not a shameful five or six months. But instead, she was going to have to waddle down the aisle with a belly on her like a watermelon and all the world knowing what she and Terry had been doing.

She felt a wave of panic jostling to get past the nausea in her throat and did what Louise had suggested at lunchtime: she closed her eyes, breathed slowly in and out until she felt calmer, and told herself about all the good things.

For a start there was Terry, whom she loved more than anything else in her entire life. And there was the baby that they both loved to death already, even if it was coming at the wrong time. *And* they were getting married in only five more weeks. Irene was right: she'd still only be four months pregnant then and if she chose a pattern with a high waist and an A-line skirt and wore a girdle (but not one that was too tight — she didn't want to squash the baby) people might not even notice. So it wasn't all bad, was it?

Beatrice Button climbed off her stool at the head of the work table and came to peer over Daisy's shoulder.

Daisy knew she was there but didn't look up from her work, terrified she would make a hole in the hat with her stitch unpicker if she didn't pay attention. She was a funny woman, Miss Button. She was in her early fifties, Daisy guessed, very short and rather round, but her clothes always fitted her perfectly. She said that to patronize any other store would be disloyal and only ever wore clothes from Dunbar & Jones, whether they were off the peg — which wasn't often because of her rather odd shape — or garments she'd had made by the store's dressmakers. When she and Miss Willow arrived at work together, which they did every day because of their living arrangements, they looked more than a little bit like Laurel and Hardy, though no one dared say that to their faces.

Miss Button said, 'You look a little green around the gills, Daisy. Are you not feeling well?'

Alarmed, Daisy replied, 'No, I'm all right, Miss Button, thank you.'

Miss Button gave Daisy a look. 'You don't look all right. Do you need to go to the sick bay?'

'No, thank you,' Daisy lied. Her nausea had suddenly worsened and her mouth was starting to water. Through clenched teeth she added, 'I might just go and get a drink, though, if that's all right.'

'Of course it is.'

Daisy got off her stool and hurried from the workroom, heading for the toilets. Banging into a cubicle, she knelt in front of the bowl just in time as her lunch came up in a hot, stinging gush. She waited for a minute until she was sure it was all out, spat a couple of times and wiped her mouth on a wad of toilet paper, then flushed the loo.

In the mirror above the handbasin, she looked a fright. Her eyes were red and watery and her face was very pale, but she felt a lot better. This seemed to be the pattern her body had established — feeling sick just before breakfast then OK after she'd eaten, then sick again until lunch, then again afterwards until she finally threw up. But at least she got to enjoy her afternoon tea.

On the way back she bumped into Terry, who was hovering in the corridor that led along to the millinery workroom. His tie was knotted crookedly, the tail of his shirt wasn't tucked in properly, his kind brown eyes were full of concern and his usual shy smile was noticeably absent.

'Are you all right? I saw you rushing into the toilets,' he said in a loud whisper. 'Are you feeling sick? Because if you are, I've got these for you.' He handed Daisy a paper bag; she opened it and saw that it contained home-made oat biscuits. 'Mum said they're good for morning sickness. A bit late today, though, obviously.'

Daisy looked up at Terry's lovely, gentle face and wanted to kiss him, but didn't in case she smelled of sick. Instead, she pushed back a lock of his dark brown hair that had flopped over his forehead. 'Oh, that's so nice of her, tell her thank you very much,' she said, wishing her own mother were a bit more like Terry's.

'She made them this morning,' he went on, 'so they should last a few days. She says you're meant to have them with a cup of tea whenever you feel squiffy.'

'Oh, right,' Daisy said, not convinced that Miss Button would be too happy about her setting up her own little tea party on the workroom table.

Terry touched her hand. 'Are you really all right? You don't have to keep on working, you know, not if you're not feeling well. I can give you a bit of money until we're married.'

Daisy felt her eyes brim with tears at his thoughtfulness. 'That's a lovely thing to say, but it's only another five weeks.' She lowered her voice, not wanting three-quarters of Dunbar & Jones's office staff and all of the tailors, dressmakers and milliners to hear. 'And it's only morning sickness, it'll go away soon.'

'Are you sure?'

Daisy nodded, though she wasn't.

'Miss Button isn't giving you a rough time, is she?'

'No, only when I make a mistake,' Daisy replied. 'But she does that to everyone when they make mistakes, especially when we're busy.' And to be fair, Miss Button was firm, that was all, and she had to be that because it was her job.

65

'We're flat out, too,' Terry said. 'I'd better get back. Wait for me after work?'

As she watched him hurry off, Daisy told herself yet again what a lucky girl she was to have a boy as wonderful as Terry.

Louise got off the tram at Avondale, savouring the pleasurable anticipation she always felt when she went to pick up Susan after work. For months now Rob had been putting in long hours at the garage where he worked in Parnell, so she usually collected Susan from her parents' home, then walked her the two blocks to the small house they were renting. But they wouldn't be paying good money to a landlord for much longer. They couldn't afford much, but it would be marvellous to have their own place and be able to do what they liked with it. And when Rob got the raise his boss had been hinting at lately, there might even be enough money for her to stop work and be a proper mother. She knew that Susan was well looked after during the day — despite Rob's mother carping on about it incessantly — and she enjoyed working at Dunbar & Jones, but deep down she wanted to be at home with her daughter. It wasn't right, bringing a child into the world then abandoning it five days a week to go out to work, but Susan deserved a proper home.

Louise opened the gate to her mother's house and hurried down the path, calling out as she went, 'Susan! Mummy's here!'

There was a bang as the fly screen on the back door flew open, then the sound of little feet belting around the side of the house. Susan appeared a moment later in her favourite pink dress with the frill around the hem and little black patent leather shoes, with her chestnut curls flying and most of her hairclips missing. In her hand was a large piece of paper, which she was waving madly.

'Mummy! Mummy, look what I drawed!'

Louise crouched down. 'Hello, sweetheart! What is it?'

Susan held up the paper for her mother to see. 'It's a horsie! There's his legs and there's his tail, and there's his ears and . . . that other thing.'

'His mane? Gosh, what an excellent picture! Did Grandma buy you some new crayons?'

'Yes. I got red and green, and yellow, and . . . red. And . .' Susan trailed off, her finger in her mouth. 'I forget the rest.'

'Well, you must have got brown, because you've coloured the horsie in brown, haven't you? And blue, because here's the beach.'

'No, it's not the beach, it's a lake!' Susan pointed. 'See? Here's a birdie, cleaning his teeth in it.'

'So he is!'

'We had skibetti for lunch,' Susan said, indicating a smear of orange down the front of her dress. 'But I didn't clean my teeth after.'

Louise stood up. 'I wouldn't worry about it, sweetheart. Twice a day is probably enough. Where's Grandma?'

'Inside. We done baking. She's cleaning up.'

'We *did* baking,' Louise corrected. 'What did you make?'

'Come and have a look,' Susan said, taking Louise's hand. 'We saved some for you and Daddy.'

Louise allowed her small daughter to lead her around to the rear of the house and up the back steps. Her mother's kitchen was cool and a little dim after the bright sunshine outside.

Marion Bourke was standing at the sink washing dishes. She wore slippers but was bare-legged, her varicose veins making fat purple worms over her ankles and pale calves.

'Hello, love,' she said. 'Good day at work?'

'Busy,' Louise replied.

'Cuppa?'

'No, thanks, Mum, I need to get home and get tea on. How was madam today?'

Marion dried her hands on a tea-towel. 'Madam was an absolute princess, as always. Helped me with the housework and then we went for a walk to the shops, didn't we?' Susan nodded energetically. 'And after lunch we did some drawing and then a bit of baking.' Marion nodded towards the kitchen table, where a small pile of greyish, rubbery-looking pikelets sat on a plate. Raising an amused eyebrow, she said, 'They've been on the floor twice, but we got most of the fluff off.'

'They're for you and Daddy,' Susan said proudly.

'Yummy,' Louise replied enthusiastically. 'Shall we save them for supper tonight?'

Susan nodded, but she'd lost interest in the pikelets. Eccles, the Bourkes' cat, had slunk into the kitchen and was weaving around the legs of the table, taking care to keep well out of Susan's reach.

'Can I pat him?' she asked her grandmother.

'If he'll let you.'

Susan made a lunge for the cat, but he saw her coming and streaked for the back door, his claws scrabbling on the worn lino.

'Eccles doesn't like me,' Susan declared sadly.

Marion said, 'Yes, he does, sweetie. He's just being a grumpy-bum today.'

In fact, Eccles was always a grumpy-bum around Susan, who adored him but, on the rare occasions she managed to pick him up, almost squeezed the life out of him in her enthusiasm.

'Come on, missy,' Louise urged gently. 'We have to go home and cook Daddy's tea, so say goodbye to Grandma, there's a good girl.'

Marion bent down far enough for Susan to kiss her cheek.

'Bye-bye, Gran,' Susan said.

'See you tomorrow, love. Don't forget your pikelets!'

Louise asked, 'Will about quarter to eight be all right? I need to get in early.'

'Shall I feed you breakfast then, madam?' Marion said to Susan. 'Porridge and golden syrup?'

Susan clapped her hands and charged outside, yelling 'Podge and *syrup*, podge and *syrup!*', and scaring the wits out of Eccles, who was hiding under the lemon tree.

'Thanks, Mum,' Louise said. 'I mean it.'

Marion kissed her daughter. 'I wouldn't miss it, love. She keeps me young, she really does.'

That night Allie lay in bed, doing her best to get to sleep because she had a busy day tomorrow, but failing miserably. She'd had a hot cup of cocoa and a long bath to relax. She'd tried counting sheep but had given up when she'd got to a thousand. She'd imagined herself lying on the beach at Mission Bay in her togs, the sun warm on her skin, the breeze so light she could barely feel it, and the small waves hissing in and out, in and out, in and out, lulling her closer and closer to sleep, but that hadn't worked either. Then she'd read for half an hour, a book she'd pinched out of Donna's satchel — Mickey Spillane's latest, *Kiss Me, Deadly*, which had been banned by the school, so God only knew where she'd got it — but found the story quite unpleasantly violent and gave up on it.

Now she was lying in the dark, her bedroom window open and the blind up a little to let in the smell of the sea, still thinking about Sonny Manaia and her date with him the following night. She was looking forward to it, and feeling nervous about it, in roughly equal measures. When she'd said to Irene that she hardly knew him, it had been the truth: she'd never even spoken to him before Monday. He'd come into the cafeteria one morning with a group of the lads from stores and you couldn't help noticing him. He was nice-looking and had sort of a confident air about him and seemed to have plenty of mates.

And of course he was Maori, and there weren't many Maoris working at Dunbar & Jones. Allie tried to count them in her head. She thought there might be two blokes in stores, and there was Hori who drove one of the delivery vans. And one of the girls in the typing pool was part-Maori, she knew that. So those four, plus Sonny, made five — not many in a staff of nearly four hundred and fifty. There was the girl who had modelled in the dress department's spring fashion show, a really beautiful young woman, but Allie didn't count her because she wasn't sure if she actually was Maori, or whether she was from some exotic faraway country. Somewhere foreign probably, with her stunning looks. And anyway she wasn't a house model so she wasn't on the Dunbar & Jones payroll.

70

And who was Sonny Manaia, anyway? What had he been doing before he came to work at Dunbar & Jones? Where did he come from and where did he live? She didn't even know what age he was, though she suspected he couldn't be that much older than she was. And why did he want to take her out? She wasn't the sort of girl who stood out in a crowd, though sometimes she did laugh a bit loudly in the cafeteria: she couldn't help it once she got going. What if she didn't turn out to be what he'd been expecting?

She'd been out with boys before, of course, and had had a boyfriend, Derek, for six months, but it hadn't lasted. What she'd initially taken for a reserved and cautious nature had turned out to be dullness and a distinct lack of initiative, and she'd grown tired of always being the one to decide what they were going to do on Friday and Saturday nights, so eventually she told him it wasn't working out and that was that. So why was she so nervous about this date?

She was also worried about what she was going to wear. She knew it shouldn't be that important, but she kept turning it over and over in her head. She'd told Irene she had decided on her grey skirt and Irene's bright blue top, but when she'd tried them on together that night the outfit had looked a bit, well, tarty, to be honest. Well, certainly much closer to racy than . . . not racy. Especially with her black platform heels that made her two and a half inches taller than she actually was. Oh God, how tall was Sonny? She couldn't remember. What if she towered over him? Perhaps she should take another pair of shoes in her bag just in case. But would they go in? Only her flats would fit in her handbag, and they wouldn't match the rest of her outfit.

She threw her blankets off, sat up and exclaimed, 'Oh, for God's sake!'

Almost immediately there was a tap on her bedroom door. It was her mother.

'Can't sleep?' Colleen asked.

She had on her slippers and her old chenille dressing gown, which had once been a deep apricot colour and was now so faded it was almost white, and her hair was pulled back in a plait that hung down past her shoulders. She wasn't a particularly vain woman, but she was proud of her hair, which was still thick and lustrous and not yet showing any signs of grey. Sid, thinking he was being complimentary, had once said that grey would never show anyway in all that lovely deep gold, but Colleen had been out of sorts for days, insisting that if she did have grey hairs they *would* be visible, so obviously she didn't have any. Sid had kept his mouth shut about her hair after that.

'No,' Allie said. 'Can't you either?'

'Had to go to the lav.' Colleen sat down on Allie's bed. 'Why can't you sleep?'

Allie shrugged. 'Don't know, really.'

'It's that boy you're going out with tomorrow night, isn't it?'

After a moment, Allie said, 'Yes.'

Colleen waited for a minute. 'Well, what about him?'

Allie made a face. 'I can't decide what to wear.'

'Is that all? Really?'

'I don't know. Yes, I think so.'

Colleen pulled at a loose thread on her dressing gown. 'If it's about what your father said last night, I wouldn't be too worried about it. You know what he can be like.'

When Allie had told her parents that she was going to

the pictures with a Maori boy, Colleen had said 'That's nice, love', and Sid had said 'Well, make sure he pays, keep an eye on your purse and don't stop off at the pub or you'll never get him out', then laughed his head off. Colleen had had a go at him and said that was a bit like the pot calling the kettle black, and Sid had said it was just a joke, and everyone knew the Maoris liked a drink and had a very communal view of money and property. Colleen had said she'd never heard anything so derogatory in her life and Sid had said what was 'derogatory' when it was at home and retreated behind his paper, not quite sure what he'd done wrong.

'No, it wasn't that,' Allie replied. She was used to her father being tactless and saying the wrong thing. 'It's just that, well, I think I quite like him and I just want to get it right tomorrow night, that's all.'

'Look, love,' Colleen said, 'he's asked *you* out, not your wardrobe. Go out and have a good time. It doesn't matter what you wear and it doesn't matter if he's a Maori or from Mars, as long as you enjoy yourself. All right?'

Her mother always had such a knack for putting things in perspective. Feeling a lot better, Allie went back to bed, and this time she fell asleep straight away.

Chapter Four

Allie spent half the day with butterflies in her stomach at the thought of going out with Sonny, and the other half berating herself for feeling like a silly schoolgirl. Fortunately, she was kept extremely busy, getting garments ready for the fashion show Dunbar & Jones was presenting the next night, as well as attending to an apparently endless stream of customers.

She did, however, see Sonny at lunchtime in the cafeteria. He stopped at her table and said 'Still on for tonight?', which made Allie go bright red and robbed her of the ability to say anything sensible, so she only nodded while Irene, Louise and Daisy looked on with gleeful interest.

During afternoon tea she ducked down to the cosmetics department on the ground floor where Bev, the Helena Rubenstein girl, was arranging a pile of Apple Blossom perfume and talc gift packs on the counter.

'Hi, Allie. What can I do you for?'

'Hi, Bev. I'm after a new lipstick and some mascara.'

Bev's eyebrows went up. 'Big date?'

'Could be.'

'Any particular colour?' Bev asked as she carefully balanced the last pack on the top of her display.

'I've been told it has to be a pink one.'

'By who?' Bev frowned. 'Or is it "whom"?'

'Irene. She did my face for me yesterday and reckons the tangerine I usually wear isn't right for my skin tone.'

'But darling, tangerine is your signature colour!' Bev exclaimed.

'Cut it out,' Allie said. 'So what have you got in pink?'

Bev beckoned her along the counter to the display of Helena Rubenstein lipsticks. 'Rose Mauve?' she suggested, picking out a tester and winding the lipstick out of its case. 'Give us your hand.'

Allie held her hand out, palm down.

'Other way,' Bev said. 'Your fingertips. They're the closest to your natural lip colour.'

Well, Allie thought, that was something she hadn't known until today.

Bev applied a dash of the lipstick to the tip of Allie's forefinger and studied the effect critically. She looked at Allie's face. 'Too deep, I reckon. What about Tender Pink?'

'Sounds nice,' Allie agreed, and stuck out her middle finger this time.

'That's a better colour for you,' Bev said. 'Do you want to try some on your lips?' She retrieved a tissue from beneath the counter, gave the tip of the lipstick a good wipe, then used a tiny brush to collect some of the colour. 'Have a seat.'

Allie climbed up onto the high wooden chair on the customer side of the counter and sat very still while Bev came around and applied the lipstick.

'Actually, I don't know about that one, either,' Bev said when she'd finished. 'It's too red, makes you look more like Tender Loin. What colour did Irene put on you?'

Allie shrugged. 'I don't know. It was really pretty, though, a nice pearly pink.'

Bev tapped her teeth thoughtfully with the handle of the lipstick brush. 'I might ask Anita what she's got.'

She walked down to the other end of the counter and came back a moment later with Anita, who was the Elizabeth Arden girl.

'Hi,' Anita said, holding up a lipstick. 'Have you tried this? It's the new colour Elizabeth Arden put out for the coronation. It's called Perfection Pink and there's a rouge to go with it.'

The colour looked good on Allie, so she put it on her staff account along with a cake of mascara that had its own little brush. She didn't buy the matching rouge, though. It cost too much.

But by the time the store closed at five o'clock she'd almost convinced herself she'd changed her mind about going out. Buying the lipstick had only made her feel even more nervous and all the way home she dithered yet again over what to wear, finally deciding at her front gate that she'd wear the grey skirt and blue top after all. She ran herself a long bath, eliciting protest from Donna and Pauline in case there wasn't any hot water left for theirs, and sat in it for half an hour until the water had gone tepid. She washed her hair, shaved her legs with her father's razor and pinched some of her mother's good talc after she'd dried herself.

Tea was put on the table just as she was ducking down

the hall to her bedroom, a towel wrapped, turban style, around her wet hair.

'I don't want anything to eat, thanks, Mum,' Allie called. 'My hair will dry funny.'

'You *will* have something to eat,' Colleen replied. 'You're not going out on an empty stomach.'

So Allie sat down at the kitchen table in her dressing gown with the towel still on her hair.

Sid said, 'Oh, look, it's Lawrence of Arabia.'

'Stop that, Sid,' Colleen said as she set plates of chops, beans and potatoes on the table.

Donna and Pauline were staring at Allie.

'Your face is bright red from the bath,' Donna taunted.

'Yes, and there's a *huge* pimple on your chin,' Pauline added gleefully.

'Is there?' Allie's hand flew to her face.

'No, there isn't,' Colleen said as she sat down. 'Don't be mean, girls. Leave your sister alone.'

Donna and Pauline smirked into their plates.

'What's he like then, this bloke?' Pauline asked.

'Fellow,' Colleen corrected.

Donna said, 'Is he coming to pick you up?'

'I'm meeting him in town,' Allie replied.

'Bugger,' Donna swore. 'We wanted to see him.'

'I beg your pardon!' Colleen said, glaring at Donna. 'What?'

'You just watch your mouth, young lady. Where you get language like that from I don't know.'

'Jesus bloody Christ,' Sid said as he missed his mouth with his fork and spilt beans down his front.

'Sid!' Colleen was losing her temper now.

Allie started laughing. And then Sid joined in, which

Donna and Pauline took as a sign to giggle hysterically themselves.

'Honestly, sometimes I wonder about you lot,' Colleen remonstrated, but she got up and went to the fridge in search of the butter so no one could see she was smiling.

Allie bolted a chop, a mouthful of potato and six beans, then said 'Excuse me' as she pushed her chair back from the table.

Colleen looked up. 'Is that all you're going to eat?'

'I'm not that hungry.' In fact, Allie's stomach felt as though there were a hundred angry sparrows in it, all fluttering madly to get out.

'Oh, go on then.' Colleen said, remembering what it was like to be young and getting ready to go out on a date.

Allie went to her room, shut the door and sat down in front of her dressing table. She lit a cigarette and left it burning in the ashtray, took the towel off her hair and felt her heart sink. Hurrying into the bathroom, she ran hot water over her comb, rewet the renegade sections of her hair, then dashed back to her room and bunged in half a dozen rollers. While she waited for it to set she started on her make-up.

Though she'd been impressed with what Irene had done yesterday, the result had made her feel sort of uncomfortable and self-conscious — it just wasn't her. So tonight she left off the eyeshadow, though she did try some of her new mascara. She had to have several goes, however, because it wasn't as easy to put on as Irene had made it look, and she couldn't seem to stop her hand from shaking.

When her hair had dried, she took out the rollers and brushed it until it shone, then lacquered it vigorously so it would stay in place. After she'd changed into her going-out clothes, which included a new pair of twelve-denier stockings that had cost her ten shillings and ninepence, even with her staff discount, she applied her new rose-coloured lipstick and sprayed her wrists and throat with White Magnolia perfume.

'You'd better be worth it, Sonny Manaia,' she said to her reflection in the mirror. This date had cost her a fortune.

Sid whistled when she went out into the kitchen. 'Look at our little girl, Col,' he said. 'All grown up.'

Colleen frowned. 'Yes, I can see that. You don't think that skirt's a little on the snug side?'

'No,' Allie replied, resisting the urge to tug it down because she knew it wouldn't budge. She'd be in trouble if she had to run for the bus.

'Hasn't he got a car?' Pauline demanded.

'I don't know, I didn't ask.' Which wasn't strictly true; Allie had automatically assumed Sonny didn't own one.

'Fancy not having a car!' Donna said.

'Donna, what did I say to you before?' Colleen warned.

'I'm just saying—'

'Well, don't.'

'I'll be off, then,' Allie said, edging towards the door.

Colleen asked, 'What time do you think you'll be home?'

'About half ten, I suppose. I'll get the late bus.'

'You be careful, love,' Colleen added.

Allie knew her mother wasn't just referring to going into town on her own. 'I will, don't worry.'

By the time the bus slowed at the Wellesley Street stop Allie was convinced that Sonny wouldn't be there. But he was, standing just outside the Civic Theatre. It was nearly dark now, but not so dark that she couldn't see that Sonny was grinning broadly at her. It wasn't even remotely cold but she caught herself shivering.

'Hi,' he said.

'Hello.'

Sonny took his hands out of his pockets. 'You look nice.'

'Thank you. So do you.'

Out of his work clothes, he looked very smart, if slightly ill at ease. He was wearing grey trousers, a blue shirt without a tie, a dark grey sports coat and highly polished black shoes. He was freshly shaven and close up he smelled of something that reminded Allie of wood smoke, but sweeter. Cedar?

'We're twins,' he said, nodding at her own blue and grey outfit.

'So we are,' Allie said.

And so they stood there, awkwardly saying nothing as people walked around them heading into the theatre.

Sonny looked at his watch. 'Film starts in ten minutes. You want to go in?'

As Sonny paid for their tickets, Allie thought take that, Dad, you narrow-minded old bugger.

She loved the Civic Theatre with its exotic Moorish-themed foyer and perpetual promise of fantasy and excitement. She was staring up at the domed, ornately decorated ceiling when she realized that Sonny was talking to her.

'Pardon?'

Sonny nodded towards the refreshments counter. 'Do

you fancy an ice cream or chocolates or anything?'

'No, thanks,' Allie said. 'We had a big tea.' Untrue, but she was far too nervous to eat anything now.

'We'll find our seats, then, eh?'

Allie waited while their tickets were torn in half, then followed Sonny up the carpeted stairs into the auditorium, marvelling as she always did at the lofty midnight-blue ceiling sprinkled with hundreds of glittering stars.

Apologizing and squeezing their way past people, they found their seats and sat down, looking down at a stage that seemed to be miles below them.

'Hope there isn't a fire,' Sonny remarked, 'we'd never get out.'

Allie laughed.

There was another short silence, then they both spoke at once.

'Sorry,' Sonny said, 'go on.'

'I was just going to say, do you like cowboy films?'

'Yeah, they're OK. Do you?'

'They're OK,' Allie echoed. She cast about for something else to say. 'What about war films, do you like those?'

'Not really. Load of rubbish, most of them.'

Allie wasn't sure how to respond to that. Normally she was good at conversation, even with people she didn't know, but she was making very heavy weather of it at the moment. Eventually she said, 'Busy at work?'

'Flat out. Everybody wanting things for Christmas and for the queen so there's lots of stuff coming in and going out. What about you?'

'The same.' She waited a beat before she went on. 'So when did you start at Dunbar & Jones?'

'Beginning of October.'

Allie nodded with satisfaction. 'Yes, that's about when I first noticed you.'

Sonny turned to her, looking very pleased with himself. 'Ah, so you'd already noticed me, had you?'

Wishing that the lights had already gone down so he couldn't see the blood rushing to her face, Allie said, 'The first time I saw you, I mean. In the caf.'

'I noticed you the day I started, sitting there with your friends with that beautiful big smile of yours and that lovely hair.'

Allie was so startled she could only stare at him.

Sonny laughed. 'What? It's true. You've got fantastic hair.'

'Well, um, thank you,' Allie said, thoroughly unused to such compliments, particularly from men. 'I get it from my mother, even though she's Irish. Most people think Irish women have dark hair, but my mother's really fair. Or she was — it's fading a bit now she's getting older.'

Aware she was prattling, Allie stopped, though Sonny seemed to be quite absorbed by what she was saying. This close she could see he had a line of small, pink scars marking the brown skin of his face, going from the outside of his right cheekbone and disappearing under his jaw. It looked as though he'd run into a particularly nasty length of barbed wire.

'Got any brothers or sisters?' he asked. Clearly he was struggling for things to say as well.

'Two younger sisters, fifteen and fourteen.'

He nodded. 'Both your parents still alive?'

'Yes,' Allie said, slightly shocked. 'Aren't yours?'

'Mum is. My old man died a couple of years ago.'

Allie felt awful. 'God, I'm sorry.'

Sonny shrugged. 'He wasn't much to write home about. Sometimes I think we're better off.'

'Do you have brothers and sisters?' Allie asked, unnerved by Sonny's response and deliberately changing the subject.

'Five older brothers and sisters, and five younger ones.'

'There's *eleven* of you?'

Sonny smiled. 'We don't all live at home. There's no room since we moved, anyway. I'm the oldest still there, and I'll be shifting out as soon as I get set up.' He must have seen the question in her face because he added, 'I'm twenty-three.'

'Oh. I'm—'

'Twenty, I know.'

Allie frowned.

'I asked Terry at work,' Sonny said. 'She's hapu, his girlfriend, isn't she?'

'Pardon?'

'That girl he goes with. She's . . .' he held his hands out over his stomach, '. . . having a baby.'

'And did Terry tell you that as well?' Allie didn't think Daisy would be very pleased.

'Yeah. He was having a bit of a worry one day, and he told me about it.' Sonny shrugged again. 'It's all right, it's none of my business. He's a nice bloke, Terry.'

'Mmm, he is. And Daisy's lovely, too. It's a secret, though, about the baby.'

Sonny grinned. 'Won't be a secret when it gets born six months after the wedding, though, will it?'

Annoyed, Allie said, 'And that's funny, is it?'

'Not really, but it happens, doesn't it? And like I said, it's none of my business. Good on him, though. Some blokes would run a mile.'

As Allie was pondering how very true this was, the lights dimmed, a rash of coughing washed through the auditorium, and, below them, heavy curtains swept silently back from the cinema screen.

First up was a newsreel showing something about the establishment of a new Egg Marketing Authority and an item about the Wattie's cannery in Hawke's Bay, neither of which was very interesting, and another on the New Zealand soldiers who were still stationed in Korea, even though the war had ended in July.

'I hardly know anything about the Korean War,' Allie said when the newsreel had finished.

'Most people don't,' Sonny answered shortly.

'It's awful, though, don't you think? We had soldiers there for nearly three years and nobody seemed to give a toss. Nobody at home, anyway.'

'Suited some people,' Sonny said.

Allie looked at him. 'What do you mean?'

'Well, look at the sheep farmers, for a start. Wool prices just about tripled overnight.'

But before Allie could ask Sonny how on earth he knew that, the main feature started. Unfortunately, at the same time, two women sat down in the seats in front of Allie, one of them wearing a hat so large it almost completely blocked the screen.

'Bugger,' Allie said under her breath, and leaned as far to the right as she could. She could have moved to the left, of course, but she didn't want to do that in case Sonny thought it was just an excuse for her to fall all over him.

'Can't you see?' he asked.

'Not really.'

Sonny slid forward in his seat, tapped the woman on the

shoulder and said, 'Hey, lady, excuse me, but my girlfriend can't see through your bloody big hat. Can you take it off, please?'

Utterly affronted, the woman turned around. Above the silhouette of her hat, Allie could just see the top third of a group of desperadoes gathering on the outskirts of a wild west town, but not much else.

'I *beg* your pardon?' the woman said.

'I said, can you take your hat off? It's in the way.'

'I've never heard anything so outrageous in my life!'

'Haven't you? You can't get out much, then.'

Allie laughed out loud, then clapped her hand to her mouth.

The woman turned to her companion and announced, 'Come on Edith, we're finding somewhere else to sit. I refuse to be harangued by . . . by *his* sort!'

'Better?' Sonny asked after they'd gone.

'Much, thank you.' Allie knew that if she'd been by herself she wouldn't have had the nerve to say anything.

They settled in to watch the film, which Allie found much more entertaining than she'd expected. During the big fistfight, Sonny's arm, which was lying along the back of Allie's seat, inched down until it rested across her shoulders. She froze for a moment, then let herself lean into him. She quickly realized how uncomfortable she was, but decided it was worth putting up with.

As the credits rolled up the screen, Allie sat up straight in her seat, easing the crick in her neck. The lights came on and Sonny took his arm away.

'Well, that wasn't bad, was it?' Allie said.

Sonny turned to her and sang 'Do not forsake me, oh my daaarlin' '.

'I'll try not to.'

Grinning, Sonny stood up and stretched until Allie was sure she heard his spine crack. 'A bit hard on your arse, these seats.'

Allie's bum was numb, too, but she certainly wasn't going to rub it to get the circulation going in the middle of the Civic Theatre.

They waited until their row had cleared, then shuffled along until they reached the aisle, waiting for a gap in the stream of people heading out of the auditorium. When someone moved in front of Allie, Sonny reached back, took her hand and drew her up next to him. His hand was warm and a little rough at the base of his fingers. He squeezed and Allie squeezed back.

'Well,' she said, when they'd been disgorged into the foyer, 'thank you for that. I really enjoyed it.'

'Good. So did I.' Sonny smoothed his hair back from his forehead. 'Want to go for a drink or something?'

'A drink?' Allie was surprised; her hand was already in her bag feeling around for her bus money.

'The Wintergarden downstairs is open. Or we could get a coffee or something.'

'I'm not sure.' Allie knew her mother would worry if she wasn't home when she'd said. 'I've got work tomorrow.'

'So have I.'

'No. Thanks, Sonny, but I'd better not. I've had a lovely night, though.'

'Tomorrow night?'

'I'm sorry, I'm busy.' And she was, with the fashion show.

'Another time, then,' he said.

Allie suddenly realized that she'd played her hand badly,

and felt almost winded with disappointment. 'Yes, another time.'

Outside it was still pleasantly warm and there were plenty of people out and about. Christmas and royal tour decorations mounted on telegraph poles and the façades of buildings sparkled and gleamed in the street lights, lending Queen Street a particularly festive air. Further down the street she could see Dunbar & Jones's giant kiwi and lion flashing away twenty feet above the footpath.

Sonny let go of her hand. 'Allie, I didn't mean "another time" as in let's forget about it. I meant, will you go out with me again?'

Her spirits suddenly soaring again, Allie shocked herself by saying, 'No, why don't *you* come out with *me*? Do you like dancing?'

'Well, they don't call me the King of Swing for nothing.'

'Who calls you the King of Swing?'

Sonny grinned. 'No one, actually, but they should.'

'Well, some Friday nights a group of us from work go to the Peter Pan. Terry and Daisy usually go, and Louise and her husband Rob. You know Louise, the tall, thin girl with the chestnut hair?'

Sonny nodded.

'And sometimes Irene as well, though her husband doesn't like going out much so she's usually on her own.'

'Irene's the dark one with the . . .'

'Yes, that's her.' Allie felt a stab of irritation. 'Obviously you've noticed her.'

'Who hasn't?' Sonny said. 'She's a beaut-looking woman.'

'Yes, she is,' Allie admitted.

'Not my cup of tea, though,' Sonny said. He reached up to her hair and gently wound a strand of it around his finger. 'I like my women all shiny and golden.'

Shiny, golden and bright red, Allie thought, as she felt her face burn.

He saw her embarrassment, and rescued her from it. 'So, yeah, I'd like to come dancing with you,' he said. 'This Friday, you reckon?'

Allie nodded.

'I'll look forward to it.'

'So will I.' Reluctantly, Allie looked at her watch. 'I've got to go now, though, or I'll miss my bus.'

'I can give you a lift home.'

'Oh. I didn't think you had . . .' Not wanting him to embarrass *him* now, Allie stopped.

'A car?' Sonny said. 'I don't, but I've got my brother's truck. It's not very flash, but it'll get you home.' He looked doubtful for a moment. 'Probably. Where do you live?'

'Orakei.'

'Well, that's easy. So do I.'

'Really?' Allie was delighted. 'What street?'

'Kitemoana.'

Allie held Sonny's almost defiant gaze, willing her face not to betray what she was ashamed to be thinking: how could a boy as bright and capable and well dressed as Sonny Manaia come from somewhere like Kitemoana Street? 'That's good,' she said. 'I live in Coates Ave, so it's not too far out of your way.'

'Right, then,' Sonny said, and Allie saw in his eyes that he knew exactly what she'd been thinking. 'Truck's parked up the road.'

He took her hand again and they turned into Wellesley

Street and started walking up the hill. They crossed Albert Street, then Sonny stopped.

The truck was old — much older than her father's Morris 8. She didn't know much about vehicles, but this one looked pre-First World War, never mind Second World War. It had a small, square cab and a wooden deck, and long curving mudguards over the front wheels. It also had rust everywhere and dents in the bonnet and in the passenger door. It might have been painted green once, but it was hard to tell.

Sonny was watching her. 'I'm getting something of my own in a few days,' he said, 'but beggars can't be choosers, and at the moment I'm a beggar.'

He opened the passenger door and held Allie's elbow as she climbed in, then went around to the driver's side. Allie's window was down so she wound the handle — the frame came up, but there was no glass in it. She looked at Sonny and they both burst out laughing.

'Told you,' he said.

'I think it's . . . quaint,' Allie said.

'I think it's a heap of shit.'

That set them off again. Sonny started the motor and they rattled up Wellesley Street for a few yards before he did a U-turn, coasted down the hill with the engine back-firing loudly so that people on the footpath turned around to look, then turned left into Queen Street.

The truck was very noisy, so Allie didn't say much during the ride home. Sonny lit a cigarette, offered her one and then lit it for her with a shiny metal lighter. The smoke hovered in the cab for a second, then was sucked out through the missing window. When he shut the motor off outside her gate the silence seemed almost deafening.

They sat for a minute, saying nothing.

'Well,' Sonny said eventually. He got his cigarettes out again. 'Another smoke?'

'No, thanks.'

He put the pack away and gazed down the street. 'Sky's nice and clear.'

'Yes, it is,' Allie replied. Her nerves were humming like a tuning fork and she wished he would either say goodnight or kiss her. The tension was killing her.

He swivelled in his seat to face her, and she was just about to thank him again for a lovely night when he bent forward and brushed his lips against hers. It wasn't a proper kiss, but it was very nice. He pulled back so he could see her properly, slid his hand into her hair and swept it back off her face.

But, to Allie's instant embarrassment, his fingers caught in a patch of hardened lacquer.

'Whoops, sorry,' he said, wiggling his fingers gently to extricate them, which only made it worse. He sat there for a moment, his hand caught just above Allie's ear, then started to laugh.

Allie was mortified now.

He moved closer. 'Hang on,' he said and, gripping the hair near her scalp with his free hand, jiggled the other one until his fingers became disentangled. 'Sorry,' he said again, still grinning.

There was nothing Allie could say that wouldn't sound completely inane, so she leaned over and kissed him. Immediately his arms came up and settled around her, pulling her against him. His lips were smooth and warm, and she could feel his heart beating beneath his shirt. She slid her hand over his chest, and was mildly pleased to note that he wasn't wearing a singlet, which would have reminded her too much of her father and his baggy braces.

They kissed for several long minutes, and when Allie finally pulled away she was convinced she was only seconds away from melting completely. She was panting slightly and knew that if she didn't go inside now, she might do something she'd regret. Or not regret at all, which would be even more dangerous.

'I'd better go,' she murmured, and was relieved when Sonny nodded.

'I'd walk you in, but . . . I can't,' he said, looking down at his lap.

Allie looked down herself: the lump in his trousers was plain to see but he didn't seem at all embarrassed by it.

'Best not,' she agreed. She opened the truck door and climbed out. 'See you tomorrow at work?'

'You will.'

She was halfway down the path when he called out softly, 'Allie?'

She stopped.

'Next time, don't put any of that stuff in your hair, eh?'

Chapter Five

I rene set her cup of tea on the table and sat down.

'Well, how did it go?' She'd been dying to catch up with Allie, but she'd come in late and hadn't been able to sneak away from the typing pool.

Allie broke her Belgian biscuit in half, then licked her finger and collected the crumbs of pink icing that had fallen off. 'Great, actually, considering Sonny nearly started a fight with a lady at the pictures, the truck he took me home in was older than my nan and only held together by rust, and I had so much lacquer in my hair that he got his hand stuck in it,' she said, bracing herself for her friends' response.

She was actually feeling a bit flat. She hadn't seen Sonny yet today, and prayed that he wasn't avoiding her.

Daisy paused, one of Terry's mother's oat biscuits halfway to her mouth. '*Really?* Why did he nearly get in a fight with a lady?'

'Because she sat down in front of us with a bloody great hat on that completely blocked my view, and wouldn't take it off even though he asked nicely. Well, quite nicely.'

'Did he hit her?' Daisy's eyes were huge.

Allie rolled her eyes. 'Of course he didn't hit her! She said she refused to be "harangued" by his sort — I think she meant a Maori — and moved to another seat, which suited me.'

'Was it his truck?' Irene asked.

'It was his brother's. He'd borrowed it for the night.'

Irene said, 'Well, that'll make for a memorable summer romance, won't it, swanning around town in an old borrowed wreck of a truck.'

'He's getting something of his own, soon,' Allie said defensively.

'And why was there so much lacquer in your hair?' Irene asked.

'Because Mum made me eat tea and it dried funny.'

The others nodded in sympathy — hair could be like that, and at the most inopportune times.

Louise lit a cigarette. 'Was the film any good?'

Allie nodded. 'I didn't think it would be, but it was more of a love story than a western. Well, not a love story, not like, you know, *A Place in the Sun*. More of a *loyalty* story, really.'

'Sounds great,' Irene said.

'No, it was. You should go and see it.'

But Irene was too busy thinking about her own personal love story. Or whatever it was. She was seeing Vince Reynolds today at lunchtime and had agreed to meet him in the basement. It was a bit tacky, she had to admit, hiding in grubby little storerooms just to get away from prying eyes, but there was no other way they could manage any time alone together. And it added to the excitement, sneaking around like that. She was definitely looking forward to it, but hadn't decided yet how far she would let him go — just far enough, she thought, to make sure he stayed interested.

'Will you be seeing Sonny again?' Daisy asked.

'Actually, I've invited him to come to the Peter Pan this Friday night,' Allie said. 'We're going, aren't we?'

'Well, we are,' Daisy replied. 'What about you and Rob?' she asked Louise.

'That's the plan.'

Allie was pleased. 'You'll like him, I know you will.'

'Terry says he's a good bloke,' Daisy said. 'Anyway, at lunchtime I'm picking material for my bridesmaids' dresses. Who wants to come and help?'

'I will,' Louise volunteered. 'What colour have you decided on?'

'I haven't, yet. That's the trouble.'

'How are you going to get your dress, and three bridesmaids' dresses, sewn by the end of January?' Irene asked, who couldn't sew a straight line if her life depended on it.

'Mum's going to help me with mine, and my Aunty Di's doing the bridesmaids'.'

'Well, I'll help you pick,' Allie said.

Daisy looked at Irene, who said with genuine regret, 'I'd love to, Daisy, I really would, but I'm busy today. I'll help you with your shoes and headgear, though.'

Daisy smiled, relieved. Irene was so very good at clothes, whereas she always felt she never quite got it right. And she very much wanted her wedding day to be perfect.

'The thing is,' Daisy said, 'my sister isn't blonde like me, she's got more sort of copper in her hair, and I wanted the bridesmaids — and her of course, but she's the maid of honour because she's already married — to wear peach. And she won't. She says she'll look like a faded carrot.'

'She will, too,' Louise said bluntly. She'd met Daisy's sister, whose hair was a lot closer to ginger than it was to copper. 'What about the other bridesmaids?'

'My cousins? They've both got dark hair.'

'Well, what about pale blue? That'll suit everyone.'

'I don't know,' Daisy said. She looked at Louise. 'It's a bit, um, unvirginal, isn't it?'

'Only on the bride. And you're wearing white, aren't you?'

'Yes.'

Allie winked at Daisy. 'You wore a blue suit when you got married, didn't you, Lou? I've seen the photos. Were you not, well, virginal?'

Louise tapped the side of her freckled nose. 'That's for me to know and you to find out.'

Daisy, who had been assuming that she was one of the very few New Zealand girls to go to the altar without her virginity intact, and was now paying the price for it, stared. 'Had you already . . . were you and Rob . . .' She didn't seem to know how to finish the sentence.

Louise made a production of looking furtively over her shoulder, then leaned forward conspiratorially. 'Yes, we were. It's much more common than you think it is, you know!'

Daisy looked mildly scandalized, but noticeably relieved.

'But that's not why I got married in a blue suit,' Louise

went on. 'It was in 1948 and you just couldn't get nice fabric then, remember, even though it was after rationing ended. So I had a suit.'

'So blue would work, wouldn't it, Daisy?' Allie asked.

Daisy didn't look convinced. 'Blue's a winter colour and I'm having a summer wedding.'

'Well, what are summer colours, then?'

Daisy thought for a moment. 'Yellow?'

'Yellow would work for your cousins, but not for your sister,' Louise said. 'She'd look awful.'

'Well, I don't know then,' Daisy said, now looking as though she might burst into tears at any moment. 'What colour did the queen's bridesmaids wear?'

Louise sighed. 'I don't know. White, probably. Look, your sister doesn't have to wear the same colour as your cousins, does she? Why don't you put them in peach and your sister in something darker, something more coffee-coloured, perhaps?'

'Brown? Yuck!'

'No, not brown. I was thinking more of a deep, bronzy caramel, something like that. Something that won't clash with her hair.'

'That sounds nice,' Allie said, and Daisy agreed.

The peach fabric was easy and they found a pretty nylon straight away. But they spent the next half-hour perusing every bolt of material in the dress fabrics department that was remotely caramel-coloured, until Daisy eventually chose something she was happy with.

'Now all I need are the patterns,' she said.

Allie looked at her watch. 'I have to go back to work now.'

'So do I,' Louise said.

'Well, what about tomorrow? Can we look tomorrow?' Daisy suggested.

Allie caught Louise's eye briefly. 'I've got something on tomorrow at lunchtime, sorry, Daisy. What about on Monday?'

'I really wanted the patterns by the weekend,' Daisy grumbled, clearly disappointed. 'Lou, can you help?'

'I'm sorry, I've got something on as well. Let's make it Monday, eh?'

'I suppose,' Daisy said.

She looked so dejected that Allie felt quite sorry for her. 'Look, why don't you come to the fashion show tonight? I can get you free tickets and you might get some ideas for dresses, especially as we're having a bridal segment.'

'Yes, please,' Daisy said, perking up.

'Can you get me a ticket?' Louise asked. 'I wouldn't mind a look myself.'

Allie nodded. 'Miss Willow's quite generous with the tickets, even though she's not supposed to be. I'll give them to you at afternoon tea.'

While Allie, Louise and Daisy were in the fabrics department, Irene was standing on the landing of the staff stairs leading down to the basement, looking at her watch. She was five minutes late meeting Vince, and that was exactly how she meant it to be.

She opened her handbag, took out a small mirror and a tissue, blotted her lips then checked her reflection to make sure there was a hint of colour left. It wouldn't do to get lipstick on Vince's clothes and have his wife ask where it had come from. But she didn't want to meet him with completely bare lips either — that wouldn't be very sexy at all.

When she was ready she descended the stairs, her heels clattering on the wooden risers. The lift actually went all the way down to the basement, so the storeroom staff could bring up large and heavy items after hours when there were no customers in the shop, but she didn't want to draw attention to herself by using it.

When she got to the bottom she pushed open the door and left the echoey stairwell. In front of her was a long, whitewashed hallway, its walls made of bricks laid by workmen almost a hundred years ago when Auckland was still a new town. She reached out and ran her fingers across some, feeling how cold they were, yet dry: there was no dampness down here at all. It was in fact the perfect place to store goods of all kinds, and that was exactly its function: in its huge double basement, Dunbar & Jones harboured an absolute Aladdin's cave of delights.

The flooring reserves were stored there — carpets, rugs and enormous rolls of linoleum — as well as items eventually destined for the furnishings floor, along with rows and rows of muslin-draped bolts of dress fabrics. The remaining area was packed with smaller items such as bales of mercery, wools and manchester linens not yet opened.

Packing materials, office supplies, old kitchen equipment and the emergency generator lined one wall, and on the back wall, near the delivery ramp descending from the narrow lane running behind the store, were located the store's cleaning supplies, the gas meter, the Lamson blower and the main switchboard for the electricity. The electricity supply came into the basement from a pole on the corner of Queen and Wyndham Streets, then crossed the ceiling unenclosed to the switchboard, from where it was distributed throughout most areas in the three Dunbar & Jones buildings via a maze of wiring.

Irene never liked coming down to the basement and, fortunately, rarely needed to. The main storage area was huge with a low ceiling lit only by bare bulbs, and the smaller rooms off to one side, where she was now, were no better. She imagined as she walked down the hallway that there were enormous spiders lurking in dark corners above her, just waiting to abseil down on glistening threads and catch in her hair. Or, even worse, drop down the back of her blouse. It was the most unromantic place she could imagine for a liaison, but then she and Vince didn't have a lot of choice.

Irene and Vince. She tried it out a couple of times in her head, quite liking the sound of it. Mrs Vince Reynolds. No, she'd be Mrs Irene Reynolds, because she was a modern woman. It sounded a lot classier than Irene Baxter. Not that it mattered, because she didn't want to marry Vince, and there was the small matter of her already being married. And accountants probably made a lot more money than floor-walkers, even in posh shops like Dunbar & Jones.

Something touched her shoulder and she nearly screamed.

'Vince, you sod!'

Vince was genuinely apologetic this time. 'Sorry, honey, but you went straight past. We're in here.'

He turned her into a small room stacked almost to the ceiling with cardboard boxes, folded trestle tables and a five-foot high, pale pink papier mâché egg left over from that year's Easter window displays. The single bulb was quite bright in here, casting a harsh yellow light everywhere except in the corners.

'Nice,' Irene remarked, looking around.

'Best I could do,' Vince said. 'Should I have brought a mattress in?'

'A mattress? What for?' Irene had already made up her mind that she wasn't going to be doing anything requiring a mattress.

Vince said, 'Well, you know, to lie on.' He added quickly, 'Not that I'm assuming anything, of course. It was just if we wanted a bit of a cuddle.'

Irene lowered her head slightly, tilted it and looked up at him through her thick, black eyelashes. 'Mr Reynolds, I was hoping that if we were to have . . . a cuddle, it would be in a much more salubrious place than this. I think I'm worth that.'

'Oh, you are, darling, you most certainly are,' Vince agreed fervently, though his hopes for something more than just a kiss and a cuddle had just been severely dented. But he loved it when Irene used clever words — she was such an intoxicating mixture of brains and sex appeal. And he especially loved it when she called him Mr Reynolds; it made him feel so in command and, well, virile.

'And we've only got half an hour,' Irene pointed out. 'I have to be back at work at one.'

Vince thought they could achieve quite a lot in half an hour, but didn't say so. 'Well, we'll just have to make the most of it, won't we? Are you cold?'

Irene wasn't; it was cool down here but it certainly wasn't cold. She was shivering, though, from excitement. 'A little,' she said.

'Then come and sit by me,' Vince invited. He sat down on a cardboard box, which immediately collapsed beneath him, sending him lurching sideways.

Irene laughed, a loud peal that sounded harsh in the small room.

'Shit,' Vince said, getting up and dusting off his smart trousers. He tested another box and sat down again, but cautiously this time. 'Come here, Irene, come and sit with me.'

Irene stepped over and sat down next to him, perching her bottom on the very edge of the box. He tucked his arm around her, moved over slightly to give her more room, and started kissing her.

Irene responded enthusiastically, enjoying his obvious ardour and the strength she could feel in his arms. He might have a fairly sedentary job at Dunbar & Jones, but he obviously kept himself in shape, which was a pleasant surprise.

After several long minutes, Vince pulled back and looked at her. His face was flushed and his eyes were filled with the sexual longing Irene found intoxicating.

'You're a gorgeous woman, Irene,' he murmured huskily. 'You remind me so much of Veronica Lake with that long sweep of hair falling across your face. Except that you're a brunette, of course.'

'Ted thinks I look like Hedy Lamarr,' Irene said. 'He calls me that every morning when I come in.'

'Ted Horrocks? What would he know?'

'Is that a note of jealousy I hear in your voice, Vince?' Irene asked playfully.

'Hardly. Ted's seventy if he's a day, silly old bugger.'

'He's sixty-four and I like him.'

Vince said, 'Well, I like *you* and we're wasting time, so bugger Ted.'

He leaned in again for another kiss, and this time his

free hand settled on Irene's waist. A few moments later it had crept up to her left breast and lingered there, lightly rubbing over the rayon of her summer blouse. Irene felt her nipples rise, and arched her back slightly to push her breast into Vince's cupped hand. He groaned and moved his mouth from her lips to her neck, nuzzling the white skin beneath her ear.

And then he bit.

Irene jumped, the sensation sending shockwaves of lust through her body, and terror into her heart. 'For God's sake, Vince, don't make a mark!'

'I won't,' he mumbled, his mouth still pressed against her skin. 'I'll be gentle.'

Irene didn't actually want him to be gentle, but she did want him to be discreet: explaining to Martin how she'd managed to get a love bite on her neck would be very tricky.

'I'll do it to you,' she threatened.

'God, would you?' Vince said, raising his head and exposing his own throat. The skin there was pale, and Irene could see the blue of that night's stubble already beginning to show through.

She bent her head and bit, tasting the tang of light sweat and cologne. Vince groaned and grasped her hand, pushing it into his lap where she could feel his straining erection.

'Irene,' he said through gritted teeth, 'let me make love to you. Please!'

Thrilled though she was, she still had the presence of mind to remove her hand. 'No, not here. I don't want to do it here.'

Vince groaned again, this time in obvious frustration.

Worried that she might have overdone it — or rather,

underdone it — Irene said, 'But we can still have fun, can't we?' and began to slowly unbutton her blouse.

Vince sat mesmerized as the fabric fell open to reveal the twin cones of her satin bra, pointing directly at him. He reached out with both hands, like a child about to receive an eagerly anticipated treat. But then he detoured and his fingers eased her blouse off her pale shoulders and let it slide down her arms, where it rested at her elbows like a shawl.

She trembled as he began to kiss her shoulders and then her décolletage, his tongue travelling ever closer to her cleavage. When his thumbs hooked under the straps of her bra and slid them off her shoulders, releasing her heavy white breasts with their erect, dusky pink nipples, she gasped.

'Oh my God, Irene, they're magnificent!' Vince marvelled, running his fingertips over the firm flesh. He cupped his hands under her breasts and lifted them slightly. 'You're an absolute cracker of a girl, you really are.'

Irene closed her eyes, bathing in the warmth of his adoration. When he began to lick her nipples she slid her hands through his hair and dug her fingers into his skull, her sense of satisfaction turning to excitement. She squirmed, and felt heat coursing through her body and her face and neck reddening.

Vince tugged her blouse out of her waistband and slid it off completely, then reached behind her to unhook her bra. When she was naked from the waist up, he grasped both of her wrists in one hand and held them up, pinning them against the boxes stacked behind them.

'God give me strength,' he said, gazing lasciviously at her.

He slid his free hand up her thigh until his fingers met flesh above stocking. Then, letting her wrists go, he pushed up her skirt until the white triangle of her pants was visible.

As he lifted the lacy edge of the flimsy fabric, Irene stopped his hand, even though she was very much ready for him to do anything he liked. 'No, Vince, I'd love to, I really would, but it's the wrong time and place. Couldn't we find somewhere, well, nicer?'

Extracting his hand from beneath her skirt and sighing heavily, Vince sat back. His was sweating freely now, the bulge in his trousers still very evident.

'Where do you live?' he asked.

'Eden Terrace.'

'Does your husband ever go out by himself? At night, I mean?'

'Hardly ever. He doesn't even go out with me, let alone without me. And, well, I don't think I'd want to do it in my house, Vince.'

'Christ, I'd do it in mine, but my wife sticks to me like shit to a blanket. We only go out when we're both invited, and even then Cynthia watches me like a bloody hawk.'

'Why? Have you done this sort of thing before?'

'No,' he said, rather too quickly. 'She's just a very possessive sort of woman.'

'So we can't go to your house?'

'No.'

'Not even at lunchtime?' Irene suggested.

Vince shook his head. 'Cynthia doesn't go out to work.'

Irene felt her heart sink. Was it possible that they actually couldn't find an opportunity to be together? Was it going to be that difficult? And would he lose interest if it was?

Vince leaned forward with his elbows on his knees and his face in his hands.

When he didn't say anything for over a minute, Irene asked, 'Vince? Are you all right?'

He looked up, his face a picture of disappointment. 'I don't know what to suggest, Irene, I really don't. And I want to be with you so much, you have to understand that. You mean . . .' He trailed off, staring at the floor again.

Irene hung on for as long as she could, but finally had to ask, 'I mean what, Vince? What were you going to say?'

Vince swept his hand back through his hair, took a deep breath and turned to face her. 'I wasn't going to say this in case it frightened you off, but bugger it. Irene, you mean the absolute world to me. I think about you night and day, and every time I see you I go weak at the knees and I want to take you in my arms and make love to you. I can't help it, darling, you're just so beautiful and so bloody sexy.' He thumped his thigh angrily with a closed fist. 'God, *why* couldn't I have met you earlier! But I didn't and I'm married to someone else and . . . and wanting you is driving me insane and we can't bloody well do anything *about* it!'

Shocked at his passionate declaration, and reeling from the sense of power it gave her, Irene felt both elated and panicked. This was it, this was what she had wanted all along, and now she was going to lose it, all because they couldn't find a bloody bed!

'What if we got a hotel room?' she suggested desperately.

'No, Irene, those rent-by-the-hour places are flea-pits and you're worth more than that,' he said, echoing her earlier words. He shook his head in anguished resignation. 'No, it's no good, I'm going to have to get a job somewhere else. I can't go on like this, seeing you every day and not being able to have you.'

Irene made a decision. She picked up his hands and settled them around her waist. 'Well, we'll do it here then.'

Vince's face lit up. 'Are you sure?'

Irene nodded.

Vince kissed the tip of her nose. 'God, girl, you have no idea what this means to me.'

He pulled her to her feet and wrapped his arms around her, kissing her passionately, this time on her mouth, and running his hands across her naked back and over her buttocks. After a minute he eased her skirt up to her hips and hooked his thumbs into the waistband of her pants, then slid them down her legs. They dropped to the floor and Irene stepped neatly out of them. Vince pushed her gently backwards and she sat down on the edge of the carton, shivering as he parted her legs so that the tangle of her black pubic hair was exposed between white skin and the pale beige gleam of her silk stockings.

Vince gave a low whistle of appreciation, then, standing before her, shrugged out of his suit jacket and loosened his tie. Shaking visibly, he placed Irene's hand on his belt buckle, groaning slightly as she undid it, then with more fervour as she opened the buttons of his fly. His erection popped up, straining at the fabric of his underpants. Shoving both his pants and his trousers down to his knees, he knelt on the floor and positioned himself. Irene guided him into her, gasping as his length filled her with one deep, slippery stroke. She lifted her legs and wrapped them around his waist.

Panting already, Vince murmured in her ear, 'Jesus Christ, I'm not going to last long. Hold on, babe.'

Irene did, and moments later Vince gave three or four almighty thrusts, then shuddered and gradually subsided onto her. She stroked his hair and waited. When his breathing had slowed somewhat, he withdrew and pushed himself back onto his naked haunches.

'I've been waiting for that for a long time,' he declared, still breathless. 'And, my God, it was worth it. Irene Baxter, I think I love you.'

Irene laughed, delighted. He'd said it! And as she gazed into his dark, slightly glazed eyes, she began to believe that what she felt for him could quite easily be love, too, or something very close to it; she was sure nothing else could make her feel like this.

Vince got to his feet. 'Christ, my legs feel like jelly,' he said, staggering slightly as he yanked up his trousers. He reached for his jacket, took the handkerchief neatly folded into the breast pocket and handed it to her. 'Here, use this to clean yourself up.'

Irene mopped at the wetness between her legs, then handed back the handkerchief, which had Vince's initials embroidered in one corner. Vince looked at it, then stuffed it behind the cartons.

'Well, I can hardly take that home for Cynthia to wash, can I?'

Irene retrieved her underwear from the floor and put on her bra and blouse. Then, while Vince was tucking in his shirt and putting on his jacket, she fished a mirror out of her bag, combed her hair and put on fresh lipstick.

'We'd better go upstairs separately,' Vince said as he smoothed his hair into place. 'That was fantastic, darling. When can we do it again?'

Irene giggled. 'As soon as possible, I hope.'

'Me, too. Tomorrow?'

'I can't, I've got something on.'

'What about Sunday. Are you going to the staff picnic?'

'Yes, but Martin's coming as well. Well, he said he would, unless he has to go into the office. Are you?'

'Yes, but with Cynthia, of course. Still, you never know, we might be able to sneak away for a few minutes.' He looked at his watch. 'Bugger. Speaking of minutes, I have to get back to work.' He pecked Irene on the cheek. 'See you at afternoon tea?'

Five minutes after Vince ducked out into the hallway, Irene left herself, feeling as though her feet had wings.

Keith Beaumont stood in his office on the first floor and stared out of the window at the opposite side of Wyndham Street. The shop he was looking at was a draper's, selling blue jeans at a much lower price than Dunbar & Jones. Still, they were probably badly made from inferior fabric, so he wasn't worried. He opened the top drawer of his desk, eyeing the hip flask of scotch longingly, but reached for his cigarettes instead. He slid one out of the packet and lit it, watching the pale smoke swirl up into the air and luxuriating, if only fleetingly, in the sense of calmness it gave him.

He sat down and smoked the cigarette to the butt, then ground it out in his ashtray. After remaining still for a long moment, he rubbed his face vigorously with his hands as though he could scrub away what he was terrified was written all over it.

He was fifty-five years old and had been manager of Dunbar & Jones for eight years now. He was doing well

— he had his eye on everything that went on in the store, he met his targets every quarter and he was respected by his boss Maxwell Jones if not by the rest of his staff, many of whom, he knew, were frightened of him. He was also an inveterate gambler and had been skimming between two and three hundred pounds off the store's takings every fortnight for the past eighteen months. It had been surprisingly easy, though he'd worried himself sick when he'd started.

The first thing he had done was tell the woman who supervised the accounts office that he was about to instigate a regular programme of spot audits of the books, carried out by himself, of course. From then on, every fortnight after the staff had gone home at the end of the day, he simply went into the accounts office upstairs and altered the figures for the previous two weeks' takings. He did it in increments — thirty pounds from one day, thirteen from another and forty-five from another — and he did it so that the shortfall looked like customer returns, then he took the money out of the safe before it could be banked the following day. He also constantly practised different handwriting styles so he could manufacture bogus returns dockets, which ensured that everything balanced. He couldn't do it with the credit accounts, of course, because the money for those sales was paid once a month and often by cheque, so he confined himself to cash sales. But that still gave him plenty of scope because, though most of Dunbar & Jones's biggest-spending customers had credit accounts, the majority of purchases were still made by people who paid cash.

It had worried him for a long time that one day someone in accounts would question a returns docket and actually talk to the sales assistant who had purportedly filled it out.

So, to circumvent that, he had told Max Jones that he was becoming concerned about the number of returns the store was experiencing — though everyone knew that returns were common and unavoidable — and that he was going to keep an eye on them. He then told the cash office supervisor that any discrepancies in returns dockets must go to him first, and that he would deal with them personally. He would be questioning the sales assistant concerned very closely about why the customer had felt compelled to return their purchase and establishing whether there had been a failure of duty to deliver the highest possible quality of customer service. The accounts office supervisor was a decent, kind-hearted woman: rather than get someone into trouble over what was probably fickle or difficult customer behaviour, he knew she would probably keep the returns dockets to herself. So far this assessment had been spot on — none of the returns dockets had ever been questioned and Keith had actually received a small bonus from Max Jones for being so vigilant and innovative.

Of course, he had telephoned his bookmaker as soon as he'd got the bonus, put it all on a horse running at Addington that afternoon and lost the lot.

Keith's operation was now running very smoothly, but the longer it went on the more nervous he was becoming. He wasn't a bad man, he knew that; it was just that no matter how hard he tried — and he had tried very hard indeed — he couldn't keep away from the horses and the dogs, or anything else his bookie could find for him, legal or illegal. Only he never did it in public. He never went to the track, well, not any more, he certainly never went to the TAB, and he hid his copies of *Best Bets* at the bottom of the lockable drawer of his desk. He even refrained from having a flutter in the Melbourne Cup sweepstakes the staff held every November, making a point of refusing to take part.

He had a responsible, well-paid job, he had significant standing in the community, he had a lovely home, a good wife, Nora, and three wonderful grown-up children, and he was constantly in debt to his bookie and almost everyone else with whom he had financial dealings. He lost far more often than he won, but he knew, deep in his heart, that one day he would have *that* win, the really big one that would solve all his money problems and still give him enough to bet with impunity for the rest of his life. Or at least until the next big win came along.

But he'd found himself in terrible financial strife and had had to remortgage his house to get himself out of it, though Nora didn't know that. And he'd been stockpiling some of the money he'd stolen from Dunbar & Jones, about fifteen hundred pounds, which he'd hidden in the kitchen of the White Room on the first floor, in a metal box at the back of a high cupboard. To be extra safe, he carried the keys to the box and the cupboard constantly in his trouser pocket. It was quite a performance whenever he changed his suit, but it was worth it for the comfort and security of knowing that they were there. He told himself that this money was only to be used in a dire emergency, and not for placing bets every day, but it nearly killed him thinking about it, in that dark, airless box all by itself, just crying out to be handed over to his bookie. And he dreamed about it constantly, that one day he would open up his *Best Bets* and there it would be, the horse that every fibre of his being would tell him was going to win — an unknown, an outsider that would attract huge winnings. He would go into the White Room, unlock the cupboard, take the money and put it all on that horse, and in a matter of hours his life would change forever.

He always woke up sweating from that particular dream, and spent most of the following day physically forcing himself not to take the money, or at least stopping himself from repeatedly checking that it was still there. And every time he took money from the store's safe he took a little downstairs and added it to his 'emergency box'.

Keith lit another cigarette. He had a meeting with Max Jones in five minutes, and, though he knew by now that his operation was foolproof, he still sweated every time his boss asked to see him. To steady his nerves he opened his top drawer and took a quick swing from the flask of scotch. Which reminded him — he was running out of breath mints.

Chapter Six

Allie didn't go home after work, but the staff cafeteria provided sandwiches and cups of tea at a quarter past five for everyone required to work late, so she didn't go hungry.

She freshened up and made her way downstairs to the White Room, where the fashion show was to be held and where she would meet Miss Willow and Rhonda Kendrick, another salesgirl from the dress department who would also be helping out tonight. Dunbar & Jones presented four fashion shows a year at the start of each season to showcase both the lines imported from overseas and the store's own designs. They were very prestigious affairs catering to the store's wealthier female clients and attendance was generally by invitation only, except for a limited number of tickets which were always at a premium.

The first-floor foyer was quite a large area, normally furnished with comfortable couches where patrons could gather if they were going into the White Room for lunch or, after hours, to a dinner or a private function. On the opposite side of the foyer were the executive offices, the credit office, and toilets discreetly positioned behind a partitioning wall which held a telephone for the use of customers by day, or restaurant patrons by night. Between the offices on one side, and the White Room on the other, was the wide archway opening onto the dress department.

But this evening the couches had been temporarily removed and the space was crowded with display staff flitting anxiously about. In front of the archway, storemen were calmly erecting a wooden frame on which would shortly be hung a series of black curtains: the models would make their costume changes in the dress department, then walk to the left behind the curtains to appear elegantly and effortlessly in the doorway of the White Room.

'Excuse me, miss, but are you one of the models?' a voice behind Allie asked.

She smiled and turned around. 'Hi. I didn't think you were at work today.'

Sonny looked genuinely pleased to see her, which made her feel better than she had felt all day. 'Been flat out,' he said. 'No time for smoko or lunch.'

'You must be starving then,' Allie said. 'There are sandwiches in the caf.'

'Nah. I went down the street before to the pie cart and got some chips.'

'Chips won't keep you going.' Allie winced slightly as she realized that this was exactly the sort of thing her mother would say.

Sonny transferred his hammer from one hand to the other and shrugged cheerfully. 'So, *are* you a model? You could be, you know.'

Allie blushed but managed to explain that she was a dresser, helping the models to change.

'Bit of a circus, this, isn't it?' Sonny observed, looking around. 'You'd think the queen was turning up.'

'No, that's not for another week,' Allie said, taking him seriously. 'The fashion shows are always like this, everyone running around like chooks with their heads chopped off, but it all usually goes well once we start.'

Sonny nodded. 'And it's all so a room full of rich women can sit around having cups of tea and looking at clothes and then spend piles of money on them?'

Allie wanted to protest, but his interpretation of the event was actually fairly accurate. This time she shrugged.

'So is this what you're too busy doing tonight to go out with me?' he asked, then grinned. 'Well, that's all right. I thought you might have another bloke.'

Allie frowned. 'But I've already asked you out dancing tomorrow night. Why would I do that if I had another bloke?'

'I dunno. Greedy?' Sonny suggested, and then laughed at the look of affront on her face. 'Nah, you're not that sort of girl, are you.' He made it a statement rather than a question. He almost added, not like that Irene, but thought better of it: one of the lads had spotted her slinking out of the basement behind that flash bugger Vince Reynolds, but it was none of his business and there'd be no point to telling Allie — they were mates and she probably wouldn't thank him for it.

Miss Willow hurried up, looking agitated.

'Allie, there you are! We've been fluffing about for ages, waiting for you! Come along now, we need to sort out the garments. The models will be here shortly.'

'Sorry, Miss Willow.' As Allie headed into the dress department she shot Sonny a sorry-but-I've-got-to-go look.

He smiled and gave her a little wave, then went back to his hammering.

Ruby Willow strode across the floor, heading for the discreet staff door in the back wall that led to a series of small storerooms. In one were five portable clothes racks, already hung with the garments for the show, as well as several empty trolleys. During the day Ruby had selected the clothes to be shown and sent them up to the tailoring workshop to be steamed and ironed, but now they had to be sorted into the order in which they would be worn. Rhonda hovered nearby, looking anxious. She was a very good salesgirl but tended to get upset easily, especially under pressure.

'What are we showing first?' Allie asked. Though this was the fourth fashion show she had attended as a staff member, it was the first time Miss Willow had asked her to help with dressing the models, and she wanted to be sure of the procedure.

Ruby perched her glasses on her nose and consulted her list. 'Day dresses with hats, followed by leisure wear, then swimsuits, then Young Miss while the adult models are having a break.'

Allie cast her eye over the racks. 'So we want day dresses on the first rack and leisure wear on the second?'

'Yes, and the hats on two of those trolleys. Miss Button's doing the compering for the hats. But we'd better put swimsuits at the end of the second rack — Young Miss, evening wear and ball gowns will take up all of the next two. And mantles and bridal can go on the last one.'

There would be six models tonight — four young women, and two fifteen-year-old girls for the Young Miss fashions. Between them they would model around a hundred garments and ensembles, including lines from Dior, Balmain and Balenciaga, as well as couture clothes designed in-house.

'Are they doing their own make-up?' Allie asked.

'Yes. Well, they're bringing two make-up artists with them, if that's what you mean.'

A make-up table had been set up behind the dressing rooms, where there would be no chance of the models accidentally being seen from the foyer. Dunbar & Jones prided themselves on presenting only the most glamorous models, and the illusion would be irreparably spoiled if they were to be spotted wandering about like mortal women with curlers in their hair, bare feet and no make-up.

Minutes later the models appeared like a small flock of exotic, twittering birds, escorted by Miranda de Saint-Castin, who ran the modelling agency. She was tall, slender, raven-haired, very self-assured and always impeccably attired, but ever since Miss Willow had told Allie in confidence that Madame de Saint-Castin's real name was Mabel Biggs and that she originally came from Bulls, Allie hadn't been able to regard her in quite the same light.

As usual, the models had come along in their casual clothes — slacks, sleeveless blouses and flat shoes. With them were their two make-up artists and a hair stylist. Allie saw that the stunning-looking dark girl was here again: even without make-up she was easily the most beautiful and exotic-looking of them all.

Madame de Saint-Castin clapped her gloved hands. 'Now, girls, we have an hour before the parade starts and I want to get your maquillage started. Tea? Is there tea?'

'Tea?' the dark girl said disparagingly. 'What about something stronger?'

The other models laughed, though Madame didn't.

While Miss Willow sent Rhonda up to the cafeteria to get pots of tea organized, Allie found a chair and placed it near the make-up table so she could watch. Tending to a girl with long, almost platinum-blonde locks, the hair stylist first brushed the hair out, then began to back-comb it until it sat up from the crown by several inches. She then took the hair from the front and swept it back over the teased section, making a smooth dome, and tucked the ends into a ponytail fashioned from the rest of the hair. This was then twisted around several times to form a gleaming knot and pinned to the back of the model's head, creating a very elegant and tailored effect. The stylist then sprayed the whole thing with enough lacquer to cement bricks together. The model sat very still the whole time, not even blinking when the make-up artist skilfully applied several coats of thick black mascara to her lashes. When her make-up and hair had been completed, the model rose from the table, lit a cigarette and wandered over to the tea trolley. The Young Miss models received similar treatment, though their make-up was lighter and their hairstyles less elaborate.

At half past six, thirty minutes before the fashion show was due to start, Allie checked the White Room to make sure that everything had been set up properly. As usual, the tables and chairs had been rearranged to create a temporary runway down the middle of the room. It made for a tight squeeze, but the audience didn't seem to mind — in fact the tables right next to the runway seemed to be the most coveted. A lectern, with Dunbar & Jones's distinctive logo on the front, had been set up at the far end, where Miss Willow and Miss Button would stand and describe each outfit as the models appeared. Behind the lectern was the most enormous flower arrangement, which the store's florist had been working on all day. It was crammed with roses and other summer blooms, and the delicious scent filled the room.

At a quarter to seven the audience started to arrive, and Allie made her way back to the dress department ready to help the first model, who happened to be the lovely dark girl. Allie knocked outside the dressing room, but didn't know where to look when she saw that the girl was completely naked.

'Oh, I beg your pardon,' she said, mortified.

The girl waved her hand dismissively.

'Shall I wait outside?' Allie suggested.

'No, you're supposed to be helping me, aren't you?' the girl said, though she looked amused rather than angry. She had the widest eyes, the most gorgeous caramel-coloured skin and the most perfect nose and mouth Allie had ever seen, and she couldn't help staring.

'Yes, I'm your dresser,' she said nervously. 'Um, sorry, but what was your name?'

'Heliopolis,' the girl said. 'What's yours?'

'Allie. That's an unusual name. Lovely, though.'

'What? Allie?'

'No, your name, Heliopolis. Is it foreign?'

'It's Egyptian.'

'Oh. Is that where you're from?' Allie asked. She knew the girl had to have come from somewhere exotic.

'No, I'm from here. Auckland.'

'Oh, right. Your family's Egyptian, though?'

'No, my family's from New Zealand.' Allie must have looked confused because the girl rolled her eyes. 'Heliopolis is the hospital in Egypt where my uncle died in the First World War. I'm named for him,' she said slightly crossly, as though she'd had to explain it a thousand times. 'But most people call me Polly. I'm Maori, not Egyptian.' She picked up some undergarments from the dressing-room chair and started to undo the hooks on them.

Allie felt silly. 'Sorry, I just thought—'

'Most people do,' Polly interrupted. 'Most people don't believe that a Maori girl could model couture clothes for Pakeha women.' She slipped her arms into a bra and turned her back so Allie could do it up. 'I am, though, eh? I'm doing all right, too. One day I'm going to Paris and I'll be a world-class model.'

Allie didn't doubt it.

Polly pulled on a girdle and wriggled it up over her hips, then sat on the chair and began to roll on a pair of very sheer stockings. The bra made her breasts look like two bullets, and Allie didn't think she needed the girdle because her stomach was already firm and flat, but she supposed Polly had to have something to hold her stockings up.

Polly stood and studied her reflection in the mirror. 'What am I wearing out first?'

Allie stepped outside the dressing room to fetch the first outfit. When she returned, Polly was smoking a cigarette and drinking from a small bottle.

'Want some?' she said, offering it to Allie.

'What is it?'

'Gin.'

'Er, no thanks.' Allie wasn't at all sure that Madame de Saint-Castin would approve of drinking alcohol during a show. Neither would Miss Willow, for that matter.

'Come on, a sip won't hurt,' Polly insisted.

'It will. I'd be fired if Miss Willow found out.'

Polly shrugged, took another swig and slipped the bottle back under her street clothes, which were lying in a heap in the corner.

Allie handed her the first dress, zipping it up when Polly had stepped into it and fluffing the pleats so that it sat properly. The bright floral pattern looked spectacular against Polly's darker, glowing skin. She dropped her cigarette butt into her teacup, slipped on high-heeled sandals, gloves and a hat, grabbed the handbag and stole that Allie was holding out to her, and sauntered out of the dressing room.

Allie followed her out to the black curtain, where they waited for Miss Willow to introduce the proceedings.

'Good evening, ladies,' Ruby began in her clear, ringing voice. 'It is my pleasure to welcome you here tonight to Dunbar & Jones's latest seasonal couture collection. We will, as usual, begin with a special selection of day dresses and accessories, then move on to leisure wear and swimming costumes, with our latest line in latex floral bathing caps imported especially from France. This will be followed by Young Miss, with our new summer range of Teena Louise, which I'm sure many of you mothers are anxious to view on behalf of your lovely daughters. There will then be a short interval with refreshments, after which we will recommence with evening wear and ball gowns, followed by mantles and, of course, bridal wear, the jewel in our *haute couture* crown.

'Please note that your programmes provide an indication of the price of the items you see here, should you wish to place an order at the end of the evening. Remember, ladies, these ensembles have not yet been displayed on the shop floor and as our valued customers you are seeing them here first. I know that many of you will be attending events to honour the imminent visit of Her Majesty the Queen next week, not to mention the many and varied Christmas engagements you have planned over the festive season, so I hope that you may perhaps see something here tonight that will fulfil your particular requirements. So, thank you for your attention, and we will now begin.'

Ruby nodded at the pianist sitting behind his baby grand just inside the entrance to the White Room and he launched into Nat King Cole's 'Mona Lisa'.

Peering through a gap in the curtain, Allie spotted Louise and Daisy sitting at a table in the third row back from the runway, both dressed in their smartest clothes. It was a treat for them to be here tonight, and an even bigger treat for Donna and Pauline. Allie spied her sisters sitting against the far wall, without their hats and gloves, which they must have ditched somewhere along the way. Her mother wouldn't have let them out tonight if they weren't dressed like the little ladies Colleen thought they should be. And, bloody hell, was Donna smoking a cigarette?

Allie straightened up as Polly glided past her to the end of the curtain and stepped out onto the runway, her beauty and the elegance of her outfit eliciting murmurs of appreciation from the audience.

Ruby put her glasses back on and consulted her notes. 'Tonight Polly is modelling one of our in-house designs, a day dress suitable for an afternoon event or a garden party, in elegant charmeuse with a tableau of aqua blue flowers on a pale coral background. As you can see, this style is designed to accentuate a shapely silhouette with a small waist. The dress is available in a range of sizes, and the

122

fabric is available from our own dress fabrics department and can be made up to your requirements.'

Polly did another circuit of the runway.

'Polly is wearing this beautiful frock,' Ruby went on, 'with French elbow-length coral suede gloves, a gorgeous deep coral, imported all-wool stole for those slightly cooler summer afternoons, a soft leather handbag in aqua blue, and matching high-heeled leather peep-toe sandals with ankle straps. Polly's divine hat is, of course, one of our own millinery department's wonderful creations, and I will invite my colleague Miss Beatrice Button to comment on that.'

Miss Button, so short she almost couldn't see over the top of the lectern, stepped up and cleared her throat.

'We are very proud of this particular creation,' she began, 'because as you can see it captures all of the elements of today's finest millinery trends. Into a timeless picture-hat style featuring a widened east to west brim with grosgrain trimming, we have incorporated an ornamental bird, its pink and coral plumage designed to directly complement the tones in our model's dress. The crown and the brim are of novelty straw, which is both light and airy. I am sure you will find that this hat will become an essential piece in your summer wardrobe this year.'

Miss Button stepped down and Ruby Willow took her place. Passing the next model on her way out onto the runway, Polly disappeared behind the curtain, whipping the example of 'today's finest millinery trends' off her head and tossing it aside as she hurried towards the dressing rooms, Allie close behind.

And so it went for the next forty minutes, a mad dash to get the models changed into their next outfits, a few minutes' reprieve, then another rush. By the interval Allie was quite frazzled, so she could imagine how the models themselves were feeling. The second half of the show, however, featured the 'glamour gowns', so there was no opportunity to slow down before the show ended.

The bridal ensembles were particularly tricky to get the models into, as there was the dress itself and the special lingerie that went under it, the shoes, stockings and decorative garter, jewellery and, finally, the headgear. So while two of the older girls and the two teens modelled the evening gowns and the mantles, Allie assisted the three 'brides' into their ensembles. Polly, wearing Dior, looked absolutely stunning in the startling whiteness of the gown and its long veil, her small waist accentuated and her generous breasts moulded by the stiff satin of the bodice.

While they waited behind the curtain for the evening wear models to come off, Allie slipped out into the foyer and went to stand at the back of the White Room, wanting to see the reaction to the bridal wear with her own eyes. The first two gowns — a Balenciaga and then a Dunbar & Jones design — went down very well, eliciting gasps of admiration from the women in the audience, including Daisy, who sat with her hands clasped and her mouth open in delight, obviously imagining herself walking down the aisle in one of the fabulous, frothy creations. The Dior, however, literally stole the limelight, as Miss Button deliberately turned off all the lights except for those above the runway to highlight the gown's shimmering beauty. Or was it Polly's beauty that was making such a stunning impact? She certainly looked like a fairy princess, albeit a very chic, modern one, gliding along the runway, the beading on the dress glittering and the white satin giving off a soft light of its own.

Raising her hands to applaud, Allie inadvertently elbowed someone and glanced behind her to apologize.

'I thought you'd gone,' she said, smiling as Sonny did his best to blend into the shadows. 'I didn't realize you liked couture fashion.'

'I don't,' he muttered.

'Gorgeous dress, though, isn't it?'

'It's all right.'

'Of course, the model certainly helps. She's gorgeous as well,' Allie noted.

'She always was.'

Allie went very still, a hot shard of jealousy lodging uncomfortably in her chest. 'Oh. Do you know her?'

Sonny nodded.

Allie knew she should leave it alone, but all the common sense she'd ever possessed deserted her and the words were out of her mouth before she could clamp it shut. 'How well?' she said, trying to make the question sound casual, but it still came out rather aggressively.

'Very. She's my sister.'

Allie worked her way steadily through the discarded clothes and accessories strewn across the floor outside the dressing rooms. Now that she thought about it, there was quite a resemblance between Polly and Sonny. He was a little darker, but their facial features were similar. Allie wondered if the colour of Maori children's skin got lighter as more and more of them were born. Could a thing like Maoriness get diluted the more it was used? No, probably not, she thought, and smiled to herself for being such a twit.

Sonny had asked her if she wanted to go somewhere for

a cup of coffee, so she was hurrying to get everything tidied up before she could leave. There were shoes and hats and bags and roll-up jeans and knitwear and dresses and scarves and bathing caps everywhere.

'I think that was very successful, don't you?' Miss Willow said, her arms full of shoes. 'Especially the off-the-peg formal daywear. We've taken lots of orders for that. It's the queen, I expect.'

'Probably,' Allie agreed. 'Do you want us to put everything away tonight?'

'No, I don't think so,' Ruby replied. 'I'm quite exhausted after all that and the display people are coming in early tomorrow to tidy up the White Room, so why don't we come in early as well? That is, if you haven't planned a night out on the town,' she added slyly.

Allie blushed. 'Well, actually, I am going out for coffee, but it definitely won't be a late night.'

'With your Maori chap? Well, you'll certainly make a splash in your Dunbar & Jones uniform, dear.'

'What? Oh bugger,' Allie said as she realized she was still in her work clothes. 'Oh, I beg your pardon, Miss Willow.'

'Indeed,' Ruby said, 'though I have heard worse, you know.' She looked thoughtful. 'Look, why don't you take something off the shop floor to wear?'

'I can't actually afford it at the moment,' Allie replied uncomfortably.

'Did I say anything about paying for it?' Ruby leaned closer. 'Just between you, me and the gate post, I have myself been known, on occasion, to, er, borrow the odd item to wear to a special function. And Miss Button certainly flits around town in a remarkably extensive selection of hats, given her modest income. As long as you don't damage or stain it and you have it back in the morning, it can go upstairs with the rest of the garments from the show to be cleaned and pressed, and no one will be any the wiser.'

Allie didn't know what to say: the idea of Miss Willow borrowing clothes from the shop floor, wearing them, then putting them back on the racks was both shocking and astonishing.

'Don't look at me like that, dear,' Ruby said mildly. 'I've been doing it for years and no one's ever caught me out. And there's no harm done. I like to think that in a way I'm actually fulfilling the role of a poster girl for Dunbar & Jones. Well, not a poster *girl* as such, more a poster middle-aged spinster, but people know I work here, and if I'm well dressed then surely they'll assume that all my clothes come from the store, don't you think? And they do, of course; it's just that I don't always pay for them. So, really, I suppose I can say I'm in advertising these days, as well as sales.'

She said it with such conviction, and sounded so much like Donna and Pauline when they were trying to justify away something naughty they'd done, that Allie laughed.

Ruby smiled, though a little ruefully. 'Yes, I know, it does sound, well, somewhat creative, but one has to have one's small victories, even if they're silent, doesn't one? And I know what you're thinking, Allie. You have a very expressive face — you'll never be any good at poker, you know. No, unfortunately all is not what it seems in terms of my position here at Dunbar & Jones. There's so much more I could achieve if only I wore trousers instead of a dress. But I don't, and by the time that changes, if it ever does, I'll be long gone.' She plucked a handkerchief from her sleeve, picked up her glasses and polished them vigorously. 'But perhaps that's a conversation for another day. I suggest you select something from the racks, discreetly of course, then go out and enjoy yourself.'

'Thank you, Miss Willow,' Allie said. 'I'll be very careful with what I choose, I promise.'

'I'm sure you will be, Allie. You're that sort of person.'

It didn't take Allie long to select an indigo pencil skirt and a pale lilac, three-quarter-sleeved top; her work shoes were black and only had a low heel, but they would look all right. She changed in one of the dressing rooms, using the mirror to comb her hair and put on fresh lipstick. Then she rolled up her work uniform, but when she tried to stuff it into her bag it was obvious that it wasn't going to fit, so she stowed it under the dress department counter; she could wear her other uniform tomorrow.

Sonny was waiting for her at the side door onto Wyndham Street, leaning against one of the store's plate-glass windows and having a cigarette.

'Sorry, I got held up. Have you been waiting long? '

'It's OK,' Sonny said, grinding his smoke out under the heel of his boot. He was wearing his work clothes but also had on a pea coat, with the collar turned up. He kissed her cheek lightly. 'So where are we going?'

'I don't know. I thought you had somewhere in mind.'

'Not really. Where do you want to go?'

'We're not really dressed for the Wintergarden, are we?'

'Nope. What about a coffee bar?'

'That would be nice.'

'There's a good one in the back of Currie's, up the street.'

128

'Currie's Milkbar?'

Sonny nodded.

'Isn't that where the milkbar cowboys go?' Allie said. 'I've heard it's a bit rough there.'

'Only when the teds turn up,' Sonny replied. 'You'll be OK with me, and if you don't like it we'll go somewhere else. There's always Somervell's.'

Allie knew Somervell's Milkbar, having been there once with Irene after the pictures six months ago. All sorts of people congregated there and it was becoming a hangout for Auckland's more 'alternative' types — artists and strange writers like that Frank Sargeson — but evidently teddy boys and their girlfriends sometimes turned up as well.

Allie was well aware of the teddy boys because her father expounded on them weekly without fail, insisting that the bodgies, as he called them, were nothing more than juvenile delinquents and long-haired layabouts who went around wearing poncy bloody clothes and giving the streets of Auckland a bad name. A good war would fix them, he reckoned, and why the government hadn't rounded them all up and sent them off to Korea, he didn't know. And of course, whenever he went on like this, Donna and Pauline would launch into impassioned explanations that they weren't bodgies and their girlfriends weren't widgies — they were teddy boys and anyone with half a brain knew that. Which would cause their father to rattle his newspaper at them and point out that the press was calling them bodgies, so that's what they were. Then Donna and Pauline would say that the papers didn't know their arseholes from their earholes, and that would make their mother bang a pot or something on the bench and tell them that that was enough, and to all shut up.

Allie and Sonny walked up Queen Street hand in hand, stopping to look into Smith & Caughey's display windows so Allie could see what the opposition were doing, until they came to Currie's, which seemed fairly quiet. Mind you, it was only eight o'clock. They went inside and sat down in a booth towards the back. Johnny Ray was on the juke box and the lighting in the rear of the shop was subdued and intimate, unlike at the front where it bounced glaringly off the white formica counter tops and the gleaming chrome of the shop's fittings.

Sonny ordered black coffee for himself and white for Allie, from a waitress who wore a straight skirt with a slit up the side, a tight black polo-neck, her long hair in a ponytail, and a name badge that said 'Candy'.

Allie rather liked the look of the girl's ponytail. What luxury it would be to go around with your hair done like that every day. No more curlers and lacquer, just a quick brush and an elastic band and that was it.

'So how long has Polly been a model?' she asked.

'About two years, I think,' Sonny replied. 'I dunno, I've been working away for a while so I'm not sure when she started.'

'And is she your little sister?'

Sonny nodded. 'Next in line after me.'

'She's very beautiful.'

'She's very tutu.'

'Sorry?'

'She's naughty. She drinks too much and runs around with the wrong people and gets in trouble all the time. Poor old Mum's just about going round the bend.'

'And does she live at home?'

'More or less.'

Allie leaned back as the waitress set their coffees on the table. 'Well, she won't get to be a world-famous model if she behaves like that.'

'Won't she?' Sonny said.

Allie looked at him for a second. 'I don't know, actually. I just thought models would have to be well behaved.'

Sonny shrugged. 'Well, don't ask me. All I know is that Polly's a pain in the arse most of the time.'

'Beautiful, though,' Allie said, stirring her coffee to cool it down.

'Yeah, that's the trouble.'

They sat in companionable silence. Then Sonny said, 'Are we still on for tomorrow night? The dancing?'

Allie nodded.

'Shall I come and pick you up? It'll only be in the truck.'

'That would be nice, thank you.'

'It won't,' Sonny said, 'but I'll have my own transport soon.' He shovelled three teaspoons of sugar into his coffee. 'It's my brother's twenty-first this weekend, on Saturday night. Do you want to come?'

Allie felt a delicious sense of anticipation steal over her. Counting tonight, that would make four dates with Sonny in one week. And that must mean that he was as interested in her as she was in him, mustn't it? 'Yes, I'd like that!'

'Nothing flash. Just a party.'

'It sounds great,' Allie said, already thinking about what to wear. Would it be in a hall, or somewhere outdoors? She opened her mouth to ask, but then frowned and said instead, 'What's that noise? Like thunder. Can you hear it?'

Sonny listened. 'Motorbikes.'

'Sounds like a lot of them.'

The noise grew louder and louder until it peaked in a rumbling, blatting roar that made the hairs on Allie's arms spring up. She half stood for a better view of the street outside. 'They're stopping here!'

Sonny turned around, had a look, then turned back again. 'Don't worry about it.'

But Allie was worried. She could see something like a dozen motorcycles pulling up in front of the milkbar, their riders revving loudly and backing up to the footpath before dismounting.

'What if they come in?' Allie said anxiously. 'Will they come in, do you think?'

Sonny touched her hand across the table. 'Don't worry, drink your coffee.'

Allie obeyed, but didn't take her eyes off the door.

They did come in, a dozen of them, some with girls trailing behind them. Their clothing was menacing, to say the least. Most of the lads wore leather flying jackets with the sheepskin collars turned up, jeans and heavy work boots. When the one at the front turned around, Allie saw that there was an image of an eagle emblazoned on the back of his jacket above the words 'Currie's Cowboys'.

Everyone in the milkbar stared at them in silence, and there was a sudden tension in the air. The cowboys sat down at the tables near the front while their leader sauntered up to the counter, leaned against it and propped his boot on the footrest.

'Hokey-pokey milkshake, doll, when you're ready,' he said to the waitress.

The chatter started up again, and Allie breathed a sigh of relief. Perhaps there wouldn't be trouble after all. She was vaguely concerned for her own safety, but more than that she had a horrible image in her head of the headline that would be splashed across the next morning's *Herald* — 'DUNBAR & JONES SALESGIRL AT CENTRE OF MILKBAR BRAWL'.

The cowboy leader paid and sat down next to a very pretty girl wearing tight black capri pants, a low-cut black sweater and a pink scarf at her throat. He stuck two straws into the milkshake and they bent their heads over it, giggling.

Sonny drained his coffee, then inclined his head towards Allie's cup. 'Do you want a refill?'

'No, thanks. I'd better be getting home soon. I have to get to work early tomorrow.'

'I'll give you a lift.'

'OK, thanks, but I'll go straight in this time,' Allie said. 'Donna and Pauline were watching us last night through the curtains and this morning they—' She stopped.

The cowboy leader was walking towards their booth. He came to a halt in front of them and stood for a long moment, his thumbs caught in the pockets of his jeans, staring down at Sonny.

Allie tensed as Sonny pushed his cup away and slowly raised his eyes to the cowboy's face.

Then he said, 'G'day, Gary.'

'Hey, Sonny. All right?'

'Yep. Yourself?'

'Can't complain.'

Sonny said, 'This is my girl, Allie.'

'Pleased to meetcha,' Gary said, then asked Sonny, 'Going down the club tomorrow night?'

'Nah, going dancing.'

'Yeah? Whereabouts?'

'The Peter Pan.'

'We been banned from there,' Gary said. 'But, you know, I can't dance anyway.' He looked over at his friends, who were getting up. 'Well, gotta go, we got some teds to beat the shit out of.'

Sonny and Allie watched as Gary and his mates slouched out of the milkbar, climbed onto their motorbikes and, with a great deal of engine-revving and yelling out to one another, roared off up Queen Street.

Chapter Seven

Daisy was still feeling sick, and tired and down in the dumps. The wedding gowns last night had been absolutely gorgeous, but she knew she wouldn't be wearing anything remotely like that. Still, at least she could get some nice material, and her mother was good with a sewing machine.

She looked at the clock on the wall above the rows of hat blocks and saw that it was ten minutes to twelve — nearly her lunchtime. She'd just stitched a line of grosgrain ribbon onto the brim of a hat, but it looked rather odd and she wondered if she'd put it in the wrong place. Daisy put up her hand so that Miss Button would come over. She preferred the girls to do this if they wanted something — she said it was more sensible than them all queuing up in front of her and making the room untidy, and anyway she needed the exercise.

'I'm sorry, Miss Button, but am I putting the ribbon on in the right place? I seem to be having a bit of a dozy time today.'

Beatrice Button privately thought that Daisy had a dozy

135

time most days, but she was never unkind enough to say so. And besides, the girl was sweet, her sewing was very neat and tidy, and she did have a certain creative flair.

'No, dear, it should be on the outside of the brim, not next to the crown.'

Daisy's pretty, endearing little face fell and her huge grey eyes filled with tears.

'It's all right,' Beatrice said. 'Just unpick it and put a new piece on in the right place.'

'And I can't seem to get this peony right either,' Daisy complained. 'The petals keep going funny.'

Beatrice glanced up at the clock herself. 'Why don't you ask me about that after lunch, Daisy? I've got an appointment and I really do need to go in a minute.'

Daisy nodded, feeling more despondent than ever. Everyone was doing something today at lunchtime except her. Nyla and Peg, her two best friends in the millinery workroom, had already gone, and even Terry was too busy to meet her. She supposed she would have to eat her lunch by herself. Sighing, she carefully put down the hat and stuck her needle into a pincushion so it wouldn't get lost. Retrieving her bag from the shelf beneath the table, she went to the toilet, which she seemed to be doing a lot lately, washed her hands and put on a bit of lipstick. What now? A boring old sandwich and a cup of tea in the caf, she supposed. But when she came out again she bumped into Allie, leaning with theatrical nonchalance against the wall.

'I thought you had something on today?' Daisy said, trying not to sound grumpy.

'I have,' Allie replied, tucking her arm through Daisy's. 'Come on.'

'Come on where?'

'You'll see.'

Allie led Daisy all the way down the stairs to the ground floor, then out onto the crowded street.

'Where are we going?' Daisy said again.

'Just wait and see, will you? It's not far.'

Mystified, Daisy allowed herself to be pulled along until they came to the Kia Ora Tearooms, not far up the street.

'What are we doing here?' Daisy said, now thoroughly confused.

Smiling to herself, Allie didn't reply. Instead she led Daisy past the tables filled with lunchtime customers and through to a private room at the back of the shop.

As they entered, Daisy saw Irene, Louise, Nyla, Peg and Miss Button sitting around a table wearing silly smiles on their faces.

'Surprise!' Louise exclaimed. 'We're having your Dunbar & Jones bridal shower!'

Daisy burst into tears.

'Oh dear,' Beatrice said, digging for a handkerchief in her bag. 'Have we given you a fright?'

Daisy took the handkerchief and honked into it. 'No, I just, well, I didn't expect this, that's all.'

'Well, a girl only gets married once, you know,' Peg declared.

'But it's not till the end of January,' Daisy protested.

'We know,' Louise said, 'but we'll all be off on our holidays after next week, and you'll be busy getting everything ready for the wedding when we get back, so we thought we'd have it now. Now come and sit down, we've ordered a lovely lunch. But first . . .' She reached behind her and produced an elegantly wrapped parcel. 'Ta-da! Come and open your presents!'

'I don't know what to say,' Daisy said as she sat down.

'Don't say anything,' Allie suggested. 'Just open your presents.'

Daisy pulled hesitantly at the ribbon around the parcel.

'Oh, just tear it off, it's only paper!' Irene said, giggling.

'But it's really pretty!' Daisy ripped it open anyway, then gasped, 'Louise, it's lovely!' She held up a beautifully embroidered damask tablecloth so everyone could see.

Allie waited for the oohs and aahs to die down before she handed Daisy her present, about which she'd thought very carefully.

Daisy opened it, and started crying again.

'It's a length of guipure lace,' Allie explained. 'For your wedding dress.'

'I know,' Daisy said, wiping at her tears. 'It's beautiful. It must have cost you a fortune!' She managed a giggle. 'The queen will be so jealous!'

'Bound to be,' Irene said. 'Now open mine.'

Irene's present was a crystal salad set. She'd decided against the Indian rug, thinking that Daisy was more of a salad set sort of girl.

'Thank you, Irene. It's very classy and such a lovely pattern. You can come and have the first salad with it after we're married.'

Nyla and Peg's gift was a hand-painted Sèvres porcelain sandwich tray.

'We chipped in together,' Nyla explained. 'We're both a bit broke at the moment.'

Beatrice presented her gift last, a very pretty silver condiment set. 'It's from Miss Willow as well,' she said. Then she passed over another parcel, wrapped in yellow paper.

'This is just for you. Open it when you're by yourself.'

'Oh. Thank you very much.' Not sure what else to do, Daisy slipped the parcel into her bag just as their lunch arrived.

Irene reached for a potato-topped savoury. 'Yum, I'm starving.' She bit into it, and laughed as a globule of hot mince squirted out and plopped onto the table top.

'You're in a chirpy mood today,' Allie observed. 'Did you win the art union?'

Irene shook her head, and swallowed. 'No. But it's a beautiful day and Daisy's getting married and it's Christmas and everything's all right, isn't it?'

Allie supposed it was, though she suspected there was more to Irene's good mood than she was letting on. Something to do with Vince Reynolds, perhaps? He'd given Irene a particularly sleazy wink at morning tea.

'We're all going dancing tonight at the Peter Pan,' Louise told Nyla and Peg. 'Do you want to come?'

'I can't,' Nyla replied morosely. 'I'm babysitting my little brother. My parents are going out.'

'Can I bring Jim?' Peg asked, referring to her husband. 'Or is it a girls' night out?'

'Rob's coming,' Louise said, reaching for a ham and egg sandwich.

Irene added, 'And Allie's bringing a man.'

'Have you got a new man?' Peg asked excitedly.

'That Maori boy from stores,' Irene said. 'Sonny Manaia.'

'The one with the duck's arse hairdo and the twinkly brown eyes?' Nyla was impressed.

Allie nodded, half proud and half embarrassed.

'He's nice. How long have you been going out?' Peg said,

139

dissecting her sandwich and scraping the piccalilli off the ham.

Daisy was fascinated. 'Don't you like piccalilli?' She couldn't eat it herself, at the moment — the thought of any pickle, in fact, turned her stomach. On the other hand, she was getting through a jar of Marmite every week, so she supposed it evened out.

'I hate cauliflower,' Peg explained. 'And sometimes they put cauliflower in piccalilli.'

'We've only been out twice,' Allie said, suddenly overwhelmed with a need to talk about Sonny. 'The pictures on Wednesday night, and last night after the fashion show we went for a coffee.' She paused for a deliberate second. 'At Currie's Milkbar.'

Nyla's thinly plucked eyebrows went up. 'Isn't a bit rough there?'

'Not really, though some cowboys did stop by when we were having our coffee.'

'Weren't you scared?' Peg asked.

'A bit,' Allie said, and couldn't resist adding, 'but the leader, Gary, was a really nice sort.'

'You met him?' Irene asked, clearly a little miffed because, for a change, someone else had done something more daring.

'My dad says he'll skin me alive if he hears I've been anywhere near a milkbar,' Nyla said. 'Though I have to say I do like those motorbikes they ride. They're so . . .' She stopped, obviously searching for a suitable description.

'Sexy,' Irene said.

They all looked at her, uncomfortable with the bluntness of the word.

'Well, they are, aren't they?' Irene protested. 'All that

140

power and noise and the way the girls sit on the back with their legs around the boys. It's sexy.'

'Not my cup of tea, I'm afraid,' Beatrice said lightly. 'The closest I've ever been to a motorbike is the bicycle I had when I was a child. And even then I wasn't very successful at riding it. My legs were too short, you see.'

Allie laughed as merrily as everyone else, though she was finding it slightly peculiar, having lunch with Miss Button, but Louise had said they should invite her because she was Daisy's boss, and Daisy liked her. And she did seem to be a good sort. Like Miss Willow, really. Only Miss Button was half the height and twice as wide.

'I propose a toast,' Louise said, holding up her tea cup. 'To Daisy and Terry. May they have a very successful marriage, loads of well-behaved children and a long and happy life together.'

Everyone lifted their cups and said, 'To Daisy and Terry', and Peg added, 'Pity it's not champagne. Or even sherry.'

Allie shot a glance at Miss Button, who only nodded.

'I'm partial to a drop of good sherry myself,' she said. 'But we'd better not roll back to work smelling like we've been in a public bar all morning. Mr Beaumont would have kittens.'

Daisy snorted tea out of her nose, which made everyone else laugh. Then, disconcertingly, Daisy's giggles turned into tears.

'I'm sorry,' she said after several moments, dabbing at her eyes with a paper serviette that had a smear of piccalilli on it. 'I seem to be bawling all the time these days. It must be—' She stopped, remembering that Nyla and Peg and Miss Button weren't supposed to know about her condition. 'I mean, I was feeling so rotten this morning — I think I

141

must be nervous about the wedding or something. But it's lovely to have such good friends.' She looked hesitantly at Allie. 'And it will be all right, won't it?'

Allie patted her hand. 'Of course it will, silly.'

They were ten minutes late back to work, but as Miss Button was with them they felt they had a certain level of dispensation.

Keith Beaumont didn't, though. Unfortunately, he was having a conversation with Ted Horrocks just as they all trooped through the front door, and he ostentatiously checked his watch.

Allie ducked her head and stared hard at a display of royal tour mementos: silk scarves patterned with images of Buckingham Palace, cups and saucers, cake plates, teapots, brooches, pens and pencils, and special folding seats you could sit on while you waited for the queen to go past. Allie wished she was sitting on one now, preferably on her own back lawn.

'This is an unusual time for staff on the twelve-to-one lunch shift to be returning to work, isn't it, Miss Button?' Keith was in a very bad mood because he'd just lost yet another fifty pounds at Addington. Bloody trots — he knew he should have stuck to the gallops or the dogs. He'd never been any good at picking form for pacers.

'Yes, I'm afraid it is, Mr Beaumont,' Beatrice said, and sighed. 'And as the senior staff member in the party I take full responsibility.'

'I trust there's a good reason for your tardiness?'

'Of course,' Beatrice replied. She leaned closer to Mr Beaumont, as if to impart a confidence, but barely lowered her voice at all. 'We were out at lunch and one of our party unfortunately suffered a slight accident.'

Mr Beaumont looked wary. 'Accident? What sort of accident?'

'*Women's* problems, Mr Beaumont,' Beatrice declared earnestly. 'One of us is experiencing *women's* problems and we were unforeseeably delayed.'

While Allie and the others looked on in horrified glee, Mr Beaumont's face went the colour of a ripe tomato. He tugged at the hem of his waistcoat. 'Yes, well . . .' he said, then turned and strode off.

'That was a bit naughty, Beatrice,' Ted said, trying not to smirk.

'Yes, I suppose it was, wasn't it?' Beatrice replied, thoroughly unrepentant. 'But he shouldn't be so nosy, or such a stickler for the rules. It is Christmas, after all. Come on, girls, let's get back to work, shall we?'

When Allie apologized and explained why she was late back from lunch, Miss Willow only laughed, though she made a half-hearted effort not to.

'Yes, well, they've never seen eye to eye, Miss Button and Mr Beaumont,' she said. 'But don't be late again, please, Allie. We're terribly busy.'

'I know, I'm sorry,' Allie said again.

By five o'clock Allie's feet were killing her and she'd barely squeezed in ten minutes for a cuppa and a cigarette at afternoon tea. Friday afternoons were always busy, but today, the last late shopping night before Christmas, was particularly hectic. The store closed at eight o'clock; she would get a thirty-minute break at six, but there were still another two and a half hours of serving panicking women who didn't know what they wanted, or only wanted what they couldn't, or shouldn't, have. Women were the most difficult customers, Allie thought. They seemed to invest so much hope in the clothes they bought, expecting the garments alone to transform them.

And there would be no time to go home tonight before she went out, so she'd brought her clothes into work, as had Louise and Daisy, so the three of them would change in the staff loos before they headed up to the Peter Pan. Irene still didn't know if she was coming, but she was an office girl so she could get away at five o'clock anyway.

By eight Allie was so exhausted that if she hadn't been going out with Sonny, she might have told the others that she was just too tired, and gone home for an early night. But by the time they'd changed into their glad rags she felt a little better, and as the three of them hurried down the stairs to the side door on Wyndham Street, she realized that she was excited.

Ted Horrocks was waiting to let them out. He considered that, just as it was his job to greet customers as they entered the store during the day, it was also his job to farewell the staff at night. It was something he enjoyed, especially on Fridays, because many of the younger ones were on their way out and he loved to see them all bright-eyed and bushy-tailed and looking forward to an evening on the town.

'Big night, girls?' he asked as he held the heavy glass door open for them.

'The Peter Pan,' Louise said.

'Ah,' Ted said, 'dancing the night away, eh? Well, have a marvellous time.'

Daisy looked at him. 'Why don't you come with us?'

Ted's ruddy face beamed. He knew he'd never take up the offer — he was far too old for that sort of thing — but he was extremely chuffed. 'Thank you very much, I must say. I have been known to cut rather a spectacular rug in my time, but I don't think Mrs Horrocks would be very happy.'

'If you went out on the town with three girls?' Louise teased.

'No, if I left her at home,' Ted replied. 'No, she'll be putting the kettle on by now and getting out the baking tin. She does a tremendous sultana cake, does my Natalie, and we always have a slice or two with a cup of tea on Friday nights. It's one of the real pleasures of my life.'

Allie said shrewdly, 'What, the sultana cake or sharing it with Mrs Horrocks?'

'Well, girls, put it like this — if it was cardboard we were eating it wouldn't make much difference to how I felt about it.'

Allie got that nice warm feeling she sometimes had with her parents: it must be wonderful to love someone that much.

'Well, we'll have a dance for you, shall we?' she offered.

'That would be just the ticket,' Ted said. 'Now, have a lovely night, eh?'

Smiling to himself, he closed the door behind them.

They were the last out — even Mr Max and that twit Keith Beaumont had left on time tonight. Must be all the posh Christmas dos they had to rush off to, Ted thought, though he wouldn't swap places with either of them for quids, not when he had Mrs Horrocks and sultana cake to go home to.

He started his rounds of the store, checking that every

window was closed properly, every door locked, and every tap turned off in the kitchens and the restrooms. When he'd done that he rubbed his hands in anticipation, because now it was time to do one of his favourite jobs — turning on the lights on the Christmas tree in front of the big front doors. In all the time he'd been with Dunbar & Jones, the lights had never been switched on until precisely the weekend before Christmas. It had started when that sharp-tongued old matriarch Isobel Dunbar had been running the place — probably, he suspected, because she was too mean to pay for the electricity until she absolutely had to — but now it had become a tradition.

He made his way downstairs, leaving strategic lights burning on each floor — 'We want the store to be lit up like a *castle*, Ted,' Mr Max said every year, 'a veritable *fairy* castle where people will all want to come and spend their Christmas bonuses' — until he reached the ground floor. He circled the Christmas tree, its topmost point almost reaching the high ceiling and crowned with a porcelain-faced Christmas fairy, relishing the way that the glass balls and satin bows and tinsel decorations already glittered. When he retired — which, he'd decided, wouldn't be too far away now, because even he had to admit that he was getting a bit too old to be belting up and down three flights of stairs every morning and night — he was going to say thank you, but he didn't want a gold watch or a mantle clock or whatever Mr Max's secretary thought he should have. He was going to ask for a miniature version of this very tree, complete with decorations, that he could put up every Christmas in his own front room and look at to remind him of all the satisfying years he'd had at Dunbar & Jones. Yes, that's definitely what he was going to do.

He reached down to the power point set into the floor, and plugged in the cable leading from the thousands of tiny lights on the tree to the power socket. Then, out loud, he counted 'One, two, three!' and switched it on. The tree lit up dazzlingly and, stepping back, Ted had to admit that it really did look like something you might find in a fairy castle. It was just beautiful, there was no other word to describe it. And already, a couple outside had their faces pressed against the glass doors looking in at the spectacle. Ted waved, and they waved merrily back.

Whistling, he collected his rucksack — a cherished memento of his army days — and made his way to the side door where he let himself out, and strode happily off up Wyndham Street.

Behind him, in the basement of Dunbar & Jones, the ancient electrical wires strung across the ceiling began slowly to heat up.

Allie's face lit up like the store's Christmas tree when she saw Sonny waiting on the street. He was with Terry and they'd both obviously had a quick tidy-up. Sonny was wearing the same clothes he'd had on to go to the pictures, and Terry was looking fairly smart himself in a sports coat and a loud blue tie with hand-painted ducks flying across it.

'You're wearing it!' Daisy exclaimed delightedly as she yanked the bottom of the tie. 'I gave it to him for his birthday,' she said to Allie. 'I ordered it from a catalogue. It's different, don't you think?'

'Yes, it is,' Allie answered truthfully, trying not to catch anyone's eye.

Sonny was wearing a tie, too, which didn't match his outfit: Allie thought she might have seen it on Terry a couple of times.

Louise looked at her watch. 'Come on, let's go. I'm meeting Rob there at half past eight. He'll worry if I'm not there on time.'

So they headed off up Queen Street, Allie arm in arm with Sonny, and Daisy holding Terry's hand.

'You look nice,' Sonny said to Allie.

She was wearing her full satin skirt in midnight blue, a violet lurex top and shoes with heels low enough for energetic dancing.

'Thank you,' she replied. 'So do you.'

'I've only got the one decent set of clobber,' he said.

Allie could claim a reasonable wardrobe only because she got a discount at work. 'You look pretty good to me.'

Sonny smiled at her and squeezed her waist.

The Peter Pan was already crowded, noisy and filling up with a blue cloud of cigarette smoke. Alcohol wasn't served there because of the liquor laws, but the girls each had a small flask hidden in their bags, knowing they wouldn't be searched. The band hadn't started yet, but they were on stage tuning up and tapping microphones.

The girls found seats at a large, round table while Terry and Sonny fetched jugs of orange juice from the bar. Rob had been waiting outside the cabaret for Louise, and they sat together now, sharing a joke. Watching them, Allie thought how lucky Louise was. Rob was a good-looking bloke, fit and strong and with all the character traits a girl — well, most girls — liked in a man. He was hard-working and generous and kind, and he clearly thought the world of Louise. And of Susan. He wanted to own his own garage one day, but not until after he and Louise had bought a home, which Allie thought was very sensible, if not the tiniest bit boring. She couldn't see herself being that level-headed about money. Not that she frittered hers, what there was of it, but she did give quite a lot to her mother, and she bought things for Donna and Pauline, and she bought shoes and, well . . . it just sort of disappeared. And Louise just seemed so much more grown up, even though she was only three years older than Allie. She supposed it was being married and having a child. Would she feel grown up when all that happened to her? On the one hand she was getting a little worried that it wouldn't, but on the other hand she was quite happy being single. Well, she had believed she was, before she'd met Sonny.

She glanced at him and saw that he was watching her. He smiled. 'Penny for your thoughts?'

The question gave her a tiny fright. 'Just relaxing, really,' she replied. She could hardly say she was thinking about marriage and having children and taking out a mortgage, which would surely send him running for the hills.

Lighting a cigarette, Louise nodded towards the door. 'Here comes trouble.'

Irene was standing in the doorway, pausing, no doubt, for maximum impact. She was wearing a scarlet satin dress with narrow shoulder straps, a very tight bodice and a tiny waist. But tonight the skirt was full, unlike the snug pencil skirts she usually favoured. The colour of the dress perfectly set off her pale, luminous skin and gleaming black hair, which fell over her shoulders and was fastened on one side with a diamante clip. She carried a minuscule black evening bag that matched her high-heeled satin sandals.

Allie immediately felt like a frump.

Terry muttered, 'Crikey!'

'Terry!' Daisy said. 'Though she does look very pretty, doesn't she?'

'I'm not sure if "pretty" is *quite* the right word,' Louise countered.

Allie glanced at Sonny to gauge his reaction, but he was half under the table topping up his orange juice with gin from the flask in her bag.

Irene waved out and sailed over, a sea of admiring glances following her.

'Hi,' she said, over the sound of the band, and pulled up a chair. As Irene sat down and leaned back, her rigidly corseted and jutting breasts seemed to point straight at Sonny.

Rob said in Louise's ear, 'Christ, she could take a spider's eye out with one of those,' and they both dissolved into a fit of giggles.

'Couldn't you get Martin to come out?' Allie said across the table.

Irene scowled. 'No. He had some important papers to read. Has anyone got any booze?'

'In my bag on the floor,' Allie replied.

Irene poured herself a glass of juice and bobbed down beneath the table. Reappearing a moment later, she quaffed half of her drink in one go, then wiped her mouth with the back of her hand. It was a very masculine thing to do, but somehow Irene managed to make it look stylish.

'Who wants to dance?' she asked.

Terry declined politely, and Rob didn't hear because he was talking to Louise again.

Irene suggested, 'What about you, Sonny? Fancy a dance?'

'No thanks,' Sonny said, sipping his drink.

Leaning forward so that her cleavage was even more evident, Irene wheedled, 'Oh, come on, I don't bite.'

Sonny looked as though he didn't believe her. Then, to Allie's surprise, he said, 'Yeah, all right then.'

He took off his jacket and he and Irene moved onto the dance floor, which was already filling with whirling couples. The band, renowned for playing popular, up-tempo dance tunes, was clearly on form tonight. But Allie barely noticed as she stared after Sonny and Irene, feeling hurt, annoyed and a bit of a fool. Sonny hadn't even danced with her yet! She could feel Daisy and Louise looking at her, but refused to meet their eyes.

On the floor Sonny took Irene's hand and launched into a jive. He whipped her through a spin, brought her back in a return, then did a few basic jive steps before sending her out and reeling her back in again.

'You're good on your feet,' Irene said.

'You're not so bad yourself,' he replied, doing a very tidy spin of his own.

Irene glanced over his shoulder to where the others were still sitting, and remarked benignly, 'Allie looks annoyed.'

'You would too if some sheila'd just dragged your bloke onto the dance floor.'

'I didn't drag you,' Irene said quickly. 'I asked and you said yes.'

Sonny did another spin. 'Only because I wanted to get something straight. You want to think before you do things, Irene. About other people, for a start.'

Irene didn't like the way the conversation was going. She stopped dancing and parked her hands on her satin-clad hips. 'What do you mean?'

Sonny also stopped. 'I think you probably know, eh.'

Irene did, actually. She looked at the floor for a moment, then sighed. 'You're right, I suppose. Sometimes I don't think.'

'And I'm not on the market,' Sonny added. 'If that's what you had in mind.'

Her confidence returning as quickly as it had ebbed, Irene laughed. 'No, it wasn't, actually. I only wanted a dance. I like to dance.'

'Just making it clear.'

Irene thought it was time to make herself clear. 'Look, Mr Fancy Feet, you might be smooth and handsome, but you're Allie's bloke and Allie's my friend. I don't do that to my friends.'

'Glad to hear it,' Sonny said.

They shared a look of mutual understanding that could almost be construed as respect, then resumed dancing.

When the song finished, an amused Irene said with exaggerated formality, 'Thank you, Mr Manaia.'

Sonny nodded and said after a moment, 'You're all right.'

'So are you,' Irene replied, and they made their way back to their table.

'Sorry about that,' Sonny said as he sat down next to Allie. 'Had to get something straightened out.'

'And did you?' Allie asked, still feeling somewhat bruised.

'Yep.' He paused. 'That Irene's a good mate.'

Startled, Allie said, 'Of yours?'

Sonny kissed the end of her nose. 'No, of yours.'

Peg and her husband Jim arrived then, and they all shuffled their chairs around to squeeze them in.

Allie danced almost constantly with Sonny, and when they took breaks he stayed beside her and talked to her, except when he, Terry, Rob and Jim ducked outside for a beer from Terry's car. Allie felt wonderfully light-headed, almost drunk, even though she'd only had a couple of gin and oranges, and she caught herself wishing that the evening would never end. Poor Daisy, who'd had the same amount to drink, actually was drunk, but then she was in a delicate condition. Irene was having a marvellous time — her backside was only ever on her chair for a few minutes before someone would come up and ask her to dance and she'd be off again, whirling and spinning, laughing and flirting like mad.

At eleven-thirty Rob and Louise announced that they were off to collect Susan. Terry glanced at Daisy's drooping eyelids and said that they should probably go, too, and did anyone else want a lift home? Allie and Sonny accepted as Sonny didn't have the truck.

When they were halfway down the cabaret steps, Sonny stopped and frowned.

'What is it?' Allie asked, and when he nodded at something across the street, she followed his gaze.

There were several cars parked there, with more than a dozen teddy boys slouched around them. Allie felt her stomach lurch: she knew they were just ordinary Kiwi lads, but for some reason they looked menacing in their stovepipe trousers, draped jackets, skinny ties and chunky shoes. She had heard, too, that they all carried flick-knives.

'What are they doing?' she asked nervously.

Sonny shrugged. 'Waiting?'

'What for?'

'Trouble, probably. Come on, let's go.'

Terry was waving out from his car a short way down the street, and they had almost reached it when the unmistakable thunder of motorcycle engines filled the air.

Sonny muttered, 'Shit.' He flicked his cigarette into the gutter and gestured for Allie and Daisy to hurry up and get into the car.

They scrambled in, just in time to see the cowboys come rumbling and back-firing up street, the lights from store windows and street lamps reflecting off the chrome and gleaming paint of their motorcycles. Allie recognized Gary in the lead, but her heart almost stopped when she also realized that one of the pillion passengers, her arms tight around the waist of a denim- and leather-clad boy, was Donna, wearing tight capri pants and a very skimpy halter-neck top.

The cowboys cruised slowly past the teds, who gave them the fingers and yelled abuse. Then, deliberately stopping traffic in both directions, the motorbikes turned in the middle of the street and came back. Drawn by the noise, people were pouring out of the Peter Pan and gathering on the footpath.

Terry started the car. 'Time to go, I think.'

'My sister's on one of those motorbikes!' Allie blurted.

'What, Pauline?' Terry looked as shocked as Allie felt.

'No, bloody Donna.'

Terry said, 'Sorry, Allie, but I'm not grabbing her. I'll get my head kicked in.'

'Where's Sonny?' Allie looked around wildly. And then she spotted him, standing very still on the footpath, watching the teds. She wound down her window and called out to him.

He turned his head, but didn't take his eyes off the teddy boys.

'Donna's on one of those motorbikes!' she shouted.

Sonny did look at her then. 'Your sister?'

Allie nodded.

Sonny swore. Then, almost inevitably, a bottle spun through the air and smashed against one of the teds' cars, and they surged into the street, hitting and kicking out at the cowboys going past. Two went down, the big machines crashing onto the tarseal in a shower of sparks, the riders and pillion passengers scrambling out of the way. Realizing what had happened, the rest of the cowboys wheeled around, parked, leapt off their bikes and lunged across the street, throwing themselves at the teds. In an instant there were fists and boots everywhere, people yelling and swearing, and high-pitched screams from the girls of both gangs.

Watching from the safety of the car Daisy shrieked herself, and Allie gasped as a cowboy girl launched herself at a ted girl and yanked her hair viciously, then slapped her face.

'Bloody hell,' Terry said.

Allie looked for Sonny again but he'd gone. She spotted him a moment later in the middle of the mêlée, lashing out with his fists while also trying to pull a ted off Gary, who was face-down on the road. Then someone lurched up to him and punched him in the head, and he went down himself.

'Oh God, Terry, help him!' Allie wailed.

But Terry, his face the colour of porridge in the bright light of the street lamps, swallowed and said nothing.

Then a new noise was added to the din — police sirens.

A car and two vans screeched to a halt, disgorging cop after cop. The teds melted away and the cowboys ran for their bikes and roared off, though the police managed to collar several from each gang, bundling them unceremoniously into separate vans. It was all over in a few minutes, and the crowd outside the Peter Pan began to disperse, hurried along by several stony-faced constables.

Allie's door was yanked open and Sonny fell in, a handkerchief clamped over his bleeding nose. 'Put your foot down, Terry,' he said in a muffled voice.

Soon they were driving along Parnell Road, heading for Orakei.

'Are you all right?' Allie asked when she trusted her voice enough to speak. Her knees felt like jelly even though she was sitting down, and her heart was only just beginning to settle back into its regular rhythm.

Sonny nodded.

Terry cleared his throat. 'Allie, sorry I couldn't do anything about Donna. Or give you a hand, Sonny. I . . . just couldn't.'

Sonny waved his hand. 'Don't worry about it. It was just a stupid bloody scrap.'

'I'll kill Donna when I see her,' Allie said grimly.

They were silent again for a while. Then, just as they turned into Coates Avenue, Daisy asked, 'Did one of those cowboys throw that bottle?'

'I didn't see,' Allie said.

Sonny dabbed at his nose. The bleeding had stopped so he wound down the window and threw the bloodied handkerchief out. 'Someone on the footpath chucked it.'

'I'd better go straight in,' Allie told Sonny when Terry had stopped the car.

'Sorry about what happened,' he said. 'But Gary's a mate.'

'I know,' Allie replied. 'It's all right.'

'Are we still on for tomorrow night?'

'Yes. Why wouldn't we be?'

Sonny looked relieved. 'I'll pick you up at six then, eh? Meet me on the corner of Kepa Road. Oh, and wear long pants.'

Mystified, Allie looked at him. 'Why?'

'Wait and see,' Sonny said.

After Terry had dropped her off at home, Daisy crept into her bedroom so she wouldn't wake her parents, closed the door, and opened Miss Button's secret present. It was a set of white, exquisitely knitted baby clothes — a gown, a jacket, a bonnet and booties. The card tucked into the tiny garments said, 'To Daisy and Terry, congratulations and very best wishes regarding your soon-to-be new arrival. If there is anything we can help with, please let us know, from Beatrice Button and Ruby Willow.'

Daisy cried for the fourth time that day.

Chapter Eight

Allie sat up and lifted the blind at the window — another lovely, bright sunny day. Throwing off the covers, she slid out of bed and looked in the mirror. God. She hadn't taken her make-up off last night and she looked a sight.

The floorboards were cool on her bare feet as she padded down the hall to the bathroom. She splashed cold water on her face and rubbed off the worst of the smeared mascara, then went out into the kitchen.

Everyone was there except Donna, and Allie felt her heart sink.

'Morning, Sleeping Beauty,' her father said, turning over a page of the *Herald*. 'You get in a stoush last night?'

'What?' Allie said, appalled. Was it in the papers?

'A stoush. You've got black eyes.'

'Oh. No, that's just make-up.' Allie gave an inward sigh of relief. 'Where's Donna?'

'She stayed at Maureen's house last night,' Colleen said, breaking eggs into a spitting frying pan.

Allie nodded. That made sense. Maureen was Donna's

friend from school, and they were always getting into trouble together.

'Except I wasn't allowed to go,' Pauline complained.

'You weren't invited,' Colleen said, shaking the pan so the eggs wouldn't stick.

Pauline scowled. 'It's not fair, I never get invited to stay at anyone's house.'

'For Christ's sake, Pauline, give it a rest, will you?' Sid had been hearing this all morning. He snapped his paper shut. 'Bugger-all in that today,' he added, 'except there's been another scrap in Queen Street between those lads on the motorbikes and those bloody bodgies.'

'Teddy boys,' Pauline corrected.

Sid didn't take the bait. Colleen put his breakfast in front of him. 'Thanks, love, this looks good,' he said, enthusiastically rupturing his fried eggs with a fork. 'Who's helping me in the garden today?'

'Not me,' Pauline said immediately.

Allie said, 'I will, if you like.'

Sid shovelled in a mouthful of food and talked through it. 'Thought I'd put in some beans and a bit of beetroot, maybe some broccoli—'

Pauline pulled a disgusted face. 'Yuck.'

'—and some celery, and I might even have a go at some snow peas.'

Colleen sat down at the table with her own breakfast. 'Snow peas? They're a bit posh, aren't they?'

'Dunno, but Bill reckons they're just the ticket in a salad with a bit of lettuce and a hard-boiled egg. His missus grows them.'

Buttering a piece of toast, Colleen said, 'When do we ever eat salads?'

'Never,' Sid replied, 'but maybe we should start.' He poked the roll of fat bulging over the waistband of his trousers. 'That's how you get rid of one of these, isn't it? Eating rabbit food?'

'But you've had that tummy for years, love.'

'That's right, but it occurred to me recently that the sheilas haven't been whistling at me half as much as they used to, and I thought maybe it was the spare tyre.'

Fork halfway to her mouth, Colleen stared incredulously at her husband, then burst out laughing.

'What?' Sid said, trying to look wounded. Then he started laughing too.

Allie was giggling so much she had to put her cup back in its saucer.

Pauline, who had a pained expression on her face, said, 'God, Dad, you're pathetic.'

'That's enough, Pauline,' Colleen warned, though there was no bite to her words. 'At least your father can laugh at himself.'

Pauline muttered something under her breath, grabbed a piece of toast, and slouched out of the kitchen.

'Bloody teenagers,' Sid said cheerfully.

Allie sat on an upturned bucket, smoking a cigarette and watching her father swear as he tried to separate clumps of baby celery plants.

'I'm buggered if I know why they can't wrap each one up individually,' he said.

'That'd be a lot of newspaper, though, wouldn't it?' Allie countered.

'Yes, but it only ends up around fish and chips anyway, doesn't it?'

'I suppose,' Allie said. She looked up as Donna appeared around the side of the house. Her sister was wearing a knee-length skirt and demure cotton blouse — no sign of last night's rather revealing outfit — and the sort of sour yet shifty expression that only Donna could manufacture.

Sid said, 'Hello stranger. Have a nice night?'

'It was OK,' Donna said, not meeting his eye. She hurried up the back steps and disappeared into the house.

Allie stood up, flicked her fag end into the nasturtiums behind the bomb shelter and followed her sister inside.

She caught up with her in the hall. 'Where were you last night?' she demanded.

'At Maureen's,' Donna said.

'All night?'

'Yes.'

'Liar.'

'I am not!'

'You bloody well are,' Allie said. 'I saw you in Queen Street at about half past eleven, on the back of some bloke's motorbike!'

Donna glared at her, clearly trying to decide whether to continue lying or not. 'So?' she said, shrugging.

'You were right in the middle of that bloody fight!' Allie snapped.

'So what if I was?' Donna replied blithely. 'You were there too!'

'Donna, I'm twenty years old. You're only fifteen! And *I* wasn't wrapped around a milkbar cowboy!'

'Well, at least I wasn't wrapped around a *Maori* boy.'

Allie felt the last of her self-control slip away and she punched her sister on the arm.

'Ow! What was that for?' Donna cried.

161

'What's happening out there?' Colleen called from the kitchen.

Allie lowered her voice and hissed, 'For being so bloody rude! How dare you say that about Sonny!'

'What? That he's a Maori?' Donna said, rubbing her arm. 'Well, he is, isn't he?'

'It was the way you said it. As an insult.'

'I think you're hearing things, Allie.'

'I think you're being a bitch, Donna. Why?'

Donna was quiet for a moment. Then she shrugged again and made a vaguely remorseful face. 'I don't know. Sorry.'

'And where was Maureen last night? Did her mother know you were in town?'

'Not exactly.'

'What do you mean, "not exactly"? Did you sneak out?'

'Didn't have to. Mrs Johnson was at the housie.'

Allie frowned: she bet her mother hadn't known that. 'And where did you get those pants and the top? Mum'd have a fit if she saw you wearing them. You looked closer to twenty-one than fifteen.'

When Donna's face lit up, Allie knew she'd said the wrong thing.

'Yeah, I did, didn't I? Kev says I looked beaut.'

'Who the hell's Kev?'

'Kevin Donovan, from school?'

Allie cast her mind back: all she could recall of Kevin Donovan was a pair of knobbly knees beneath baggy school shorts and a bad case of acne. 'Kevin Donovan's a milkbar cowboy?' she said disbelievingly.

Donna nodded proudly. 'And my boyfriend.'

'Oh, don't be so bloody stupid. You're not old enough to have a boyfriend.'

'I am so,' Donna shot back, then burst out laughing. 'You should see your face.'

'It's not funny, Donna. You could have been hurt last night. Or arrested. And motorbikes can be very dangerous.'

'Oh, they are not.'

'Well, if I even *hear* you've been out with Kevin Donovan again, I'm telling Mum,' Allie threatened.

'I'm telling Mum,' Donna mimicked in a silly voice. Then, with a toss of her long blonde ponytail, she flounced into the bedroom she shared with Pauline and slammed the door in Allie's face.

Allie stared at the door for a moment, then turned away to see her mother standing at the other end of the hallway.

'What was that in aid of?' Colleen asked.

'Oh, you know. Just Donna being Donna,' Allie said.

Colleen made an I-know-what-you-mean face. 'Will you be wanting tea tonight before you go out?'

'No, thanks, Mum. I think there'll be food there.'

'Allie, where exactly is this party you're going to?'

'It's a twenty-first so I think it must be in a hall somewhere. Or it might be outside or in a marquee, because Sonny said to wear slacks. I don't think it's a dress-up thing.'

Colleen didn't look entirely pleased. 'Well, you be careful, Allie. You might not know anyone else there.'

'I will, Mum, don't worry.'

Allie took her time dawdling back from the shop that afternoon, enjoying the balmy weather. She fancied Sonny so much it almost hurt, and whenever she thought about him, which was frequently, her stomach flipped and she got fluttery feelings in the most embarrassing places. He had such beautiful eyes, and lovely muscled arms and a deliciously firm belly, which she'd felt through his shirt the other night. When he'd kissed her she'd wanted it to last for ever, and now she was starting to think that she wanted it to go further. The idea of it made her feel nervous and horribly excited — nothing like the way she'd felt, or not felt, about Derek.

Poor old Derek hadn't been bad-looking, and they'd kissed plenty of times, which had been nice, she supposed, but things had never advanced beyond that. It was just that . . . well, he just hadn't set her on fire. She used to catch herself looking at him sometimes, trying to imagine what he'd be like in twenty years' time, and in her mind's eye he always came out exactly the same: sitting on a couch reading the paper or talking about the All Blacks with her father. Except he might be a bit fatter. Yes, he would definitely be fatter. In fact, he would probably be a lot like her dad, and, though she loved her father very much, she certainly didn't want to marry him. Mind you, her father had a wonderful sense of humour, which made up for a lot. Derek, unfortunately, hadn't. She'd once told him a very long, absolutely hilarious joke, making her father laugh himself sick and almost wetting her own pants in the process, and all Derek had said at the end was, were there any more date scones? She supposed that had been a warning sign, really.

She sat down on a wall and lit a cigarette.

Sonny was nothing like Derek, though, and he certainly had a sense of humour, though it was a little drier than what she was used to. And even if he hadn't had a witty bone in his body, she didn't think she would care because he was just so bloody *sexy*. Irene's word really did describe him perfectly. The question was: what was she going to do about it? She was a virgin, but it wasn't that she was deliberately saving herself for marriage or anything like that: she just hadn't met anyone who'd tempted her enough. But now she had. And if she did sleep with Sonny, presuming that he wanted to sleep with her — which she thought was a fairly safe bet — would he still want to be with her afterwards? Or would he think she was easy and cheap? It wasn't fair. Boys could go around sleeping with as many girls as they could talk into dropping their knickers and no one blinked an eye, but if a girl did it — or even just behaved as though she would *like* to do it, as Irene did — people were very disapproving and sometimes even quite nasty.

She decided she should probably talk to her mother about it.

Colleen was peeling potatoes at the kitchen sink, Donna and Pauline had disappeared somewhere and Sid was still at the pub.

'Shall I do some carrots?' Allie asked.

Colleen nodded. 'There's some in the cupboard.'

Allie started peeling, flicking the damp shreds of orange skin off her knife into the sink. 'Are these out of Dad's garden?'

'No, you know he's not very good with carrots.'

Sid wasn't really very good with anything in his garden, if they were honest, but he prided himself on having one, so no one ever said anything rude when misshapen and undersized vegetables appeared on their plates, not even Donna and Pauline.

Allie scraped steadily away for a few minutes, wondering how to phrase what she wanted to ask.

'Mum?'

'Mmm?'

'I think I need some advice.'

Colleen stopped what she was doing and went very still. 'What about, love?' she said. There was a slight wobble in her voice.

'It's, well, it's to do with Sonny.'

Colleen put her potato and her knife down and leaned her hands on the bench, as though bracing herself for bad news. 'Go on.'

'Well, I really like him, Mum. And I think . . .' Allie paused, then rushed on. 'I think I'd quite like to sleep with him.'

There, she'd said it.

Exhaling loudly, Colleen exclaimed, 'God almighty, Allison, I thought you were going to tell me you'd already done it and now you're pregnant!'

Allie stared at her mother. 'Mum! I only went out with him for the first time on Wednesday night!'

Colleen shoved a strand of hair off her forehead with the back of her hand, leaving a sliver of potato peel stuck to her temple. She glanced at Allie and started to giggle.

'What?' Allie asked, picking the peel off and flicking it into the sink.

'I suppose that would be a bit of a record, wouldn't it?'

Colleen said. 'Though it has happened, believe me.'

'Well, not to me, it hasn't,' Allie replied.

'And thank Christ for that.' Colleen reached for her knife again. 'What is it you want to know?'

'Well, just what you think, really. Should I or shouldn't I?'

Colleen finished peeling her potato and dropped it into the pot. Then she said, 'I don't think you should.'

'Oh.' Allie wasn't really surprised.

'For two reasons,' Colleen said. She rinsed the vegetable knife under the tap and wiped the blade on the bench cloth. 'The first is I don't want you getting into trouble. It can happen like that, you know. I had a girlfriend when I was about your age who only did it the once and got caught. It could ruin your life, Allie.'

Allie felt an irrational pang of hurt. 'Like yours was, you mean?'

Colleen winced inwardly. 'Oh, of course not, love. I wouldn't trade you or your little madam sisters for anything, I really wouldn't. But your father and I would probably have our own home by now, if we'd had the time to work and save up. And we'd have had you anyway, love, just not quite so soon.'

'Would you still have married Dad?'

Colleen smiled. 'Not if your nan had had anything to say about it.' She thought for a moment. 'I really don't know. But I did, and I'm glad I did. I wouldn't trade him, either, despite what it might look like sometimes. But it's a huge risk, Allie, and I don't think it's one you should take.'

'Even if I — if we — used something?'

'Even then. They don't always work, you know. That's

how we got Pauline. But for God's sake don't tell her that, we'd never hear the end of her being an unwanted child. Which she isn't, of course.'

Colleen ran the cold tap over the potatoes so they wouldn't go brown, and set the pot on the stove. She turned the knob to start the gas, and swore when nothing happened. Digging a shilling out of her purse she handed it to Allie, who went out to the back porch and dropped it into the meter.

Taking a plate of stewing steak out of the fridge, Colleen laid the pieces one by one on the chopping board. 'Have you really thought about this, love? About what you would do if you did get caught?'

'Not really,' Allie said truthfully.

'Well, you'd have to marry him.'

'Would I?'

Colleen cut into a piece of meat, trimming off the fat and putting it to one side. It wasn't particularly good meat, but it was all she could afford when she'd gone to the butcher's yesterday, and it would taste all right stewed with the carrots, a bit of celery and plenty of salt and pepper.

'What else could you do?' she said. 'Go away to Wellington and everyone knowing what's happened but pretending that they don't, and then come back six months later with a flat belly but no baby and a broken heart? Do you really want that, Allie? Do you?'

Allie was startled at the vehemence in her mother's voice.

'Because that's what would have to happen, you know,' Colleen went on. 'You couldn't keep it. I wouldn't mind it if we had another little one in the house, but it would be a bloody great millstone around your neck until the day you die. People don't forget that sort of thing, Allie. And they don't forgive.'

'Wouldn't it be my business, though, not anyone else's?'

'You try telling that to your Mr Max at Dunbar & Jones, missy. And anywhere else you might go looking for a job. I'm telling you, it's not the sort of thing people turn a blind eye to.'

Allie was quiet for a moment. 'And what if Sonny and I did get married?' Then she laughed. 'This is silly, Mum. I haven't even done it yet and we're talking about weddings!'

Colleen banged the knife onto the chopping board, making Allie jump. 'No, we're *not* talking about weddings, Allie, we're talking about the rest of your life. Look, he's a local Maori boy, isn't he? Didn't you say he lives up on Kitemoana Street?'

Allie nodded.

'Well, I've no doubt he's a nice lad, otherwise you wouldn't be so keen on him, but what do you think your life would be like if you married him? A Maori boy?'

'Well, like yours and Dad's, I suppose.'

'Oh, don't be so bloody stupid, Allie! It would be *much* harder than this! You know that!'

'No I don't.'

Colleen took a deep breath, calming herself. 'Allie, love, he'll never get a decent job no matter how clever he is; he'll never make a lot of money and he'll always be treated as a second-class citizen. And people will treat you the same way, for marrying him.'

'But why?' Allie was amazed, and quite shocked, to hear

her mother talking like this. What about what she'd said the other night, when her father had made rude remarks about Maori people, even if he had only been joking? Her mother had been genuinely cross about that. Or was it different when it came to the notion of her daughter actually spending her life with a Maori boy, rather than just going out with one a few times?

'Because that's the way it is,' Colleen said. 'Whether you like it or not, whether *I* like it or not, and whether that poor boy likes it or not. People will look down on you, and your poor bloody kids will be stuck in the middle of it with the worst of both worlds.'

'But that's not fair!'

'Life's not fair, Allie.' Colleen finished trimming the meat and dropped the fat on top of the scraps in the sink. 'I'm sorry, love, but that really is the way it is. And I don't want that sort of life for you.'

Allie was sorry now she'd ever brought the subject up. But it didn't change anything: she still wanted Sonny so badly she ached.

She had planned to spend ages getting ready, but in the end she felt too upset about what her mother had said. She brushed her hair until it shone then pulled it back in a ponytail like the girl in the milkbar, patted some powder onto her nose, which had gone pink from being in the sun all day, and put on some lipstick. She dressed in a white short-sleeved shirt, snug-fitting rolled-up denim jeans and flats, and tied a light jumper around her waist. Sonny had said to wear longs, so she hoped being this casual would be all right.

At twenty to six she said goodbye to her parents — but quickly, so that her mother couldn't say anything else that might dampen her spirits — walked down to the end of Coates Avenue to where it met Kepa Road, and sat down in a bus shelter to wait. To her right, Orakei Basin glittered in the low, late afternoon sun, and she could smell a hint of mud and mangroves on the light breeze.

At five past six she looked at her watch, then again at ten past, then again at a quarter past. What if he'd forgotten? Or, far worse than that, what if he'd changed his mind? A very unpleasant worm of anxiety began to uncurl in the pit of her stomach. Why had he asked her to wait here for him? If he was going to pick her up, what was wrong with coming to her house?

She chewed nervously on the edge of a fingernail, then sat on her hands so she couldn't. A car went past with two young men in it; they waved out and tooted the horn, but she didn't respond.

At twenty past, just as she'd decided to give it another ten minutes at the most and then she was going back home and Sonny Manaia could stick his good looks and his charm up his backside, a motorbike roared up the street. It slowed as it approached, and she saw with enormous relief that it was him.

He coasted to a halt in front of the bus-stop. 'Hey, sweetheart, want a ride?' he said, grinning from ear to ear. 'Beaut, eh?'

Very long and low and currently emitting a loud, rumbling purr, the motorbike was all sparkling red paint and gleaming chrome, with a fringed, black leather seat, three headlamps, mirrors on the handlebars and white rims on the black tyres. Sonny, sitting proudly astride the machine, wore jeans, a dark shirt open at the neck and a pair of heavy leather boots.

'What sort is it?' Allie asked.

'This,' he said with an expansive, downward sweep of his arm, 'is the finest motorcycle ever made: a 1953 Indian Chief with an 80-cubic-inch motor that'll leave everyone else in this town in the dust. Hop on.'

Allie hesitated. 'I've never been on a motorbike before.' Unlike my little sister, she thought sourly.

'Nothing to it. Just climb on and hold tight!'

Allie secured her bag over her shoulder, stepped up and swung her right leg over the seat.

'Move up, so you're close behind me,' Sonny said. 'Have you got your feet on the pegs?' He twisted around to make sure. 'You can either hold on to the bar behind the seat, or put your arms around me.'

He turned back and she wrapped her arms tightly around his waist and pressed the insides of her thighs against his flanks. This close to him she could smell his hair and his skin, and feel his heart beating against her.

'All right?' he asked over his shoulder. 'Hang on then,' he said, and nudged the bike into gear.

It rolled forward, lulling Allie into a false sense of security. She relaxed fractionally and Sonny opened the throttle, sending her lurching backwards and clutching wildly at his shirt.

'Hang on!' he yelled, laughing.

Allie hunched behind him, terrified, as he shot off up Kepa Road. Her ponytail whipped out behind her and her jumper flapped like a sail as she hung on as tightly as she could. At the intersection of Kepa Road and Kupe Street he turned left, leaning the bike over so far that Allie panicked and, digging her fingers into Sonny's chest, leaned the opposite way, causing the back of the bike to wobble alarmingly.

Sonny slowed, pulled over to the side of the street and stopped. He turned around.

'You've got to lean into the corners, the same way as me, or we'll fall off.'

Her heart pounding, Allie looked at him doubtfully.

'Trust me,' Sonny said. 'You'll be OK, I promise.'

He took off again, slowly at first to make sure she was settled on the pillion seat properly, then faster as he felt her relax against his back.

Soon, as she started to get the hang of it, Allie began to smile. Then, as Sonny went even faster, swooping into corners and accelerating smoothly out of them, she found herself laughing out loud. Her eyes were watering, an early evening bug collided painfully with her cheek, and if she didn't pay attention to when Sonny changed gear her nose banged against the back of his head, but she felt indescribably free and alive. It was so much better than being in a bus or a tram. She could taste the sea in the air and smell the summer gardens as they roared past and the faintly acrid stink of warm tar off the road and, best of all, she could feel the wind.

'Good, eh?' Sonny yelled over his shoulder.

'Fantastic!' Allie called back.

'Shall we go for a burn along the waterfront?'

Allie nodded.

Sonny headed down towards Ngapipi Road and followed it around Orakei Basin. Ahead and to her left, Allie could see the stark concrete line of the sewer pipe stretching across the shallows of Hobson Bay before it marched onto land again. They turned right onto Tamaki Drive, roared around Hobson and Pokanoa Points and along into Okahu Bay where the sewer pipe cut directly across the shallows.

Sonny followed the shoreline around Okahu Bay, then turned off Tamaki Drive onto Kitemoana Street. The road took them uphill to a cluster of several dozen new state houses in a cul-de-sac, squatting on raw, unlandscaped sections with barely a tree in sight, though grass was starting to grow on some of the lawns and bright, white footpaths had been laid on both sides of the road. In the middle of the road, kicking a battered football around, was a group of little kids, who didn't bother to get out of the way to let Sonny through. He rode around them, then slowed outside a house near the end of the cul-de-sac. The street here was lined with an assortment of cars and trucks, the windows and front door of the house were wide open and Allie could hear music and raised voices.

Sonny rode over the footpath onto the patchy grass of the front lawn and turned off the motor. 'Hop off,' he said.

Allie obeyed. 'Where are we?'

'My mum's place,' Sonny answered, dismounting himself. He looked at her. 'This is where the party is.'

'Oh. Right,' Allie said, very relieved that she hadn't got all dolled up, then feeling sharply ashamed for it.

Sonny laughed. 'It's not what you're used to, I know.'

'No,' Allie began, 'it's just that . . .'

'You don't go to many parties full of noisy, pissed Maoris,' he finished for her.

'No, it's not that!' Allie protested.

'Yes it is. It's written all over your face. And you're going red,' he added.

174

Allie's felt her cheeks burn even more, and a spark of anger flared. 'That's mean, Sonny. You could have told me.'

'I would have, if you'd asked, but you didn't. And I told you it wasn't flash.' He gave her a quick kiss and took her hand. 'Come on, no one'll bite.'

Irene hurled a plate against the wall where it smashed, showering the floor with shards of china. She hated the plate anyway — Martin's mother had given it to them as a Christmas present the year before and it had a hand-painted picture of a particularly gormless-looking cocker spaniel puppy on it.

Martin finally folded his paper and set it aside. There were shadows of fatigue beneath his intelligent blue eyes, a dent between them where his glasses rested and his black hair stuck up from his habit of absentmindedly running his hand through it. 'Obviously you're not very happy, Irene.'

'No I am *not* happy, Martin!' Irene shouted. 'I'm bored absolutely bloody rigid and I'm sick to death of sitting in this dreary bloody little flat night after night while everyone else is going out and having fun! It's Saturday night, Martin. Why the hell can't *we* ever go out?'

Martin pinched the bridge of his nose and squeezed his eyes shut. This had been going on for nearly an hour now — Irene winding herself up into a state until she finally got his attention. He was always — *always* — aware of what mood she was in, and more often than not the reason behind it as well, but it just wasn't in his nature to be as passionate as she was. He much preferred to discuss matters rationally, without the yelling and the histrionics, but he knew that

Irene was incapable of that: it was one of the reasons he loved her so much.

He opened his eyes and looked at her. She was gorgeous with her dark hair all over the place and her eyes flashing and her hands on her wonderful, curvy hips.

'But darling, you went out last night,' he said, and immediately regretted it.

'Yes, by *myself!*' Irene shot back. 'Because you were too bloody *tired*, as usual!'

'I'm sorry, I really am. But we're so busy. It's just that time of the year, I'm afraid.'

'You're always too bloody busy,' Irene said, adding maliciously, 'Sometimes I think you just don't want to take me out. Are you ashamed of me, is that it?' She knew it wasn't true, but she knew it would upset him.

'Oh God, no, of course I'm not ashamed of you, Irene. Why on earth would I be?'

'Because I'm not posh and well-spoken and *educated* like the other wives.'

'What other wives?'

'Oh, don't be so bloody thick, Martin! You know who I'm talking about — those stuck-up bloody women married to the blokes in your office!'

Martin sighed, though he did it very surreptitiously so Irene wouldn't pounce on him. The other wives weren't particularly friendly, but, he suspected, it was because they were jealous — of Irene's beauty, her marvellous figure, her flair and the way their husbands looked at her when they thought they weren't being observed. None of the men had ever said anything to Martin, except that he was a very lucky man, but he knew they envied him. He was so proud of her on the rare occasions when he actually did have the energy to go out, even though she could be a little, well, over the top sometimes. He wished he wasn't so tired all the time, but he was worried that if he didn't work hard, he would never be offered a partnership, and then there wouldn't be the money to buy Irene all those things he knew she wanted so much.

His mother always said, privately, of course, that Irene would hold him back, that he would never advance at Hart, Bullock and Associates with her as his wife, but Martin knew she was wrong. Irene was a very kind girl at heart, and generous and extremely bright, and if she did sometimes come across as selfish and demanding, well, he couldn't entirely blame her, having to live in a poky little bachelor flat like this, married to a man she thought was dull and having to go to work every day in someone else's office typing all sorts of boring letters and accounts. Irene was the sort of woman who needed to be pampered and adored, and until he earned enough he just couldn't give her that. But he would one day, in the not too distant future, and then his lovely, tempestuous wife would be happy. And when Irene was happy, everything was very good indeed.

But not tonight, not with bits of his mother's ugly dog plate all over the floor and Irene standing there looking around for something else to hurl. He hoped she wouldn't choose the Royal Crown Derby cup and saucer — that was his and it had cost quite a lot. But at least she *was* angry. He dreaded the day she stopped railing at him about not going out, because that would be the day she'd decided she didn't care any more, and not long after that, he was certain, she would pack her suitcases and leave him. And if that happened, he didn't know what he'd do.

'Is that really what's upsetting you?' he asked cautiously. 'Not being posh and stuck-up?'

Irene flopped down on the sofa, and Martin knew his cup and saucer were safe.

'No,' she replied grudgingly. 'I'm *bored*, Martin. I want us to go dancing together. I feel a fool going out by myself all the time. People will think my husband isn't interested in me.'

Martin raised an eyebrow. 'Since when have you ever been bothered by what people think?'

Irene scowled. 'Oh, shut up.'

She looked so genuinely miserable sitting there that Martin realized he would do just about anything to cheer her up. He wondered if sex would make her happy. It usually did. He also thought about the fat pile of documents in his briefcase that he'd been asked to have checked and corrected by first thing on Monday morning, and said, 'I'll come to your staff picnic tomorrow if you like.'

'Oh. Well,' Irene said. 'Good.'

Martin could tell by her lack of enthusiasm that she wasn't entirely pleased. His heart sank: she must be having one of her 'flirtations' with someone at Dunbar & Jones. He knew about these, though she wasn't aware that he knew, and had decided some time ago to tolerate them if they kept her amused. And, more importantly, still married to him. They hurt him a lot but, as far as he'd been able to ascertain, they'd never amounted to much — just harmless little games that boosted her ego and stopped her from becoming too bored. He was terrified, however, that if he made a fuss she would actually run off with someone, and God knew there were plenty of men out there who would be happy to oblige.

'And maybe later in the week we *could* go dancing,' he suggested, though he knew he'd be hellishly busy every evening until Christmas.

Irene got off the sofa and came and sat on his knee.

'That would be nice, baby,' she said, resting her head on his shoulder and rubbing her hand slowly over his chest.

Martin tightened his arms around her and closed his eyes, thanking God for giving him such a gorgeous wife, but wishing He'd made her just a little less manipulative.

Chapter Nine

'Come and meet my mother first,' Sonny said, leading Allie by the hand down the path at the side of the house.

There was an enormous green and brown tent pitched on the back lawn, its sides rolled up to reveal a crowd of people sitting on an assortment of chairs, benches and boxes, singing, shouting and generally making lots of noise. But Sonny turned her up the concrete steps to the back door and urged her inside.

They stepped into a kitchen not dissimilar to the one in Allie's house, though this one was obviously somewhat newer. There were banks of bright, lemon-painted cupboards, a stove and a good-sized bench, though Allie wondered where the fridge was. The kitchen table, covered with oilcloth, was piled high with food — bowls of cockles, mussels, pipis and something bright orange and sloppy that Allie hadn't seen before, baskets of sliced, buttered bread, four or five trifles, and heaped plates of lamingtons. Around the table sat five children between the ages of about four and seven, dipping saveloys into a plate of tomato sauce and smearing their faces with it. They stared at Allie with enormous brown eyes.

'Hello, Aunty Maria,' Sonny said to an older woman standing at the stove frying something that smelled delicious.

'Kia ora, Sonny, love,' the woman said, offering her brown, wrinkled cheek for a kiss.

'This is my girlfriend, Allie.'

'Hello, Allie, dear,' Aunty Maria said, kissing Allie on both cheeks and giving her a hell of a fright because she wasn't used to that sort of familiarity from people she didn't know.

'Where's Mum?' Sonny asked.

'In the sitting room having a rest.'

'Is she asleep?'

Aunty Maria shook her head. 'Having a cuppa.'

His mother did seem to be asleep. She sat on an old sofa with her feet, clad in a pair of men's tartan slippers, up on a footstool. Her cup of tea was balanced on the arm of the sofa, still full.

Allie thought she was possibly the most striking-looking woman she had ever seen. Her long hair was still dark, with a hint of steel grey at her wide temples, and worn in a long plait that hung over her shoulder, and her brown face showed only a few wrinkles, radiating out from her closed eyes and running from her nose down to the corners of her mouth. Her lips were full and proud, and she wore no make-up at all. In her pierced ears were small gold hoops and she was dressed in a blue and grey-patterned dress, a black cardigan and a flowered apron. She was solid but shapely and her legs were bare.

'Mum?' Sonny whispered.

One large brown eye opened, then both. 'Hello, son.'

'Sorry, were you asleep?'

'Just dozing.'

'Mum, this is Allie. Allie, this is my mum, Te Awhina — Awhi — Manaia.'

'Hello, Mrs Manaia,' Allie said.

Awhi Manaia hoisted herself up on the sofa and set her feet on the floor. 'Kia ora, dear. We've been hearing all about you.'

Sonny touched the side of her cup. 'Your tea's gone cold. I'll get you a fresh one, eh?'

He took the cup and saucer away, leaving Allie standing in the middle of the room feeling silly.

'Sit down, dear.'

Allie sat in an armchair so old that the pattern had worn almost completely off the arms. There was a large mat made of woven flax or some similar fibre on the wooden floor but no curtains at the windows, and dozens of framed photographs on the walls, mostly of old Maori men scowling at the camera and serious but beautiful women, their hair long and thick and cascading over their shoulders. Some of the women had tattooed faces, and several wore feathered cloaks over European dresses. On the mantelpiece above the tiled fireplace was propped a framed photograph of a handsome but ferocious-looking man in a military uniform. A velvet ribbon had been tied across the top of the photo — pinned to this were seven gleaming military medals. Flanking the photo was a pair of beautiful little Asian dolls with porcelain faces wearing traditional costumes. Kimonos? Apart from the photographs and the dolls, the room was relatively bare, but it was spotlessly clean. There was a baby asleep in a carry-cot on the floor; Allie couldn't see its face but she could hear its tiny snores.

Awhi noticed Allie looking at the photo on the mantelpiece. 'That was my husband, Sonny's father, Pera. He passed last year.'

Allie could see Sonny in his father's face, except that Sonny's features weren't — usually — anywhere near as grim.

Awhi laboriously pushed herself off the couch and bent over the carry-cot, moving the fluffy pink blanket away from the baby's face. 'This is Polly's baby, my mokopuna.' She straightened up. 'You know my daughter Polly, eh? She said you were at the department store where Sonny works.'

Allie nodded. 'Did your husband serve in the war?' she asked, mainly because she couldn't think of anything else to say.

'Ae, Maori Battalion,' Awhi said, sitting down again. 'Greece, Crete, Italy, North Africa, he was at all of those places.'

'Did he bring those dolls home from Japan?'

'Eh? No, he didn't go to Japan. Sonny sent me those.'

Allie stared at Awhi. 'Sonny was in Japan?'

'Ae. On leave, from Kayforce in South Korea.' Awhi gave Allie an odd look. 'He only came home in August.'

A silence descended between them. Allie, stunned, wondered why Sonny had never said anything about being a soldier. She could hear the kettle whistling in the kitchen, and Sonny saying something to Aunty Maria and laughing. She wished he would hurry up and come back. She looked at the photographs again, then at the floor, then finally risked a glance at Mrs Manaia, who was staring back at her.

'My Sonny is a good boy,' she said.

Allie wasn't sure what to say to that, so she just nodded politely.

'Not like some of my other kids,' Awhi went on. 'Bloody no-hopers, some of them.'

Allie couldn't even nod to that.

'I don't want him getting in any trouble.'

Now Allie didn't know what she meant. 'Sorry?' she said.

'I don't want him having any little ones like this one here,' Awhi said, nodding at the baby in the carry-cot. 'Not yet. And I don't want him to have to marry a Pakeha girl because he's made a mistake.'

God, and Allie had thought *her* mother was blunt! She felt colour flood into her face.

Watching her, Awhi said shrewdly, 'I know you're thinking, what is this rude old Maori woman saying about me? What a cheek! But I can see you're a very pretty girl, and I know Sonny thinks a lot of you, and all I'm saying is you both need to watch out. You might think it would all be happy families to be together, but it won't.' She gave a wry little smile. 'Your mother has said the same thing, I expect. She would be a stupid woman and a bad mother if she hasn't.'

Allie had no idea how to respond, but fortunately just then a little boy stuck his head around the door. 'Nanny, Aunty says what do we put the fried breads in? We've run out of bowls.'

'There's a basin in the washhouse,' Awhi said. 'But clean it first. *Properly!*' she called after him as he retreated. She turned back to Allie. 'I'm sorry, dear, I can see you're a nice girl, but I don't want my Sonny to make a mistake. If you want to love him, that's all right. Just don't hopukia him, eh? That's all.'

Allie had no idea what hopukia meant, but Sonny,

standing in the doorway holding a steaming cup of tea and frowning, obviously did. She looked at him for explanation.

He said, 'It means capture. Mum, you said you wouldn't say anything!'

Awhi shrugged. 'I'm getting old, I forget.'

'Bullshit,' Sonny said.

'Just looking out for you, son.' Awhi held out her hand for the cup. 'I was just saying you want to be careful, that's all. I don't want any more mokopuna just yet.'

Even Sonny went red then. He changed the subject. 'Aunty Maria says the food's nearly ready and what time is the hangi coming up?'

'Now,' Awhi said. 'Go and help your brothers with it.'

'Come and meet everyone,' Sonny said, holding out his hand for Allie to take.

As they left the room, Allie glanced back at Mrs Manaia. She winked, and Allie very clearly saw Sonny in her face as well.

'You said no one would bite,' she complained as they walked down the back steps.

'Sorry. Mum can be like that sometimes. Since the old man died she's sort of taken over running the family. She's only doing what she thinks is best.' Sonny smiled. 'Actually, my father never ran the family, he only thought he did. Bad-tempered old bastard that he was.'

At least fifty brown faces looked up expectantly as Allie followed Sonny into the tent. And that was only the adults. There seemed to be children everywhere, perched on knees, playing on the ground, sitting on the roof of the shed at the end of the lawn, playing cricket with a ratty old bat and three sticks for stumps.

Allie recognized only two faces — Hori the driver from Dunbar & Jones, who waved, and Polly, a bottle of beer in one hand and a cigarette in the other, who nodded then went back to talking to the man beside her. Allie felt completely out of her depth.

Sonny sensed her discomfort. 'Do you want to see the hangi coming up?'

Taking a firm, proprietorial grip on her hand, he led her around the back of the tent to where a group of men were leaning on shovels, gazing at a mound of gently steaming dirt.

'This is my brother Harry,' he said, nodding at a slightly older and bigger version of himself.

Harry nodded back, a cigarette dangling out of his mouth.

'And this is Oscar. It's his twenty-first.'

Oscar nodded as well.

Sonny didn't introduce the other men, though they all looked at Allie with undisguised interest. One of them scraped some dirt off the mound and revealed the corner of a sack, which he then lifted, letting out a small billow of steam.

'She's ready,' he said.

The others started shovelling the dirt off the mound, then dragged away the sacks, exposing a layer of steaming white cloths. These were also removed, revealing a series of tightly packed wire baskets set into a hole. When the heavy baskets were lifted out, wafting a delicious smell of pork and chicken after them, Allie saw that they had been sitting on top of a bed of hot stones.

'Do you do all your cooking like this?' she whispered to Sonny.

'Hell no, we'd starve to death!' he replied. 'It takes seven or eight hours to do a decent hangi.'

Wrapping cloths around their hands, the men carried the hot baskets into the tent and set them on a long trestle table. Several women, including Aunty Maria, started to unpack the baskets and arrange the food on paper plates. As well as chicken and pork, there were also mutton and potatoes, pumpkin and kumara, and something Allie didn't recognize.

'What's that?' she asked, pointing at the long, glistening segments of what might or might not be meat.

'Eel,' Sonny said, picking a bit off a plate.

Aunty Maria slapped his hand.

The children had congregated around the table, their eyes huge as they contemplated the feast.

'Go away!' Aunty Maria said, flapping a tea-towel at them as though they were particularly large flies. 'Go inside and help Nanny bring out the other food. And no pinching it on the way!'

The kids scampered off, jostling and shoving each other to be first through the back door.

When the food had all been brought out, including large bowls of cream and jugs of custard for the steamed puddings that Aunty Maria, to Allie's fascination, had decanted from half a dozen large fruit tins, a dapper old man in a cream panama hat hoisted himself to his feet and everyone fell silent as he began to intone something in Maori. Glancing around, Allie saw that everyone had their heads down and their eyes closed, and rather self-consciously followed suit.

When the old man had finished, the women began to pile the rest of the food onto plates and hand them to the more elderly people, who remained seated. Then the children were allowed to help themselves, then the younger adults. Allie, not sure of how you did things at a Maori function, hung back and was grateful when Sonny brought her a plate containing chicken and pork, a sliver of the eel, potato and kumara, and a piece of Aunty Maria's fried bread. She tried that first — it was still warm, soft in the middle and crispy around the edges, very greasy and utterly delicious. A couple of these a day, Allie thought, and I'd soon be letting out the seams on all my skirts.

The noise in the tent didn't decrease even though everyone was busy eating, but Allie still felt awkward. Hers was the only white face there, and she was sure that everyone was staring at her because of it. She knew they were probably only curious, but she still felt as though that was the reason. At one point, Sonny, working his way through the mound of food on his plate, caught her eye and mouthed 'All right?' And suddenly she was.

When a large dent had been made in the food, and people were sitting back and opening fresh bottles of beer and the women had covered what was left on the table with pieces of muslin, Sonny began to introduce Allie to more people, whose names, she knew, she would never remember.

'This is my mate, Whare,' Sonny said, pulling up a chair for Allie on the edge of a group sitting just outside the tent.

Whare was somewhere in his twenties with a clean-shaven face, and hair parted on the side and slicked down with at least a pot of Brylcreem. He smiled at Allie then went back to tuning the guitar resting on his knee.

'And this here's Reuben, another mate.'

Bleary-eyed, Reuben waggled his fingers cheerfully at Allie, then startled her by prising the top off a bottle of DB with his teeth.

'Skite,' Sonny said, amused.

Reuben grinned. He started to say something, muddled his words, had another unsuccessful attempt, then gave up and took a swig from his bottle.

'Party started at lunchtime,' Sonny explained.

Allie nodded in sudden understanding. A lot of people seemed to be rather drunk, but if they'd been at it since midday, especially with the sun blazing away all afternoon, that explained a lot.

Sonny's brother Harry came over and sat down next to Reuben. He reeked of alcohol — Allie could smell it from six feet away. While she watched, he opened another bottle.

'You work with Sonny, eh?' Whare said, plucking a guitar string and cocking his head to hear the note better over the chatter and laughter.

'I work at Dunbar & Jones, yes,' she replied, absurdly grateful that one of Sonny's friends was actually talking to her. For some reason, she'd been harbouring a fear that none of them would, that they might perhaps disapprove of her. Like his mother had, though Mrs Manaia hadn't actually *disapproved*, as such — it was more that she'd just spoken her mind.

'She sells frocks,' Polly said, pushing her way into the group and sitting on Reuben's knee. 'Fancy ones.' She took a drink from her bottle, realized it was empty, and threw it across the lawn.

'Pick that up, Polly,' Sonny said. 'It'll get smashed and someone will stand on it.'

'You pick it up.' Polly helped herself to Reuben's beer.

'Oi, that's mine!' he complained.

'Tough. S'mine now,' Polly shot back.

She had on skin-tight red capri pants, a sleeveless black top and flat black mules with very pointy toes. She wore no make-up on her stunning face, and her black hair was pulled back in an untidy ponytail. Allie thought she looked incredibly sophisticated, though she'd obviously had quite a skinful.

'Do you want a beer?' Sonny asked Allie.

She'd said no earlier, but she felt like one now.

'I'll see if I can find a glass,' Sonny said, and disappeared towards the house.

Harry squinted at Allie thoughtfully. 'Stand up for a minute?' he said.

'Sorry?'

'Stand up for a minute.'

Mystified, Allie did as she was asked.

'Now turn around.'

Worried now that she might have sat in something, Allie turned her back to Harry.

'No,' he said after a moment, 'nothing there. You can sit back down now.'

Allie glanced at Reuben, Polly and Whare, who were grinning widely, and sat down again, feeling embarrassed.

'I'm sorry, I don't understand,' she said.

Harry said, 'Well, Sonny thinks the sun shines out of your arse, but I can't see anything.'

The others laughed their heads off.

Sonny came back carrying two bottles of beer and a cup. 'What's so funny? I couldn't find a glass so you'll have to have this.' He filled it with beer and handed it to Allie,

190

whose face was flaming. 'What's the matter?'

'Nothing.'

Sonny immediately glared at Harry. 'Lay off, eh?'

Harry lifted his hands in a parody of innocence. Sonny sat down, his hand resting protectively on Allie's shoulder.

Weaving through the crowd, Sonny's mother made her way towards them, carrying the baby and a bottle with a plastic teat on it. 'Polly?' she said, holding out the bottle.

Busy with Reuben, Polly didn't look up.

'Polly!' Awhi said again, more tersely.

Polly stopped whispering in Reuben's ear. 'What?'

'Bubba needs a feed.'

'Well, feed her then.'

'No, girl, you feed her, she's your baby!' Awhi snapped.

Polly reluctantly took her daughter, settling her in her arms and plugging the teat into her mouth. The baby's arms reached up, her fingers open like little starfish, then her tiny hands closed over the bottle.

Awhi glared for a moment, then marched off, her slippers flapping.

The baby suckled, making happy slurping noises, while Polly impatiently swung her elegantly crossed leg. Someone called out to her across the tent and she waved.

'That'll do,' she said, whipping the bottle away from the baby. The teat slipped out with an audible pop, leaving her daughter with a bewildered expression on her little face and her arms waving.

'Jesus, Polly, she's hardly had any!' Sonny said.

'Well, you bloody do it, then!' Polly thrust the baby and the bottle at him and ducked off.

Sonny stared down at the infant in his arms. 'Do you want to hold her?'

Allie, entranced by the baby's big dark eyes, lovely caramel-coloured skin and tuft of black hair sticking straight up, cradled her, then gave her the bottle again.

'What's her name?' she asked.

'Gina.'

'And she's about ten months?'

'Nine,' Sonny said.

'Doesn't Polly want her?' Allie said, then snapped her mouth shut, mortified that she'd said it out loud.

Harry snorted. 'Polly doesn't want anything that might wreck her fun.'

Allie was horrified that anyone could have produced something as lovely as this little thing and not be devoted to it. 'But she's so beautiful,' she said, staring down at the small face gazing serenely back at her, lips firmly clamped around the bottle's teat.

'She is, eh?' Sonny said quietly.

'Won't her husband help?' Allie asked.

Harry laughed this time, but it wasn't a nice sound. 'What husband? She won't even tell us who the bloody father is.'

Allie didn't know what to say, so she kept her gaze on Gina, whose eyes were starting to close. When the baby's hands slipped off the bottle, she said, 'I think she's going to sleep.'

Sonny looked around for Polly, but she'd disappeared. 'I'll take her,' he offered.

Allie carefully passed the baby to him, and watched as he settled her little body low against his chest and rocked her. 'You're good with babies.'

'Plenty of practice,' Sonny replied. 'I was ten when our youngest brother came along. That's Paroa. The old man was overseas when he was born. Poor little bugger didn't even know who Dad was when he came home. Cried and hid from him for about a week.'

'Are all your brothers and sisters here tonight?'

'Well, Gilbert ain't,' Harry said, lighting a cigarette.

'Gilbert's in Mount Eden,' Sonny said matter-of-factly. 'But Wiremu's here, he's the oldest, he's thirty-two. Noah's here, Gilbert comes after him, then Hareta, she's got four kids, then Harry, then me, then Oscar, you met him before. Then Polly, Hine, Ruth and Paroa. Mum had Paroa when she was forty-one. Bit of a surprise, he was.'

'You must have lots of nieces and nephews,' Allie remarked.

Sonny thought about it. 'Seventeen.'

'Is it hard work buying Christmas presents for them all?' Allie recalled the agonizing that went into her shopping every year, making sure she found exactly the right gift for everyone in her family.

'Nah,' Sonny said. 'We just have a big feed at Christmas time, we don't have presents. We used to—'

'But then we got kicked off our land,' Harry interrupted.

There was an uncomfortable silence, except for Whare, who went on quietly strumming his guitar.

'Shut up, Harry,' Sonny warned.

'Why? Just because she's here?' Harry asked, nodding at Allie.

'There's a time and place.' Sonny's voice was sharp now.

'I bet she doesn't even know what I'm talking about,' Harry said disgustedly.

Everyone looked at Allie, who wanted to disappear. 'I think I might have read something in the papers last year,' she mumbled.

'Harry, I said shut the bloody hell *up*.' Sonny glared at his brother for a long, unpleasant moment.

Uncomfortably aware that her presence was the cause of the tension, Allie said quickly to Sonny, 'Can I hold the baby again?'

He passed her over and Allie cradled her in her arms. 'I think she's gone to sleep. Shall I take her inside?'

Sonny's eyes met hers and she saw that he realized she wanted to escape.

'That's a good idea. Polly's room is the one at the end of the hall. Just put her down in her cot, she'll be fine.' Then he touched her hand, and she knew that he understood.

She gathered the baby to her and, carefully stepping over outstretched legs, made her way to the back door. The kitchen was empty, as was the sitting room, and the hallway seemed very dim after the bright sunshine outside. The door to the room at the end was closed. She knocked, but when no one answered she went in.

There was a bunk along one wall, a cot against another, a single bed with its head against the third and a battered chest of drawers beneath the window. The walls were bare except for a painted wooden crucifix, the blood on Jesus's hands and feet a violent crimson. Over the crucifix someone had hung a long necklace of tiny pale yellow shells.

Allie gently laid Gina, now soundly asleep, in her cot, wondering whether the baby should be on her back or her tummy. She couldn't remember how her mother had put Donna and Pauline down when they were small.

'On her back,' Awhi said from the doorway.

Allie started at Mrs Manaia's sudden appearance. She hastily turned the baby over, feeling irrationally guilty, as though she'd been caught stealing Gina rather than just putting her to bed.

Awhi stepped into the room. 'She can't breathe if she's on her puku.'

'Sorry,' Allie apologized, feeling even worse.

'Never mind.' Awhi sat down on the single bed. 'Don't you come from a big family?'

'Not really. I've only got two sisters.'

'Younger or older?'

'Younger.'

Awhi nodded as though this meant something. 'Not like Sonny, eh?'

'No,' Allie replied, vaguely alarmed that Mrs Manaia seemed to be settling in for some sort of talk.

'I heard Harry outside,' Awhi said after a moment. 'Talking about the land.' She picked up the end of her plait and examined it for spilt ends. 'Sonny doesn't like his brother doing that, but Harry's got a big mouth. And his wairua is angry, like his father's was.' She looked up at Allie. 'His soul. He'll go the same way as Gilbert soon — too much booze, in trouble with the law.'

There wasn't much Allie could say.

Awhi went to the cot and pulled the blanket up over Gina's little bare feet. 'Do you know much about the land?' she asked when she'd sat down again.

'Not really,' Allie replied, assuming Mrs Manaia meant the Maori land at Orakei.

'Do you want to know?'

Allie was too scared to say no, and Awhi took her silence as a yes.

'Good,' she said. 'You should hear it, if you plan on getting to know my boy.' She patted the bed. 'Sit down, girl, and I'll tell you.'

Allie sat, her hands clasped nervously in her lap. In her cot, Gina made a series of little snuffling noises.

Awhi swept her arm in a wide arc, the evening sun catching the dull gold of her wedding ring. 'All this used to belong to us, to Ngati Whatua, the sea and the hills around it and all the land under the city. Our roots have always been in this soil. When the Treaty was signed we invited Governor Hobson to make a town here, and we sold thousands of acres for that purpose, but we always wanted to keep Orakei for ourselves. Always. Orakei was never for sale. Our ancestor Te Kawau sought a deed to make Orakei safe, but he never got it. *We* never got it.' She gave a small sigh of frustration. 'Then came the Native Land Court. They gave Orakei to thirteen of us, thirteen Ngati Whatua, and we believed it would be all right because we thought the thirteen would only be trustees.'

Allie nodded, though she didn't know the first thing about the Native Land Court. 'When was that?'

'It was in 1869.' Awhi gave Allie a quick, wry smile. '*Well* before *my* time. But then the Public Works took some of the land for defence, and then the court divided the rest between those thirteen and made them outright owners.'

Even more confused now, Allie asked hesitantly, 'But you *were* the owners, weren't you? Ngati Whatua?'

Awhi shook her head. 'We don't have the same ideas about ownership as Pakeha. No one person ever owns the land. That's not the Ngati Whatua way. It's not the *Maori* way. Well, it didn't used to be.' She spread her slippered feet slightly and set her elbows on her knees, staring down

196

between them at the bedroom's bare wooden floor. 'For us Maori, the land is everything. It feeds us and shelters us, and it tells us who we are. It's where we . . . anchor ourselves, it's where we belong. Losing the land is like losing our mother.' Awhi was silent for a long moment, then she straightened up. 'Anyway, without tribal permission, some of the thirteen leased the land to Pakeha. Some of us without title stayed on in the village, but others left to find homes somewhere else.' She frowned. 'I think now we all should have stayed.'

Gina gave a distressed little squawk. Allie and Awhi both stood, but Allie quickly sat back down, embarrassed. Awhi tucked Gina in more snugly.

'Only a baby dream,' she said as she sat on the bed again. 'The Pakeha lessees asked Parliament for the right to buy our land outright, and the Auckland City Council and some crooked MPs passed a Bill to take the whole Orakei block, except for our papakainga, our village, at Okahu Bay. Apirana Ngata tried to stop it but he couldn't.' Awhi sighed again, and this time it was an exhalation of unadulterated despair. 'And then they laid that sewer pipe across the shore right in front of our village. The sewage poisoned our shellfish beds so we couldn't eat kai moana any more, and we couldn't get out to sea, and the pipe made the village flood. Then the laws all got changed so the land at Okahu Bay could be sold, and that was when some of the people started selling it off outright.'

Allie noted that Awhi had gone from saying 'us' and 'we' to 'some people': they must be the Ngati Whatua who'd let the side down. If all this was true, it was no wonder some of the Maoris were angry and bitter.

Awhi said, 'After that, the government made it so that the

land could only be sold to them. And some of the people did sell it. Some were just greedy, but some sold because they thought the village would be spared, or that we'd get house sites reserved for us.'

'When was this?' Allie asked.

'About 1912, 1913. Then about fifteen years ago all these new houses started going up around Orakei, these state houses, and the council asked the government to help them buy the last of our land and kick us off so they could have it for more new houses. There weren't many of us living in the village by then because there wasn't much left — not even enough land to grow our own food. But we stayed. We had no running water and no electricity, but we stayed.'

Allie calculated that Sonny must have been about eight or nine at the time. What an awful thing for him, for them all, to have to go through. And the younger children would have been very little then. How had Mrs Manaia managed?

'Was that hard?' she asked, remembering what the village had looked like a few years ago — a ramshackle collection of dilapidated cottages and buildings, the earth around them bare and the fences falling down.

'It was very hard,' Awhi said, 'especially with the babies. They got sick all the time. That always made me angry. But then at the start of the war our kinswoman Te Puea Herangi from the Waikato came to help us. She had the ear of the prime minister, Mr Fraser, and the trade unions. And Mr Fraser said there'd be new houses for us above the village but that we could keep our old marae. He said we could have a new meeting house, too. Well, we wanted that, but we still wanted to keep our village too so we never moved. But in 1950 Sid Holland just came and took the land! Just took it!' Awhi shook her head in disbelief. 'He was a bugger, that man. A real bugger.'

Allie was sure her father would agree.

'All we had left then was the urupa, the cemetery. Well, you can't live in a bloody cemetery, can you?'

Allie supposed not.

'There was compensation money paid, but no one would touch it so it went to the Maori trustee. And then they built these houses up here on Kitemoana Street and some people moved in last year. And when they moved, their houses were demolished behind them. But still some of us stayed. And then someone burnt down our old meeting house, Te Puru-o-Tamaki, so we had just about nothing left then.' Awhi smoothed her apron over her knees. 'But everyone *still* wouldn't leave, because, you know, the village is our home — it's where our heart is. And that's when we got burnt out. They came and set fire to our homes and the old ones had to be carried out screaming and crying, and one old koro, my friend's father, ran back in because he wanted to die where he believed he belonged.'

Allie remembered seeing something about that in the paper — it had been in July of the previous year. She risked a look at Mrs Manaia's face, and saw that her full lips were pressed hard together and that her eyes were bright with tears.

'So here we are,' she said after a long moment, 'booted up to Boot Hill, with no marae, no meeting house, no land, no mana, no nothing.'

'But isn't it nice having a new house?' Allie asked, and Mrs Manaia gave her a look of such gentle pity that she knew she'd just said something unutterably stupid.

'They're too small, e hine, and they don't suit us. People

199

are leaving and families are falling apart. Many of our elders have died since they came up here, of broken hearts. Without family, and without the land, we are nothing. And now Te Puea's gone as well. Everything has gone, everything that made us who we were.'

They sat in silence, Allie trying not to but feeling as though she was personally responsible because she was a Pakeha, and wishing she'd brought her bag inside so she could have a cigarette and give her shaking hands something to do.

Chapter Ten

By ten o'clock more people had arrived and the party was in full swing; to be heard Allie had to yell at Sonny over the noise. It was fun, though. Whare had stopped fiddling with his guitar and was now playing it so energetically that Allie was worried his fingers might start to bleed. He had a lovely voice and he'd been joined by three others on guitars.

They played only a few songs that Allie knew. She was able to sing along to 'Silent Night', but only in English when just about everyone else was singing it in Maori, and the chorus to 'Maori Battalion' but not the verses, shouting along with everyone else, 'Maori Battalion march to *victory*, Maori Battalion staunch and true!' She especially enjoyed the final '*Au-e!* Ake, ake, kia kaha e!' 'Blue Smoke' she also knew, and parts of 'Now is the Hour', and she was delighted when Whare started in on 'Ha-ere Mai', which she particularly liked.

Into Sonny's ear she sang, 'Ha-ere mai, everything is ka pai, you're here at last, you're really here at last', then sat back, wondering if she might not have had a bit much to drink.

But he only smiled and kissed the tip of her nose. 'That's what I should be singing to you. Because you are, you're really here at last.'

'At your mum's house on Kitemoana Street?'

'No, with me. It doesn't matter where it is, as long as it's with me.'

Allie snuggled up to him and he stroked her ponytail.

'You're not wearing any of that sticky stuff on your hair,' he said.

Allie giggled. 'Well, no, not after last time.'

'And none of that stuff on your face. I think you're prettier without it.' He gazed at her for a moment. 'Do you want to go for a ride?'

Allie's face lit up. 'On the motorbike?'

'Yeah, come on.'

He took her hand and they went around the front where he carefully removed three small children who were sitting on the seat of his bike one behind the other, noisily going 'Brooom, *brooooom!'*

'You kids be careful of that, it's not a toy,' Sonny said.

''Tis!' the middle one insisted, his shorts at half-mast. None of them had shoes, but they were all wearing enormous grins.

'It's very late,' Allie said. 'Shouldn't you be tucked up in bed by now?'

'No,' the smallest one replied defiantly.

'Well, you should go inside anyway,' Sonny said. 'And don't play on the roads in the dark. You might get run over.'

Three small heads looked up, then down the street: not a moving vehicle was in sight.

'Go on, go inside,' Sonny said again, aiming a very

gentle kick at the closest one. 'Ask Aunty Maria if there's any steamed pudding left.'

The kids looked at each other, their eyes sparkling, then shot off towards the house.

'Little buggers,' Sonny said, but he was grinning.

They rode down to Tamaki Drive, then turned right and followed the shoreline around to Mission Bay. Allie pulled off the elastic band holding back her hair, relishing the feel of the cool evening air on her scalp. It was even more exhilarating being on the bike at night, almost like riding through velvet.

Sonny pulled up at the side of the road, then turned off the motor. Silence rolled over them after the deep, rumbling throb of the engine. A car went past, its tyres swishing on the still warm tarseal. Another was parked a hundred yards away, the two heads silhouetted close together in the front seat suggesting that the occupants were aware of nothing but themselves.

His hands in his pockets, Sonny asked casually, 'Want to go for a walk along the beach?'

Allie looked out across the long expanse of sand, pale silver in the moonlight, and listened for a second to the soft hiss of small waves as they touched the shore.

'OK, that would be nice.'

Holding hands, they walked across the stretch of grass between the road and the beach, then stepped down onto the sand. Sonny unlaced his boots, tugged them off, then pulled off his socks and stuffed them inside.

'What?' he said, as he became aware that Allie was watching him. 'You don't walk down the beach with your shoes on.'

So Allie kicked off her shoes and set them neatly next to

his boots. The sand felt cool and moist between her toes, even though she knew they were far enough above the high-tide line for it not to have been submerged all day. They wandered down to the ocean's edge, and stood for a moment, gazing out to sea.

'What can you see?' Sonny asked.

'Nothing,' Allie said truthfully. It was too dark to discern where the ocean joined the sky, although the surface of the water sparkled under the moon for what looked like miles and miles. 'I can smell it, though. Sort of a cross between chalk and salt.'

'It's not chalk,' Sonny replied. 'That's the smell of rain coming.'

'Oh, I hope not, or the work picnic tomorrow might be cancelled.'

'It'll only be a shower,' Sonny said. He turned and started walking down the beach.

Catching up with him, Allie asked, 'What was it like, when you were kicked off your land last year?'

'I don't know, I was away. But I think it was the last straw for the old man. He was always a hard bastard and he got all those medals in the war and all the rest of it, but he knew we couldn't win when it came to the land and it killed him.'

'What happened to him?'

'Drank himself to death.'

Allie was silent for several minutes. Then she asked, 'How do *you* feel about it? About getting kicked off your land.'

Sonny stopped walking, and sighed. 'Don't take this the wrong way, Allie, but I'm not sure you'd understand. But for us the land's important, more important than anything else. And especially Orakei, our traditional home. It was all ours once, all this around Auckland, and when we lost more and more of it, Okahu Bay was sort of our last stand. And now that's gone, too. And so have we.' He tapped his chest. 'In here.'

'I know, you mother told me,' Allie said, but Sonny had turned away.

They started walking again.

'Why didn't you tell me you were in South Korea?' she asked.

Sonny shrugged. 'Dunno. It just . . . it was just something I did, that's all.'

'Did you join the army especially?'

'No. I went into camp for call-up just before the war started, so I thought I might as well have a go at what I'd been trained for. And the old man and my uncles had all been to war, so I just carried it on. Let's sit down, eh?'

They wandered over to the grass at the edge of the sand and made themselves comfortable at the shadowed base of an enormous, ancient pohutukawa. Even in the moonlight its heavy mantle of bristly crimson flowers was visible, a sign that this year's summer would be long and hot. Sonny put his arm around Allie and they looked out at the sighing sea.

She jumped slightly as he suddenly turned and kissed her lingeringly, his hand sliding from her shoulder down her arm before settling on her waist, making her surreptitiously suck in her stomach. His mouth tasted faintly of beer, cigarettes and hangi-ed chicken. His lips were soft and warm and the tip of his tongue danced lightly against hers. She shivered uncontrollably.

Sonny pulled back. 'Cold?'

'No, just . . . no.'

'Can I keep going?'

Oh, please, please, please! 'If you like.'

'No, only if *you* like, Allie. It's up to you.'

Allie nodded, too embarrassed to say how very much she wanted him to continue.

He kissed her again and this time his arms slid around her, his hands petting and stroking her face, her hair, her neck and her breasts over her shirt. The muscles in his arms and shoulders were hard, and his skin smelled of fresh sweat and that cedar smell again, and he was getting very close to needing a shave. She felt warm and safe and very excited, the slippery heat between her legs increasing by the second and making her squirm. She'd been waiting all night for this, she knew it now, and wondered how she could have behaved so normally all evening in front of his friends and family, all the while knowing that everything that she and Sonny said and did and thought would lead up to this.

But first she had something to tell him. She pressed her face against his warm neck so she wouldn't have to look at him. 'Sonny? I haven't done this before.'

She felt the muscles move in his throat as he swallowed, then he pulled back so he could see her.

'I know,' he said. 'That's why it's up to you.'

Allie bit her lip at the understanding in his voice. 'I don't want you to be disappointed.'

Sonny stared at her for a second, then laughed. 'Disappointed? Christ, girl, I've been thinking about this non-stop for weeks! I'm not going to be disappointed!'

'Yes, but it's just that, um, I'm not sure what to do,' Allie whispered.

'It's easy,' Sonny said. 'You just do this' — and he kissed

her — 'and this' — and he kissed her again — 'and then this' — and then he started unbuttoning her shirt. Slipping his hand inside and then into her bra to caress her nipple, he murmured, 'OK?'

'Very,' she said, closing her eyes. But when he tried to slip her shirt off, she grasped his wrist. 'What if someone comes past?'

But a moment later the shirt was off and Sonny was unhooking the back of her bra. He slipped the straps down her arms and took it off, leaving her bare from the waist up, the gentle night breeze playing across her skin and giving her goosebumps, before handing her the shirt to put back on. He ran his fingers lightly over her belly and breasts, then tugged his own shirt out of his jeans, pulled it off over his head and tossed it aside. His stomach was flat and muscled, he had hardly any hair on his chest and his small, dark nipples were erect. Allie looked down; so were hers, embarrassingly so.

Kissing her shoulder and licking a wet trail from there up to her ear, Sonny murmured, 'Still OK?'

Allie giggled. 'Still OK.'

He pushed her gently back onto the grass; it was kikuyu, coarse and pleasantly scratchy against her hot skin. Grunting slightly, he rolled on top of her, supporting his weight on his elbows and smiling down at her.

'I've got you now,' he said.

'You have,' she replied, loving the way his skin felt against hers, and marvelling at how hard his erection was. It was digging into her pubic bone and she wondered if it was getting squashed between them. She thrust up her hips slightly. 'Are you comfortable? You're not getting . . . sore down there?'

'Not sore, no. And don't do that or it'll be over before we get started.'

Lifting her up a little, he slid his arms under her back so she was cradled beneath him, then began slowly to rub himself against her, his breathing becoming heavier as he covered her face and eyes and throat with kisses. Allie raised her legs and clamped her thighs around his buttocks, holding him tightly and instinctively moving against him, feeling a natural rhythm beginning and wanting desperately to get her jeans off so that their flesh touched everywhere. She moaned and then squeaked as he gave a particularly energetic thrust that almost knocked the breath out of her.

'Oh, Jesus,' Sonny said. 'I can't wait much longer.'

'Neither can I,' Allie replied, and she'd never meant anything more.

He rolled off her, reached down to the zip on her jeans and slowly pulled it down, making every fraction of her skin beneath it crawl with anticipation. Then he was tugging her jeans to her knees and, finally, off over her bare feet. His hand slid down her flat belly, under her pants and into her pubic hair, where his fingers began to massage gently at first, then more insistently. Allie wriggled, feeling the prickly grass beneath her back and the breeze on her skin and more desire for Sonny than she'd ever imagined was possible.

When he undid his own trousers and pushed them down his thighs, she couldn't stop herself from staring; he wasn't wearing underpants and his erection sprang straight up, grazing against his muscled stomach as he sat up to shove his jeans down past his knees. She'd never seen a penis before, and certainly not an erect one, and it was sort of what she'd expected, and sort of not. She reached out and touched it, making it jerk upwards. She hadn't realized that the skin would be so silky, or the end of it quite so, well, purple. Or would Miss Willow call it heliotrope? Allie clamped her lips tight against the nervous, excited giggle that seemed to want desperately to escape.

Sonny rolled on top of her again, nudging her legs open with his thighs.

'Ready?' he whispered.

She nodded, her face pressed against his neck. She felt his fingers on her, opening her, and then he pushed. She gasped as a sharp little pain stabbed her, and then it was gone.

'OK?'

Not trusting herself to speak she nodded again and moved her hips, centring herself beneath him and making herself more comfortable on the grass. Sonny sighed and rested for a moment, his forehead against hers, then began to thrust, slowly at first but then faster and faster. Allie curled herself around him, holding on until he threw his head back, exposing the taut sinews in his neck and the sheen of sweat on his throat, and shuddered once, then again, then once more. A moment later he slowly subsided on top of her.

Allie gazed up at the black branches of the pohutukawa canopied above them, feeling Sonny's heart thudding against her ribs until, after several minutes, it began to beat more calmly. He said something into her shoulder and she thought it might have been 'God almighty'.

He rolled half off her, propped himself on one elbow and smiled ruefully down at her. 'Sorry, love, that wasn't a very good first time for you, was it?'

'It was lovely,' Allie said, running her finger playfully down his nose.

And then she had a thought so horrible she actually cried out.

'Oh, no, Sonny, we didn't use anything!' How could she have been so bloody stupid? She sat up and scrabbled for her clothes. 'Oh, God, what am I going to do?'

'It's all right,' he said, sitting up himself, although to Allie's ears he sounded a lot more confident than he suddenly looked.

'It is *not*. What if I'm pregnant? What am I going to do?'

He took hold of her hand. 'Calm down, sweetheart, come on. Don't worry, it's not that bad.'

'It bloody is!' she almost yelled, snatching her hand back.

'Shut up, love,' he said gently, taking her hand again. 'When's your, you know, your bleeding due?' He inclined his head towards her belly.

'My period? Why?'

'When's it due?'

She had to think for a moment. 'Monday. Maybe Tuesday. Why?'

'Because you can't get pregnant just before it starts.'

'Who told you that?' she replied, wavering between disbelief and hope.

'Mum. The old man was useless at that sort of thing.'

'Are you sure?' she demanded, her heart still galloping.

Sonny nodded. 'I think we're fairly safe.'

Allie was slightly mollified by his use of the word 'we' rather than the very lonely-sounding 'you'. But she still said, 'You could have used something.'

'I know. I've got something in my pocket, but I got carried away. I'm really sorry.'

Allie suddenly became aware that they were sitting almost naked on Mission Bay beach. 'We should get dressed. Someone might see us.'

They got back into their clothes, Allie pulling a face as a trickle of semen dribbled out of her. She hadn't realized that it would come out quite so soon, if at all, but given her blind panic a minute ago, she was very pleased that it had.

Then all of a sudden her eyes prickled and she wanted to cry. She turned away from Sonny, so he couldn't see her face.

'What's the matter?' he said, coming to stand behind her and wrapping his arms around her.

'I don't know,' she said. 'But, apart from the fright, that was lovely.'

'So are you,' Sonny replied, giving her a gentle squeeze.

Leaning her head back against his shoulder, Allie whispered, 'And so are you.'

Chapter Eleven

When Allie got up to go to the toilet the next morning she felt agitated, worried and very grumpy. But when she came out that had all evaporated because there had been a pink smear of blood on the paper, which surely meant that she hadn't been caught out the night before? Her usual pattern was that she would spot one day, nothing would happen the next day then her period would start properly the following day, and she would know she was safe. That *they* were safe.

She crossed the back porch into the kitchen and put the kettle on the stove. No one else was up. Good — she could have the bathroom to herself for a while. But when she got there the door was closed. She knocked on it sharply.

'Go away!' It was Donna.

Allie could hear the sound of the bath running. 'I need to go first, Donna,' she called. 'I'm going out this morning.'

'Too bad. So am I.'

Sometimes, Allie thought, she could easily murder her little sister and would happily swing for it.

'Well, hurry up! And don't take all the hot water!'

By the time Donna came out, with her hair in a towelling turban and wafting her hands about because she'd done her bloody nails in there as well, it was nearly half past nine. Allie ran herself a short bath, because as predicted there was hardly any hot water left, and lowered herself into it, wincing as the warm water stung between her legs. It had hurt when she'd peed as well. The memory of what had caused it made her stomach do a slow, thrilled flip.

She soaped herself everywhere and washed her hair, because it stank of smoke even though she'd been outside nearly all of the previous night, and ran her hands over her legs, thinking that perhaps she should shave them even though she would be wearing longs today. But when she climbed out of the bath and opened the bathroom cabinet to grab her father's razor, she noticed that where it usually sat was now a small metal box with a padlock on it. She laughed and closed the cabinet again.

Breakfast was the usual Sunday morning affair — late and unhurried. Colleen wanted to know who'd used all the hot water. No one said anything. Sid was reading *Best Bets*.

'Did you have a nice time last night?' Colleen asked.

Allie nodded, her mouth full of toast. She swallowed. 'Yes, it was great.'

'And where was it, the party, in the end?'

'Someone's house, on the back lawn.' Allie thought that it would save a lot of unnecessary questions if she didn't say that it had been a house on Kitemoana Street.

'And what time are you going out today?'

Allie wished her mother would stop interrogating her, although she supposed she just wanted to know what was going on. 'Eleven o'clock, it's supposed to start.'

'Sounds like a yawn to me,' Pauline said. 'A picnic at the Domain.'

'Will there be teddy bears?' Donna asked sarcastically.

'As long as it's not bloody teddy boys,' Sid muttered from behind his *Best Bets*.

'Will you put that bloody thing away?' Colleen said crossly. 'We hardly ever get to sit down as a family these days.'

'Yes, we do,' Sid said. 'We do it twice a day.'

'Yes, but we never . . . oh, never mind,' Colleen grumbled as she got up to put more bread under the grill. Over her shoulder she said, 'It would just be nice to sit and talk about things for a change, instead of bickering about everything and then rushing off in all directions. Sunday's supposed to be a day of rest. And for families.'

'I am resting,' Sid said. 'Are we going to meet this bloke of yours today, Allie?'

Allie nodded. 'He's picking me up.' She was a bit nervous, not sure that her parents would appreciate Sonny's motorbike quite as much as she did.

'Will he come in?' Pauline asked.

'I suppose so.'

Allie wasn't much looking forward to that either, knowing the way her family could behave. With luck she could get away with just quickly introducing him, then, pleading lateness, they could race off and leave her parents and sisters to talk about him as much as they liked. She glanced up at the clock. 'I've got to go and get ready.'

After she'd cleaned her teeth, done her hair and put on a dash of make-up, she went back out to the kitchen, sat down and lit a cigarette. Her father was still there, making a little pile of hand-rolled smokes. Her mother was rolling out pastry on the bench, Pauline was reading a book and Donna, despite insisting earlier that she had to go out, was still there.

'Perhaps we should all go and wait in the sitting room,' Colleen suggested.

Allie looked at her mother in horror. 'What for?'

'We always use the sitting room when we're receiving company,' her mother replied. She was smiling to herself, but Allie couldn't see it because Colleen had her back turned.

'We do not,' Sid said, who was grumpy now because Colleen had used yesterday's newspaper to wrap up apple peelings before he'd quite finished with it. 'We never have that sort of company.'

'We want to make the right impression, though, don't we?' Colleen said.

Allie, realizing her mother was having her on, relaxed. 'He'll only be here a few minutes and then we'll be gone.'

Pauline cocked her head. 'Is that him now?'

Allie recognized the low rumbling sound of the motorbike's engine. Donna and Pauline leapt up from the table and pounded down the hall to peer out through the sitting room windows.

'It's him, he's here!' Pauline shouted, loud enough for Sonny to hear from the street.

Half a minute later there was a knock at the back porch. The door was already open: Allie jumped up but Donna had already yelled out, 'Come in!'

Sonny appeared in the doorway. His hair had been freshly combed — ten seconds ago, Allie suspected — and he was wearing corduroy trousers and an open-necked shirt. He looked very handsome. Allie wanted to give him a kiss but didn't think it would be the thing to do in front of her parents.

'Everyone, this is my friend, Sonny Manaia. Sonny, this is my dad, Sid, and my mum, Colleen, and this is Donna and Pauline.'

Sonny said hello. Donna and Pauline simpered, Colleen smiled brightly and Sid stuck out his hand. 'Pleased to meetcha,' he said, pumping Sonny's arm up and down. 'Have a seat.'

Sonny looked at Allie, who said, 'I think we should make a move. We don't want to be late.'

'Ah, it's only a picnic,' Sid protested. 'Come on, sit down, lad, have a cuppa. Put the kettle on, Col, there's a love.'

Allie's heart sank. But it turned out to be quite a pleasant half-hour, despite her sisters whispering and tittering on one side of the table and her mother rummaging about in the cupboards trying to find biscuits that weren't stale and saying if it had been just a little later Sonny could have had a nice slice of hot apple pie. Sonny immediately asked her father what he thought about the All Black test in Wales the day before, and Sid's eyes lit up — 'We were robbed, boy, robbed' — and he didn't shut up for the next twenty minutes. But eventually, after making a show of looking at both her watch and the clock repeatedly, Allie managed to drag Sonny away. Unfortunately, the whole family followed them outside to wave them off.

'Oh,' Colleen said when she saw the motorbike. 'I'm not sure I like the look of that. Is it safe?'

'In good hands, it is,' Sonny replied.

'Yes, motorbikes can be very dangerous, Allie,' Donna said, smirking.

Allie gave her a dirty look.

'She's a beauty, isn't she?' Sid said admiringly. 'I used to have a motorbike, you know, a BSA. Lovely machine. Allie's mother and I used to take some pretty hair-raising spins on it, didn't we, love?'

'You never told us about that, Mum,' Allie said.

'Yes, well, you be careful,' Colleen said quickly. 'People have been known to come a real cropper off motorbikes.'

'I'll be very careful, Mrs Roberts,' Sonny assured her.

'Yes, you do that,' she replied, holding his gaze a moment too long and leaving Allie with the uncomfortable feeling that it might not only be motorbikes her mother was referring to.

Sonny smiled his most charming smile, which was very charming indeed. 'Right, then. Thanks for the cup of tea. Are we off?'

Allie nodded and stepped back as Sonny swung his leg over the bike and turned the engine on. She hopped on and waved back at her family as Sonny cruised with exaggerated care down to the intersection with Kepa Road before he let out the throttle and roared off.

They crossed Orakei Bridge and rode into town, then turned onto one of the little winding streets leading up to the Domain.

'Where's it supposed to be?' Sonny called over his shoulder.

'Winter Garden and Fernery.'

He turned up a narrow side road that would take them past the War Memorial Museum, monolithic and pale and looking like the bottom tier of a particularly utilitarian wedding cake, and around to the other side of the hill. Everywhere, Allie could see evidence of preparations for the royal tour. Apparently, the queen was going to visit the

217

hospital on Thursday, then drive around the Domain in an open car during a rally of children's groups. She felt sorry for the queen in a way — by the end of her tour her poor arm would just about be falling off from so much waving.

Ahead of them, Allie could see the domed roof of the grand brick-and-glass building housing the Winter Garden.

She pointed and Sonny changed down a gear, slowing as they approached.

Maxwell Jones was also a little late for the Dunbar & Jones staff Christmas picnic. He sat impatiently in one of the elegantly upholstered chairs in the foyer of his home in Remuera Road, the case containing his Santa suit on the floor beside him, tapping his foot, checking his watch and waiting for his family to hurry up and come downstairs. Anton, his driver, was already waiting outside with the car, dressed in his customary plain dark suit, as Max thought it was rather pretentious to be driven around by someone wearing a uniform covered in shiny buttons, as if he were royalty or something.

His wife, Estelle, had woken up this morning with one of her bad 'heads' and had had to stay in bed until it had subsided, which had put them behind schedule. Then the children had performed, saying that they didn't want to spend all day at the Domain hanging about with children they didn't know and probably wouldn't like, when they could be with their friends. But Max had put his foot down: he liked to promote the idea of family values and cohesion, both among his staff and as part of the store's ethos, so his wife and children would accompany him.

He had married late, not until he was thirty-eight: until then the store had taken up all of his time, and his interest. But one day his father, James, had taken him aside and asked him outright if he wasn't one of those pansy fellows. When Max, unsure whether to laugh or be mortally offended, had said no, he wasn't, his father had pointed out that it would probably be tactical, and at the very least practical, if he found himself a suitable wife in the not too distant future. Someone who would be an asset at social functions, who could hostess private events held at the Jones residence, and who could provide him with children who would reinforce the store's reputation and image as a family business. His father had also hinted that, unlike Max's grandmother Isobel, he had no intention of keeping a stranglehold on the store's reins until he finally collapsed and died at his desk, and that Max's time might come sooner rather than later.

So Max had gone out and found himself a wife, which hadn't been too difficult. He was moderately good-looking, personable and heir to one of the most successful retail enterprises in the country. He had chosen Estelle, a renowned social butterfly and daughter of a very well-to-do banker and his wife, who had pots of old money from down south. Estelle was a lot younger than Max — twenty-seven when they married — was very pretty, charming and popular, and not terribly bright. Now, ten years later, she was still attractive and charming, and still not very bright. If Max didn't keep an eye on her chequebook and how much she spent, she invariably found herself in all sorts of trouble. They could afford her extravagances, but it wouldn't do for her to go around running up debts all over town. Estelle was, however, as predicted by his father, a delightful hostess, a real asset to Max, and not a bad mother, either, given the material she had to work with.

Max sighed. He had no idea why two of his three children were turning out the way they were. The youngest, five-year-old Emily, was still quite a sweetie, but then she wasn't old enough yet to be anything else. However, nine-year-old Philip and eight-year-old Amanda were little horrors, even if he did say so himself. They were spoilt, arrogant and really quite rude. If Grandmother Isobel had still been around she would have sorted them out, he was sure of that, but they ran riot over Estelle and he didn't have the time, and anyway it wasn't his job. He wondered, quite often, if sending them away to boarding school would do the trick.

But his children and his failure to arrive at his own company's staff picnic on time weren't the only things bothering him this morning. He was concerned about a report he'd received some weeks ago from a maintenance firm he had contracted to assess the extent of work required on the store over the next two years. The three buildings comprising Dunbar & Jones were on the whole sound, but there were some matters that would definitely need attention before too long. These included the lifts, which were getting a bit long in the tooth and needed a thorough overhaul, and the fact that there were cracks in the façades of the middle and Wyndham Street buildings. Also, some of the windows couldn't be opened, the electrical wiring required modernizing in some areas, the bolts attaching the fire escape to the back wall of the building were showing signs of corrosion, and the cisterns in the staff toilets were on their way out. None of it was urgent, but something would have to be done within the next year.

Max hadn't been surprised — the buildings were, after all, really quite old. Work on the fire escape, in fact, was already under way, since that was a matter of staff safety. He wasn't looking forward to paying for it all, however. Dunbar & Jones could bear it, but the expense would make a bit of a hole in the company's future profits, which wouldn't endear him to the shareholders. But there was no way around it.

The second thing bothering him was his store manager, Keith Beaumont. Keith wasn't a bad sort, and indeed he was a very efficient manager in his fashion, but for some time there had been a regular discrepancy in the accounts. The office supervisor had come to him some months ago, concerned that, on a disconcerting number of occasions, neither she nor her staff had been able to balance the books. Furthermore, she had gone over the accounts very carefully and eventually noticed that some of the dockets for returned items appeared to have been tampered with. She had interviewed her staff very rigorously indeed and was satisfied that none of those she supervised directly were responsible. Max believed her. She was a very conscientious woman, with a high regard for her staff and a genuine concern for their welfare. She had come to him, not with a desire to dob someone in, but to protect her workers.

So Max had told her to leave it with him and to go on as though nothing were amiss, while he tried to get to the bottom of the problem. Not wanting to create an atmosphere of inquisition, or to alert whoever was responsible, he had not discussed the matter with anyone else, but had begun to double-check the accounts himself. When he realized that this would achieve nothing more than confirmation of the docket fiddling, he decided to take another approach and keep an eye out for anyone on his staff who was spending more than they should or otherwise generally acting in a furtive manner. That hadn't worked, either. There were far too many employees for a start, and plenty of them had run up enormous staff accounts, though he was only looking for people spending actual cash, and a disturbing number of them seemed to act furtively on a regular basis.

Then, several weeks ago, Anton had mentioned in passing that Keith Beaumont used the same bookie that he did, and very regularly by all accounts, and the penny had wobbled, if not dropped. Max had no proof, but Keith had been behaving rather oddly over the past year or so for no apparent reason, and he had access to the accounts office and the safe any time he liked, and the authority to cover up any discrepancies that might be of his own making. It saddened Max, the possibility that Keith might be embezzling from Dunbar & Jones, but, if he was, the week before Christmas was not the time to do anything about firing him, especially with the queen coming and the possibility of it getting into the papers. But what if Keith was indeed embezzling, and got it into his head to make off with all of the Christmas takings? Max sighed. Oh God, perhaps he should talk to Keith this week after all.

'I'm sorry, darling, we're ready now,' Estelle said from the top of the stairs. As Max watched, she descended, followed by the three children, Philip and Amanda dragging their feet noticeably.

Max had suggested to Estelle that the children didn't wear their smartest clothes out of deference to the parents on his staff who might not be able to dress their own children in quite the same, expensive, fashion, and she had chosen wisely: the children looked smart, but not ostentatious. Estelle was wearing a very pretty pale pink frock, a large straw sunhat, and a simple rope of pearls at her throat and her pearl earrings. Max himself had forgone his suit and tie in favour of casual, but smart, trousers and a cream shirt, though he still couldn't decide whether to wear the sleeves down or rolled up.

He collected his Santa case and stood up. 'Good. Right, we'll go then, shall we?

Grumbling, Philip and Amanda preceded him out of the door and climbed into the back seat of the car, a Rover 75 sedan purchased late the year before and still smelling very satisfyingly of new leather. The children's bad mood disinclined anyone to say anything on the short trip to the Domain, except for Emily, who hummed the whole way in between pointing out what she considered to be sights worthy of note.

As the car approached the Winter Garden and Fernery, Max saw that many of his staff had already arrived. A colourful, shifting throng of people was milling about outside the Winter Garden building, and several vans, carrying the food prepared by specially engaged caterers (who had cost a fortune), were parked in an orderly row along the narrow road in front of it. They would never all fit into the building, so the plan was for everyone to lay out their picnic rugs on the Domain grass at the edge of the sportsfield and help themselves to the buffet. No alcohol would be served because it was Sunday, and anyway Max didn't agree with his staff drinking in public, especially when onlookers might be aware that it was the Dunbar &

Jones Christmas function. There would be various games throughout the afternoon, and at three-thirty Max himself would duck off, dress in his Santa costume, then reappear in the Rover bearing an enormous sack containing a gift for every child attending the picnic. It was the part of the proceedings he particularly enjoyed.

'Here comes Mr Max,' Louise said.

She, Susan and Rob had spread their rug on the ground not too far from the public toilets. Though well out of nappies, Susan was still occasionally caught short, especially when she was excited, and Louise didn't want to have to spend her afternoon traipsing all over the Domain for the loos.

'Nice car,' Rob commented. It was a lovely, warm day and he was dying for a beer.

Daisy and Terry were sitting next to them, Daisy wearing the yellow halter-neck sun frock she'd made especially. It was an A-line with the waist starting quite high and concealed her little bump nicely.

'Doesn't Mrs Max look lovely,' she said as the Jones family alighted from their car. 'And what lovely children. I bet they're well behaved.'

'I bet they aren't. No one has perfect children, Daisy,' Louise said, keeping an eye on Susan, who had found an ants' nest at the base of a tree and was poking it energetically with a stick.

'Is that Allie and Sonny?' Terry asked, shielding his eyes against the sun and watching a motorbike cruising down the hill. 'Crikey, that's an Indian Chief. When did Sonny get that?'

'Beaut motorbike,' Rob said in admiration, when Sonny and Allie joined them.

'Yeah, it's all right, eh?' Sonny replied, and he, Terry and Rob wandered over to have a look at it.

'You look a box of birds, Allie,' said Daisy.

'Do I?'

'Good night out, was it?' Louise asked knowingly.

Allie, her cheeks going pink, nodded.

'Where was it, in the end?'

'At his mum's house, in Kitemoana Street.'

'Really?' Louise pulled a dubious face. 'How was that?'

'It was really good, actually. He's got a huge family and they were nearly all there and there was a huge feed, a hangi, and guitars and all sorts. It was fun.'

'Did you meet his parents?' Daisy asked.

'Well, his father's passed away but I met his mother.'

'Was she nice?'

Allie hesitated. 'She's, um, very straightforward. But, yes, she was nice.'

'What sort of house do they live in? Was it . . . clean?'

'Don't be silly, Daisy. It was fine. Isn't Irene here yet?'

As if on cue, Irene and Martin appeared, walking across the grass from the direction of the museum.

'Oh . . . my . . . God,' Louise said, unable to take her eyes off Irene.

Neither, it appeared, could anyone else as heads rapidly turned in her direction.

'What the hell has she got on?' Louise asked.

What Irene had on was an eye-watering flamingo-pink 'play suit'. The shorts sat snugly on her waist but ended only inches below her buttocks, giving everyone an eyeful of her firm, bare thighs. The top was a sleeveless shirt, with several buttons undone to display plenty of cleavage, and tied under the bust to show off her enviably flat midriff. On her feet were matching pink high-heeled wedge sandals, and her hair was tied back with a pink-and-black-patterned chiffon scarf. Martin walked a few feet behind her, very unselfconsciously, Allie thought, given that nearly five hundred people were staring at them.

'Hi!' Irene called out as they approached.

Bug-eyed, Sonny, Terry and Rob managed to say hello.

Martin produced a rug from the bag he was carrying, laid it on the grass with a flourish, and he and Irene sat down.

'Love your outfit,' Louise said.

'Yes, it's fun, isn't it?' Irene replied. Catching the expression on Louise's face, she laughed. 'Well, someone has to make a spectacle of themselves today, so I thought it might as well be me.'

'I really like it,' Daisy said, enviously eyeing Irene's flat stomach.

'Hello, Martin,' Allie said.

She'd met Martin several times before and, to her surprise, had found she rather liked him. Based on Irene's frequent complaints, she'd been expecting some boring old bloke with no sense of humour and terrible dress sense, but he was only in his late twenties, and was actually quite nice-looking, even if he did wear glasses, and in her opinion his clothes always looked fine. Conservative, yes, but nicely cut and of very good quality.

'Hi, Allie. How are you?' Martin's voice was warm.

'Good, thanks. I don't think you've met my boyfriend, Sonny Manaia?' Boyfriend: even just the word gave Allie a warm and slightly smug feeling of pride and happiness.

226

Martin shook hands with Sonny. He already knew Rob and Terry.

'Good day for it,' he said.

'What time's the food?' Irene asked. 'I'm so hungry I could eat a baby's bum through the bars of a cot.'

'Irene!' Daisy exclaimed, a hand protectively on her belly.

'What? Oh, sorry, but I haven't had anything to eat for hours.'

'Looks like they're getting it ready now,' Terry said, nodding towards the vans where the caterers were unloading trestle tables, stacks of plates, serving utensils, boxes and trays of food and various other bits and pieces.

In fifteen minutes it had all been set up, and the word went around that everyone was to collect a plate and form orderly queues at the ends of the tables.

'Look, there's Miss Willow and Miss Button,' Daisy said as they were waiting in line. She waved enthusiastically.

When they'd loaded up their plates with sandwiches, sausage rolls, savouries and cake, and grapes and water-melon from the enormous fruit platter, they returned to their rugs and sat down to enjoy it. Then there were cups of tea or coffee from several enormous urns, and cigarette smoke rose as everyone lounged about in the sunshine.

As the caterers began to clear away the picnic things, Mr Max, who had eaten his lunch with his own family and those of the very upper echelon of Dunbar & Jones's management hierarchy, moved to the centre of the mosaic of rugs, blankets and deckchairs and made an announcement.

'Shortly,' he began, almost shouting so that everyone could hear him, 'we'll start the afternoon's games off with an egg-and-spoon race, followed by a three-legged race, a sack race and then light-the-cigarette. Children will have their own special games, of course. For those of you who don't want to tear up and down the sportsfield making fools of yourselves' — polite laughter from everyone — 'there will be cricket, quoits and croquet. Lastly, I've heard it rumoured, and this is mainly for the benefit of the little ones here today, that . . .' he paused, stretching the moment out as long as possible, 'that, yes, Santa Claus himself will be putting in an appearance!'

All around him, children, not all coached by their parents, let out an enthusiastic 'Yay!'

Mr Max beamed. 'Yes, that's right! *And*, I believe he might just have a little something for all of you!'

A very hearty 'Yay!' this time.

'So, grown-ups, perhaps we should now get under way. Oh, and thank you all very much for putting in such a lot of hard work during the year, and especially that concerning the preparations for Her Majesty's arrival on Wednesday, which I'm sure you're all looking forward to as much as my family and I are.'

There was a round of applause, and everyone made a move towards the sportsfield.

'He's a good sort, Mr Max, isn't he?' Daisy said. 'And of course, hats, dresses and lingerie will win the prize again.'

Irene snorted. 'Not likely. Accounts and typists have got some strong runners this year.'

'Except that no one will be doing much actual running, will they?' Allie countered. 'Not while they're balancing eggs or with their legs tied to someone else's.'

The department whose individual members accrued the most points in the games would receive an engraved trophy and a free morning tea in the cafeteria for every person. After the competition's inaugural year, there had been complaints that chocolates and condiments, for example, hadn't had a hope of competing successfully against a department as big as, say, floorings, so now the departments had been divided up into more or less equal groups, which meant that Allie, Louise and Daisy were on the same team. Only Irene was in a different group.

As announced, the egg-and-spoon was first. There were several dozen heats in each event, but fortunately each race only covered fifty yards. Daisy, who refused to run properly in case she jiggled the baby, came last in hers, but Irene, who was a powerful runner once she kicked her sandals off, and who had very good hand-eye co-ordination, won hers.

None of them did well in the sack race, they were laughing so much, but Allie and Louise both came first in their heats in the three-legged race, although Allie whacked Sonny on the nose with her elbow and made his eyes water, and grazed her knee when she fell over at the end. The light-the-cigarette race was possibly the most fun, and the most dangerous, though it did preclude non-smokers. The idea was that teams of equal numbers lined up, a lit cigarette was handed to the first ones to go, who then belted down the field to their partner or team-mate waiting at the other end, who had to light a cigarette off the first one, without anyone using their hands. A bit of fun for those grabbing the opportunity for a quick cuddle, much hilarity for spectators, and the odd cigarette burn.

At two-thirty, the games adjourned for afternoon tea and everyone collapsed onto their rugs. Irene, noticing that Vince Reynolds had moved his rug closer to hers and Martin's, even though he had brought his trout of a wife Cynthia with him, set about tidying her hair and applying fresh lipstick. Sonny and Allie lay on their backs, surreptitiously holding hands, staring up at the sky and telling each other what shapes the clouds were. Rob was talking to Terry about cars while Louise and Daisy had taken Susan for a walk to the toilet. Ted Horrocks was tucking into a slice of fruit cake and telling his wife that it wasn't a patch on hers, and Ruby Willow and Beatrice Button were trying to decide whether the caterers had used real tea or those dreadful new bags Lipton had put out. The latter, they suspected.

Max Jones was sitting quietly, watching everyone and congratulating himself on another successful staff Christmas party and wishing it could always be like this — everyone happy and working together and having a good time.

Keith Beaumont, who had come with his wife and was sitting on the outskirts of the managerial party, had worked himself into a state of considerable anxiety. Max Jones had been staring at him on and off all day. Did he somehow know? He couldn't, Keith was sure of it, but that dread was still there, eating away at him like a particularly virulent cancer. And he couldn't even go and place a bet to alleviate his discomfort because it was Sunday and nothing was running. The best he could do was to keep on topping up his orange squash with gin and hope that no one would notice. Nora had, and had been giving him some very quizzical looks, which only reminded him of the extent to which he was letting her down.

Irene waited until Cynthia had turned away to talk to

someone, then caught Vince's eye; he raised one eyebrow, then nodded almost imperceptibly. Then he got up, brushed off his trousers and sauntered towards the toilets. Irene gave it a minute, announced that she was absolutely bursting and walked off after him.

Allie, sitting up and ferreting through her handbag for her cigarettes, saw the whole thing. Appalled, she glanced at Martin. He was lying propped on one elbow with his ankles crossed, stripping the leaves off a twig and looking after his wife. He turned his head and met Allie's gaze.

She swallowed, wanting suddenly, desperately, to say that she was sorry.

'It's all right,' Martin said, sitting up. 'I know.'

Allie stared at him.

'Well, I know about these little "entanglements" she has.' He gave a rueful little smile. 'But, you see, I don't want to lose her.'

Irene followed the little concrete path around the back of the toilet block to the ladies' entrance, smiling at Daisy, Louise and Susan as they came out, and out of the corner of her eye saw Vince standing a short distance away, half concealed behind some bushes. She waited until the others had gone, then hurried over to him, her sandals crunching over dead leaves and desiccated undergrowth.

He drew her further into the shelter of the bushes. 'Christ,' he said, 'I thought I was never going to give her the slip.' Running his hands up and down her back, he covered her face with kisses. 'What about your husband? Did he notice?'

Irene laughed. 'No, he never notices anything I do.'

Plucking feverishly at the knot of fabric under her bust, Vince said, 'Quick, we've only got about five minutes.' He yanked open her shirt and pushed her bra up, groaning as her breasts were exposed.

'Five minutes for what?' Irene said, startled.

Vince's hand snaked down and cupped her pubic bone. 'For this, darling, for this.'

'What? No, not here!'

'We'll be all right, love, it'll only take a minute.' He grabbed her hand and pushed it against his erection. 'See?'

'But someone might catch us!' Irene was uncharacteristically disconcerted: she'd assumed they'd only be having a slap and a tickle, not that he would want this. Not here.

'Oh, God, Irene, please,' he begged. He grasped her hands. 'Look, I'm going to talk to my wife. I can't keep on like this, seeing you every day and not being able to have you. I'm going to tell her I want a divorce.'

Irene's mouth fell open. 'A divorce?'

Vince nodded. 'We'll run away. I've got money put aside. We'll go to Australia — I've got contacts there.' His face lit up. 'Or what about America? Would you like to go to America, Irene? We could make a fortune — they say anyone can there!' He shook her, but not too hard. 'Don't you understand? I love you! And I have to have you!'

Irene slid her arms around his neck, so that her face was only inches away from his. She felt overwhelmed by his admission. He might have been half-joking the last time he'd said it, but he meant it now, she was sure of it. 'I love you, too, Vince, I really do,' she said, and kissed him urgently.

'Then let me make love to you, Irene.'

She wanted to say yes, desperate to savour that heady sensation of victory and power as her body reduced him to a gasping, quivering mess, but, oh Christ, not here, not in the bushes outside the Auckland Domain public toilets.

'If you really loved me you'd wait until tomorrow,' she murmured into his ear, her body pressed hard against him. 'We could go down to the basement again at lunchtime.'

He groaned in frustration. 'I can't wait until then. At least help me, Irene,' he said, grasping her hand again and pushing it down the front of his trousers.

And, overcome by visions of the two of them running off together, to a place where they could start a new life and make plenty of money and buy everything they wanted — a big house, a flash car, clothes and maybe even jewels for her — she did what he wanted.

'That wasn't bad, was it, for a work do?' Allie said. 'Wasn't Mr Max good with the kids?'

'Yeah, he's not a bad bloke. For a boss,' Sonny replied.

'I really enjoyed myself. The races were a laugh.'

'Not as much fun as last night, though.'

Allie smiled. 'No, it wasn't, was it?'

The picnic had finished and they were having an ice cream at Mission Bay on the way home.

'Everything all right?' he asked, nodding down at her stomach.

'A bit sore this morning, but my you-know-what started, so that's all right.'

'Jesus, I'll say,' Sonny said, and breathed an enormous sigh of relief.

Allie looked at him. 'I thought you said you weren't worried?'

'I lied.'

'But what about what you said about not being able to fall just before a period? Did you just make that up?'

'No. But, you know, sometimes what you want isn't what you get.'

Allie thought about that for a minute. 'Yes, I suppose you're right. I suppose anything can happen sometimes, things you've never even thought about.'

'You've got ice cream on your nose.'

'Have I?' Allie nearly went cross-eyed trying to see.

Sonny wiped the little blob of hokey-pokey off with the tip of his finger. Then he kissed her, tasting it on her lips. 'We would have been all right, though, Allie. No matter what.'

Part Two

Fire

Chapter Twelve

In the kitchen of her parents' house in Grey Lynn, Daisy did her best to force down a piece of dry toast, but gave up after only a few bites.

Her mother, standing over her in her dressing gown, frowned. 'You have to eat something, Daisy. You can't go to work on an empty stomach.'

'I know, Mum. I've tried, I really have.'

'What about a boiled egg?'

At the thought of the runny yellow yoke and the possibly undercooked white, all watery and stringy, Daisy gagged. Her hand over her mouth, she shook her head.

Agnes Farr shook her own head, but in despair. Daisy had bitterly disappointed her, but now that it had happened, she was determined that the wedding would go ahead with as much dignity as possible, even if people did suspect why her daughter was walking down the aisle at such short notice. Daisy's dress was going to be tasteful and elegant, the flowers would be perfect, the food memorable and the whole day something that would do the Farr family proud.

'A cup of tea, then? With sugar,' she suggested.

Daisy shoved her chair back and lurched out of the kitchen, heading for the toilet. The door slammed and Agnes heard her retching. She put the kettle on.

When Daisy came back, her face pale and her hands shaking slightly, she said, 'At least I got it out before work this time.'

Agnes didn't answer. Daisy might have been stupid enough to get herself in the family way, but that didn't mean that the pair of them had to sit around discussing it as though it were some happy, planned event mother and daughter could share. She would talk about the wedding, yes, but not the baby. It was wrong, and it was humiliating, having a daughter so simple-minded and . . . *lustful* that she could fall into such an old trap. On the other hand, Daisy had to look after herself. If she didn't, that would be just one more thing for people to talk about.

And Agnes felt guilty, although she wasn't about to admit that to anyone, not even Harold, Daisy's father. If she had taken Daisy aside when her monthlies had started and explained to her about how these things worked — about how you could get into trouble so easily and that was why you shouldn't tempt fate at all, at least, not until you were safely married — all this might have been avoided. But she hadn't. She hated talking about that sort of thing almost as much as she hated doing it, which, thank God, Harold had finally accepted. So she had hoped, prayed even, that Daisy would be bright enough to just not get herself into that situation. But she hadn't been. A part of Agnes wanted to take her little blonde Daisy in her arms and cuddle her and tell her it would all be all right, but then she didn't want to touch her at all because she had been so . . . deliberately wanton.

So she said nothing, just kept on with making the fresh pot of tea.

'I'm getting the material for my dress today,' Daisy said, feeling her mother's hostility and wanting to say something — anything — to gain her approval. She shuffled her chair further under the table so her mother couldn't see the firm lump of her belly. 'And Terry said he's happy to wear a morning suit. You can hire them from work, you know, really smart ones.'

Agnes nodded in grim satisfaction. 'No, I didn't think he'd actually own one.'

Well, how many people actually do? Daisy wanted to say. 'He's not that keen on the top hat, though,' she added, and waited for the heavy scowling silence that meant her mother didn't approve.

But it didn't come. Agnes sat down at the table. 'They can be ostentatious, top hats, especially when the ceremony is only going to be in a small church. At St Andrew's, perhaps, but you're not getting married at St Andrew's.'

Heartened, Daisy said, 'I thought we could start cutting out the material tonight. If we made space in the sitting room we could do it in there.'

Agnes actually smiled, happy to be able to say something to Daisy that didn't convey her disappointment and disapproval. 'Yes, we could, couldn't we? But you'll have to come straight home from work because I expect it will take us half the night, with the amount of fabric in that skirt.'

Daisy looked at her mother, feeling a tiny glimmer of hope that things might, after all, be all right. 'Oh, I will, Mum, I'll come straight home, I promise.'

'Hurry up, sweetheart, you'll make us late for work,' Louise said to Susan, who was playing with her Weet-bix, shunting the last few soggy mouthfuls around her bowl.

'Sir Edmund Hirraly eats Weet-bix,' Susan announced.

'Hillary, Edmund *Hill*ary,' Louise corrected as she put away the last of the breakfast things. 'Come on, we have to go in a minute.'

Susan scooped up her Weet-bix, shoved it in her mouth, swallowed and smiled. 'See, I knocked the bastard off!'

'*Su*san!' Louise looked up as Rob came into the kitchen. 'Did you hear that?'

Laughing, Rob said, 'I wonder where she got that from?'

'Dad, probably,' Louise said, smiling herself now. 'He's been saying it ever since Hillary climbed Everest.'

Rob collected his lunch-box from the bench. 'Are we right?'

'Got to brush my teeth,' Susan said as she climbed down from her chair. 'Grandma says they'll fall out like hers if I don't brush them.'

'They will, too,' Rob said.

'An' then I'll have to go to the *murder house!*'

'Honestly, where does she get this stuff?' Louise asked when Susan had disappeared into the bathroom.

Rob shrugged. 'You know what kids are like.'

'I know what my father's like. I'll have to have a word.'

Louise's father, Neville Bourke, delighted in his small granddaughter. He took her for walks and to the park and down to the shops, and thought her three-year-old observations of other people and of life in general were hilarious. At the moment, he was teaching her the fine art of doing armpit farts.

'Don't worry about it, love. Susan thinks the sun shines out of him. And they have fun together. They're OK.'

'I suppose,' Louise said grudgingly. 'What time do you think you'll be home tonight?'

Although she caught the tram home after work because of Rob's often late hours at the garage, he always took her into town in the morning on his way in, the pair of them dropping Susan off at Louise's parents' on the way. Usually she was first home, and tonight she was planning to cook Rob's favourite meal because it was his birthday: mashed potatoes, peas and a nice piece of steak, with apple crumble and cream for pudding.

'Why?' he asked, his eyes twinkling. 'Will there be something tasty waiting for me?'

'There might be, if you're good.'

Rob grabbed her around the waist and pulled her to him. 'And will there be a nice tea as well?'

'Oh, get away!' Louise said, laughing and pushing him gently.

'That's mean, Mummy,' Susan said from the doorway.

'We're just playing, love,' Rob said, pinching Louise's bottom as she turned away from him.

She jumped, but kept a more-or-less straight face. 'Have you got everything? Your spare pants? Peter?'

Peter was Susan's precious toy rabbit, once white and sporting pale yellow overalls, but now naked and almost grey from excessive cuddling and washing, despite frequent applications of Reckitt's Blue in the rinse water.

Susan held up her pink plastic satchel.

'Good, let's go then,' Rob said, fishing in his pocket for the keys to his truck.

Louise locked the back door behind them and five

minutes later they arrived at her parents' house. The truck idling, Rob waited at the kerb while she took Susan inside.

Her little shoes making a racket on the lino, Susan pounded into the kitchen yelling, 'Grandma, Grandpa! I knocked the—'

'That'll do, sweetie,' Louise said as her mother appeared.

'An' I got a new Buzzy Bee at the Bundar & Jones picnic!' Susan opened her satchel and held up the toy. 'The wings go round and make a clackity noise, see?'

'Isn't that lovely,' Marion said admiringly. 'And it's got a string. You could pull it up and down the path outside, couldn't you?'

'No, it can go on the floor as well!' Susan insisted, putting the Buzzy Bee down and whizzing it around and around so that its wings clacked furiously.

'I take it she enjoyed the work do, then?' Marion said to Louise.

'Had a great time, especially when Santa turned up. And she won the under-fives' egg-and-spoon and got a little present for that as well.'

'Well, that was a good haul,' Marion observed, 'accidentally' standing on Buzzy Bee's string to shut it up. 'Will you be back at the usual time?'

'Gran, you're treading on Buzzy Bee!'

'Ooh, so I am! Tell you what, let's put him up on the table to keep him safe, shall we?'

'It's a girl bee.'

Louise said, 'I won't be late. It's Rob's birthday, remember.'

'All right, I'll see you then.' Marion gave her a peck on the cheek.

Louise bent down to Susan, who was sidling up to the table to retrieve her toy. 'Bye, sweetie,' she said. 'See you tonight, all right? Be good for Grandma.'

'Bye, Mummy.'

'Let's go out to the gate and wave goodbye to Mum and Dad, shall we?' Marion suggested.

Buzzy Bee temporarily forgotten, Susan nodded vigorously. Waving was one of her favourite things at the moment: she'd been practising and practising for when the queen came to visit all the little children.

As Louise and Rob drove off, Marion lifted Susan up and held her as she waved madly after the retreating truck.

'Bye, Daddy!' she yelled. 'Bye, Mummy!'

As Allie got off the bus then dodged through the traffic across to Dunbar & Jones, she wondered if Sonny was at work yet. She was very tempted to sneak around to the narrow lane at the back of the building to see if his motorbike was parked there, but decided against it. She would see him soon enough, she hoped.

'Good morning, Sunshine!' Ted Horrocks said, standing just inside the big glass doors and tipping his cap to her. 'Another marvellous summer's day and only four more left until we all get a nice bit of time off!'

'That'll be lovely, won't it?' Allie agreed. 'Going away?'

'Only up to Waipu, as usual,' Ted said. 'My brother lives up there and we're always welcome. Lovely spot. And yourself?'

'I don't know. I think I'll just wait and see what happens.'

'Probably a wise move. See what that young man of yours is up to, eh?'

Startled, Allie said, 'How do you know about that?'

Ted winked. 'You don't get to be commissionaire in a store this size without developing good observation skills. And I wish you all the best. Seems a nice lad, that Sonny.'

'He is,' Allie said, feeling a wide, silly smile spreading across her face. 'See you later!'

Ted tipped his cap again as she raced off towards the escalator, waving at the hosiery, scarves and cosmetics girls as she went. Alighting on the first floor she caught sight of Louise in lingerie, straightening the boxes of undergarments that lined the high shelves behind the counter. She waved but didn't stop, knowing it would make her late.

As always, Miss Willow was already at work in the dress department, putting out extra stock for the last, hectic week before Christmas. Rhonda was already in as well, following Miss Willow around, her arms piled high with skirts and blouses.

'Good morning, Allie,' Miss Willow said. 'Recovered from yesterday?'

'The three-legged race, you mean?' Allie pulled the hem of her dress up to her knees, revealing a small, red graze. 'I expect I'll live.'

'Well, at least we kept the trophy, so it wasn't in vain. Beatrice and I enjoyed ourselves.'

'Yes, it was fun, wasn't it?'

'Unfortunately, however, it's back to work today. I'd like you to help Rhonda to finish putting out this stock, please, then we'll have a look and see if we need to bring anything else out. I'm expecting us to be very busy this week, especially from Wednesday onwards while Her Majesty is in town, and I don't want to be running backwards and forwards replenishing shelves and racks.'

Allie tucked her handbag under the counter and got to work. At ten to nine, just before Ted opened the store's doors to the public, Sonny appeared at the top of the escalator, making Allie's heart leap when she caught sight of him.

'Hi, sweetheart,' he said.

Rhonda heard, tittered and went pink.

'Hi, Sonny,' Allie replied, delighted to see him but very aware that she was supposed to be working.

Sonny looked casually around, as though he had all day, then leaned on the counter.

'Busy tonight?'

Allie was very tempted to say no, but she was. 'I promised Mum I'd help her do the mince pies for Christmas.'

'Those ones with the fruit and all that?' Sonny said. 'I'm really good at those. D'you think she'd like some extra help?'

Allie looked at him sceptically.

'No, I am,' he insisted. 'I find that if you put in extra cinnamon, and brazil nuts as well as almonds, you can't miss.'

Allie could feel Miss Willow standing behind her, and she knew she was smiling.

'Don't forget about the suet,' Miss Willow said. 'If you don't get that right, you might as well not bother.'

'Too right,' Sonny agreed, nodding like a jack-in-the-box. 'Nothing worse than when the mince sticks to the roof of your mouth. It has to melt,' he added, drawing the word out and doing a theatrical little flourish with his hand.

Trying very hard not to laugh, Allie said, 'All right then, come around if you like. But I warn you, Mum's a bit precious about her mince pies. She might not take to you handing out advice like . . . like someone who makes better ones than she does. And anyway, where did you learn how to make Christmas mince?'

'From my mate Willie, the battery cook in South Korea. And if your mum tells me to stick his world-famous recipe . . . back in my pocket, I will.'

Allie did laugh then. 'Will you be at morning tea?'

'Nah. Me and Hori have to deliver a sideboard to Epsom at eleven, so we probably won't be back 'til lunch. But I'll see you then, eh?'

'That would be nice,' Allie said.

Sonny blew her a kiss, and it was her turn to go pink.

'I just think it was a really mean thing to do,' Daisy said, dunking her biscuit into her cup of tea and trying to keep her voice down so no one at the surrounding tables would hear. 'I mean, I know Irene's an awful flirt, but I never thought she'd, you know, go that far. Especially not with poor Martin right there!'

Louise and Daisy had spotted Vince Reynolds lurking in the bushes behind the toilets at the Domain, and when Irene had swanned past them as they'd come out they'd put two and two together. Louise thought it was utterly disgraceful.

'I don't understand her,' she said. 'Martin's a perfectly nice bloke. Well, he'd have to be, wouldn't he, to put up with her shenanigans? So why does she have to carry on like that? And particularly with someone as revolting as Vince bloody Reynolds! What's wrong with her? Lots of women would kill to have a lovely bloke like Martin.'

Allie could see that Louise was really upset, and knew it was because she actually liked Irene — when she wasn't behaving like a tart.

'Do you think it's because she's dissatisfied?' Daisy asked.

'Dissatisfied?' Louise snapped. 'How the hell could she be dissatisfied? She's got a good job with prospects, a freehold home, a car that doesn't leak when it rains. It's more than a lot of us have got.'

'Well, she likes to be the centre of attention, doesn't she, and maybe she isn't, with Martin. Maybe she needs more.'

Allie and Louise stared at Daisy, startled at the depth of her perception. It wasn't like her at all.

'Too bad,' Louise said bluntly. 'Nobody ever gets *everything* they want, do they? And she'll have even less if Martin ever finds out.'

After a long silence, Allie spoke up: 'He already knows.' And she told them about what he'd said at the picnic.

Daisy's eyes filled with tears. 'That's really sad. Poor Martin.'

'And she knows he knows?' Louise was appalled. 'God, what a bitch.'

'No, I don't think so,' Allie said. 'And I think he's too frightened to confront her about it in case she packs up and leaves him.'

Daisy sniffed loudly. 'He must really love her. That's so sad.'

'Oh, shut up, Daisy,' Louise said, though there was no malice in it. 'But you're right, it is sad.'

'But what can we do about it?' Allie hated to think that everyone might not be as in love with life as she now was. 'Shall we talk to her about it?'

'No,' Louise replied, lighting a cigarette. 'We won't. Because it's none of our business, it's for Irene and Martin to sort out. It's their marriage.'

Daisy looked up. 'Shssh, here she comes.'

Weaving her way through the cafeteria tables, Irene pulled up a seat, set her cup of tea and a cheese scone on the table, and sat down.

'What?' she said as she noticed the others looking at her. Except for Louise, who was pointedly staring in the opposite direction. 'Have I got something stuck in my teeth?'

'No,' Daisy said hurriedly. 'We were just, um, drinking our tea.'

'You're a hopeless liar, Daisy,' Irene said. The moment she'd sat down she'd felt something, a coldness, coming from the other girls. No, not a coldness, more an air of, well, mistrust. 'Right, what's going on?' she demanded.

This was the last thing she needed. She had letters to type piled up to the ceiling on her desk, Martin had hardly said anything at all to her last night, just moped around with that wounded look he got sometimes but insisting that nothing was wrong whenever she asked — and on top of all that she felt guilty about what she'd done yesterday. And because she felt guilty she'd started doubting herself, asking herself whether she did actually deserve to have or feel anything good, and when that happened, as always, she needed reassurance. She hoped Vince would be around at lunchtime.

'We saw you and Vince yesterday,' Daisy blurted.

The blood drained from Irene's face for a second, then rushed back, staining her cheeks pink.

'Daisy!' Allie exclaimed, appalled.

'I don't like there being secrets,' Daisy said, her voice wobbling. 'We're all supposed to be friends, aren't we? Secrets ruin everything.'

'I don't know what you're talking about,' Irene said, and

it sounded a particularly feeble denial even to her own ears.

Louise angrily ground out her cigarette in the ashtray. 'Oh, come off it, Irene, you do so. It's not on. Flirting's one thing, but having an affair's another. And if *we* all know, who else does? Martin's bound to find out. And you'll lose your job.'

Instantly on the defensive, Irene snapped back, 'He'll only find out if someone tells him. I suppose that's going to be you, is it?'

'No, it won't,' Louise said. 'But I'd be lying if I said it didn't bother me.'

'Well, I'm sorry if it *bothers* you, Miss High and Mighty, but it's actually none of your business. Or yours, or yours,' Irene added to Allie and Daisy, who leaned back in their chairs, shocked at the vehemence in her words.

The people at the next table turned around and Irene lowered her voice.

'Don't you *dare* judge me! You've got no idea what it's like going home to someone like Martin, sitting there watching him doing bloody paperwork night after night before he stumbles off to bed early, and then having to lie there listening to him snore his head off because he's out for the count! Have you? I bet you don't. It's *boring*, that's what it is.' After a second, she added, 'And it's lonely.'

She put her hands in her face, and just for a moment Allie thought she was going to cry. Instead, she took a deep breath, looked up and said, 'I know what you must think of me, and that's up to you. But if I can't make myself happy, who the hell will?'

And with that she stood up and walked off, leaving her tea and scone untouched.

Allie, Louise and Daisy looked at each other, but no one said anything.

Irene took the stairs to the ground floor and went outside onto Wyndham Street, where she lit a cigarette and dragged on it furiously until she felt her heart-rate begin to slow down. A middle-aged man going past looked her up and down and leered, so she gave him the filthiest look she could muster, feeling a certain level of satisfaction when his eyes widened in surprise and he sped up.

How the hell could she have explained to them what was happening? They wouldn't understand, not even Allie, who seemed to have the most open-minded and tolerant view of life, even if she was sometimes quite naïve. Louise was a good, decent girl, but she was so old-fashioned with her ideas of steadily putting money in the bank and saving for a house — a lot like Martin, really — and rushing home to cook Rob's meals and making sure that little girl of hers could read her Dick and bloody Janes even before she got to primary school. And she was really quite judgemental, Louise. But she was honest, and loyal, and it hurt Irene very much to know she had upset her. And Daisy, well, poor Daisy with her little blonde head crowded with wedding dress patterns and her belly full of Terry's baby. She was kind and generous but she was just too young, and Irene had been dismayed to see the wounded look in her eyes, her realization that she, Irene, appeared to be gambling away everything that Daisy yearned for.

She took one last drag on her cigarette and flicked the butt into the gutter.

Well, they didn't understand, and that was just that. But

it wouldn't stop her — she was going to spend her lunch break down in the basement with Vince if it was the last thing she did.

Upstairs, in his office on the first floor, Keith Beaumont sat at his desk, sweating freely and staring at the handwritten note in front of him.

> Keith,
> I have a matter I'd like to discuss with you in private. I wonder if you can spare a minute some time after lunch today — say, 2.30 PM? — and pop into my office.
> Thank you.
> Yours sincerely
> Max Jones

It had appeared on his blotter pad while he'd been in the toilet: since that bloody staff picnic yesterday his bowels had been giving him gyp, cramping and making him pass the most appalling gas. Now, his innards rumbling and banging like a set of unlagged old pipes, he felt an urgent need to empty them again.

It could be about anything, he thought. God, it could even be about getting that stupid sports trophy engraved, or something equally trivial.

But he didn't think so.

Chapter Thirteen

Jock McLean, stores manager and supervisor of Dunbar & Jones's basement, finished his fag. He'd missed smoko because he'd helped to load up the van for the Epsom delivery, but he was buggered if he was going without his mid-morning cigarette. All of the other lads were out at the moment, too, so he'd be on his tod for the next hour or so.

He went back inside through the Wyndham Street door, trying to keep in the background to minimize the possibility of customers seeing him in his old grey work coat with the red Dunbar & Jones logo on the pocket. He'd had his smoke in the service lane behind the store, but, because he was a conscientious sort of bloke, he'd locked the big set of sliding metal doors from the lane into the basement so no one could get in and pinch anything. Not that anyone'd get far with a bloody great roll of linoleum balanced on their shoulders, or a dining suite or a grandfather clock. Still, it was better to be safe than sorry.

He passed through the staff door at the rear of manchester, then trotted down the steps leading to the basement, wondering what his wife had put on his sandwiches today. She could be quite inventive sometimes, but he never looked before lunchtime because he quite liked the surprise of discovery. Last week it had been sliced left-over sausages with gravy one day, and then cheese and celery the next, but the week before it had been brisket and pickle four days in a row, because she'd been a bit short with the housekeeping. His absolute favourite was cold savoury mince, and judging from delicious aroma coming from his lunch-box, he suspected it might be that today. Fingers crossed.

When he reached the bottom of the steps he stepped into the basement and closed the door behind him. Then he stopped, all thoughts of savoury mince gone.

There was something wrong.

'Anyone down here?' he called, his voice echoing around the cavernous space and bouncing off the piles of goods stacked neatly in gloomy corners, against shadowed walls and in rows along the floor.

No one replied, but that odd, sharp smell was still there, tickling the hairs in his nostrils and reminding him of something he couldn't quite put his finger on.

He slowly walked further into the basement, noting that the big sliding doors were still closed, turning his head this way and that, trying to locate the source of the smell. It was almost . . . metallic, and a little bit acrid, and now he could hear a faint buzzing noise as well.

The sound led him over to the wall where the main switchboard was, and then he saw it: a cable drooping from the ceiling, not yet broken but with the rubber peeling away in several places and tiny sparks fizzing along it. He squinted and saw that most of the wires inside the cable had come apart, making it sag, and that it was now held

253

together by only two or three strands. It hadn't been like that before he'd gone for his smoke, he was sure of it!

Jock swore — if the cable broke, Dunbar & Jones would lose most of its electricity. Then he winced, thinking of the thousands of pounds that would be lost in sales if the store had to be closed. This week of all bloody weeks! There was an emergency generator for that very reason, but he knew for a fact that it wasn't particularly reliable. But if he could somehow shore up the cable, perhaps by wrapping some sort of tape around it, disaster might be averted at least until an electrician could be called in. But who knew how long that would take? He'd always said they needed one on site. He would have to be extremely careful, though, because there was a hell of a lot of current surging through the bloody thing, and he didn't fancy being fried. Perhaps it would be wiser just to ask Mr Beaumont for permission to ring the electrician.

Without taking his eyes off the cable, just in case it did something untoward, like break, Jock walked over to the telephone mounted on the wall and dialled Keith Beaumont's extension. The phone rang and rang, but no one picked it up. He hung up and tried again, but with the same result: the bugger must be away from his desk. Typical.

Perhaps he'd just have a closer look at the wires, to see if he couldn't do anything himself before he tried Beaumont again. Wishing that one of the lads were here with him, he set up a ladder near, but not directly under, the still-sparking cable. He climbed to the second-to-top rung and peered at the cable, wondering how much longer it would last before it broke altogether.

And that was when it did break. The lights flickered and

254

the live end of the cable swung down and hit Jock in the face, burning his cheek and causing him to fling up his hands to bat it away. One hand touched the bare wires and involuntarily closed around them, sending volt after volt of electricity coursing through him. His body spasmed as the electrical energy travelled along his blood vessels, nerves and bones, searing tissue as it went, and both hips were dislocated as he was hurled off the ladder. He hit the floor and rolled several yards, coming to a stop some feet from the lift doors. Although smoke wafted out of his clothes and from the melted ruin of his hand, he was still sufficiently conscious to register that the emergency generator had kicked in.

Unable to make any sound other than a low whimpering, he dragged himself over to the lift on his elbows and managed to reach up and hit the button that would summon it to the basement. Miraculously, it arrived almost immediately, and when the cage opened Jock collapsed halfway across the threshold, the last life wheezing out of him as his face hit the floor. A moment later his clothes burst into flames.

Behind him, the slowly swinging live cable continued to spit sparks, one of which was propelled far enough to land in a bucket filled with used cleaning rags. For a moment there was nothing, then a small 'whoomph' as the rags caught and flames shot up into the air. In less than a minute they had jumped gleefully from the bucket up to a shelf holding a tin of varnish, four of naphthalene, five bottles of furniture polish and Jock's spare packet of Desert Gold. When they had all been consumed, feeding the flames until they were twenty times their original size and rapidly becoming white hot in intensity, the conflagration moved onto a skip filled

255

with shredded paper for packing, then, hungrily, reached out for the huge rolls of linoleum and carpet.

Thirty feet away, the lift door began to close, then rattle open again, close, then rattle open again, jamming on Jock's incinerating body.

On the floors above, most people had noticed the lights flicker briefly, but nothing else. On the second floor, however, Walter the lift boy, who had left his post to dash off for a quick wee, stood outside the lift jabbing the 'up' button repeatedly, trying to get it back and wondering why it wasn't responding. Some idiot must be holding the door open downstairs.

On the ground floor, a sales assistant from manchester on her way up to the credit office via the staff stairs stopped in the stairwell and sniffed. Was that smoke? Had someone been having a sneaky fag in here? But it didn't really smell like tobacco smoke — it was stronger than that, and quite nasty.

Deciding that she should really tell someone, she turned back and quietly informed her supervisor of what she'd noticed. The supervisor, Mrs Wolfe, immediately telephoned Keith Beaumont, who was back at his desk by now, his bowels thoroughly emptied but his nerves still in tatters.

He snatched up his telephone and barked into it, but after a second went very still.

'In the ground-floor stairwell?' he repeated. When the voice on the other end confirmed it, he said, 'Well, stay at your post and I'll be down in a second. And don't tell anyone else, for God's sake, we don't want a stampede.'

He put down the phone and stared sightlessly at his

blotter, the hateful little note now safely in his pocket. What could smoke in the staff stairwell mean? Should he inform Max Jones? No — it was probably just a false alarm, some staff member having an illicit cigarette. He'd find out who it was, though, and they could well be looking at their final pay packet by the end of the day. Smoking in the stairwell was strictly forbidden.

He descended to the ground floor via the public stairs and strode into the manchester department. The supervisor was standing over by a display of Egyptian cotton sheeting, whispering into some other woman's ear: he hoped she wasn't spreading rumours.

'Mrs Wolfe!' he snapped. 'A word?'

Mrs Wolfe hurried over, her eyes darting nervously about and her face exhibiting definite signs of panic.

He deliberately kept his voice low. 'The smoke, exactly where did this girl notice it?' he asked. Adding hastily, 'If that's what it was, of course.'

'On the ground-floor landing, she said.'

'Well, I'll go and have a look myself. Go back to work. And *don't* say anything to anyone else, do you understand?'

Mrs Wolfe nodded and scuttled off.

Keith went through the staff door and onto the landing. The girl had been right, there was smoke in here, and quite a lot of it. He blinked, wondering if it was growing thicker even as he stood there, or whether that was only his imagination.

But he still didn't want to tell Max Jones. The longer he put off seeing him for any reason at all, the better. So he went back out into manchester, giving Mrs Wolfe a stern look as he passed her, and hurried through the store to the

257

main door, where he knew he would find Ted Horrocks, who knew everything there was to know about the three buildings that made up Dunbar & Jones.

Ted's normally ruddy face blanched when he told him. 'Smoke? In the stairwell?' he repeated — rather stupidly, Keith thought.

'I can't tell where it's coming from.'

'Basement, probably,' Ted said, and started walking quickly towards the manchester department, his back straight and his arms swinging as he marched off.

Keith had to trot to catch up. 'I don't think there's any reason to panic just yet, Ted,' he said, and was disconcerted to note that the commissionaire didn't even respond.

Ted went straight out the back to the stairwell. He stood for a moment, sniffing and apparently listening, then began to descend the steps one at a time, gripping the iron handrail firmly. Keith followed him all the way down to the bottom.

'It's down here, all right,' Ted said, eyeing the lazy grey wisps escaping from beneath the door leading into the basement. 'Come on, we need to get everyone out. How long did the fire brigade say they'd be?'

'Er, I haven't rung them yet,' Keith said.

'*What?*' Ted couldn't believe his ears. 'Well, get on the bloody phone and alert them, man!' He turned around and belted back up the stairs, heading for the fire extinguisher on the wall behind the lift shaft.

By the time he got back down to the basement landing, Beaumont had disappeared. But now, Ted could hear an ominous crackling coming from behind the door and his heart sank. If the fire was that big, one piddling fire extinguisher wasn't going to put it out.

On the first floor, Keith rapped on the door to Max Jones's office, but didn't wait to be invited in.

Max, sitting behind his desk, looked up, then after a moment carefully put the lid on his pen. 'Ah, Keith, you saw my note, I gather.' He glanced at his watch. 'You're a little early.'

'There's a fire in the basement,' Keith blurted. 'Ted Horrocks is down there with a fire extinguisher now.'

Max felt his heart lurch sickeningly. 'What? Has anyone called the fire brigade?'

'I thought I'd check with you first,' Keith said.

'Do it now,' Max ordered, and waited white-lipped while Keith made the call. Then he ran out into the foyer outside his office and, using his elbow to smash the glass, pushed the button to activate the fire alarm.

Nothing happened.

Downstairs, Ted kicked open the basement door and was almost knocked flat by a pulsing wall of heat and flame. He dropped the fire extinguisher and scrabbled back up the stairs, smelling his hair ignite and feeling the skin on his cheeks and forehead begin to tighten.

At the top of the stairs, he staggered through into the manchester department, slammed the door behind him and said to the nearest girl, 'There's a fire. Tell everyone to get out now,' then fell flat on his face.

George Lynch, senior salesman in men's shoes, ran across and bent over him. 'Ted? Ted! What's going on?'

'Fire,' Ted gasped. 'Get everyone out.'

And so it began, the evacuation of the ground floor, packed with Christmas shoppers and their children and around fifty of Dunbar & Jones's staff. Word spread instantly and, though there hadn't been a proper fire drill since the war, the heads of departments began to herd their customers and staff quietly out of the building and onto Queen and Wyndham Streets, speaking in measured, if strained, voices, urging people to go carefully, not to run, to leave any large parcels or bags behind, to keep hold of small children and, above all, not to panic, all the while fighting the urge to scream in terror themselves and sprint for the nearest exit. Several women did scream when Ted was carried past them on a litter made from sheets from the manchester department, his eyes already swollen closed and his face an alarming, shiny crimson colour.

On the first floor, Max and Keith approached each customer individually and explained that there appeared to be a slight problem with a small amount of smoke in the basement and, though there was absolutely no need to panic, could they please make their way as quickly as possible to the nearest ground-floor exit. To his staff, Max simply said, 'Get out. Now.'

Ruby Willow heard him, but instead of heading for the public staircase, she quietly slipped through the staff door in the rear of the dress department and up the staff stairs.

When they were satisfied that the first floor had been completely cleared, Max and Keith ascended the public stairs, checking as they went, until they reached the second floor, where, as they had suspected, there were only a handful of customers. Floorings, soft furnishings and furniture were not popular items at Christmas time, and the floor was cleared very quickly.

'We've got to warn the people in the cafeteria,' Max urged. 'And the workrooms.'

His heart was thudding in his chest and he was starting to feel dizzy, as though he might faint at any moment. He was terrified — of the fire itself, of his business being ruined beyond redemption and, most of all, of the possible deaths of his staff, the ghosts of whom, he knew, would haunt him for the rest of his days.

Keith, also terrified and aware that there suddenly seemed to be smoke seeping into every part of the store, decided it was time he got out himself, and told Max he was going back downstairs to recheck the first floor.

Then the lights went out.

Peg, who was on the late lunch shift, said 'Bugger, that's all we need', and walked over to the window. It faced east and from her vantage point she could see down to the busy wharves and right out across the harbour, but only a portion of the lower end of Queen Street.

'There's a whole lot of people on the street,' she remarked.

'It's the week before Christmas,' Nyla snapped, annoyed that the power had gone out because she needed to use the steam press.

'No, I mean they're all over the road. And the traffic's stopped.'

Nyla came over and joined her. 'Look, there's a fire engine. And another one. There must be a fire somewhere.'

'I thought I heard sirens,' Daisy said.

Beatrice Button looked up from the hat she was working on. 'Are they stopping?'

Nyla stood on tiptoe. 'I can't see, they've gone out of sight. But I can't hear the sirens any more.'

Very calmly, Beatrice said, 'Girls, just to be on the safe side, I think we should go and find out what's happening.'

Daisy, Nyla and Peg stared at her.

'Do you think the fire's here, at Dunbar & Jones?' Peg asked nervously.

'Of course not,' Beatrice replied. 'But if there is a fire, and it's in a building close to us, it might be a good idea to go outside.'

She set her work aside and stood up. 'Now, grab your things, but only if they're handy, and we'll go and see, shall we?'

Mopping his sweating face with his handkerchief, Keith trotted down the public stairs to the first-floor landing, then continued on down towards the ground floor. The temperature seemed to be increasing with every step he took, and the smoke was certainly much denser down here now, stinging his eyes and catching in his throat and making him cough.

When he reached the bottom of the stairs, he grasped the handle of the door closing off the stairwell, then screamed and whipped his hand back; the handle was red hot. Flapping his arm wildly, he pulled his jacket sleeve down over his other hand and snatched the door open, and was immediately sent reeling by a blast of air as hot as a furnace. Flames exploded into the stairwell, and Keith only just managed to kick the door shut again. He staggered dazedly back up the stairs, burnt hand forgotten, then slumped against the wall on the first-floor landing to regain his breath. Through the window, he could see on Wyndham Street below, and on Queen Street to his left, that four fire engines had arrived, and that the police were halting traffic on both streets and erecting barricades. He was horrified. Had it been only twenty minutes since he'd gone down to the basement and seen just a few wisps of smoke down there? What had happened? How had the fire escalated so quickly?

He tried the window, but it had been painted shut and wouldn't budge. If he could smash it, though, he could get out that way and crawl across the roof of the verandah and then jump off — it would be a drop of only about ten feet at the most. He started coughing again, and realized that the smoke was getting denser by the second.

And then it hit him, with far more force than his terror of being caught in the fire. His beautiful money, his precious emergency box, was locked in the White Room kitchen!

He spun away from the window then, and almost banged into Max Jones.

'Keith, what are you doing?'

'Just having a last look—'

'No, come on, man, it's not safe. Get upstairs! Now!'

Max grabbed Keith's sleeve and started pulling him up the stairs. He fell over on the landing and barked his shin atrociously, but Max kept on yanking and pulling him, not letting him go and making sure he kept going up.

'It's the most ghastly shock, I know,' Max said between great gasps for air, 'but we're management, Keith.' He took a firmer grip on Keith's jacket. 'They're relying on us, we can't let them down.'

But Keith, fumbling in his pocket to make sure he hadn't lost his keys, wasn't listening.

Irene hurried down the public stairs. She was late meeting Vince, but this time she really didn't want to be: she was that desperate to see him, to feel his arms around her and be comforted. And she was worried. She had stopped off at furnishings to make sure he was still coming but hadn't been able to find him. Or anyone, actually. But perhaps he was already down there, or maybe it was something to do with the power going out. In the back of her mind she had heard sirens outside but the sound had hardly registered.

Then, suddenly, Mr Beaumont and Mr Max were staggering towards her up the stairs like a pair of drunks, Mr Max calling out something she didn't quite catch. They both looked very peculiar, dishevelled and, well, rather grubby. And why could she smell smoke?

Mr Max barked, 'Go back upstairs, there's a fire.'

'What?'

'In the basement, and it's spreading. Get back upstairs.'

Irene gasped. But what if Vince was already down there, waiting for her?

'I'm going down,' she said.

Max grabbed her arm. 'You can't get out, not this way. The fire's reached the ground floor and the bottom of the public stairwell is blocked off.'

Irene's eyes widened. 'Oh Jesus, it's serious, isn't it?'

Wishing she would just shut up and get moving, Keith snapped, 'Go on, go back up!'

'But what about everyone on the ground floor?' Irene exclaimed, the magnitude of the situation finally sinking in. 'And the first floor? And how will we get out if we go back up?'

'The ground, first and second floors have been cleared. The fire brigade are here, they'll get us out,' Max said.

He started to lead Irene back up the stairs, but she wrenched her arm out of his grasp.

'But there's dozens and dozens of people still up there! It's lunchtime, they're in the caf! And what about the workrooms? How will we all get out?'

She lunged over to the window and looked out over Wyndham Street. The footpath opposite was empty except for firemen, but when she pressed her face against the glass and looked to the left she could see the crowds of people behind the barricade across Queen Street.

Max pulled her gently away. He knew she was a staff member because he'd seen her in the typing pool, but he couldn't remember her name. 'Come on, Miss, let's go up and see what we can do, shall we?'

Numbly, Irene turned to him and nodded, then let him lead her back up the stairs.

At the top they crossed the floorings department and headed for the staff stairs beyond the showroom, the only access from that point on to the floor above. Reluctantly, Keith followed Max and Irene into the staff stairwell, consoling himself with the thought that there still might be time. There had to be.

Halfway up the stairs, Irene stopped and said, 'Did you hear that?'

'What?' Keith said impatiently.

'That banging. I heard something banging.'

'Where?' Max asked.

'On the landing, I think.'

Max clapped his hand to his sweating forehead. 'Oh God, I didn't check the lavatory.'

He dashed back down the stairs and hammered on the door to the second-floor landing toilet. It was ancient and dank and smelly and hardly anyone used it, preferring instead to take the extra few minutes to whip up to the more wholesome staff toilets upstairs.

The response was immediate — someone inside yelled that they were locked in and to let them out.

Max unlocked the door and Terry came staggering out. 'Smoke!' he exclaimed. 'I can smell smoke!'

'There's a fire in the basement,' Max said, and propelled him towards the stairs.

Terry blinked like someone who has been rudely awakened by the bedroom curtains being whipped open on a bright, sunny morning. 'I was in the dunny,' he said to Irene, 'and then the lights went out and I couldn't get the bloody door open.'

'Come on,' she said. 'Daisy's probably upstairs.'

And then regretted it, because if Daisy *was* upstairs, that meant she wasn't outside, down on the street, safe.

By twelve-thirty-five the ground floor was a roiling chaos of smoke and flames. The fire had burnt up from the basement through the wooden floor and was relentlessly consuming everything in its way: the manchester and fine linen especially imported from overseas, the smart suits and hats in menswear, rows of handmade Italian leather shoes, hundreds of uniforms for Auckland's poshest schools, silk scarves and stockings in the haberdashery department. At the cosmetics bar, pots of expensive face creams and lotions heated up and burst, and lipsticks liquefied instantly. Tea services, coffee pots, trays and cake stands in the silverware department tarnished, warped and then melted, and china plates and vases, and the glass shelves displaying them, exploded.

Then, with a series of bangs so loud that war veterans watching in the street involuntarily dived for cover, the huge plate-glass windows along both street frontages blew out, showering the footpaths and several firemen and constables outside with glass. A great groan went up from the crowd, and everyone rapidly moved back a few feet.

Inside the building, the fresh supply of air sucked in through the holes in the display windows fuelled the fire anew, sending the flames reaching even higher until they grazed, then began to feed on, the ceiling above. Within seconds, the ceiling started to disintegrate, drawing more air up into the first floor. In the basement, the walls of the lift car finally burned completely away, as had poor Jock McLean, causing the smoke and fumes from the heart of the fire to be rapidly drawn up the shaft and spew out onto every floor except for the third, which the lift didn't reach. The escalator well was also acting as a flue, allowing even more smoke and ash to dance through the first and second floors.

Until now the staff stairs had been relatively free of smoke, as someone had had the foresight to close the doors opening onto them from the shop floors. But as soon as the fire, fed by the new influx of air, burned through the basement door at the bottom of the stairs, the smoke began to billow upwards, filling and gradually poisoning the stairwell.

Allie almost choked on her egg sandwich as someone came running into the caf, slid over on the lino, then struggled to their feet and screamed, 'Fire! There's a fire — get out!'

She glanced at Louise, who was frowning.

There was a moment of almost complete silence, then everyone started talking at once and a couple of people started moving towards the door. Allie and Louise watched them for a moment, then got up and headed for the door themselves. Suddenly there were people running, and someone started to scream. Something banged into Allie and she almost fell over, but Louise grabbed her arm and hauled her to her feet again. Then came the sound of breaking glass: heads turned, attentions caught for a moment by a man standing on the cafeteria counter, waving his arms.

'Slow down!' he shouted over the noise. 'Everyone slow down! Walk, don't run! Slow down!'

The stampede receded to a mad rush, and Allie found that she had a fraction more space in which to move.

'Where is it?' someone next to her said in a panicked voice. 'Where's the fire?'

They were propelled out of the caf and into the hallway that led along to the third-floor offices, which, though wide, was a tight squeeze for the ninety or so panic-stricken people jammed into it. And that was when Allie saw Daisy, pressed back against a wall clutching her handbag to her stomach and looking utterly terrified. Miss Button was behind her, and so were Peg and Nyla.

Allie waved out. Daisy saw her and screamed, '*I can't find Terry!*'

Louise and Allie pushed and shoved through the jostling river of people until they reached her.

'There's a fire,' Daisy warbled, tears streaking her cheeks. 'I can't find Terry!'

Miss Button said breathlessly, 'We were just heading downstairs.'

Louise, her face so pale that her freckles stood out in sharp relief, nodded and hooked her arm through Daisy's. 'So are we. Come on, let's see if we can find him on the way, eh?'

They merged back into the crowd, allowing themselves to be carried along towards the staff stairs that would take them down to the second floor. Some people were crying now, and whoever had started screaming was still doing it. Or perhaps it was someone else now.

Beatrice tugged on Allie's sleeve. 'Have you seen Ruby? Miss Willow, I mean?' And then her round face lit up as she spotted Ruby at the other end of the hallway, waving madly.

Someone yelled for everyone to be quiet for a minute; Allie couldn't see who it was but it sounded like the man on the cafeteria counter. When he climbed up onto a chair, she saw that it was. She thought his name might be Norm O'Brien. Or was it O'Reilly? Anyway, she wasn't sure, but she knew he worked in appliances on the second floor.

'We're going to go down the staff stairs,' he announced as the noise died down.

'Who made you the boss?' someone called. Allie turned around; it was Vincent Reynolds.

'Look, you can get up here on this chair if you like,' Norm said. 'What's *your* plan for getting us out of here?'

There was no response.

Norm went on. 'If the power's off, the lift won't be working and neither will the escalator. And if the fire's taken hold, there could be smoke in the public stairwell.'

'Won't that mean there'll be smoke in the staff stairwell, too?' someone asked.

'With a bit of luck someone will have closed all the doors opening onto it, so maybe the smoke won't have got in yet.' He paused. 'And if it has, then we might just have to go down as far as we can, then climb out the windows.'

There was a rash of muttering, but Norm stopped it by raising his hand. 'Look, it sounds drastic, I know, but what's the alternative?' he asked. 'Wait here and hope someone comes to rescue us? Don't know about you, but I'd rather have a go at getting out before it's too late.'

Someone pushed his way over to Norm's chair, a tall man wearing a suit, then turned to face the crowd.

'Who's he?' Allie muttered to Louise. She'd seen him around, but hadn't had any dealings with him.

Beatrice heard her. 'That's Colin Crowley, the head accountant.'

Mr Crowley cleared his throat, as though preparing to announce that year's dividends to a meeting of Dunbar & Jones's shareholders. 'I say we stay where we are. The fire brigade is down below, they have ladders and rescue equipment, and they're experienced professionals who know exactly what to do. However, Mr O'Brien has just suggested that we all go trotting down those stairs, quite possibly through a wall of toxic smoke and fumes, then hurl ourselves out of windows if necessary. It doesn't add up. It's not a risk I'm willing to take, and I don't think anyone else should, either.'

'Typical accountant,' Louise whispered.

There was another round of muttering, punctuated by the occasional sob, then some people started moving towards the door to the stairwell, while others stayed where they were, clearly not sure whose advice to listen to. After a few minutes, by far the largest group stood clustered around the stairwell, Norm O'Brien at the front doing his best to keep everyone calm before they went down.

The exercise started off in an orderly manner, but then a bottleneck developed at the top of the stairs, and people began shoving.

'Hey, cut it oot!' someone shouted, and Allie saw that it was the big Scottish woman who ran the staff cafeteria. She had arms like hams and hands bigger than most men's, and she'd raised one of them now, threatening a girl who was trying to wriggle her way to the front of the queue. 'Ah'll boot yis erse if ye cannae wait ye turn! Yis ent the only bugger wantin' tae get oota here! Jist settle doon, ken?'

Fighting an irrational but hysterical urge to laugh, Allie said to Louise, 'What did she say?'

The Scottish woman waded in and started hauling people back, eliciting exclamations of outrage and some muffled swearing, but the bottleneck unjammed itself and people began to descend the stairs in tandem, which was all the narrow, unlit stairwell would allow.

When it came to their turn Louise tightened her grip on Daisy, Allie took hold of Beatrice's hand, Peg and Nyla linked arms and Ruby brought up the rear. They were about halfway down the flight when someone near the top fell, setting off a chain reaction below them as people went down like lines of dominoes. Allie was shoved into the wall and hit her face hard enough to make her lip bleed; Beatrice was knocked to her knees.

Struggling to turn around against the seething mass of

people trying to right themselves, Allie held out her hand. 'Are you all right?'

Beatrice, her bun knocked skewwhiff and her spectacles hanging off one ear, nodded. 'I've ruined a perfectly good pair of stockings, though.'

Allie helped her up, then looked around for the others, relieved to see them only a few steps further down. The stairwell had always ponged to some extent, of age and worn wood, but now it stank of smoke, and of sweat and fear.

They started shuffling forward again, feeling the floor with their feet so as not to fall down the next step. Then the procession bumped to a halt again.

'What's happening?' someone further up shouted.

A disembodied voice from the front called back, 'There's someone coming up.'

They waited for what seemed like an age. Then the voice ordered, 'Turn around, go back up.'

'Why?' Beatrice demanded.

'We can't get out this way. Turn around.'

Someone burst into tears.

They all turned and shuffled back up to the landing, then out into the hallway again.

The last group to leave the stairwell were coughing and spluttering and rubbing streaming eyes with filthy hands.

'*Terry!*' Daisy shrieked and, shoving people out of her way, threw her arms around him.

He hugged her back, his face buried in her hair. He was sweating heavily and his face was scarlet from coughing. 'Thank God,' he kept saying as he rocked Daisy. 'Thank God, thank God.'

'I thought you were caught in the fire,' she sobbed.

'I was stuck in the second-floor lav. Mr Max let me out.'

Allie, delighted for Daisy, prayed that Sonny was still out doing his delivery. If he had been in the basement when the fire had started . . . But he would have escaped, she was sure of it.

Then she noticed the others who had come up the stairs: Mr Max, whose shirt tails were hanging out, and an equally scruffy Mr Beaumont, who was bending over with his hands on knees. He couldn't stop coughing and there were long strings of saliva swinging out of his mouth. Allie looked away. Then she saw Irene. Her hair was all over the place, she'd lost a shoe and her face was dirty, and Allie had never been so pleased to see her.

Allie waved out and Irene came over. They hugged, then Irene stepped back.

'Have you seen Vince?'

'He's here somewhere. I saw him before,' Allie replied.

Irene spotted him and called out, but he didn't seem to hear her.

'I'm so glad you're safe,' Allie said.

'I'm not yet,' Irene answered, her voice low. 'None of us are. We can't get out the way we just came up.'

Allie's heart sank. 'Why not?'

'There's too much smoke. I was going down the public stairs when Mr Max and Mr Beaumont told me I couldn't go that way because it was blocked by the fire. So we went to the staff stairs on the second floor and there was smoke coming up them from the floors below. Mr Beaumont had a coughing fit and we had to cover our faces so we could breathe better. We were only in there for a few minutes and the smoke just got worse and worse. We nearly passed out, all of us.' Irene's voice started to waver. 'Mr Beaumont said the fire's actually burning out of control on the ground floor. He burned his hand.'

Allie put her arm around her, feeling the slim shoulders twitching and shaking.

'We'll get out, Irene, don't worry.'

Irene stared back at her. Her lipstick had disappeared and there was a shadowy smudge of mascara under each eye. 'Will we, Allie? Will we really?'

Allie didn't answer. She was too frightened to speak.

Chapter Fourteen

Sonny looked at his watch and swore. He'd miss Allie completely at this rate: her lunch break would be over by the time he got back.

The sideboard had taken ages to deliver because the old bint who'd bought it couldn't decide where she wanted it. First it was 'Against this wall, thanks, boys.' Then it was 'No, I think it might look better over here', followed by 'No, perhaps it was better where you first had it.' And it had weighed a bloody ton, not the sort of thing you could easily heft between the two of you and trot all over the house with.

He glanced at Hori. 'How long till we get back, d'you reckon?'

'Dunno. Twenty minutes? Fifteen, if we're lucky.'

'Put your foot down, eh?'

'You in a hurry?'

'Yeah.'

Hori gave Sonny a sly look. 'To see that sheila of yours?'

'Maybe.'

'Maybe definitely,' Hori said, smirking. 'She's nice, though, eh, that Allie.'

Sonny nodded. They drove on in silence for a while, through Newmarket to Khyber Pass Road, then on to Symonds Street. At the intersection with Karangahape Road, Sonny pointed through the windscreen. 'What's that? Can you see that?'

'What?'

'Smoke, over there on the right. Where's it coming from?'

Hori squinted. 'Dunno. Queen Street?'

As he watched the huge, roiling black clouds rising above the tall city buildings, a feeling of dread settled in the pit of Sonny's stomach and his hand tightened on the door handle.

They turned off Karangahape Road and into Queen Street, and Hori narrowly missed driving into the back of the car in front of him. Below them, stretching down Queen Street, was a long line of vehicles, all stationary. At the front of the traffic jam, dark smoke was pouring out of the first-floor windows of a building on the left-hand side of the street.

Sonny immediately knew which building it was. 'Jesus Christ, that's Dunbar & Jones,' he said, and flung open the van door. 'Come on!'

Hori shouted 'What about the van!' after Sonny's retreating figure, then shrugged, reversed a few feet, moved the van closer to the footpath, and ran after him.

They dodged through the crowd clogging the footpath and the street, elbowing people out of the way to get past. When Sonny spotted a cluster of Dunbar & Jones staff members huddled behind the barrier the police had erected, he barged over and demanded, 'Has anyone seen Allie Roberts, the blonde girl from the dress department?'

Mrs Wolfe, who knew Allie, said in a wavering voice, 'I don't think she's out yet. I haven't seen her.'

Ice settling on his heart, Sonny said, 'Is this everyone who's out?'

Mrs Wolfe nodded. 'The ground floor's been cleared. We were told to stand here, so everyone who comes out can be counted. That way they'll know . . .' She trailed off.

'Are the firemen in yet? What about the top floor?'

Starting to cry now, Mrs Wolfe blurted, 'They can't go in, the fire's in the stairwells.'

'*What about the top floor?*'

'I don't *know!*' Mrs Wolfe wailed. 'I think they're still in there!'

Sonny turned to watch the dozens of firemen, now furiously playing high-pressure hoses onto the first-floor windows facing both Queen and Wyndham Streets. Several teams were attempting to raise extension ladders against the building's façade, but the verandah over the footpath was proving an obstacle: even from the very top of the ladders, the windows would still be out of reach. Another three fire engines arrived, nosing their way through the traffic and into the cleared section of street in front of the building.

Sonny eyed the police barrier across Wyndham Street, behind which a crowd was also gathering, and decided he'd have a better chance where he was. He ducked under the barrier and, dodging around fire trucks and leaping over hoses, sprinted straight for Dunbar & Jones's front door.

'Hey, you!' a policeman yelled. '*Stop!*'

Sonny ignored him and sped up. He'd almost reached the door when he was tackled by a pair of constables, who wrestled him to the ground. Avoiding his kicks and punches as best they could, they dragged him back behind the barrier.

But they weren't unsympathetic. 'Sorry, lad,' the older of the two said as they bundled him into a police car, 'but you can't go in there. It's too dangerous.'

'My girl's in there,' Sonny protested, blood trickling from his nose from where he'd hit the footpath. 'I've got to get her out!'

'I know, lad, I'm sorry. The fire brigade is doing the best they can. Now, are you going to sit here quietly or do I have to handcuff you to the car door?"

Sonny didn't reply.

Ruefully, the policeman reached into his jacket.

In Coates Avenue, Sid was looking for his painting overalls in the washhouse and wondering if they were on the line, when he heard someone come pounding down the path at the side of the house. A second later Bill stuck his head around the door, looking very perturbed.

'Have you heard? Dunbar & Jones is on fire. It's on the radio. Your Allie works there, doesn't she?'

Sid straightened up. 'Ah God, oh no,' he said, and closed his eyes.

Bill grabbed his sleeve. 'Hurry up, we'll go over in the van.'

Then Sid was in the passenger seat and Bill was tearing towards the city, hitting his horn and swerving around anyone in his way.

Several miles away behind the counter in the Mission Bay

Tea Shoppe, Colleen was making a pot of tea and only half listening to what her customer was saying. Then, suddenly, she registered.

'A fire? At Dunbar & Jones?'

'Yes! A big one!' the old lady said, lifting her handkerchief and pressing it against her wrinkled mouth in distress. 'They're saying there's people trapped inside. Isn't it terrible?'

Colleen dropped the teapot, not even noticing when the hot water scalded her legs. Ducking from behind the counter she ran to the bus-stop just outside the shop, crying out in fear and frustration when she saw that a bus wasn't due for another thirty minutes. She sank to her knees, covered her face with her hands and burst into tears.

In Remuera Road, Estelle Jones sat in her large, beautifully decorated living room and stared unseeingly at the vase of cream roses she'd just finished arranging, wondering if she would see her husband again and wishing she'd said goodbye properly to him this morning. She'd not even bothered to look up from the book she was reading, only offered him a silent cheek to kiss as he left.

In Avondale, Marion and Neville Bourke stared at each other in horror across the kitchen table, then Marion started to weep and had to tell Susan it was because she'd just peeled a big, fat onion.

Agnes Farr stood absolutely still in the middle of her sitting

279

room, her hands over her mouth and her eyes squeezed shut, thinking of all the things she'd never said to her precious younger daughter.

Rob Taylor dropped his spanner, leapt into his truck and screeched out onto Parnell Road, leaving a wake of exhaust fumes behind him. Leaning on the horn the whole way, he raced down into Beach Road, then into Customs Street, only to discover that he couldn't drive any further. Swearing loudly, and terrified at the thought that his lovely Louise might be somewhere inside that huge dark cloud rising above Queen Street, he abandoned his truck and started running. But the footpath was also jammed, and it took him almost ten minutes to make his way to the front of the crowd. And when he had, when he gazed up into the streams of black smoke and hot, orange flames pouring out of the first-floor windows of Dunbar & Jones, his heart almost stopped.

In Kitemoana Street, Awhi Manaia marched out of her kitchen and roundly kicked a bucket someone had left on the back steps. It sailed down the raggedy back lawn, followed by her slipper, and hit the ground in a series of tinny clanks. She stomped down after it, retrieved her slipper, then retreated to the back steps and sat down, willing herself not to weep. Sonny was her special child, the Manaia she had always believed would hold the family together, after she and her brothers and sisters had died. It was part of the reason that her husband had been so hard on the boy. Pera hadn't wanted him to grow soft in any way, to allow him to sit on his backside and do nothing about what was happening to Ngati Whatua but whine, as some of the others had started to do. Though in some ways she couldn't blame them — it had been, and would continue to be, a long and bitter struggle — but doing nothing but whine was tantamount to giving up.

Pera had had a vision for Sonny, and the boy had begun to fulfil it of his own free will when he'd signed up to go with the artillery to South Korea. Pera had been so proud that day. He'd been a war hero himself, with the Maori Battalion. But when he'd come home, wanting to use his mana to lead his people, he'd discovered that things had changed while he'd been away. The government had been steadily eating away at the land and at the souls of Maori, and he was still treated by the Pakeha with the same disdain and disrespect he'd experienced before he'd gone away. It had torn at his heart and embittered him terribly, and he had retreated into a dark place of alcohol and violence.

And as he had sunk further into the mire, he'd become increasingly convinced that Sonny would be the salvation of Ngati Whatua, though he had never once, to Awhi's knowledge, told his son that. Instead he had only stepped up his drinking and started beating the boy, and his brothers and sisters — and, yes, even Awhi herself. Pera's brothers had tried to intervene several times, but that had only earned them a beating too. Sonny had been sixteen when his father had first hit him, and very near to becoming a man, but he'd kept his fists to himself and taken it. Later, though, Sonny had told Awhi that if his father did it again, there would come a time when he would fight back — and he would not pull his punches.

And of course it had happened again, many times, until

one night just before Christmas 1949 when Awhi had sent Sonny down to the pub to make sure his father got home in one piece, because she knew he would be blind drunk. When Sonny had discovered his father slobbering over some slut in an alleyway behind the hotel, he had dragged him off and beaten him so badly that Pera had been unable to get out of bed for four days. Neither he nor Sonny had told the rest of the family, but Awhi had seen the grazes on Sonny's knuckles and the blood on his shirt, and had known in her heart what had happened. Then, a few months later, Sonny had come to her about it, and Awhi had seen how much it had hurt him to tell her the truth.

Yet Pera had still been delighted when Sonny had signed up the following year, insisting to Awhi that the boy had the makings of a fine warrior and leader, refusing to accept that Sonny despised him by then and was probably only enlisting to get away from him. Or perhaps even to atone for the beating he had administered to his father. Awhi knew it hadn't sat well with Sonny, that he was ashamed of hitting a man so drunk he could barely stand, and of allowing himself to lose control.

But Awhi had not been delighted when Sonny had joined up. It had been bad enough when Pera had gone, but he had been older, and a much harder man than Sonny would ever be: she had known that if anyone would come home from the battlefields of the Mediterranean and Europe, it would be Pera. She just hadn't realized how changed her husband would be when he did return. But Sonny was different. He was special. A leader, yes, but a gentle one, who would lead with common sense (which most of her other children seemed not to have been blessed with) and empathy and wisdom and a quiet strength, not the sort that relied on violence and bullying. And now he was probably trapped in a burning building and she might never see him again.

She stared angrily at her slippers for a moment, then covered her face with her apron and started to keen.

Natalie Horrocks pushed herself creakily out of her chair, turned the radio off and went into the kitchen to gather together the ingredients for a sultana cake. Ted would be wanting a slice when he got home.

Martin Baxter already knew what had happened, because he was standing in the crowd outside Dunbar & Jones, staring up at the conflagration with tears streaming down his face.

Max had to raise his voice almost to a shout to make himself heard.

'The fire escape! Has anyone tried the fire escape?'

'We thought we'd be able to get down the stairs,' Norm said defensively.

There was a brief lull, then a handful of people started to move away from the stairwell. And then they were running, down the narrow corridor that led to the tailoring and soft furnishings workrooms on the north-west side of the top floor.

'Where *is* the fire escape?' Allie asked.

'You get to it through the tailoring workroom,' Terry said. 'Come on.'

By the time they got there, a crowd had gathered around

the long sash window that also served as an exit to the fire escape.

Max struggled with the window latch, fearing for a long, horrible second that it wasn't going to open. He bent down, hooked his fingers into the handles and wrenched up the window, letting in a rush of smoke-tainted air and a flurry of ash.

Leaning out, he saw that smoke was pouring out of the ground and first-floor windows all along the length of the service lane. And then he caught sight of something so dreadful that he moaned aloud in despair: an entire section of the fire escape had been removed between the third and first floors, creating a gap of about twelve feet, a gap that would be impossible to negotiate.

Slowly, he pulled his head back in and turned around, unable to meet anyone's eyes. Then he took a deep breath, and straightened his shoulders.

'The maintenance programme . . .' he began. 'The contractors have started on the fire escape. I'm so sorry . . .'

Stunned faces stared back at him.

'What?' someone said disbelievingly.

'The fire escape . . . it's out of order,' Max said. 'We can't use it.'

Standing at the rear of the group, Keith began to slowly step backwards. No one was watching him: they were all looking at Max Jones. When he reached the door, he slipped out into the corridor and hurried back to the head of the staff stairs.

They were all in the cafeteria now, many standing at the windows looking down at Queen Street, where the people and the fire engines looked tiny.

'Do they know we're still up here?' someone asked.

'Someone would have taken note of everyone who's already got out, surely?' There was a hint of panic in the question.

'But what if they haven't?' asked a girl from women's shoes, sounding very close to tears.

'They will. Ted Horrocks will have seen to that.'

'Well, I'm going to wave something to make sure they *do* know,' the girl said, hysteria creeping into her voice now. Her eyes were very bright and there were two spots of red high on her cheeks.

She darted behind the cafeteria counter, opened a few cupboards and came back with a red-and-white-checked tablecloth. Gripping one corner of it, she opened the window and flapped the cloth madly. Below, a sea of small white faces turned up towards her, then the waving started.

'They've seen us!' she said excitedly.

'Yes, and now what?' Irene muttered. She had tried to talk to Vince a moment ago but he'd ignored her again, leaving her hurt and uncomprehending.

The girl hung precariously out of the window for a moment, then turned back to face everyone in the caf.

'It's really not that far down, you know,' she said. 'There's a ledge just under the window, quite a wide one, and a sort of a ridge above the window straight under that. If we could get onto that ledge, we could keep going and climb all the way down! And the verandah's there as well, we could drop onto that.' She seemed to think that this was an absolutely marvellous idea. 'I'm going to have a go.'

'No,' Max said, walking towards her.

'Go away! You're not the boss any more!' the girl shouted, starting to cry. 'I'm not going to sit here and just wait! I'm *not!*'

'Christ, what the hell is she doing?' Irene said, alarmed.

The girl had pushed the window all the way open, and was now kneeling on the ledge, facing inwards, her bum sticking out into the air. Taking a good grip on the sill, she pushed herself out and let herself drop until all that could be seen of her were her white knuckles. Max lunged but then even the knuckles disappeared, and several people gasped in shock and fright.

Reluctantly, Max peered out of the window.

'God, she's on the ledge!'

A handful of people rushed to the other windows to see, but nearly everyone else stayed where they were, not wanting to watch what they believed would be inevitable.

Max exclaimed, 'She's letting herself down onto the top of the next window. She's nearly got it!'

Then the onlookers at the window screamed and reeled back in horror. Max stood there for a while, still looking down, then eventually turned away.

Daisy started to cry and Terry put his arm around her, looking as though he'd like to weep too.

'Did she fall?' she blurted through her tears. 'She fell, didn't she? We aren't going to get out, are we?' A bubble of snot formed at her nostril and Terry wiped it away with his sleeve. 'We'll die and I won't get to wear my wedding dress.'

'Daisy?' Irene said calmly. 'Listen to me. We bloody well

will get out, you know. There's probably about two dozen firemen coming up the stairs right now, bashing away with those axes they have. And anyway, we can't die.'

'Why not?' Daisy said, huge tears trembling on her eyelashes.

'Because it'll annoy the crap out of the queen, that's why. She'll come driving up the street in that big car of hers on Wednesday looking all over the place for Daisy Farr and Irene Baxter, and if we're not here she'll say, "Bugger, what a waste of a bloody trip that was", and go home again!'

Daisy giggled, and even Louise smiled.

'*And*,' Irene went on, 'you won't get to see whether she's wearing her fairy dress, will you? So we have to be there for that, don't we?'

Daisy nodded, and wiped her eyes. 'Do you really think the firemen are coming right now?'

'Well, if they're not, they'll be down there on that street working out how to do it.'

A little later, when Daisy had gone to get a drink of water from the sink behind the counter, Louise asked Irene, '*Do you think that*?'

'Do I think what?'

'That the firemen are coming?'

Irene looked at her. 'How the hell should I know? But what's the point in letting her wind herself into a tizz? It'll only make her feel worse. And us.'

Louise was silent for a moment. Then she said, 'Irene, I'm sorry about what I said to you this morning. What you do is your business. You're right, I did judge you, and I'm sorry.'

Irene only nodded, but Louise could see in her eyes that the apology had been accepted.

On the other side of the cafeteria, Norm stood up and clapped his hands. 'I still think we should try the stairs, smoke or not. We could cover our faces with damp cloths and make a run for it.' There was murmured agreement from some around him. 'And if the flames . . . well, if it turns out we really can't get out that way, we can always come back.'

'Hear, hear,' someone said.

'I don't think you realize what that smoke's like,' Max said anxiously. 'It's virtually impossible to breathe when you're in it.'

'I'll take my chances.' Norm glanced around. 'Is anyone with me?'

Almost everyone raised their hands, although a small group gathered around Colin Crowley did nothing. But Crowley himself stepped forward.

'You'll regret it,' he warned. 'Stay here, all of you. Think about it. They'll be here for us soon, they're bound to be. Please, don't risk it.'

Norm waited a few seconds. Then, as though Colin Crowley hadn't spoken at all, he said, 'Right, then. If some of you could get busy tearing up some tablecloths and if someone else could fill the sinks, we'll soak the cloths and tie them around our faces.'

It took only ten minutes to do as he'd suggested, and soon the majority who had decided to go were crowded into the hallway again, dripping cloths secured over mouths and noses, awaiting their turn to descend into the stairwell.

Keith had made it down the staff stairs to the second-floor landing. The smoke here was dense, but he couldn't tell if the fire was in the stairwell yet.

He pushed open the door into the back of the flooring department, and stepped through. In here the smoke was almost solid, and there was a hell of a noise — crackling and a dull roaring, though he couldn't see any flames in here, either. And there was a wind, a searing hot wind that lifted his hair and flapped the tails of his suit jacket. How strange. He hadn't expected there to be wind in the middle of a burning building.

But it didn't matter; none of it mattered. Because he was going down to the White Room to get his money. And when he'd done that, when he had it all safely in his pockets, he would break one of the windows and jump. He wouldn't die — he probably wouldn't even be hurt. It wasn't that far up. And, anyway, he was blessed. He was blessed because he had gambled away thousands and thousands of pounds over his adult lifetime and got away with it, he'd stolen from Dunbar & Jones and got away with it, and now he was going to collect his money, and get away with that, too. And when he had, he would go straight down to the railway station, board the next train out of Auckland, and just keep on going to somewhere he could start again. Hell, he might even go to Australia!

Because, now that he thought about it, his had been a terrible job. People were always peering over his shoulder, or looking at him sideways. He knew it, he'd seen them — Max bloody Jones and all those other twits on the management committee — always watching him and talking about him behind his back and waiting for him to make a mistake. But he'd show them. He'd take his money, put it only on dead certs, then use just enough of his winnings for the next bet, until one day he could afford to throw money away on outsiders, the horses you heard about in your local, the tips that people passed on with a nudge and a wink. Because you had to act on tips like that, didn't you, or you might miss out on the really big one, and how would you live with yourself if that happened?

And where the hell was the doorway that opened onto the public stairs? He'd gone through appliances: he knew that, because he'd seen the smooth, ghostly shapes of the new Whiteway automatic washing machines. Was he going in the wrong direction? Was he lost?

No, he was all right because there was the doorway over there; he could tell because it wasn't quite so dark. Something beneath his feet made a huge, drawn-out groaning noise, like some gargantuan, ancient creature on the verge of waking up, but he kept going, feeling his way, the sweat pouring down his face and soaking his shirt and his underpants as though he'd accidentally pissed himself.

When he reached the doorway he stopped for a second, trying to draw a decent breath. Had he shut the door onto the staff stairwell? He couldn't remember.

He pulled out his handkerchief and held it over his nose and mouth. Not much further to go now — just down one more flight of stairs and he'd be on the first-floor landing, and then it would just be a matter of feeling his way around to the right and into the White Room.

God, his lungs were really burning. He coughed, then coughed again, and suddenly he couldn't stop. Bending over, he vomited, tasting blood and feeling horribly dizzy as stars danced across the insides of his eyelids. And he was so tired now, too. But he was so close, so close to his beautiful money. Saying this out loud to himself over and over, he stepped into the public stairwell and reached out until he felt the wooden banister rail, smooth and very warm beneath his grip.

There was only a very hazy outline where he presumed the stairwell window was. But he kept on, his leather-soled shoes sliding over the smooth marble of the steps, until he felt the raised strip of metal on each edge. Carefully, but eagerly, he continued his shuffling descent for a few more steps, then he stepped down.

'If I don't burn to death I'll bloody drown,' Louise said, water spluttering from the cloth over her mouth.

She was trying to make jokes, but what she really wanted to do was lie down and bawl her eyes out — for herself, and for Rob, but most of all for Susan, whom she was beginning to fear she might never see again.

Allie laughed, then spluttered and coughed into her own cloth. Up ahead she could see Vince standing with his back to them. Typical, she thought — as close to the head of the queue as he could get without looking like a coward. As she watched, she noticed Irene edging her way up through the line until she reached his side.

He glanced down at her, then away again.

'Vince, I'm frightened.' Irene was absolutely petrified, though she hadn't been about to show that to the girls.

'We all are,' Vince said shortly, still looking straight ahead.

'Will you hold my hand?' she asked hesitantly.

'No.' Just the one, short syllable.

Perhaps he was so frightened himself that he didn't trust his voice. As Irene lifted her cloth to her face and tied it behind her head, the moisture ran down her cleavage and soaked into her bra. It felt cool, nice.

Up ahead, the queue started to move as the people at the front began to descend the stairs. Max Jones went first. He hadn't wanted to, insisting that it was his place to stay behind and see that everyone got out. But someone — some very kind person who could see that Mr Max was as terrified and panic-stricken as everyone else — pointed out that someone had to take the lead to make sure that the way down actually was safe. So he'd moved into the stairwell, then paused and asked if anyone had seen Keith Beaumont. When it was clear that no one had, he'd finally stepped down onto the stairs and been swallowed up by the swirling darkness.

Progress was slow, with people yelling back that it was pitch-black and much smokier than the first time they'd tried. The messages were passed back and filtered through to the ones still nervously waiting. Hardly anyone spoke.

When about a third of the group had gone down, a girl still on the upper landing started babbling that she couldn't do it, that she was terrified of the dark and had asthma and wouldn't be able to breathe. Then she fainted, landing heavily on the wooden floor.

Vince darted up the line and crouched down beside her. 'Move back, give her some air!' he commanded.

A few people shuffled back slightly, but not far enough to lose their places.

The girl moaned and Vince helped her to half sit up, cradling her in his arms and fanning his hand in front of her face.

'Oh God, I'm sorry, did I faint?'

As Irene watched incredulously, Vince said, 'Yes, but you're all right now, I've got you.' He hoisted her to her feet, settled one of her arms over his broad shoulders and slid a hand around her waist. 'I'll help you down. If you think you're going to faint again, tell me and I'll carry you.'

The girl nodded gratefully up at him, then lifted her cloth to her face.

Incensed, Irene ripped off her own cloth and elbowed her way up the queue. 'What about me!' she demanded in a hoarse whisper. 'Why can't you help me down? Why won't you even talk to me? Help me, Vince, I'm terrified!'

'We all are, Mrs Baxter,' Vince said.

Mrs Baxter? Irene stepped up to him. 'Vince, it's me you're talking to, the woman you said you loved? You're leaving your wife for me, *remember?*'

When Vince finally met her gaze, she saw that there was nothing at all in his eyes. Nothing for her, anyway. And then he blinked and she saw it: a tiny flash of irritated contempt. And that was all.

She understood then, and what she understood was so enormous, so sharp and painful that it struck at her very core. She stepped back. Vince turned away and started down the stairs, the girl leaning against him.

The queue moved on, but Irene didn't.

'Are you all right?' Allie asked when she came abreast of her.

Irene turned her head slowly towards her. 'He looked at me as though I wasn't there, Allie. He looked at me as though I was dead already.'

'Oh, don't say that, Irene, please.' Bloody, *bloody* Vince! What a bastard! Allie linked her arm though Irene's. 'Come on, we'll sort him out when we get down, eh? Don't worry about it now.'

But Irene didn't respond.

And then it was Terry and Daisy's turn. They turned and waved, their cloths tied over their faces like a couple of kids playing at bank robbers.

'I'll put the kettle on when we get down, eh?' Terry called with a terrible false cheer. Then, holding hands, they went into the darkness.

As Allie watched them disappear and silently wished them luck, she realized she needed to go to the toilet.

'Mind my place?' she said to Irene, as though they were queuing up for tickets at the pictures, then felt silly.

Irene nodded. 'Be careful.' At least she was talking again.

Allie made her way back along the hallway, turned right just before she reached the cafeteria and pushed open the door to the women's staff toilets. It wasn't as smoky in here: the windows were all closed so nothing was drifting in from outside. As she washed her hands, she glimpsed herself in the mirror above the handbasin. Her face was pale and her eyes red from the smoke and crying, but she didn't look like she was going to die.

Instead of going back down the hallway to join the others, she turned into the cafeteria. Colin Crowley's group was still in there, sitting around three of the tables, looking as though they were waiting to have their orders taken.

Allie went to stand by one of the windows overlooking Queen Street. There seemed to be thousands of people down there, to the right and to the left, everywhere but directly in front of Dunbar & Jones. That space was filled with fire trucks and hoses and firemen and policemen, all doing their best to save them. It felt very odd. Here they were stuck up here and trying to get down, and there they all were down there trying to get up. What would happen in between? she wondered almost dreamily. What would change and what would stay the same? Would *anything* be the same after this?

She leaned out of the open window and looked down. The air coming up was extremely hot and made her eyes water, and every few seconds the smoke from the floors below completely blocked her view. Below and to her left, their wire frames still attached to the front of the building at first-floor level but the papier mâché all burned away, perched the giant crown flanked by the kiwi and the lion, now both black skeletons. Allie squinted against the heat: something was jammed down behind the kiwi. She couldn't quite make it out, but it had been burnt to a crisp. Then, with a surge of nausea, she realized what it probably was — the poor girl who had fallen from the window ledge.

Oh dear, she thought inanely, what would the queen think when she got here on Wednesday? And then she giggled, but it was only the beginnings of a sob. Then there were more sobs but she managed to stop them. Her tears dried quickly, making the skin on her cheeks feel tight.

She opened her arms, set her hands against the window frame and gazed down again. Was Sonny down there? Could he see her?

She shouted out his name, twice, but didn't think he could have heard her.

'Ha-ere mai, everything is ka pai,' she whispered.

'Allie?'

It was Irene.

'It's nearly our turn.'

Allie nodded. She retied her face cloth and followed Irene back out into the hallway. It had taken a little less than fifteen minutes for everyone before them to go down, and now there were only about a dozen people left. In just five more minutes she should be on her way down.

But then Irene stopped abruptly and Allie walked straight into her.

'What?' Allie said, fresh ripples of fear running up her spine. 'What is it?'

Miss Willow and Miss Button, waiting at the head of the stairs, were clutching each other tightly and everyone else looked as though they'd just been slapped very hard across the face.

Simone from gloves stammered, 'It just went. They got on it and it just went.'

'What went?' Irene demanded. Her voice went up several octaves. '*What went?*'

'The stairs,' a man Allie didn't know said. 'Four got on them at once, they were rushing, and the whole lot just dropped — disappeared.'

He sounded bewildered and more than a little disgruntled, as though he'd just been cheated out of something.

Allie crept over to the stairwell and looked down. He was right — there was nothing left. Everything had gone: the steps, the landing, the handrail, everything. And at the very bottom, far, far down, she could see the flicker of bright, hungry flames.

Chapter Fifteen

'Can I get through? My daughter's up there, I need to get through.' Sid elbowed his way down the middle of the street.

The crowd parted and let him past, their eyes brimming with sympathy and concern.

Bill close behind, Sid wedged himself in behind the police barricade, squinting up at the burning building, his heart pounding furiously. Was she up there, his beautiful daughter?

He tapped the shoulder of a cop standing on the other side of the barricade. ''Scuse me, mate, but my daughter works in there. How can I find out if she's been brought out?'

The constable, a young, soot-spattered bloke who looked as though he'd rather be anywhere else, made a sympathetic face. 'No one's been brought out yet, sir. Sorry, but the fire brigade hasn't been able to find a way in. So far.'

'Has *no one* got out?' Sid exclaimed, appalled.

'Oh, yes, quite a few,' the cop said, pleased to actually be able to impart a bit of good news. 'They're all over there.' He waved a hand. 'She's probably there with them. And there's a list they're ticking off. You could have a look at that.'

Sid and Bill made their way over to the large, bedraggled-looking group on the footpath. Some of them were filthy, others simply looked stunned.

'Allie Roberts!' Sid shouted. 'Has anyone seen Allison Roberts?'

A wall of blank faces stared back at him. Then someone spoke up, a woman holding a blood-stained handkerchief to her nose.

'She was on the top floor. She was coming down after us. But I don't know if . . .' she trailed off, clearly lost for words.

'Have you seen her since then?' Bill asked.

Reluctantly, the woman shook her head.

'Where's that list?' Sid demanded. 'That cop over there said there's a list.'

The woman retreated into the crowd, then reappeared a moment later. 'This is George Lynch,' she said. 'He's ticking everyone off.'

George asked, 'Who are you looking for?'

'My daughter, Allie Roberts. She works in the dress department.'

George nodded and ran his finger down the list, turned the page, then flicked it back again. He met Sid's gaze and looked quickly away. 'I'm sorry, Mr Roberts, but she isn't here. But she could be outside somewhere and we just haven't seen her yet.'

Sid's heart sank, but he nodded his thanks and walked away, back towards the young policeman.

'Hey, Sherlock!' he called. 'Who's the head honcho here, for the fire brigade?' He felt Bill's hand settle on his shoulder.

'Are you talking to me?' the constable said, looking non-plussed.

Bill murmured, 'Calm down, Sid.'

Sid ignored him. 'Yes, boy — you!'

The young cop pointed towards a member of the fire brigade who had his head down over a set of plans.

Sid ducked under the barricade and marched over.

'Are you the boss here?' he demanded.

The fireman glanced up. His eyes were reddened by smoke and there were bits of black stuff stuck in his teeth. 'I'm the senior station officer, yes.'

'Well, get your arse into gear and get those fucking ladders up! My daughter's up there!' Sid shouted right into his face.

The fire chief stepped wearily back. This fire was the worst he'd attended in his twenty-four years of service, and it was tearing him apart, having to stand around down here on the ground like a useless bloody idiot, knowing that there were still people in there.

'We're doing everything we can, sir,' he said.

'*No you aren't!*' Sid roared. 'Why aren't those fucking ladders up?'

'Because the verandah's in the way. The ladders can't reach the windows. But we're looking at getting some men into—'

Sid threw a punch at him, but in his anger missed by a mile.

The crowd gasped and Bill put his hand over his eyes. Two police constables ran over and took hold of Sid's arms.

Standing well back now, the fire chief said, 'I realize you're upset, sir, but we're doing everything we can.'

'Well, it isn't *enough*, d'you hear me?' Sid shouted as the cops half dragged, half walked him towards a police car. '*It isn't bloody enough!*'

One constable opened the back door of the car while the other pushed Sid into it.

'Hello, Sid,' Sonny said.

Sid, who had whacked his head on the way in, rubbed his ear and looked at him in bewilderment. 'Sonny? What are you doing here?'

Sonny nodded at the handcuff still attached to both his wrist and the door handle. 'Had a bit of bother.'

'So did I,' Sid said, and burst into tears.

Sonny looked out the window and let him get on with it. Eventually he said, 'She's a strong one, Allie, eh? If there's a way out, she'll find it.'

Not counting Mr Crowley's lot, there were only thirteen of them left now, Allie thought. A very unlucky number.

She lit a cigarette. She'd lost her bag somewhere but had spotted a packet in someone else's, so she'd pinched them.

'Does anyone else want one?'

Irene and Louise both nodded, so she slid the packet across the table. They were back in the caf, sitting with Miss Willow and Miss Button. The others were standing over by the window. They seemed to be arguing.

'We've never smoked,' Ruby said. 'Have we, Bea?'

Beatrice shook her head. 'It was terribly fashionable in our day, though, wasn't it? All the bright young things used to do it. My sister used to have the most wonderful long, ivory holder.'

Louise said, 'Do you really think anyone's coming for

us?' She was silent for a moment. 'Or is this it?'

'Don't worry, dear,' Beatrice replied gently. 'They'll be doing their very best, I'm sure of it.'

'Yes, but is anyone *coming?*' Louise put her head in her hands. 'It's driving me spare, just bloody well sitting here. Just *waiting.*'

Nobody said what they were all thinking: that soon they would have no choice left but to jump.

Allie remarked, 'I've lost my bit of cloth.'

She felt very strange. She still had that sensation of being detached and everything seemed hazy, as though she were looking at everything with a stocking pulled over her face. She was still scared stiff, she knew that, but now it felt as though it was someone else who was terrified, not really her. She supposed it was the shock. But it was nearly funny, sitting around the table enjoying a relaxing cigarette while the floors beneath them were burning with such intensity that they could all hear the fire, and great sheets of black smoke were whipping up past the windows outside and blocking out the sky. She looked at her watch: only thirty-seven minutes since they'd all gone running out of the caf. It felt like they'd been stuck up here for ever.

She wondered what Donna and Pauline were doing. And she thought about her mother. Was she still at work? Had she heard? And what about her dad? He was supposed to be painting with Bill this afternoon, but they were probably in the pub right now. Bill was a good bloke, but he freely admitted that Sid could always lead him astray. She loved her family very much: the notion of not seeing any of them again was just . . . absurd, really.

'Is anyone here a Catholic?' Louise asked.

301

'I am,' Irene said, stubbing out her cigarette. 'Well, I was. I've lapsed.'

'So have I,' Beatrice said. 'But my family are strict Methodists, not Catholics.'

'I haven't been to church since I was thirteen,' Irene went on. 'Except for when Martin and I were married, but that was in an Anglican church.' Irene looked at Louise. 'Why? Are you?'

Louise nodded. 'I was raised a Catholic, but I don't go to church that often. But I was just thinking that someone might want to, well, you know, that we should . . .'

'Confess our sins because we're all about to die?' Irene finished for her.

There was a moment of silence. Then Louise said, 'Yes, I suppose. I'd like to, anyway, if nobody minds.' When no one objected, she took a deep breath. 'When I found out I was pregnant with Susan, I was really upset because I didn't want a baby so soon. I wanted Rob and me to work for a few years and save some money and put a deposit on a nice little house and buy all those things that married people buy together. You know, a fridge and a lounge suite and a washing machine and a decent car and all the rest of it. I certainly didn't want to be stuck in a poky little rented house boiling nappies in the copper and wondering what to do with half a pound of mince for the fifth night in a row. I was only about eight weeks at that stage and I hadn't told anyone, not even Rob.' She put her hands on the table, stared at a spot between them and didn't say anything for a few seconds. 'So I went to see a woman who I'd been told could . . . take care of that sort of thing.'

'An abortionist?' Irene said, sounding very surprised.

Louise nodded. 'And it went against everything I'd ever

302

been taught. You know — "all human life is sacred, for it is created in the image and likeness of God". But I was so angry because I wanted it to be just me and Rob. I felt like this . . . *accident* had come along and we didn't have anything ready for it and it was going to come between us before we even had a chance to really have a life together. You know, just us. So I went to see her, and she was this really kind woman and I thought she was going to be awful with dirty fingernails and a fag hanging out of her mouth and a bare mattress in a back room. And she told me very gently what she would be doing and what to expect, and was I absolutely one hundred per cent sure it was what I wanted? And I started crying and I couldn't stop and she told me to go home and think about it overnight and come back in the morning if I still wanted to go ahead. So I went home, and I did go back, but only to tell her I'd changed my mind.' Louise was crying now. 'And thank God I did, because otherwise I'd never have had Susan and, well, I can't even imagine what my life would be like without her. I never told Rob. I've never told anyone.'

She glanced around the table, looking for censure and judgment, but there was none, only soft eyes full of sympathy and love.

'So that's it, that's my confession.' She gave an enormous sigh. 'God, that feels better.'

'I've got something,' Allie said, 'though it's nothing like Louise's. But it's something that's sort of . . . stayed with me.' She reached for the cigarettes, then pushed the packet away again. 'It was when the waterfront lockout was on. I was eighteen and I was going out on a first date with a boy. His name was Brian, Brian Ingham, and he was twenty-one and I just thought he was the bee's knees. It was about three months into the lockout, I suppose, and we were going to a party with some of his friends. He was at the university and he was very posh and educated — I'd met him down at the tennis courts. And halfway through this party, people started talking about the lockout and how all the watersiders were communist shit-stirrers and ruining the country's economy and should be locked up, not out, or sent to South Korea to do a decent day's work for a change, and they were laughing but some of them were getting quite het up about it. And I was sitting there, smiling away in the new dress I'd made especially and thinking how wonderful I was getting invited out by such a clever, good-looking boy, but terrified in case I said something stupid and he never asked me out again. And anyway he turned around and asked me what my father did. And I said he owned a building company.'

'But your dad was a wharfie, wasn't he?' Louise said.

Allie nodded. 'And that night, I bloody well *knew* he was biking around Auckland with some of his watersider mates delivering food parcels to other wharfies because they couldn't even afford to buy their kids bread or milk.'

No one said anything for a moment, and Allie could see in their faces that they understood.

'Did you go out with the boy again?' Ruby asked.

'No, I never heard from him after that.'

The subsequent silence was filled by Beatrice, who said brightly, 'Well, my turn, I suppose. I'm a child of Satan.'

Ruby laughed.

'Pardon?' Irene said.

'I'm a child of Satan,' Beatrice said again. 'According to my mother and father, anyway. They were very religious, my parents. My father's dead now, of course, and my mother doesn't know what day it is.'

'Why are you a child of Satan?' Louise asked, frowning.

Beatrice raised her eyebrows questioningly at Ruby, who nodded. 'Well, you see, Ruby and I are lovers.'

Allie shot a look at Irene and Louise, but they were both staring round-eyed at the two older women.

'And we have been for over twenty years,' Beatrice went on. 'Naturally, it's not something we advertise, but we're very happy together, aren't we, Ruby?'

Ruby nodded and settled her hand on top of Beatrice's, smiling fondly at her. 'We are, dear, we are.'

'So this isn't really a confession,' Beatrice amended, 'but it is something that I wanted to . . . announce. Before whatever's going to happen here, well, happens.'

Allie didn't know what the others were thinking, but she was lost for words. Who'd have thought it? Who really even knew that women actually did that? But the more she considered it, the more sense it made. They seemed to be very close, Miss Willow and Miss Button, and neither was married, and they shared a house, and, well, it was actually quite nice, really, that they had each other. And that couldn't be a bad thing. And they were together now.

But she wasn't really alone either. Sonny wasn't here — and thank God for that in many ways — but she had Irene and Louise. Daisy had managed to get out, so she would be all right, and whatever was going to happen to the rest of them, they would face it together. Knowing that made her feel better, a little less frightened.

Louise said, 'So your parents thought you were a child of Satan because you'd . . . um, taken up with a woman?'

Beatrice suddenly made a pained face.

Allie asked, 'Are you all right?' Miss Button looked like

her father did when he was anticipating one of his more subterranean attacks of wind.

Beatrice's features relaxed slightly. 'I'm fine. A touch of indigestion, I think. No, my mother and father never realized that. It was because I'd decided to leave home. I'm the youngest daughter and they'd assumed I was going to look after them in their old age. But instead, I went off and learned how to make hats and went half-shares in a little house, and they were very disappointed with me. It was my duty to dedicate my life to them, apparently, and I let them down.'

Irene took a big breath, then let it out again slowly.

'I've got something,' she said. 'And this isn't a confession either, because I never actually did anything wrong, I understand that now, but it is something I need to get out.'

The others waited, quiet and acquiescent, knowing that whatever Irene had to say, no matter how shocking or embarrassing it might be, it would be all right, because she was one of them; she was their friend.

'There were five of us at home,' Irene began. 'I was the eldest with two brothers and two sisters. Being a Catholic my mother couldn't stop popping us out, although I think she wanted to. She got quite sick after Roy, he's the youngest, and either she couldn't have any more babies or Dad left her alone, I'm not sure which. Dad was a sharemilker and we lived out at Tuakau, in a little cottage on the farm. We all went to primary school out there and we were really poor. I mean dirt poor. We didn't wear shoes to school and our clothes were full of holes Mum was always trying to patch and darn.' Irene frowned. 'Mind you, hardly anyone wore shoes to school, not just us or the Maori kids. There were quite a few Maoris at the school and they used to ride in from all over the place on horseback, three or four of them to a horse, and I used to be really jealous because I always wanted a horse but Dad said I'd never look after it. Which was probably true.

'And we all used to help on the farm, when we were old enough. I'd help Dad in the milking shed in the mornings and in the afternoons when I got home from school, and the little ones all learned to do that as they got older. Mum didn't like it — she said it stopped us from doing our homework — but I still did mine, at night. It wasn't an easy life, I suppose, but we were happy enough, for a while anyway. Mum was a good cook and she could turn anything into something worth eating. And she grew most of our vegies and made bread and did all those sorts of things a good wife's supposed to do.' Briefly, Irene smiled. 'Unlike me. I can't cook to save myself. Poor Martin. So we were all right for food, but we hardly ever had money for anything else, which is why all of us kids went around looking like we'd got our clothes from St Vincent de Paul's. Which we did sometimes. Mum used to go into town once a month and stock up, I'm sure of it. And sometimes she'd come home from her CWI meetings with things from the other ladies, but we hardly ever had anything new. No, actually that's not true. I had a lovely coat once, that the farmer's wife gave me. It was royal blue wool and had a scarf attached to it with white fur pompoms on the ends. But Mum told me I could wear it only for best, and seeing we never went anywhere nice, it hardly ever got worn. It got handed down of course, and when it got to my two little brothers, Mum just cut the pompoms off so it didn't look so girly. But they didn't get to wear it much either, and I think by the time we all grew out of it, it was still nearly as good as the day I was given it.'

She reached for a cigarette and lit it, the others waiting patiently.

'Dad started drinking heavily when I was about six. There were only three of us kids then. He fell off the tractor one day while he was feeding out, and the back wheel ran over him and broke his pelvis. He was in hospital for quite a while and apparently when he was discharged the doctors told him he would have to find a less physical job. But hell, no, my father was a man of the land and that's where he was going to stay! According to him, anyway. He couldn't accept it. Or wouldn't. I don't know. Anyway, when he came home I would hear him and Mum arguing in the kitchen late at night because she wanted us to move into town so Dad could get a job that wouldn't be so hard on him, and he wouldn't have a bar of it. "Do I *look* like a bloody townie, woman?" he'd shout back at her. And if she went on about it, which she sometimes did, he'd just stomp out of the house and we wouldn't see him 'til milking the next morning, and he'd always stink because he'd have got stuck into the booze and slept in the barn. But we got used to that.'

Irene paused for a moment. 'And then, when I was ten, it started. A man told me one day that I was a very pretty girl, and after that he started paying me a lot of attention. By the time I was eleven I was sleeping with him.'

Louise gasped and her hand flew to her mouth. 'Having sex?' she whispered, her eyes wide with shock.

Irene nodded, her white, soot-smudged face impassive.

Ruby and Beatrice exchanged quick, horrified glances,

but Allie stared directly at Irene, marvelling at the calmness — or was it a deep, flat emptiness? — in her friend's eyes.

'And that went on for about three years,' Irene continued, 'until I started getting my periods. After that he said it would be too dangerous, that I might get pregnant, and then he left.' Her mouth twisted in a sort of half smile, half frown. 'He left me.'

'Why didn't you tell someone?' Allie said, aghast.

'I . . . I just couldn't, that's all,' Irene replied, staring down at the table top. 'And he said that if I did tell, no one would ever love me again.' She looked up and added almost casually, 'Mind you, he said that anyway. He said I was used goods and no one would want me after what he'd been doing. And that I'd always belong to him.'

'Who was he, Irene? Who was the man?' Ruby asked gently. 'Was it the farmer? Because it's not too late: he could still be brought to justice.'

Irene looked mildly surprised. 'The farmer? Hell, no, it was my father.'

The others gaped at her.

She shrugged. 'After he'd gone, we all just kept on with our lives. I went to secondary school and then secretarial college. Mum still does for the farmer out at Tuakau — his wife's a bit of an invalid and they've still got a couple of kids at home. I don't think they've got the heart to kick her out of the cottage anyway.'

'And have you seen him since? Your father?' Beatrice asked.

'No,' Irene said. 'No one has.' She pushed her hair back off her face, as though she were trying to sweep all of those bad memories out of her head. 'Shall we say a prayer? I've got one. Well, I think it's a prayer, but it might be just a poem. And I can't remember all of it, but Mum used to say it to us sometimes. When things weren't going well.' Then, for the first time since any of them had known her, Irene looked unsure of herself. 'Shall we hold hands?'

No one hesitated, and when they were linked around the table hand in hand, Irene closed her eyes and began:

> *Christ be with me, Christ within me,*
> *Christ behind me, Christ before me,*
> *Christ beside me, Christ to win me,*
> *Christ to comfort and restore me,*
> *Christ beneath me, Christ above me,*
> *Christ in quiet, Christ in danger,*
> *Christ in hearts of all that love me,*
> *Christ in mouth of friend and stranger.*

When she'd finished, Irene kept her head down for a moment. Then she looked up and smiled, and Allie thought that she seemed . . . lighter, somehow.

'I don't know why,' Irene said, 'but that prayer always comforts me. It makes me—'

But she didn't complete the sentence because someone screamed; it was Simone.

Below them, on Queen Street, a constable opened the back door of a police car and leaned in.

'If I let the pair of you out, will you give me your word that you'll stay behind the barricade?'

Sid nodded, followed, after a moment, by Sonny.

'Because if there's any more trouble, I'll have to send you down to the lock-up,' the cop warned. He removed the handcuff from Sonny's wrist. 'And I bloody well mean that. All right?'

Sid nodded again, but Sonny was already out of the car, gazing up at the flames that had now breached Dunbar & Jones's second-floor windows.

'Look!' Simone was pointing past the table at which Allie and the others were sitting.

They whipped around and there it was — a long, narrow tongue of flame flickering up the wall, blistering the paint and warping the floorboards it had burnt through. And even as they watched, the flame divided into two, then three. And then it took hold, igniting the matchlining in seconds and sending ribbons of black smoke unravelling across the ceiling.

Someone shouted, 'Move! Get out of here!' and for the second time they were up and running from the cafeteria.

Out in the hallway, Louise turned right and ran down the corridor that led to the dressmaking workroom at the far end. Allie, Irene and Ruby followed her, but Beatrice had stopped.

Ruby turned around. 'Bea! Hurry!'

Her round face a picture of terror, Beatrice called: 'The others, Ruby, they've gone towards the tailoring workroom. You're going the wrong way!' And then she grimaced and clutched at her arm.

'Bea? What's the matter?' Ruby ran back down the corridor, her spectacles on their gold chain bouncing on her chest. She glanced down and tore them off.

Beatrice collapsed against the wall and slid to the floor.

Allie, watching from the doorway of the dressmaking room, ran back after Ruby.

Smoke was beginning to billow out of the cafeteria now, and Allie saw that the flames had almost consumed one wall and were moving out across the ceiling. There was a terrible smell, sharp and noxious, and she could taste the greasy smoke in her mouth. She looked right and peered down the hallway, which was rapidly filling with smoke, but there was no sign of Simone and the others.

Beatrice's legs were splayed out in front of her. Her dress had ridden up, revealing beige stockings and an inch of pudgy blue-veined flesh above them. Kneeling beside her, Ruby briskly tapped her cheek, as though Beatrice had passed out and she was trying to revive her.

'Stop that, Ruby,' Bea mumbled. 'You're hurting my face.'

Leaning over her, Ruby demanded, 'What's wrong, Bea? Are you hurt?'

'I think I'm having a heart attack.'

'Oh, you are not,' Ruby snapped. 'Get up!'

'I can't . . . I can't seem to move.'

'Have you got your pills?

'I've lost my bag,' Beatrice said through clenched teeth, then made a groaning noise that ended in a sharp, high whimper.

The sound of an explosion came from inside the cafeteria, followed immediately by a bigger one, and a wave of burning dust and debris blew out through the open door.

'Beatrice, for God's sake *get up!*' Ruby shouted.

Beatrice muttered something and her hand fluttered weakly, but otherwise she didn't respond.

Ruby grabbed her shoulders and shook her. 'Beatrice?

Bea!' She looked up at Allie in desperation. 'I can't leave her, you know. I won't.'

Something else exploded in the caf and seconds later flames shot up from the stairwell at the other end of the hallway.

Ruby sat down on the floor. Weeping now, but silently, she slid her arm behind Beatrice's neck and pulled her tight against her. Beatrice's eyes were closed and her breathing had become very shallow. 'I'm here, love,' Ruby whispered. 'Don't worry, I'm here. I won't leave you.'

She looked up at Allie. 'There's no point waiting for me, I'm staying with Bea. Go down to the dressmaking room and barricade yourselves in there. If you can keep the smoke out you'll have a little more time.'

And then she laid her cheek against the top of Beatrice's head and closed her eyes.

Allie watched them for a second, her heart aching, before she turned away and ran back down the corridor to the dressmaking room, the heat radiating from the cafeteria almost seeming to push her along.

Irene and Louise pulled her in, then slammed the door. It was quieter in here, and there wasn't much smoke yet. They leaned against the wall, breathing heavily, not from exertion, but from panic.

Their eyes met.

'No one's coming for us, are they?' Allie said flatly.

Louise pushed herself off the wall and went over to a window. Allie and Irene followed.

The workroom was in the north-eastern corner of the building, and there were windows in two of the walls. One set looked down over Queen Street, and the other, at which they stood, faced the harbour. An alleyway separated

Dunbar & Jones from the building next to it, creating a gap that looked to be at least twelve feet wide. The building opposite was a storey shorter than the department store, so if they jumped at least they wouldn't have to leap up as well as out, but the distance between the two buildings seemed enormous.

'Can we do it?' Louise said, almost to herself.

Allie felt her bowels cramp as she stared down at the smoke-filled alleyway, and at the flames bursting from the second-floor windows. 'Oh God, I don't think I can, I really don't.'

'We'd have to push off from the windowsill,' Louise said. 'We wouldn't be able to get a running start.'

She set her thumbs against the latches on the sash window in front of her, released them and shoved. Nothing happened. She put more weight behind it; there was a muffled creak, but still nothing budged. Peering closely at the join between the sill and the actual sash, she swore. 'It's been painted shut.' She tried the windows on either side. 'They all have on this wall.'

Allie ran to the windows that overlooked Queen Street and tried one. It slid up easily. She leaned out and squinted down at the street. Smoke pouring from the windows below stung her eyes and she could feel the heat in her throat. '*Hey!*' she shrieked, waving her arms madly. '*Up here! We're trapped!*'

Carrying a wooden chair, Louise appeared at Allie's side. 'Move out of the way,' she ordered, then heaved the chair out of the window.

It arced out for a few feet then began to drop, seeming to fall for a very long time before it hit the verandah roof above the ground floor and bounced off, shattered, and finally came to rest in several pieces in the middle of the street. Allie tried not to imagine what the same fall would do to a human body.

Heads turned below them and arms came up to point.

Allie and Louise waved furiously. A group of firemen ran to a spot below them, disappearing from view as they neared the building. Then two long ladders were carried over and laboriously heaved into place, propped against the verandah.

'They've seen us!' Allie said to Irene, who was standing in the middle of the room, watching calmly. 'They're putting ladders up!'

She turned back. Nothing happened for a long minute, then a helmet appeared above the edge of the verandah. The helmet tilted and, through the smoke, she could see a white face peering up at them. A hand waved: Allie waved back. The fireman continued to climb, then another one appeared on the second ladder.

One of them shouted something.

'*What?*' Louise yelled back.

'*How many of you?*'

'*Three!*' Louise replied.

'*Anyone hurt?*'

'*No!*'

The firemen climbed further, but it was becoming obvious that the manoeuvre wasn't going to work. Allie felt sick. The men were getting higher all right, but they weren't getting any nearer; once they'd climbed past the verandah, they just kept on going straight up, the six-foot gap between them and the side of the building barely shrinking at all. In fact, they looked quite silly balanced on top of their tall ladders, which only reached up to the ceiling of the first floor anyway, swaying in the wind of the fire like small flowers on particularly lofty stalks.

Allie burst out laughing. She could feel herself beginning to lose her grip. Her head felt light and dreamy again, her heart was racing and she found herself wondering what it would be like just to jump, to stand on the window ledge with her arms outstretched like a picture of a white, radiant, burning angel she'd once seen, and just let go.

Louise turned away from the window and, apparently in slow motion, slapped her.

Allie's hand flew to her stinging cheek. 'You can't slap me!' she exclaimed, and slapped Louise back.

'Stop it, you two,' Irene said. She walked over to the window.

Below, the firemen had retreated back down to the level of the verandah roof and were now standing on it. They seemed to be performing some sort of odd dance, stepping carefully and gingerly placing their booted feet here, then a little to the left, then further to the right.

'What are they doing?' Allie asked, her stinging cheek forgotten. She felt a little better now.

Louise and Irene didn't reply, they were too busy watching the firemen below. Eventually they seemed to be satisfied with whatever they were doing and bent down and began to haul up one of the ladders. Slowly more and more rungs appeared, until the entire ladder had been dragged above the verandah. Between them, the firemen managed to wrestle it up against the building's façade, its base planted squarely on the corrugated iron roof of the verandah. Allie realized what they'd been doing — looking for places where there were struts beneath the iron, for support.

One of them started climbing again, right to the very

top of the ladder, close enough for the girls to see his dirty, heat-reddened face and his white teeth, and the look of anticipated victory in his eyes.

And then a fireball exploded out of the second-storey window in front of him and he disappeared completely, the remaining bottom half of the ladder cart-wheeling slowly out into the air before clattering down onto one of the fire engines in the street.

Allie screamed and they hurled themselves away from the window. Louise, on her backside on the floor, tentatively touched her face.

'Have I been burnt?'

Picking herself up, Irene said, 'No, but the front of your hair's gone frizzy.'

'It feels like I've been burnt,' Louise muttered, her fingers still examining the planes and hollows of her face. 'It stings.'

Allie said in a quavering voice, 'That poor fireman.'

Irene went back to the window. 'There's two more coming up onto the verandah. But they're not pulling the other ladder up. And one of them's waving. And yelling, but I can't hear what he's saying.'

They leaned out of the window again, ready in an instant to throw themselves backwards if there was another explosion.

One of the fireman was indeed shouting.

'What's he saying?' Louise demanded.

They strained to hear him.

'Is he telling us to climb down?' Allie suggested after a moment.

Louise said, 'Right-o, I'll just get my emergency ladder out of my handbag.'

'Oh, Christ,' Irene said. She had turned away from the window and was staring across the room at the doorway into the corridor.

'What?' Allie asked, then she followed the direction of Irene's gaze.

Thick black smoke was pouring in under the door, curling gracefully upwards, meeting the ceiling and rolling down again, putting out blind, sooty fingers that seemed to be searching and reaching out. For them.

Chapter Sixteen

Louise lunged for a bolt of cloth lying on the heavy wooden cutting table in the middle of the room. 'Help me!' she cried, tugging at the end of it. It was a rather fine wool, destined for Dunbar & Jones's new autumn collection of suits and coats, due on the runway in about two-and-a-half months' time.

Allie snatched up a pair of fabric shears and started cutting into the material, then simply tearing it when she had enough purchase. Louise took the cloth and wedged it against the base of the door. The smoke slowed, but still trickled inexorably through the tiny gaps at the sides and at the top.

Irene stood at one end of the cutting table, looking thoughtful.

'Could you give us a hand, Irene, if you're not too busy?' Louise snapped.

'You said emergency ladders. Isn't the display department in the room next door?'

'So?'

'Well, won't there be ladders in there? For putting up the displays?'

Louise stopped what she was doing.

'If there's more than one,' Irene went on, 'we could tie them together, hang them out the window, then climb down and drop onto the verandah roof.'

'We'll need rope,' Allie said.

Irene pointed at the cutting table. 'Use lengths of material. It's wool, it'll hold.'

'It'll still be a bloody long drop,' Louise said. 'And there're flames coming out of the windows just below us.'

Irene shrugged. 'It's better than waiting here to die, isn't it?'

They looked at each other, wondering how they would get back down the corridor, thick with noxious smoke, to retrieve the ladders from the display room. If there were any. But Irene already had the answer.

'I'll go,' she offered.

Allie and Louise stared at her.

'I'm fit,' Irene said. 'I'm fast and I can hold my breath for ages.'

'But what if there isn't just smoke in the corridor? What if it's on fire out there now as well?' Louise pointed at the bolt of cloth still on the table. 'Couldn't we just make some ropes and climb down those?'

'The flames coming out the windows will burn through them,' Irene replied flatly. 'We'll fall.'

Louise's shoulders slumped.

'I think we should draw straws,' Allie said, wanting to be fair even now, but hoping like hell that she wouldn't get the short one. She didn't know if she had it in her to be that brave.

'Look, I've said I'll go,' Irene repeated. 'And I meant it.'

'Then you'd better have this.' Louise held out her piece of tablecloth.

Irene took it.

'You'll need to wet it, won't you?' Allie said.

But there was no sink in the workroom, not even a cold cup of tea left over from someone's lunch.

'We could pee on it,' Louise suggested.

There was a moment of silence. Then Irene said, 'Not if anyone had asparagus for tea last night.'

Allie snorted violently, and a string of snot shot out of her nose, making her laugh outright. She wiped it off her top lip with her sleeve. 'Sorry.'

Irene smiled faintly. 'Forget the pee. I'll just hold the cloth over my face and breathe shallowly.'

'What about when you come back?' Louise said. 'If you're carrying ladders you won't be able to hold it in place.'

Irene ignored her and moved over to the door. 'When I say go, pull the material away from under the door and I'll run through, then shove it back when I'm out. And *don't* open the door again until I bang on it, OK?'

Louise caught Irene's gaze and held it. 'Are you sure?'

Irene nodded. 'It's only a few yards up the corridor, isn't it? It won't take me long. And it might be our last chance.'

And then her hand was on the door knob and she said, 'Go!'

As Allie yanked the material out of the way, Irene opened the door and slid through the gap. A great billow of smoke rushed in, and then the door shut again and she was gone. Coughing, Allie slid the material back into place.

'Christ,' Louise said. 'I hope she's all right.'

They waited, and waited. Louise looked at her watch. Five minutes had passed since Irene had gone: it was too long.

Then something banged against the door, and Allie

321

and Louise both lunged to open it. Allie got there first, pushing the material out of the way again with her foot. She wrenched open the door and staggered back from a wall of black smoke and flames so bright she couldn't look at it. But Irene was there, with the ladders. She cried out and thrust them through the doorway. Louise grabbed them, then yelped and let go, her hands burnt. Hooking her foot through the rungs, she flicked them backwards through the doorway into the room.

Allie reached out to pull Irene inside, but then a strange, shocking thing happened.

Irene's mouth stretched wide open and she gargled, 'Tell Martin I really did love him.'

There was nothing for the shortest of seconds, then her hair burst into flames and a moment later her shoulders ignited, and suddenly she was a black silhouette inside an incandescent ball of fire. Then the fireball doubled over, and collapsed almost gracefully onto the warping floorboards. The smell was revolting.

Louise slammed the door shut and started screaming. She went on and on and on until Allie clapped her hands over her ears and started screaming herself, just to keep Louise's shrieks out.

Then Louise's screams tapered off and she took a deep breath, hoicked and spat out bloody saliva; it landed on one of the ladders and sizzled there.

Allie took her hands away from her ears, realizing only then that she was sobbing hoarsely. Then, as an image of Irene ablaze broke into her mind again, she gave one last shriek herself, and stopped. Her heart was thudding and she knew she was about to faint, so she sat down on the floor.

Louise stared at her, her face deathly white and her eyes still impossibly wide with horror. But she spoke lucidly. 'Get up. We can't give up now. Not after that.'

Allie nodded. Slowly, she got to her feet again.

'Start cutting lengths of material,' Louise ordered, some of her self-control returned now. 'We'll open the ladders and tie them together, then knot the material around the rungs at one end and the legs of the cutting table. It weighs a ton, it shouldn't move.'

Allie set to, tearing strips of the woollen fabric to make ropes, and when the ladders were cool enough to touch, they opened them out and tied them together, effectively making one ladder that was about twenty feet long. It would take them down about one-and-a-half storeys, leaving a gap of another storey to the verandah roof, still a very long way to drop.

They made the next set of ropes about ten feet long once they were tied to the ladder and the table, hoping that would reduce the drop by a few more feet. They could have made them longer but were frightened that if the ropes were too long, the wind would start the ladder swinging and they would be thrown off.

Then, as they manoeuvred the ladder over to the window, they realized that it wasn't going to fit between the wall and the cutting table, so they had to lift it over the table and into place. The workroom stank now — of chemicals as the paint on the walls started to blister and the varnish on the floorboards heated up. There was another smell, too. It started them coughing again and made their eyes sting and stream.

They poked the end of the ladder through the window, then pushed it out as far as they could and let gravity take over. It plummeted ten feet, then bounced back up a few feet as the ropes stopped playing out, and settled against the side of the building. They couldn't be sure, but were heartened when they thought they heard the crowd below cheering and yelling encouragement.

Allie breathed a huge sigh of relief. She had been terrified that the ropes would untie or simply tear, but they hadn't. Not yet.

Looking down, she saw that the firemen were positioning a mattress, or something similar, alongside the verandah, just beneath where they would probably land if they jumped. Or fell. It looked the size of a postage stamp, but even the thought of it being there was reassuring.

Just then a figure darted out from the crowd, leapt the police barrier, and raced over to the mattress, waving its arms madly. Allie smiled. She knew who it was, even from up here, and understood that everything would be all right now, no matter what happened. She drew in a deep breath and turned to Louise.

'Ready?'

'Are you?'

Allie nodded. 'You go first.'

'No, you go.'

'No, Lou. You've got Susan. It should be you.'

Tears welled up in Louise's eyes. 'Well, don't wait until I get off, don't leave it too late.'

'I won't,' Allie promised.

They hugged quickly, then Louise tucked her skirt firmly under the elastic of her knickers, took off her shoes and stockings, and climbed up onto the window ledge. She turned her back on the crowd below, then slid her legs out over the ledge and down until she found the ropes. She twined her feet around them, let go of the ledge with one hand and grasped the rope just below it. Then she took her other hand off the ledge and began to slide down the ropes, letting herself descend jerkily as she opened and closed her hands. She didn't dare look down, but, after what seemed to be at least an hour but was probably only a minute, she felt the warm metal of the ladder beneath her feet. She paused for a moment to catch her breath and ease her aching arm muscles, then continued on down. It was easier on the ladder, although it was swaying alarming, and she started to pray over and over that the ropes wouldn't break.

From the window, Allie could only see the top of Louise's head as she descended, and occasionally the flash of her pale calves as she extended her legs to feel for the next rung. On the ground, the firemen turned their hoses onto the windows Louise would pass, trying to dampen down any flames that might leap out for her. There were also two firemen on the verandah roof now, stationed on either side of where Louise was likely to land when she dropped the last dozen or so feet. Allie wondered if they were hoping to catch her: if they didn't, or at least slow her fall, she could easily crash through the corrugated iron and tear herself to pieces.

There was an almighty bang behind Allie, and for a terrifying second she thought it might be Irene, her hair aflame and her beautiful face melting, not dead yet and come to beg her for help. But it was the door to the dressmaking room exploding inwards in a great gust of flame and smoke, and she knew that if she didn't go now, she never would.

She tore off her own shoes and stockings, hoisted her skirt and scrambled up onto the ledge. She hooked her legs around the ropes, frightened almost witless, but knowing that unless she did this she would never see Sonny or her family again.

Her eyes squeezed shut in terrified concentration, she allowed the ropes to slip slowly but steadily between her hands and feet until she reached the top rung of the ladder. Untangling her feet, she let her weight drop onto it, then screamed as she suddenly felt everything — the ropes, the ladder and herself — plummet. Her eyes flew open and she saw the plastered façade of the building blur past, then part of a window, before everything jolted to a halt and the ladder swung wildly before it righted itself again. But she knew what had happened — under her and Louise's combined weight, the cutting table must have been dragged across the floor until it hit the wall beneath the window, its momentum suddenly stopped. Then came another sharp little jolt and she risked a downwards glance just in time to see Louise roll off the edge of the verandah roof and over the side.

Taking several deep breaths to calm herself and slow her thumping heart, she counted to five, then began to feel her way down the ladder. Another quick look down told her that every face in the crowd was tilted up towards her, following her progress. She could make out Sonny fairly clearly now, waiting at the edge of the mattress on the ground with his arms stretched up as though he could catch her if she fell.

She kept going, whispering 'Good girl' out loud with every new rung she reached. Above her, flames were flickering at the window of the workroom, and she knew it would be a matter of only seconds before the ropes burned through.

Then she was on the bottom rung, gazing down at the huge, dizzying gap between the point where she hung suspended and the roof of the verandah. And suddenly she lost her nerve, physically felt it draining from her. She shut her eyes again and started to pray, straining to remember the words of Irene's prayer.

And then, through the roaring and crackling of the fire above her and the groans and shifting of the crowd below, she heard Sonny shout, '*Let go, Allie, I'll catch you!*'

It was ridiculous of course — if she landed on him she'd kill him. But somehow his words made her feel better, and suddenly she knew that she could do it.

She turned herself around so that she was facing outwards, slipped her feet off the bottom rung of the ladder and let go.

Chapter Seventeen

She felt his smooth, warm hand slip into hers and squeezed it gratefully. She had been dreading this day, and now it was here.

'All right?' he whispered into her ear.

She nodded and bit her lip, struggling to hold back the tears that had been threatening to spill out of her from the moment she'd woken up that morning. It was the day of the civic funeral for the forty-nine people who had died in the fire.

'I'm going to miss them so much.'

He tightened his grip on her hand and murmured, 'I know.'

She saw Louise in the crowd then, Rob pushing her in a wheelchair across the smooth, newly clipped grass of Waikumete Cemetery, and hurried to meet them.

Bending down to kiss Louise's cheek, she said, 'How's the leg?'

Louise tapped the plaster cast that reached from her toes all the way up to mid-thigh, the top half concealed beneath the skirt of her black dress. 'Not bad,' she said. 'Not too sore, but it's itching like hell in this heat.' She brushed away a tear that had escaped and was trickling down her cheek. 'Oh, Allie, will we ever forget this? Will we ever put it behind us?'

Allie swallowed, the lump in her throat like a hot coal now, and found that she couldn't reply. Sonny slid a hand around her waist and she leaned into the comfort and strength of his body.

Louise pointed and said angrily, 'You know, I look at that and I wonder if God really bloody well does exist.'

Allie gazed at the neat arc of coffins laid out on the bright green grass next to the open graves and nodded.

The service had been held in town that morning, and the funeral cortège — forty-nine black, wreath-bedecked hearses followed by hundreds of private cars — had taken several hours to arrive at the cemetery. But they were all there now, and soon the final rites would begin.

Ted Horrocks appeared in front of them, his hat in his hand and his wife Natalie hovering close behind him. His face was still red from the fire and he was weeping but trying to pretend that he wasn't.

'Steady, girls, we're nearly there,' he said, as though he were addressing a company of young soldiers about to go over the top for the first time.

Allie hugged him, producing from him an exclamation of surprise, pleasure and grief. She had been delighted to hear that he'd survived the fire — it would have been so unfair if he'd died, after all those years of cheerfulness and loyalty he'd given Dunbar & Jones.

Ted plonked his hat back on, and reached for his wife's hand. 'This might not be the best of times to mention it, but have you seen him?'

'Who?' Louise said.

Ted nodded behind him. Allie and Louise turned and looked, their eyes narrowing as they spotted Vince Reynolds, standing beside his wife and looking suitably sombre and grief-stricken.

'Bastard!' Louise swore. Rob settled a calming hand on her shoulder, but she shook it off.

'Right.' Allie set off across the lawn in Vince's direction.

Sonny exchanged glances with Rob, and they both shrugged, unwilling to interfere in something they both quietly agreed needed to be done.

Vince clearly hadn't seen her coming, because when Allie parked herself in front of him he started in surprise.

Whipping off his smart black homburg, he began, 'Miss, er, Roberts, isn't it? I am *so* sorry about your friend Mrs Baxter. She was—'

But he was cut horribly short because Allie lifted her hand and slapped him across his face as hard as she could. There was a shocked gasp from the people standing nearby.

'She was a fool for having anything to do with *you*, Vince Reynolds,' Allie said loudly. 'Because you took everything you wanted from her, didn't you? But when *she* needed something, even just a word of comfort, you just walked away. You didn't care and you treated her as though she was already dead.' Allie was crying hard now, her words coming out with such anger that spittle was flying. She wiped her mouth. 'And Irene knew that, you . . . you cheat! You *thief!* Irene *died* knowing that!'

She watched with some satisfaction as Vince's Adam's apple bobbed nervously up and down above his black silk tie and his face turned a deep red. She spun around,

330

stumbling only slightly as her heel dug into the cemetery lawn, and stalked off.

Maxwell Jones stepped up to the lectern and cleared his throat. He spent a second or two shuffling the pages of the eulogy he had prepared, though those near him could see that he was struggling to contain his emotions.

'We have all lost friends, family and work colleagues,' he finally began. 'They were taken from us only eight days ago, but we already know that we will miss them for ever. However, we must take comfort from the certainty that God . . . that God . . .' He trailed off, and stared down at his papers.

The crowd waited respectfully for him to recover his composure, but it seemed that he couldn't. Almost a minute passed, and finally he put his hands over his face and let out a single, strangled sob. He was led away then, and someone else took over.

But Allie barely noticed. She was too busy blinking back fresh tears as she surveyed the line of gleaming coffins. Irene was in one of them, of course, and poor little Daisy, along with her unborn child. Terry's coffin lay next to hers, and Allie hoped that they would be together, wherever they were going. And, in a way, it had been right that they had been together when the stairs had collapsed beneath them. Miss Willow and Miss Button were there too, and so was Daisy's friend Nyla from the millinery department, and Bev from cosmetics, and Simone from gloves, and Walter the lift boy. There were people she had known in the other coffins, too — workmates and friends, people whose families would never see them again. And at the end of the line were three coffins that seemed the saddest of all, containing what everyone assumed were the remains of poor Jock McLean, and Mr Beaumont, and the girl from the cash office whose body had never been found.

A lone fantail swooped low over the coffins, as though looking for something, then darted off again.

Allie shuddered as she thought yet again about how close she had come to death. When she'd dropped from the ladder, she'd fallen until she had hit the verandah roof, exactly between the two waiting firemen, then bounced and skidded madly down the hot iron surface. One of the firemen had managed to grab her arm as she'd sailed past, which had deflected her trajectory out over the street and somersaulted her instead onto the mattress below. She had landed on her side and dislocated her left shoulder and badly bruised her leg, but otherwise had been miraculously unharmed. It had all become a bit hazy after that. She remembered Sonny looking down at her with tears running down his face, and then her father there crying too. Then she'd gone in an ambulance, after which a doctor did something horrendously painful to her arm at the hospital, and then she'd gone to sleep. The next morning had been worse, though, waking up to the horror of finding out who had survived and who hadn't. In one way it had been the worst day of her life, because so many people she cared about had been lost, but in another it had been the best, because she was one of the survivors. She was alive, and so was Sonny.

After the graveside service had finished and the minister had sent the dead on their journey, mourners were given the chance to say their final farewells.

When Allie came to Irene's coffin, she laid a red rose

above the brass plate that had been inscribed with her friend's full name, Irene Esmerelda Baxter. She whispered 'Thank you', and left it at that, because, deep in her heart, she suspected that, whatever Irene had been looking for, she had finally found it. She gave Martin a quick, fierce hug and moved on.

At Daisy's coffin, she knelt down and this time placed a white rose on the lid. She glanced around self-consciously, then decided she didn't care who heard what she had to say.

'I saw the queen, Daisy, I went to see her after I got out of hospital because I knew you'd want to know what she looked like. And she really was just like a fairy princess in her long shimmering dress and that fabulous purple velvet cloak you were talking about. And, Daisy, she had the most wonderful jewels at her throat and on her fingers, and a crown that sparkled like the stars.'

Epilogue

When Allie realized that she was in fact pregnant and told Sonny that they should have been more careful on the beach at Mission Bay after all, he smiled, said it was worth it and asked her to marry him. Awhi wasn't happy about it, and neither was Colleen, but Allie and Sonny were adamant so the wedding went ahead. Sid said it nearly bankrupted him, but no one listened because it was obvious that he was more than chuffed with his new son-in-law.

Allie's baby, a beautiful little girl, was born on 16 August 1954, five months after she and Sonny were married.

The first time Sonny saw his daughter, he cried.

'She's lovely,' he said, smiling as the baby's tiny hand closed over his finger. 'What shall we call her?'

Allie gazed down at her daughter's perfect face, the determined tilt of her little nose and her shock of silky black hair.

'I think,' she said after a moment, 'we'll call her Irene.'

THE END